THE LEGEND OF
MICKEY TUSSLER

THE LEGEND OF
MICKEY TUSSLER

A NOVEL

FRANK NAPPI

Sky Pony Press
New York

Sky Pony Press books may be purchased in bulk at special discounts for sales promotion, corporate gifts, fund-raising, or educational purposes. Special editions can also be created to specifications. For details, contact the Special Sales Department, Sky Pony Press, 307 West 36th Street, 11th Floor, New York, NY 10018 or info@skyhorsepublishing.com.

Sky Pony® is a registered trademark of Skyhorse Publishing, Inc.®, a Delaware corporation.

Visit our website at www.skyponypress.com.

10 9 8 7 6 5 4 3 2 1

Library of Congress Cataloging-in-Publication Data is available on file.

ISBN: 978-1-61608-658-9

Printed in the United States of America

For Julia, Nick, and Anthony

*And for my father, Francis Nappi, whose
undaunted spirit and love of the game
continue to inspire me*

No game in the world is as tidy and dramatically neat as baseball, with cause and effect, crime and punishment, motive and result, so cleanly defined.

—**PAUL GALLICO**

THE LEGEND OF
MICKEY TUSSLER

INDIANA—1948

The dirt beneath the wheels of Arthur Murphy's car rose and swirled like the breath of angry giants, lingering in the heavy morning air even after his blue-and-white Plymouth Road King had disappeared around the bend like an apparition. He had been driving all night, with nothing for company but endless rows of cornstalks, a diamond-dotted sky, and a brown paper bag whose torn front exposed the worn words *Southern Comfort*. He rubbed his eyes with one hand—they burned from the firebrick sun that had slipped over the rolling hills of clover up ahead—and drummed the top of the steering wheel impatiently with his fingers on the other. He was getting too old for this. Twenty-six years with the Braves organization; he had played for them, coached, and was now in his third year as manager of their farm affiliate in Milwaukee. But there he was, still doing a job more commonly associated with guys half his age.

"I need you on this one, Murph," the club's owner explained. "Do yourself a favor and get your ass out there and find something to help that sorry lot you call a team or *I'll* be scouting for *managers*." He paused deliberately for effect. His forehead wrinkled. "You're a good man, Murph. But this is no time for pride, Arthur. We've lost our best prospects the last few years to Uncle Sam. Damned war. They say it's over now. Sure. It's over. But everyone wants to be a soldier

1

all of a sudden. The damned Japanese ruined everything. Feels like the whole world's against us."

Murph's stomach burned as he recalled the conversation. It may have been true, all that Dennison had said, but the owner's tone irked him. And that gratuitous line about him being a good man. Who was he kidding? Murph was inclined to consider the sentiment not so much a compliment but more as crap designed to cajole him into accepting another scouting trip that nobody else wanted. Warren Dennison, the owner of the minor-league-affiliate Brewers, didn't give a rat's ass about him. Never did.

Murph's eyelids were heavy and struggled beneath the weight of sleeplessness. The rows of fruit trees were endless and hypnotic. Many times during the drive he'd felt like a rat, negotiating a series of narrow corridors, searching for the elusive prize at the end. He rolled down the window and hit the knob on the radio. The cool air and Johnny Mercer's "Sweet Georgia Brown" got his left foot tapping.

Thoughts of his past returned as well. His life had tumbled well short of the aspirations he'd had during his playing days when he was touted as the best left-handed hitter since Ty Cobb. He recalled happily all of the attention he received those first few months. He and another young stud, Chip "Hollywood" McNally, had begun their careers in the American Association the same year. They were both lionized by everyone in the Braves organization as the finest prospects they had. Milwaukee was going to be just a brief stop en route to the big show in Boston. Both were exceptional outfielders; each could run like a deer and could hit every bag with a tracer from anywhere in the outfield. McNally was probably a little stronger, and Arthur's red hair and freckles were no match for Hollywood's square jaw and golden locks. Still, Arthur was the one that all of the real baseball people whispered about, especially around the batting cage. He was a natural. Could flat out hit. Turn on the fastball. Shoot the curve the opposite way. Had excellent power to all fields. Whitey Simpson, the manager of the Milwaukee Brewers the year he arrived, swore that Arthur was the best bad-ball hitter he had ever seen.

Arthur was maybe five or six games away from being sent to Boston when the incident occurred. They were up by one with two outs in the top half of the ninth. The first two pitches were called balls. The batter, Clyde Simmons, stepped out and tapped his spikes with the knob of his bat and smiled at the crowd.

"What the hell is he doing?" McNally yelled to Arthur from right field. "Is he for real? He hasn't touched a ball all game."

Arthur shook his head. He was tired. He scanned the grandstand from his position in center field. It had been a good game. Everyone was on his or her feet, anticipating the final out. Some were clapping, while others yelled out encouraging words through rolled-up newspapers. Most were screaming for McNally and waving signs, expressing undying affection for number nine, the handsome right fielder. He was their darling. Arthur hung his head. He was tired of that too. Hell, McNally hadn't done a damned thing all day either. Three whiffs and not one putout from the field. Arthur was three for four and had thrown out two runners at home. But that day was no different from any other. Hollywood McNally was the favorite at Borchert Field. The poster boy. Arthur never quite managed to endear himself to the crowd the way Hollywood did. The press loved him, sure; couldn't stop talking about his prowess and unlimited potential. But the hometown crowd—that was something else. They never warmed to him. So all he ever got was a smattering of placards displaying his name and number and the same group of elderly men who sat behind him each game, in suit coats and fedoras, smoking cigars and critiquing his every play. Even the diminutive second baseman, little Nat Riley, who barely broke .200 every season, had a better following—a group of fifteen scraggly kids who always sat in the same section and only cheered for him. They were a coterie of misfits, from their dirty faces and torn knees to the baseball caps each one wore askew. Lefty Wilkins used to kill Riley about his admirers.

"Hey, Nat," he always said shortly after their arrival. "The orphanage just checked in." Arthur was still trying to reconcile the gross inequity in his mind when he heard the crack of the bat. It was a

screaming liner, earmarked for the right-center-field gap. He broke
as soon as he saw the ball emerge from the faces of those seated behind home plate. "I got it! I got it!" he screamed, eating up the turf
with each stride, galloping with the grace and dexterity of a gazelle.
It was one of the things he did best.

Hollywood hadn't caught a ball all game. He had spent the ma-
jority of the afternoon tipping his hat, for no apparent reason, to the
adoring crowd each time he made his way out to right or stepped to
the plate. He was always smiling.

"Where's the camera, Hollywood?" the guys all teased the first
day he arrived. The name stuck. He was always on. Nobody at
Borchert Field would ever have known how frustrated he really was
that day at not having had the chance to show off his stuff. Now, with
the game in its later stages, opportunity had finally knocked.

He never broke stride. And he never heard Arthur calling for the
ball. His spikes glistened in the high afternoon sun, leaving behind
shards of grass that fell softly to the ground like confetti. He followed
the trajectory of the little white sphere, wedded to the vision of a
game-saving catch and the adulation that would follow.

Neither happened. They collided just as each arrived at the ball.
The sound was loud and piercing, a crack of thunder that reverberated as if it were produced in a deep canyon of stone. Those in the
little ballpark groaned and sighed, then all at once lapsed into an
eerie silence as the two men crumpled helplessly to the turf. No one
even noticed Clyde Simmons circling the bases.

The Brewers' dugout exhaled, and out poured Whitey, followed
by a handful of coaches and a few of the players. A ring formed
around their fallen teammates.

"You two idiots!" Whitey bawled. "How many times have we
practiced this? Call for the ball! Call for the damned ball! Jesus, how
many times—"

Arthur was the first to stagger to his feet. His eyes were glazed and
his forehead split at the left temple. A thin line of crimson ran down
his cheek and across his jaw, ultimately finding a resting place in the
collar of his uniform top.

"I *did* call for it," he mumbled weakly.

"Where'd you get it, Murph?" one of the coaches asked.

Arthur pointed to his shoulder. Then he looked down at McNally, who lay motionless except for the grimacing.

"I'm okay," Arthur said. "I think McNally took it worse."

He was right. Chip "Hollywood" McNally's career ended that day at Borchert Field. There would be no more flashbulbs. No one would ever scream his name again or wave a sign professing undying affection for good old number nine. A fractured skull and busted knee had taken care of that.

Arthur did not escape unscathed. Sure, he recovered. But he was never the same. He went on to have a modest but successful career as a utility player. He played for nine seasons, ending his playing career with a .277 batting average and 108 home runs. But the numbers did not tell the whole story. Oh, what he might have accomplished had it not been for that arrogant bastard McNally. His ego destroyed two careers that day. It was a long time ago, but Arthur could not forget. He still heard the sound. At night sometimes, when the air outside his bedroom window was still, he could still hear it. *Crack.* That sound. It still made him shiver. And McNally's eyes as they carried him off the field. Arthur couldn't forget those either. Those eyes. Black and venomous. And those final words.

"My ball," McNally said bitterly. "My ball."

McNally kicked around the minors for a while, refusing to believe his career was finished. People said it was one of the most pathetic things they'd ever seen. He could barely run, could not reach the cutoff man from his position, and, as the old joke goes, could not hit water if he fell out of a boat.

Then, with virtually nothing left of his pride and self-respect, he finally resigned himself to coaching jobs whenever he could get one. The million-dollar smile was gone, replaced by a bitter scowl and an irrational hatred for Arthur Murphy that just continued to fester.

The radio cut out momentarily and brought Murph back to matters at hand. He was on his way to check out some hotshot first baseman from Bargersville, Indiana. One of Dennison's cousins had spotted him during a pickup game.

"Murph, you've got to see this kid," Dennison told him. "I hear he's a real god!"

Arthur was unimpressed. He had heard it all before. If he had a dollar for every "sure thing" he was told about, he'd be somewhere else right now.

He looked down next to him at the papers on the seat and shuffled them around. "Thirty-seven twenty-one Marbury Lane," he read off one of the sheets. Without a map, the address was really of little use. "Where the hell is Marbury Lane?"

He was shaking his head, thinking about the pot roast his mom used to make for him back home. God, he loved her cooking. She could bake too. Won first prize every year in the Ladies' Auxillary bake-off at the church. Nothing warmed his insides like a half hour at the dinner table. His hunger and frustration made him miss it even more. The thought of tender meat, potatoes, and gravy-soaked biscuits was comforting. He had just closed his eyes, lost in the sweet recollection, when the reminiscence was violently shattered by a sudden jolt and then the sound of breaking glass. His arms tensed as he struggled to control the car. It swerved back and forth across the road, taking out several small trees that lined the shoulder. The blue-and-white roadster careened helplessly out of control, tossing Arthur from side to side before finally coming to rest in a shallow ditch.

With tears in his eyes, a sore neck, and a faint trickle of blood coming from his nose, he stumbled out of the car. The day was new and fresh, alive with a wind full of dust and the smell of lilies. He placed his hands on his hips and surveyed the damage. He looked the car up and down.

"Son of a bitch!" he screamed, dabbing his nose with his thumb and forefinger. Then he fired his foot against the back tire. "Jesus Christ!"

The car was a mess. His eyes scraped the dusty road behind and found the cause of the mishap. It was some sort of animal, large and lifeless, lying off to the side. He ran his hands, still trembling, through his hair.

"Perfect!" he screamed. "Just perfect!"

Up ahead, just around a bend in the road, stood a modest farmhouse. Arthur's eyes found the red silo hovering just above the arching oaks blocking his vision and his feet began to shuffle in that direction. He was thinking about all he still had to do—find Marbury Lane and get a look at this kid—as he stumbled down the road. For some reason, he suddenly perceived how dissatisfied he was with the course of his career. He had been a young man once, full of hope and promise. The next Ty Cobb. He could still hear the scouts talking about him behind the cage as he took batting practice. He was so sure that his life was going to thrive under the warm glow of baseball stardom. But all he had become was the middle-aged manager of a minor league team that had struggled the past few years just to break .500. And if that weren't intolerable enough, now he was lumbering down some godforsaken road in the middle of the sticks praying that someone could help him get where he needed to be.

The mailbox outside the farmhouse was beaten and weathered, a gray wood container nailed to a crooked stake with the name *Tussler* barely visible through all of the chips and cracks. He followed a narrow, winding path that led him past a tiny field with slanted gravestones overrun with cucumber vines and crabgrass that eventually gave way to a small stable.

"Hello," he called out. "Anyone home?"

He stepped forward and opened the door, looking curiously at the scene inside. Two horses, a couple of chickens nesting in the corner, and a few pigs eating quietly from a trough.

Not much of a farm, he thought.

The animals seemed just as unimpressed with him. They barely stirred and would probably have remained completely still had it not been for the sudden thumping from behind the far wall. He followed the sound around the stable until he found its origin. He stood, with his back and left foot flat against the side of the stable, watching in amazement at the young farm boy, standing next to a curious pattern of crab apples in the dirt—six rows across, five apples deep—firing one at a time from one hundred feet away into a wine barrel turned on its side.

Thud. Thud. Thud.

Stunned, Arthur watched as the boy shifted his weight back, cocked his right arm, then exploded forward, splitting the center of the barrel every time. He didn't have much of a windup, and the mechanics were awkward, but it was the most astounding display of power and accuracy he had ever witnessed.

Thud. Thud. Thud.

He was about to walk a little closer when he stopped suddenly, taken aback by an unusual, spastic motion the boy was performing. His throwing hand, curled into a fist, was buried inside his other, and he was rolling his arms violently. Arthur watched as each elbow rose and fell rhythmically, over and over, until at last the boy stopped just long enough to reach down in front of him to resume the awesome exhibition.

Thud. Thud. Thud.

Three more strikes. Then came the rolling of the arms. Arthur stared as the powerful young man repeated the process, time and again.

Arthur was captivated. Once the pristine rows of projectiles had vanished, he walked over to the boy. The kid was bigger up close. His face was youthful, round and fleshy, with sandy brown strands of hair that barely concealed a dark purplish line under his right eye. He must have been at least six foot five. His legs looked like two oak trees, and he had the biggest hands Arthur had ever seen.

"Excuse me," Arthur said. "Hello. I had a little accident with my car. Do you live here?"

The young giant was startled and tense. He began to chew his lower lip. His eyes darted wildly.

"I live here," he answered.

"Is there someone who can help me with my car? I mean, your parents. Is your dad around?"

The boy didn't answer. He was just standing before him, his

glance shifting from Arthur's hat to his shoes and all points in between.

"I didn't mean to bother you, son." Murph held out his hand. "I'm Arthur Murphy. My friends call me Murph."

The boy's expression softened. He pushed away the wisps of brown hair that hung carelessly in his eyes.

"Michael James Tussler, sir," he answered, pulling awkwardly at one of the straps of his overalls. "Folks round here just call me Mickey."

"Mickey, huh? Say, that's quite a shiner you got there." Murph pointed to the boy's eye.

"How's that?"

"Your eye. I was talking about your eye. How'd you get that?"

The boy fidgeted. "Aw, don't reckon Mickey remembers."

Arthur smiled softly. "Well, that's all right now. It's nice to meet you, Mickey. You've got quite an arm there. Really. I was watching you from over there. How old are you?"

The boy was biting the inside of his cheek. "I got me some pigs, sir. Want to see my pigs?"

"Uh, sure. Maybe later."

"I got six of 'em. My favorite one is named Oscar."

Arthur studied the boy. He was certainly in amazing shape. A fine athletic specimen. But there was something about him. A vacuity behind his eyes that seemed to overshadow everything else.

"Well, that sounds very nice, son. Say, how old did you say you are, Mickey?"

"Seventeen."

"Ever play baseball?"

Mickey just looked at him.

Murph thought again about Dennison's ominous admonition and how desperately grave his situation with the ball club had become.

"You, know. Baseball. Three strikes. Home run. All that good stuff."

"I don't reckon I have. I'll show you my pigs now. I got six of 'em." Then Mickey placed his hands together and began rolling his elbows once again.

"Yeah, yeah. Okay, Mickey. In a minute. But first, how's about waiting here while I run to my car. Then maybe you can show me that neat trick of yours again—you know, throwing those apples in the barrel?"

Mickey nodded blankly. Murph was gone and back in a flash, fearful that the boy might change his mind. With his breath short and erratic, Murph reached down to pick up one of the wormy specimens that had fallen outside the original makeshift grid. He tossed it in the air a couple of times. Then he reached into his pocket with his other hand and presented to Mickey a beautiful new baseball.

"What do ya say, kid?" Murph prompted, holding out both his hands. "They're almost the same exact size. Except mine is real clean and smooth. Go on. Have a feel for yourself." Murph watched as the boy's hand swallowed the ball. "Pretty neat, huh?"

Mickey ran his fingers over the laces. "Mickey likes it, sir."

Murph smiled. His heart beat on. "How about giving it a toss, Mickey? You know, right over in that barrel. Just for laughs."

The boy nodded. "Can I show you my pigs now?"

"Well, sure you can, son. But first, I'd love to see you toss that baseball into that barrel."

The monotony of the conversation sank into a vague haze through which Murph's glittering visions persisted. He placed his hand on the boy's back and nudged him gently. "What do you say, son?" he prodded. "Will you do that for me?"

"Okay, Mr. Murphy. Mickey will do it."

Murph watched with immeasurable fascination as the boy held the ball, brought his hands together, and rolled his arms. Then, like a bolt of lightning released from the heavens, the ball took flight, a streak of white radiance that cut the air with a whizzing sound before landing directly in the center of the barrel, splintering the wood. Murph's eyes widened like saucers. His breath was gone again. Then, in the flatness that followed the euphoria, Murph knew, just knew, that he had stumbled on something special.

"How's that, Mr. Murphy?"

"That's terrific kid. Terrific. Now, what do ya say I go get that ball and you do it one more time. Then we'll check on those pigs."

Mickey looked right past Arthur. His face twitched ever so slightly and his gaze was off in the distance, focused on the raucous noise at the side door of the barn.

"Godammit!" a man thundered, incensed by a baby chick that would not stay in its pen with the others. "Git back here."

Arthur turned around. An elderly man in dirty overalls and a straw hat had come through the door and was sidling over to them. He had a pitchfork in one hand and a metal bucket in the other.

"What can I do for ya, stranger? I reckon ya's lost or sumpin like that."

The appearance of the farmer altered the boy's demeanor. He became stiff and distant and rocked nervously while muttering words that Arthur could not understand.

> Slowly, silently, now the moon,
> Walks the night in her silver shoon;
> This way, and that, she peers and sees,
> Silver fruit upon silver trees.

The old farmer had a hardened look to him. He was strong too, but not like the boy. His salt-and-pepper beard was dirty and snarled and his voice strained and raspy.

"Hello," Arthur said, extending his hand to the farmer. "I'm sorry. Arthur Murphy's the name. I was just explaining to your son here —"

"Don't bother splaining nothing to him. Wasting your time." The old farmer smelled of tobacco. He had a wad of chew squirreled in his cheek and was working on a thin piece of straw that danced across his lip and in the gap between his stained teeth when he spoke.

"Well, my car is sort of banged up," Arthur continued. "I was hoping to make a phone call, if it's all right."

"Clarence Tussler. You in need of assist?" the man responded, shaking Arthur's hand.

The boy just stood nervously, cowering behind his father. "'Slowly, silently, now the moon . . .,'" he repeated, almost catatonic.

"Knock that off, boy, ya hear!" Clarence chided. "Sorry 'bout that, Mr. Murphy. He does that sometimes when he gets nervous. Some cockamamy poem his ma learned him."

"That's okay," Arthur answered. "And, yeah. Your help would be great." He was still staring at the boy. "That would be great. I could sure use a telephone. And maybe some directions."

The farmer was about to say something when out of the corner of his eye he observed a tiny ball of gossamer yellow feather, vocal and wayward.

"Son of a—!" He flew into a rage, raising his boot high above the chick until a cold shadow enveloped the helpless creature. Then, with an inescapable vengeance, he lowered his foot hard, grinding his heel into the ground with curious delight.

"Annoying little bastard," he mumbled. "That'll learn ya."

Then the irascible farmer spit out his chew, took a cigarette from his outer pocket, and lit it, his deliberate motions noticeably slower from the effort he was making to calm himself.

Murph winced. He gazed briefly at the farmer in disbelief, appearing to abandon his search for something that he suddenly felt could not possibly exist.

"Why don't ya follow me up to the house, fella," Clarence said from behind a cloud of smoke. He scratched his beard. Then he shot his son a look.

"What ya looking so stupid about, boy. Go on. Go on now. Finish with them apples, then git yer keister over to them troughs. Pigs got to eat soon."

Murph looked at Mickey, not knowing what to think. "Say, you've got some arm there, kid. It was sure nice meeting you, Mickey."

The boy just hung his head.

Clarence frowned and exhaled loudly while tapping his boot on the ground. "Well, go on, boy. You heard me."

Arthur walked alongside Clarence. Once or twice he turned

back to look at Mickey, sad and defeated, his head hanging between his massive shoulders. Clarence didn't give his son a second thought. Just rambled on about his property and the Tussler family history.

"So, what brings you out this here way, Mr. Murphy?" he asked, pulling on the handle of the aluminum screen door.

"Clarence, is that you?" a voice called from inside the house.

"Yeah, Molly, it's me. Get out here. We got us company."

The abrasive farmer tossed a sleeping cat from the chair closest to the door and motioned for Arthur to sit down.

The room was dark and oppressive. The walls were splashed with a mahogany paneling that drowned out the little light that squeezed through the heavy draperies across the windows. Papers and cartons and other random objects were strewn about the room. Clarence stood leaning against a gray stone mantel, adorned with a yellowing lace doily held in place by an old brass lantern. Next to that was a family portrait in a tarnished frame and a dusty clarinet. Arthur's eyes hurt, as if something acerbic were in the air. It smelled like cat urine or perhaps it was just mold spores. Either way, he could not stop rubbing his eyes.

"Well?" Clarence asked. "What did you say you were doing in these here parts?"

"Baseball," Arthur replied, wiping the moisture from his right eye on his shirtsleeve. "I work for the Milwaukee Brewers. I'm here to scout a local kid."

"No kidding? Hey, Molly," Clarence bellowed. "Did you hear that?"

A tiny woman with long brown hair and a faint smile entered the room, carrying a tray on which rested a sweating pitcher of lemonade. She was much younger than Clarence. She walked with her shoulders slightly hunched, as if each step were a painful deliberation. He recognized the look in her eyes—it was Mickey's. She moved carefully around her husband, like a frightened puppy negotiating a dangerous intersection. Her gentleness and timidity were incongruous with everything else he had experienced thus far.

"Pardon the intrusion, ma'am," Arthur said, removing his hat. "I had a little car trouble."

"Not at all, sir." She placed a glass on the cluttered table in front of him. "Guests are always welcome in our home." She poured the lemonade and stood uneasily next to her husband.

"Say, before I use your telephone, do you mind if I ask you a question?"

"Well, I reckon that ought to be all right. Shoot, Mr. Murphy. What's eating at you?"

"Mickey's got quite an arm. I was watching him hurl those crab apples across your property. He ever play any baseball?"

Clarence laughed incredulously. His voice became louder and even more overbearing. *"Baseball?"* he mocked. "You want Mickey to play *baseball*? Now, what in tarnation is a baseball team gonna do with a retard? Huh?"

"I don't understand."

The farmer was scratching his beard. His amusement brought forth a smile, foul and yellow.

"What my husband meant to say, Mr. Murphy, is that Mickey is a little—"

"I said exactly what I meant to say, woman," Clarence barked, raising his hand in mock attack. "Don't you be correcting me. He's a retard. Ain't much use to us on the farm and probably would be even less useful to you. Teats on a bull. That's what that boy is."

Molly frowned.

"Look, Mr. Tussler, I mean no disrespect, but I think your son has an extraordinary talent. I watched him out there."

"Now, what kind of a country fool you take me for? Huh? You watched him? What, for two minutes? He was smashing apples to mix in with the pig slop. That boy ain't got no talent. He can't find his own behind with two hands."

Arthur stood up. His eyes were bothering him again. "May I use your telephone?"

Molly led Arthur into the small kitchen. Off to the side, next to the pantry, was a kerosene heater. It was old and, by the looks of it, barely functioning. The smell ran together with the pungent odor of cabbage cooking on the stove.

"Here you are, Mr. Murphy," the woman said softly. "I'll leave you to your business."

Arthur dialed Dennison's office and explained the mishap. As he detailed the events, he could hear Molly and Clarence exchanging words in the other room.

"Why do you have to talk about him like that Clarence? Why?"

"Don't you question me now, woman," he fired back. "We got to face what we got here. I don't got to sugarcoat nothin' for nobody."

"The man says Mickey's got talent."

"Mr. Murphy is a city boy. Don't know shit from Shinola."

"But, Clarence, why can't we just—"

"Hush up, woman, ya hear? That's enough lip from you. Get back in the kitchen and finish fixing what it is you're fixing."

Arthur had finished talking to Dennison when Molly returned to the kitchen. "Thank you, ma'am," he said. "Much obliged." She would not look at him, just passed by, head down, chin resting on her chest.

He put his hat back on his head and started for the door. Clarence had taken a seat in the rocker and was whittling a piece of wood with a small knife.

"Did ya get through all right to your friend there, Mr. Murphy?"

"Yes, yes, I did. They're sending someone for me right away."

"Well, you can set yourself down here for a spell until they come for ya." Murph cringed at the thought. "If it's all the same, Mr. Tussler, I'd just as soon wait outside. But before I go, I'd like to make you an offer."

"How's that?"

"An offer. You know, money."

"Mr. Murphy, a phone call ain't but just a couple of pennies. That's all right."

Murph glanced to the side and smiled. "Well, Clarence, I'd be happy to pay for the call. I insist. But you misunderstood me. I'm talking about Mickey."

The farmer stood up. Molly came back quietly and listened by the doorway, out of view.

"Come again?"

Hell, what did he have to lose? Murph had no idea if this kid could really cut it on the diamond, but given the situation, how bad could it be?

"I'll pay you—thirty-five dollars—if you will let me sign Mickey up for a tryout. Just a tryout. No big deal. It's just a formality, really. He'll come with me, back to Milwaukee, and stay with the rest of the fellas on the team. We'll be able to give him a real good look."

Clarence was smiling. All at once the abrasive farmer was juggling crowding thoughts.

"I can assure you both, it won't be a big deal," Murph continued. "He'll be with me the entire time and should be back in a few days."

A loud sound, something like pots and pans crashing against each other, dashed the air.

"Now hold here, Mr. Murphy," Molly interrupted, as she emerged out of hiding. "You don't know anything about Mickey. He's not what you think. He's special. You don't know him. At all. You can't take him with you."

Clarence looked as though he would explode. "Pipe down, Molly," he thundered. "Don't go starting a row. Let the man finish. He was talking money with me."

"I'm not trying to start a row, Clarence. I appreciate the offer, Mr. Murphy. Really. It's nice that you like our boy. But it is just out of the question." Molly continued to duck the menacing looks Clarence was shooting.

"Please don't worry, Mrs. Tussler," Murph interrupted. "Really. It's all legit. I have papers, and everything."

"Pay her no mind, Mr. Murphy," Clarence demanded, shooting Molly a piercing look. "I'll fix her later."

She frowned again and left the room, defeated and bothered by the transparent reversal of her husband's mood. Arthur watched the conquered woman, her hands in her pockets, feet shuffling quietly, as her silhouette vanished around the corner. Then he turned to face the room once again. The slovenly farmer was smiling at him.

"Now, Mr. Murphy," he asked through narrowed lids, "you was saying?"

TUSSLER FARM—SOME YEARS BEFORE

Michael James Tussler, "Mickey," was born on a frigid evening in February, when the clouds had gathered in clumps across a gray, melancholy sky, bringing a thickening darkness and premature night to an already beleaguered town. Tree limbs and rooftops, heavy with the previous night's storm, frowned at the thickening white veil that had just begun its descent. All around, stray lines of yellow light escaped from frosty windows of the surrounding farmhouses and slid across the icy enclaves, exposing the obvious signs of distress—evergreen boughs hunched mournfully over paralyzed automobiles that had fallen victim to the natural boundaries of the landscape, which had been erased by waves of drifting snow. Barren apple saplings, tiny limbs peeking out helplessly from underneath a suffocating shroud of white. A lonely schoolhouse. It was as if the universe had suddenly sat up and cried out plaintively in defiant opposition to the new life that was destined for hardship and uncompromising cruelty.

At first, everything seemed normal. He was a beautiful baby boy, like every other. He grabbed his toes. Gurgled and cooed. He was the light of his mother's life. But before long this newfound bliss was betrayed, in a burst of consternation for the little boy. Molly always told herself that God would never give her more than she could handle. Like the man she married. She had grown up in the small town of Bakersfield. She lived according to small-town rules and adopted a small-town sensibility. The concerns of most Bakersfield folk were limited to agricultural. It was their livelihood. Good crops meant good living. And when the harvest was plentiful, and life was smiling upon them, they kicked back and drank beer and talked about hunting and fishing and how the city folk were stuck-up fools, misguided in their frivolous love for theater and music and all things cosmopolitan. Molly was surrounded by that mentality all her life. And although none of the simplicity that plagued the others seemed to run through her veins, she married small-town, as most girls there did. Who knew any better?

On a bright Sunday morning, the kind where the sun seems to be a splash of yellow sponged across a canvas of blue, she first met Clarence. It was the semiannual pancake breakfast held in the St. Agnes auditorium. He was tall and strong. He had a square jaw, rugged and cleft, and broad, hulking shoulders. He also had his own farm.

"Say there, little lady," he said to her, tugging unctuously at his overall straps. "Ain't you Otis's daughter?"

She clasped her hands behind her back and turned her face away. "Uh, ye—ye—yes. Yes, I am." Her head was down and her eyes fixed on the errant shoots of straw suspended in his bootlaces. Poor Molly. She was timid and unsure. And she was never comfortable around men, much to the chagrin of her father, who lamented that he would never see the day when his daughter would be claimed.

"Fix yourself up, Molly, for chrissakes," he always urged. "No man worth a lick ever looks twice at no mousy girl."

Molly had had one or two other opportunities with men when she was younger—but nothing had ever materialized. And as time elapsed, thirty approached like a ruthless executioner.

"Seems to me a purty little thing like you ought to be keeping company with a fella," Clarence persisted that day. She was sort of interested. It had been a long time since she'd heard such complimentary words. And she had grown tired of watching all the other girls get married and begin families of their own. She decided to give it a chance.

But little things got in the way. Little things bothered her, such as his long, bushy sideburns, reddish brown lightning bolts that angled toward his chin. His breath and teeth were equally repulsive, both tainted by the potency of tobacco juice. She managed to tolerate it for a while. They took a few walks together and even shared a soda once or twice. But his visage had grown repugnant and she could no longer feign interest in the pedestrian things he loved to prattle on about. He continued to call on her. She just kept avoiding him. Despite his persistence, Clarence found himself chasing a dream.

Things sort of righted themselves until Otis caught wind of Molly's withdrawal. "Goddammit girl, what in tarnation you thinking? You ain't getting no younger. And you ain't exactly turning too many heads neither. Now I now that there boy ain't no movie star, but by cracky he's got his own farm. His own farm, Molly. I reckon you best think twice, missy."

"But, Papa, I really don't—"

"You really don't what?" he fired back. "Like him?"

She was biting her lip. Tears formed behind her eyes but she refused to cry. "We don't have anything in common, Papa," she pleaded. "All he talks about is pigs and fishing and—"

Otis had his arms folded. His eyes were narrowed and he was chewing on the end of his pipe. "That there's yer problem, little lady. Ya know that? You think yer better than everyone else. Always fooling around with that clarinet and reading all the time. Poetry? What's the use in that? Nobody, nobody worth a damn wants to talk about that."

Not long after that conversation, Molly and Clarence were married. In the beginning, it wasn't all bad. She could recall happily riding next to him in his truck, his massive arm stretched across her chest each time he slammed on the brakes to avoid smashing into a vehicle in front of them. Her heart was timorous, but somehow she felt safe. As if he would protect her. Love her. What a mistake. One year later, she found herself living with a monster—a slovenly, bilious, self-righteous dolt—and living with the steady pulse of regret, forever beating. She prayed a lot and convinced herself that it was all just part of divine providence, another phase of God's plan for her. It comforted her to some extent, especially when she felt the pull of the world tearing at her resolve. But at many moments all the justification in the world was just not enough, such as the night he broke her nose with his open hand when he caught her playing the clarinet instead of tending to the wash.

"Now I'm sorry that this had to happen," he told her later on. "But maybe this here will learn ya not to ask fer no trouble."

All she could do was sob and nod her head. And then there was the whole thing with Mickey—a pressing concern that would not go away. Something about the child's demeanor—the way he was—did not seem right. She was powerless to identify it. Attach a name to it.

She tried to forget. Often, she and Clarence would playfully joke about the size of the boy, particularly his head.

"We must have us a regular Elber Einsteen," he mocked. Truth be told, he was more interested in the boy's musculature. Clarence was so proud of the child's unusually large size, tickled by visions of his strapping young son working the family farm. He saw it as some sort of accolade, a living testimony to his own virility.

Molly never gave much thought to that. The idiosyncratic behaviors, however, crept into her consciousness and rattled around with blinding regularity. It was the lack of pointing—Mickey didn't seem to know how to point at objects. It was the child's vacant stare and that he didn't seem to play pretend like other kids. It was the incessant rocking, back and forth.

"Aw, whatcha worried about now, Molly?" Clarence chided. "What'yre saying, woman? That my boy's some kind of retard? Leave him be. Ya hear? He'll be fine. Just fine. He's just a littler slower than the other kids. He'll catch up."

Clarence was so sure. But she knew better. A mother always knows.

Mickey was four years old when Molly's suspicions were confirmed. She was in the kitchen, pouring beeswax into candle molds while Mickey and Tommy Myers played quietly on the carpet in the other room. Heat was pouring out of the woodburning stove. The warm air washed across the tiny window above the sink and collided with the biting January wind from the other side, forming beads of condensation that caught the light being thrown from a pair of candles on the table. She ran her open palm across her forehead, then wiped the moisture on the front of her apron. She peeled off her sweater and stepped away from the candles in search of some cooler air. She smiled when she saw Tommy. He had dumped Mickey's crate of wood blocks and was sitting in the middle of the floor building a house of some sort and talking feverishly about the imaginary people who lived there. The gleam in the child's eye juxtaposed with Mickey's wooden countenance alarmed her. It had never been so clear to her as at that moment. Something was wrong. Mickey was still, except for his usual rocking back and forth. He was staring blankly at the pile of blocks yet to be used, all the while repeating the word *barn* over and over. Tears formed in her eyes as she yielded to the power of this recognition.

As the years unfurled, Clarence was forced to recognize the grim reality of life with a child who, by his estimation, was not "square." Mickey learned to talk and was fairly quick with numbers and computations. He could also memorize certain things, such as Molly's favorite poem—the one she would recite to him when he was a child and would get upset. It's the only thing that calmed him down. He was always affectionate with Molly. But certain things he could not do. Things that a farm boy was expected to do. The horrible scenes still haunted her.

"Listen, boy, you and me are gonna fix that there fence out front. Grab that hammer and follow me."

"Clarence," Molly protested. "He's only eleven years old. He can't do that. Leave him be."

Her protectiveness burdened Clarence to irritation. "Now, what did we say about sticking your nose where it don't belong, woman. Hush up. He's fine. Time he started acting like a real boy. Now I don't want to hear nothing more about it or you'll feel me."

The narrow gravel path stretched away slowly to a chain of irregular tufts of dry earth dotted here and there with patches of crabgrass and dandelions, on which a series of crooked slats of threadbare wood rested precariously. Molly watched from the window through tearful eyes as the man and the boy schlepped a metal box of tools down the path, with Clarence barking at Mickey the entire way.

She didn't want to look anymore. She just couldn't. Whenever she felt this way, her chest hurt. Tightened up as if someone had wrapped a rope around her ribs and were pulling at both ends. She had to busy herself, the same way she always did whenever the dreadful reality of her existence enveloped her this way.

She placed her hand on the closet doorknob, turned it, and reached inside. She pulled out a broom and swept feverishly, raising a tiny cloud of dust. After that, she scrubbed the countertops and washed and rewashed every plate and glass she could pull from the cabinets. As she worked, her thoughts wandered to a better time—a time when she was young, and life was effortless. She drifted past weathered red barns, sleepy cornfields, and wide, clovered pastures filled with grazing cows. She saw rustic farmhouses with wrap-around porches and flower boxes bursting with brilliant reds and yellows. She heard children, herself included, playing ring-a-levio on a lush green lawn that stretched out endlessly like a thick, beautiful blanket. She also heard the clink of horseshoes and the gentle drone of a crop duster scraping the sky. She smelled honeysuckle and wisteria, and all of a sudden she could taste the wood reed in her clarinet. It was all there. So vivid. So real. Harlequin images of life in its purest form. But the life depicted wasn't her life. Not anymore. The emptiness mastered her. She sat down for a moment, let her head fall limp into her open palms, and just wept.

The discordant song of crickets and katydids clashed on the cool breath of early evening. Darkness was pulling the sun down beyond the distant treetops. She had all but arrested the unavailing flight of her heartbreak when suddenly there broke from the somber silence the most horrible cry she had ever heard. It began softly, but soon swelled, louder and louder, escalating into a plaintive wail of pain and fear and anger all mixed together in this one dreadful shriek. She rushed to the window. Peering out, she was aghast at what she saw. It was Mickey. He was on his knees, chin pressed tightly to his chest, eyes closed and hands firmly placed over his ears. He was rocking back and forth and screaming. Clarence was standing over him ominously, wielding a freshly cut two-by-four while firing spontaneous invectives at the child before finally breaking a piece of wood over the boy's back.

"You lousy, good-fer-nothing moron! Get your ass up off the ground. I'll learn ya to hammer nails like a sissy."

The boy continued to scream. His father's voice was a dull, roaring sound crashing in his ears. His stomach tightened and his chest heaved. Then he lost control of his bladder and wet himself. It infuriated Clarence even more.

He fired another two-by-four across the yard and looked skyward in exasperation. "What the hell did I do to deserve this horseshit!" he thundered. "Jesus Christ!" With his hands on his hips, he turned to face the other direction. His eye followed the gravel path back to the farmhouse, where it caught Molly in the window, cowering behind a thin blue-and-white curtain, drying her eyes with a damp handkerchief.

MILWAUKEE

Murph introduced Mickey to the team on a day when faces were long and expectations at an all-time low. They were mired in a thirteen-game skid, and their descent in the standings had been well publicized in all the newspapers. It had them all on edge. "Listen up, fellas," Murph announced. "I want you all to meet Mickey. Mickey here is gonna be doing some pitching for us."

George "Lefty" Rogers, the team's star hurler and only southpaw on the staff, was the first to fix his narrow eyes on Mickey. Lefty was a tall, lanky fireballer himself who had, up until now, seemed destined for the majors. He'd led the league in each of the last two seasons in both wins and strikeouts. Most said only his surliness had kept him from the big show for this long. But there was a dearth of good pitching throughout the league. Another good year in the minors and it would be hard for some struggling team not to pick him up. A recent injury to his left elbow, however, had taken some velocity off his fastball and rattled his confidence. His recent decline was, as all the papers reported, a large part of what ailed the Brewers. Sitting at his locker, he had one eye on Mickey and the other locked on the equipment boy, Larry.

"I don't understand what happened today, Larry," he lamented, his long fingers curled tightly around the seams of a pearl white baseball. "This is how I always hold my curveball. Don't this look right to you?"

The first thing they all noticed was Mickey's size. At six foot five, 250 pounds, he was easily the biggest guy on the team. They wondered how such a big kid could possess enough agility to throw a baseball. And all of them worried secretly about his ability to hit one. This was especially true of Woodrow Danvers.

Woody Danvers was the Brewers' hard-hitting third baseman. He wasn't particularly big himself, but he was barrel-chested and had bulging forearms and lightning-fast wrists. His long-ball prowess and boyish good looks made him a real crowd-pleaser. He was a pretty good teammate as well—supported all the other guys enthusiastically—provided everything was going well for him. A few hits would always launch him into a garrulous fit of dizzying proportions. He'd prattle on about baseball or their families or about the most insipid things, from the smell of his girl's new perfume to his nightly routine of brushing each tooth individually and then rinsing out his mouth with some sort of homemade antiseptic and a turkey baster. It was so bad sometimes that the guys found themselves making wild excuses just to get away. But on days when he wore the collar, had nothing to show for his four at bats, he'd walk right by you as if he didn't even know you. Murph always joked that when Woody was in a slump, he wouldn't give you a second thought even if your balls were on fire.

The hulking farm boy stood there, faintly rocking, his massive right hand attached to Murph's shoulder. He was scanning the room, and Arthur could hear the faint whisper of poetic words beneath the boy's breath. His eyes darted between the spirals of white towels draped over the edge of a yellow bin and the half-dressed guys sitting on the pine bench just in front.

"Hey, Murph," Woody called. "We starting a football team or something?" Woody looked around for affirmation. He was pleased when a couple of the others chuckled.

"Don't you go getting your jockstrap all bunched up now, Danvers," Murph shot back. "Mickey here is quite a pitcher, but God knows there's only room for one glamour boy on this team." The biting comment elicited even more laughs from the guys.

The words *quite a pitcher* drew the full attention of Lefty, who abandoned his curveball grip to devote his full attention to Murph's announcement. He struggled for a moment against himself. He felt a slight throb of pain at the thought of his talent, once certain, now fleeting.

"Well, maybe he can pitch a little Murph. But, Christ, can the boy talk?"

That got the rest of them buzzing. They had all observed Mickey's reticence and unusual mannerisms and wondered what Murph was trying to pull. Over the steady murmur echoing off the stone walls of the cavernous room could be heard more audible comments laced with exasperation, such as "Now they're sending us retards" and "Welcome to the circus." Some thought Murph could be a little out of touch sometimes, but he still possessed a good ear.

The same was true for Murph's bench coach, Farley Matheson. Matheson was a good twenty, maybe thirty years Murph's senior and had been in baseball forever, although no one actually knew how old he *really* was. There was a lot of talk that Matheson played with Honus Wagner and would have become a fixture at shortstop for the Pirates if Wagner had never come along. Some said he went further back than that—that he was the third person, the one nobody ever wrote about, there that day in Elihu Phinney's cow pasture in Cooperstown, along with Abner Doubleday, hitting a makeshift ball with a piece of wood and running around in circles like a banshee. He was barely five feet tall, a grizzled geezer with hunched shoulders, a thin, wrinkled neck, and watery eyes, a garrulous old coot who talked almost exclusively in metaphor and cliché. He was truly a caricature, like some almshouse flunky swimming in his baseball flannels.

"Pipe down now. All of you. You hear?" the cantankerous old man growled. "What the hell kind of question is that? Of course he can talk. You gotta trust your skipper. The chain is only as strong as its weakest link. Ya see? That's the problem with ballplayers today. It's gonna be fine, God willing and the creek don't rise. Just give the young colt a look-see."

Lefty and most of the others sighed heavily and rolled their eyes.

"Farley's right, boys," Murph added. "Mickey's down-right friendly once you get to know him." Murph turned to his latest discovery, patted him on the back, and smiled. Mickey's face was pale and dotted with perspiration. "Say hello to the fellas, Mickey."

The smell of sweat and musty lockers was strong in the boy's nose. His eyes were still roving, and he felt a little sick. His thoughts, wild and varied, were killing him. The enormity of the scene frightened him and stole his voice.

"Now, don't be bashful, son," Murph cajoled. "It's just the fellas. They're okay, Mickey. Say hello."

Mickey fidgeted a bit, licked his lips, and after great effort managed to pass a word. "Hello," he said languidly. "Hello."

Lefty guffawed and Woody and a few of the others joined in the ruckus. Aware of the derisive laughter, Mickey's face contorted and the rocking became more severe. Murph grew restless. He was just about to lambaste the entire bunch when the sound of a locker slamming split the commotion. That sound was followed by a voice, bold and vituperative.

"Shut your yaps. All of you. This is sickening. Giggling like a bunch of schoolgirls. That's what you all are. Your manager's trying to tell you something. And when your manager's trying to tell you something, you best listen."

Raymond Miller. He was the Brewer catcher. Had been for years. He stood at just five foot nine but was built like a tank—or a boxcar—which is how he earned his nickname. Many a runner rounding third with visions of glory in his eye had his hopes, and most often his body, dashed at home plate by a collision with Boxcar. He had gotten the better of every runner who had ever tried to run him down—all except Peter Barker of the Saratoga Generals, who took out Miller's legs illegally one afternoon when he rolled across the catcher's knees, even though the ball was still in the outfield and Boxcar was standing off to the side of the plate. His left knee popped and he lay there, grimacing, as the hope of making it to the next level slipped away.

His long, sandy hair and toothy smile belied the ferocity of his competitive fire. He was the most gregarious guy you could ever meet. And he could get you laughing so hard your sides would almost split. But everyone in the league knew the other side of him. And despite his affability, and the bum knee, everyone in the league feared him as well.

He was also the unofficial assistant coach and the moral conscience of the team. Everything that happened on the field or in the clubhouse was measured against his unwavering commitment to all that was righteous and just. Lefty had learned that lesson the hard way.

The lanky left-hander arrived in camp a few years back, his ego buoyed by all sorts of propitious predictions about his ability to perform at a high level. He knew what all the scouts were saying about him.

"Aspirin tablets. The boy throws aspirin tablets!"

He strutted around the clubhouse making all sorts of vainglorious remarks about how he wouldn't be with the rest of them for too long. He also sat by himself, ate by himself, and on road trips insisted on having the room closest to the ice machine, to feed his narcissistic compunction to ice every night, sometimes three and four times, to "keep the swelling down" in his golden arm. Most of the guys turned a deaf ear to the glib commentary and self-indulgent idiosyncrasies. They figured it would all run its course. But Boxcar had little tolerance for Lefty's shenanigans. He always kept a watchful eye.

Lefty's third start for the team was an absolute gem. His fastball was hopping, his breaking ball was rolling off the table, and he was painting the black of the plate with a dizzying assortment of offspeed pitches. He was locked in. Each of the first twenty-one batters just shook his head in frustration as he made his way back to the dugout. Lefty had them baffled. And he was getting stronger with every pitch. Shivers of excitement swept through the crowd as talk of a perfect game found its way to everyone's lips.

In the Brewer's half of the seventh, however, things got a little dicey. James Borelli, their fleet-footed center fielder and target of the dubious moniker "Jimmy Llamas," was drilled right between the shoulder blades by Grady Harper, the Spartans big right-hander. Harper shrugged and claimed the ball just got away, but everyone knew better. Two innings before, Jimmy Llamas had run down a ball labeled for the left-center-field gap. The catch was legit, and a brilliant defensive play by all accounts. But Jimmy's theatrics, including a flamboyant basket catch and an inflammatory hand gesture, had really irked the Spartans. There was no intent on Jimmy's part at all. That wasn't his way. He was just a goofball. His forehead slanted quickly back to his hair, which, in a prematurely moribund stage, revealed a host of unusual imperfections on his skull. His eyes were slow and heavy and lay most often expressionless beneath bushy eyebrows of dark brown. But it was his lips—two crimson slabs of liver, full and distended—that gave him the unusual nickname. That, and his nervous penchant for squirting saliva through the gap between his two front teeth every few seconds. When they first christened him, Jimmy was less than pleased.

"Hey, what's the deal with the llama thing?" he asked defensively. "You guys riding me?"

Woody was quick to quell the anxiety. "Relax, Borelli. It's a good thing. Really." He smirked a little, then struggled for an explanation. "Uh, the way you fire that ball from center field. Yeah. That's it. It just shoots out of your hand. Like those llamas at the town fair that are always spitting at the crowd. Man, you can't get away from it. It's like lightning. So is your arm, Borelli. That's all." Woody paused for a moment, trying to measure Jimmy's blank expression.

"So that's it," Woody continued. "Isn't that right, Lefty?"

Lefty was seated at his locker in front of his favorite pinup of Rita Hayworth, rubbing some liniment over his biceps. "Yeah, yeah. Right, Woody. Whatever you say."

Jimmy's face softened. He liked that. He wasn't accustomed to complimentary remarks. He liked it so much, he adopted a bad habit of forming a gun with his thumb and index finger and firing in pantomime every time he made a spectacular catch or cut someone down from the outfield. It was just good, innocent fun. But innocent or not, Jimmy had to pay the price that day against the Spartans. Baseball has this inimitable way of regulating itself. No attorneys. No mediators or formal negotiations. It was so much easier. Blood for blood. Plain and simple. That was the code.

Boxcar knew the code. Some said he created it. So when the first Spartan stepped to the plate in the top half of the eighth, he flashed a series of signals, the last one a closed fist, tightly drawn, with the exception of a wayward thumb pointing directly at the batter. Lefty peered in, furrowed his brow, and shook him off. Boxcar repeated the sign, only to be rebuked again. He threw his hand up in disgust.

"Time!" the catcher screamed. He walked out to the pitcher's mound, eyes filled with scorn. His mask was still pulled down across his face, making it difficult for Lefty to read his intention, but his gait summoned the other seven guys on the field to take cover.

"Certainly you know what you have to do, right, Lefty?" Boxcar asked peremptorily, taking the ball from the pitcher's hand.

"Hell yeah. I've gotten this guy twice already with high heat. No need to mess with that."

Boxcar slid his mask up to the top of his head. His eyes were still ablaze. "You're kiddin' me, Rogers, right? High fastballs? Not this time. He'll see just one pitch. Stick it in his ear."

"Are you kidding me, Box? No way. Jesus, I've got a perfect game here. A perfect game. You know how many scouts are out there to-night? Do you? I can't mess with that. This is my ticket out of here."

Lefty stepped back off the mound. He stood there incredulously, hands resting on his hips in quiet defiance. Boxcar moved closer to him, coming to rest directly on the rubber, elevating his eyes to meet Lefty's. The he placed his massive hand on his shoulder and put his lips to his ear.

"You stick that damned ball in his ear, or after the game, I'll put one in yours." He smiled quickly and his eyebrows danced a little as he pressed the young athlete's bravado, savoring the signs of its steady dissolution. He rubbed up the ball, dropped it deliberately in Lefty's glove, and turned back toward the plate. Then, as if suddenly remembering something of vital importance, he came back and through the iron bars of his mask whispered, "And I'll find another spot to put my bat."

The next pitch Lefty threw was a letter-high fastball that the batter tomahawked over the 326-foot sign in left field. In mere seconds, euphoria over minor league baseball immortality and a sure ticket to the big show was replaced by a suffocating shroud of failure. The perfect game, no-hitter, and shutout had all vanished like a fickle phantom. In just a few seconds, Boxcar's disdain for Lefty leaped exponentially and dropped a veil of silence over the entire ballpark. Everyone, including every member of the Spartans, had expected retaliation.

The Brewers dropped that game to the Spartans, 4–3. It was a heart-wrenching loss. When the final out was recorded, each Brewer walked off the field in ominous silence. No one said a word to Lefty. No one dared even look at Boxcar.

They sat at their lockers and undressed with an alarming sense of urgency while Matheson, at Murph's behest, prattled on, trying to lighten the mood.

"That's all right, fellas," he babbled, unaware of the insidious subplot brewing inside the room. "Hope springs eternal, boys. I seen it all before. Ya see? I may be long in the tooth, but I seen it before. It'll be fine. Greats oaks from little acorns grow." The sentiments were met with a collective groan. Nobody really listened to Matheson anymore. Any baseball savvy the man still possessed was grotesquely overshadowed by the comedic air that attenuated his every move.

Lefty remained by himself, as usual, indulging in his postgame ritual while buckling a little under the uncomfortable weight of his teammates' furtive glances. Danvers, Pee Wee, Jimmy Llamas, and the others just sat at their lockers, waiting for the fallout. They believed, to a man, that Boxcar's will would be done. They just could not understand what was taking so long. His justice was usually swift. But it had been almost a good forty-five minutes and he was nowhere to be seen.

One by one, each man finished changing. Matheson was still yammering something about "every path having its own puddle" and how they should "bless both the flowers and the weeds" as a steady trickle of bodies began exiting the clubhouse, each irritated by the quixotic banter and by Boxcar's apparent acquiescence. Nobody knew what to make of it. Was it the proverbial calm before the storm? Or had Boxcar finally gone soft, drifting without passion or purpose, like those shriveled paper bits that hover, black and weightless, in suspended animation above a campfire?

Lefty was the last to leave. He packed his bag and leaned for a while against the cool metal of his locker. No one was in sight, and the soft rays of the dying afternoon sun were falling, drowsy under the spell of dusk. He was replaying in his mind the bizarre sequence of events that had transpired just a few hours before. He was angry with Boxcar for breaking his rhythm with his white-knight routine. He was certain that his little visit to the mound was the reason for the "fat fastball" that landed some four hundred feet from home plate. He was also queasy. Truth be told, as cavalier as Lefty purported to be, he was still a little worried about what Boxcar would do now that Lefty had failed to execute his wishes. He had heard all the stories. But the longer he stood there, his contorted face obscured by falling shadows, the more he began to think that his concern was all for naught. He laughed at himself, then threw his duffel bag over his shoulder and headed for the door.

"Going somewhere, candy ass?" a voice echoed through the indistinct air.

"Listen, Box," the pitcher explained. "This is all just a big misunderstanding."

"I don't think so." The catcher gnashed his teeth as he closed in.

"Come on now. This is ridiculous. I really thought that—"

Lefty tried to dissuade his assailant, but before he could utter another word, Boxcar dropped him with one punch.

The lanky athlete stumbled over the bleached wood bench and crashed against the lockers. He lay there, his head swirling, looking up at Boxcar's face, lit now by the glow of vindictive justice.

"If it ever happens again, you'll lose a lot more than just a perfect game. Got it?"

"Yeah," Lefty replied weakly, blanched by the humiliation.

"Got it."

Neither of them spoke about the incident again.

Matheson fitted Mickey with one of the extra jerseys, number 8, because as Mickey had explained, "it was an even number that looked the same no matter which way you turned it." Then both Murph and Matheson continued showing Mickey around. It was early afternoon and the high sun shot rays of slanted light through the dusty blinds that adorned the small, cloudy windows of the clubhouse. Murph meandered on whimsically about the team and some of the unique personalities, mindful at every turn of the boy's uneasiness.

Murph was a terrific baseball man. He could really manage the flow of a game, pulling all the right strings at just the right time, and possessed enough baseball acumen to coach at any level. But the man's real genius lay in his understanding of his players—his inimitable ability to maximize what he could get from each of them, both on and off the field. He knew just how much to stroke Lefty's ego; he spoke to Jimmy Llamas with careful deliberation, the way you would a child; he understood Woody's reticence during those interminable batting slumps and knew enough to let Boxcar dispense his own brand of justice whenever the situation necessitated such. That's why when it came time to find someone to look out for Mickey in the clubhouse, he turned to his shortstop, Pee Wee McGinty.

"Here's your locker, Mick," Murph said, smiling. "The furnace is a little loud, but it's the best spot in the whole damn joint. Right next to Pee Wee's."

Pee Wee held out his hand to Mickey. "Good to meet ya, Mickey. Welcome aboard."

The others chuckled when Pee Wee's knuckles and all five fingers disappeared, swallowed by the massive grip of their newest teammate.

Murph paused meditatively. He was wondering, as the guys jeered and guffawed, if he had done something foolish. Bringing Mickey in this soon. It had sure seemed like a good idea. Yesterday he was afloat with myriad possibilities and all sorts of visions of success. Now that the boy was here, in his clubhouse with the others, he wasn't so sure. He shot a look at Matheson, who was clapping his hands and smiling a toothless smile.

"Well, Mickey, what do ya think?" Murph continued.

The room was silent. The entire team was looking on with hypnotic eyes. Mickey was vacant. He had lost track of his thoughts and was aimlessly staring off at a point in the distance.

"Mickey," Murph repeated uncomfortably under watchful eyes. "So, what do ya think? Will this be okay for you?"

The gentle giant licked his lips and nodded spasmodically. "Yeah. Yeah. Okay. Mickey thinks that this is okay. Yeah. Okay. Okay."

Elliot "Pee Wee" McGinty stood a mere five foot five inches tall and weighed a staggering 127 pounds soaking wet. He had red, cherubic cheeks and a headful of corkscrew curls. With his uniform on and his cap pulled neatly across his brow, he looked as if he should be studying for an algebra exam or shooting marbles in the schoolyard. Only the pencil-thin line of black stubble dotting his upper lip let outsiders know he was indeed a member of the team and not some baseball lackey just along for the ride. That, and his soft hands and lightning-fast feet, both of which distinguished him as the premier shortstop in the league.

McGinty was definitely the best fit for Mickey. His dad had died when Elliot was just eleven years old. Consequently, young Elliot became responsible for looking out for his mom and his younger sister, Emily, who was born with a degenerative hearing condition that had rendered her deaf by age four. The little girl struggled, drifting through life diffidently, unable to keep pace in a world that moved too swiftly and carelessly to allow for her needs.

"Why are you crying, Em?" Pee Wee often asked. "What's wrong?"

The answer was always the same. "It's the other kids," she signed. "Nobody likes me. They look at me funny. Or walk the other way when I'm coming."

"Come on, Em, give it some time. Once they get to know you,

you'll have plenty of friends."

"I don't think so, Elliot. Nobody wants to talk to someone's hands."

Murph remembered the bus ride home from Millersport, when he and Pee Wee wound up sharing a seat up front, and Pee Wee told him all about his rough childhood. A pitch-black sky was overhead. The only visible light came like fireflies from distant farmhouses and on the rare occasion when the wheels of the bus rolled past a utility pole with a lamp. Then, for a brief second, the entire cabin would flood with light, and they would momentarily smile but watch helplessly as the white streak rolled gracefully across their faces and up and over the seats, ultimately receding like a phantom.

"I've been in this racket for a lot of years, Pee Wee," Murph lamented. "Bus rides never get any easier."

"How come you still here then?"

"Gets in your blood, boy. Like a virus or the sweet scent of a woman. Something like that. Some would say I'm still looking for something. Got some unfinished business. I don't know. I just can't help it I suppose."

Pee Wee was staring at the hole in the back of the seat in front of them. "No, I don't mean baseball. This. Here. How come you're still here—not riding first-class somewhere?"

In the safety of the darkness, Murph resurrected that dream. It wasn't the type that just faded with waking, acquiescing to the early dawn. This dream was imbued with a colossal vitality, insinuating itself into everything he saw or heard. Everything he smelled. He couldn't look at a scorecard or put a bat in his hands without hearing the calls from the crowd. Everything was haunted. The smell of freshly cut grass. The sound of flags dancing in a stiff breeze. He couldn't even eat sweet-potato pie without reminiscing about Rosie's, the little truck stop he used to frequent with the guys when he was just a rookie. The images of glory days past spilled out of his head prolifically, each bump the bus hit rattling another loose from its cell. His first game as a Brewer; the game-winning home run to win the championship; the newspaper headline that read, "Murphy

Can't Miss"; the little kids, a zealous throng that followed him around after every game, clamoring for his signature. Then he recalled the collision, and the glorious jaunt through his storied past faded, and he was left, once again, sitting in a broken-down bus staring into the dark.

"I don't understand," Pee Wee repeated. "How come you're not with the big club?"

Murph sighed. "That's a story better told on a longer ride."

The two men sat quietly for a while, gazing out blankly through the window at the deserted landscape engulfed by a blanket of darkness. There were owls, not visible to their tired eyes, hooting from distant trees just beyond the open fields. Everything seemed to be inhabited by this vast emptiness. Through the still, lonely air, all they could discern were indistinct outlines of barns and cornstalks, as vapid and impalpable as their breath against the glass.

"Say, what about you, McGinty?" Murph finally uttered softly, interrupting the silence. "What's your story?"

Pee Wee shrugged and his mouth twisted a little. "Ain't a very happy one, I'm afraid. Daddy died when I was a kid. Mama was crushed. Damn near killed her too. She just cried all the time. I had to take care of her, and my deaf sister. Didn't leave too much time for anything else."

"That is rough."

"Yeah, that's it. I know what you're saying about the whole baseball-in-your-blood thing. It's what saved me. And I even had to fight for that. All the 'he's too small' talk. But I wouldn't have any of that! Hell, the diamond is the only place where I feel right. Like all the other crap that *seems* to matter outside the ballpark ain't worth a hill of beans."

"Amen, McGinty. I hear that."

The bus rolled past one of those lighted utility poles, and an errant ray of soft white caught Pee Wee's cheek and rested momentarily on a single tear that had come to rest. Murph pretended that he didn't see.

"It ain't easy being a man when you're a little boy," Murph whispered. "Looking out for your mom, and little sister. Cripe, half the time you don't know what to do, and the other half you do all wrong. And hell—when you're your size, not too many folks take you seriously anyhow." They both chuckled.

"You're all right McGinty," Murph continued. "You know that old expression Matheson uses—'It ain't the size of the dog in the fight, but the size of the fight in the dog.' I like that one. Makes a whole lotta sense. And by the looks of things, I'd say you swallowed yourself a Saint Bernard."

Murph remembered that conversation with Pee Wee, and the tear on his cheek. He was a kid who knew what it meant to struggle. Knew what it meant to be the underdog. He was just what Mickey needed.

BORCHERT FIELD—MAY

In the cool blue twilight, with the distant lamps of the tiny town glowing like the tattered ends of lit cigars, Mickey sat down on Arthur Murphy's front porch—squeezed himself into a rickety, white rocker that protested loudly under the burly boy's weight—and fumbled nervously through the team's media guide. Murph lived just a few miles from the ballpark, a twenty-minute scamper down the narrow dirt road all the locals referred to affectionately as Diamond Drive. His place was small, a modest gray dwelling that looked as though it had been dropped indiscriminately in the middle of a pale grass field flanked by clusters of big dead trees and restless tumbleweeds. The windows, clouded casements that winced uncomfortably at the barren acreage just outside, allowed only glints of light to pass through, obscurely illuminating the austere furnishings inside. It wasn't much to speak of, but it was home and would now provide Mickey with a haven from which Murph could watch him for as long as he was with the team.

"Your picture will be on one of those pages next year," Murph said with alacrity, dragging a bench alongside the rocker. "How does that grab you, Mickey?"

The boy nodded absently, his eyes affixed to the publication.

"You know, Mick, I was planning on using you in tomorrow's

game—if the time is right. You've practiced enough. Now I kind of want you to get your feet wet. Sound okay to you?"

The boy nodded again, continuing to nourish a daydream of limitless expansion seemingly tied to the pictures before him. Murph smiled at Mickey's innocence.

"Mickey," Murph repeated louder. "Do you want to play baseball tomorrow? In the game?"

Mickey lifted his head. "Yeah. Baseball." Mickey's eyes darted wildly from side to side, like two marbles rattling around inside a glass jar. "Got any pigs here?"

"How's that?"

"Have you got any pigs? Mickey loves pigs. Got me my own back home. Name's Oscar. Oscar's my pig." Mickey jerked his head irregularly and looked all about out of haggard and homesick eyes. He blinked erratically, with great purpose, as if the fluttering of his lids would somehow clear the lenses and bring into focus the orphic surroundings.

"I tell you what, Mick," Murph said, ever mindful of the boy's emotional state. "I don't have any pigs. But if you throw for me a little tomorrow, I can sure as heck try to get my hands on one."

Mickey looked down glumly at his feet and nodded. Without a word, Murph dragged the bench even closer to Mickey, engendering a quick look from the pensive boy.

"That's a pretty serious scar you got there, Mick." Murph traced with a steady eye the jagged line of raised skin on Mickey's forehead. "How'd it happen?"

Mickey sat quietly, staring blankly ahead into the approaching darkness, while unwittingly running his thick finger over the damaged area and scowling, as if the mention of the injury had brought to his idle mind a flood of memory.

Mickey spoke slowly but did not say much of anything, selecting his words carefully as if he were feeling for stones to step on to cross a rushing stream. He could still hear Clarence roaring and was unable to articulate the terror that had seized him now, all over again.

"You moron! Of all the harebrain, bone-headed things to do.

How could you leave my good work gloves outside? Huh? How do ya suppose I wear 'em now, all soaking wet from the goddamned rain last night?"

Mickey was paralyzed. He just stood before Clarence, head down, his voice reduced to nothing but a series of spasmodic whimpers.

"'One by one the casements catch, her beams beneath the silvery thatch—'"

"I'm talking to you, boy!" Clarence wailed. "Enough of that sissy crap. Look at yer daddy when he's talking to you."

Mickey shuddered beneath the blasts of alcoholic breath, raising his eyes ever so slightly.

"Well, dimwit. What have ya got to say fer yerself?"

"I, well, I—"

"Spit it out for Christ sakes!" Clarence demanded, raising an opaque glass bottle to his lips and gulping some of its contents. "I want an answer, boy!"

"I, uh, Mickey don't really know." He began to cry. "I guess I forgot."

"You forgot! You forgot? Is that what you said?" Clarence clenched his teeth.

"Mickey forgot," the quivering boy said through surging tears. "Mickey forgot. I'm sorry."

"Of all the stupid things to say! You forgot. Holy Christ. Are you kidding me?"

Mickey withered before the tyrannical farmer, his eyes shut, ears covered while he continued to utter, "I'm sorry," over and over.

Clarence's anger boiled over. "Look at me boy!" he barked. "Look at me now!"

Mickey opened his eyes and brought his hands down away from his ears. Clarence lowered his hands as well and sank into a momentary silence. The fit appeared to have abated, and Mickey had just started to breathe a little easier when Clarence whipped the bottle out from behind his back and struck him just above the eye, shattering the bottle and splitting open the boy's forehead. Sitting there with Murph, Mickey could still feel the sting of alcohol and dirt mixing with his blood. He could feel it just the same, but was powerless to share the horror.

"Your daddy isn't a nice man, Mickey, is he?"

Mickey's emotions formed a labyrinth out of the lines on his face. "I make him mad. Very mad. On account of me being a retard."

"Is that what he calls you?"

"Yes, sir, Mr. Murphy. He gets awful sore. Mad. He's always pitching a fit about something. It's why Oscar and me get on so well. I love all my animals. They can't talk, so I reckon they can't hurt you none neither."

"Yup, sure seems that way. But not all people call you names, Mick. There are some good ones. And as far as hitting you?"

"I ain't much good at anything."

"Does he get angry at your mom too?" Murph persisted. "You know, like he does with you?"

"Mama cries a lot."

Murph, feeling oddly shaken, placed his hand on Mickey's shoulder. "You're here now, Mickey," he said reassuringly. "It's okay. Things will be different."

They sat there a while longer, talking and looking out through the shroud of dusk at the countryside as it slipped away from them in irregular waves, an almost ghostlike series of slopes that crawled quietly toward the wasted expanse of land that lay just before the distant town. Murph wondered again silently, as he engaged the boy in small talk about this and that, if he had indeed made a mistake—if maybe he was asking too much. "He's a babe in the woods, Artie," Matheson warned him after meeting Mickey for the first time. "The jackals will tear him apart." Somehow, those words meant more to him now than before. In between his colloquial exchanges with this naïve boy, Murph listened to the wind, high in the trees, and thought for a moment that he could hear whispers of disapproval. Mickey, lost in thoughts of home, heard different sounds—the screams of his maniacal father, the sobbing of Molly, and the safe, playful grunting of the pink-and-black porker he called Oscar.

The next afternoon, wisps of cottonlike clouds stretched across the azure canvas of a high sky. The sun showered the manicured diamond at Borchert Field with cascading rays of golden yellow, and the redolence of spring danced gleefully on a warm breeze. It was a beautiful day for baseball.

The Brewers faced off against the Rangers of Spokane. The game was not fraught with intense rivalry rooted in previous battles, nor did a single game played this early in the season have any real postseason implications. But the skipper of the Rangers—a haunting demon from Murph's past—altered the daily face of things and made Murph want this game just a little more than usual.

Chip McNally was such a smug, surly son of a bitch. Always was. The only thing that had changed since their playing days together was the hint of gray around his temples.

"So, Murph," he said sarcastically as he limped awkwardly up to home plate to exchange lineup cards, "I see you guys are really ripping it up these days, eh?" He flashed a toothy grin, then discharged a thin stream of tobacco juice just in front of Murph's feet.

"Don't wet your Skivvies, gimpy," Murph fired back. "You just worry about yourself."

The game was a real barn burner. The Rangers put up six runs in the top of the first inning, only to see the Brewers answer with five of their own, highlighted by a prodigious grand slam off the bat of Woody Danvers. The next few innings followed a similar pattern, with both teams exchanging runs in the third, fourth, fifth, and sixth frames. The capacity crowd was getting its money's worth.

By the time the seventh-inning stretch rolled around, and each spectator had stood up, yawned, and sung a few bars of "Take Me Out to the Ball Game," the teams had together used eight pitchers. The Rangers were content to let their fourth hurler, Billy "Rubber Arm" Bradley, go the rest of the way. He was the Ranger workhorse. The guys always joked about the resiliency of Bradley's arm. He could throw one hundred plus pitches in a game, then pitch horseshoes with the guys, split a cord of wood, pick at his banjo, and be good to go the next day if needed.

"Man, I don't know what your secret is, Billy," the Ranger catcher always joked, looking down just beyond his waist. "But whatever it is, I got to get me some of that for my little slugger."

The Brewers, however, did not have that luxury. Butch Sanders was spent. He had been laboring since the middle of the fifth inning. And to make matters worse, the bullpen was short on arms. Packey Reynolds was sidelined with turf toe, and Hobie Miller was back home in Connecticut attending the funeral for his grandfather. That left Murph with just two possibilities—Lefty, who had never made a relief appearance and was scheduled to start tomorrow's contest, and Mickey, who was sitting on the top step of the dugout, poking his finger in and out of a series of anthills that had formed around the lip of the concrete platform. Murph sighed. He took off his cap, bowed his head, and ran his palm roughly across his scalp.

Some unforeseen hope came, however, in the bottom of the eighth frame. Pee Wee lead off the inning with a four-pitch walk. Jimmy Llama's Baltimore chop eluded the bare hand of the Rangers' third baseman, who had miscalculated the ball's topspin, and another walk to Woody Danvers loaded the bases. Down 15–13, Murph realized that a well struck ball would not only tie the game but would in all likelihood give them the lead.

But the tiny sparkle of optimism that danced wildly in Murph's eyes began to wane, suffocated by the all-too-familiar doldrums of unfulfilled expectation. Buck Faber took three pipe strikes, and Clem Finster ran the count to 3–2, fouled off the next five offerings, but ultimately went down, swinging wildly at a pitch in the dirt. "Oh, Jesus Christ!" Murph said, firing his cap hard against the dugout wall. "Swinging at a fifty-five-footer? What the hell do I have to do to catch a break?"

Boxcar was next. Ordinarily, this would have been heaven-sent. Your best player at the dish with the game on the line. But the Brewers' leader was mired in a 1-for-26 slump, including three situations just like this one. Murph folded his arms and sighed. "Perfect," he muttered bitterly. "Just perfect."

The Brewer catcher strode to the plate, serenaded by a frenzy of yelling and clapping and stamping of feet that washed across the ballpark like a tidal wave. Slump or not, he was their guy.

"Boxcar! Boxcar!" the raucous crowd roared.

He tapped each cleat with the shaved knob of his bat three times, in customary fashion. A subtle tip of his helmet and two practice swings that cut the air like an airplane propeller signaled he was ready.

He dug his back foot in the soft earth. For a moment, his eyes found a black-and-white placard in the centerfield bleachers: BOX-CAR IS GOD.

It was nice to see. They had not forgotten. He smiled, but only for a fleeting moment, the glimmer of glory in his mind's eye dimming quietly beneath the haze of the impending confrontation.

"You're only as good as your last at bat," he reminded himself.

The first delivery was a fastball, high and inside. Most definitely a purpose pitch. Everyone knew that Boxcar loved to extend his arms. His biceps were thirty inches of chiseled marble, two Herculean specimens bristling with raw power, rage, and fury. The only way to neutralize that power was to tie him up. The scouting report was clear and simple: hard stuff inside, junk away. He knew the routine. H-e was a catcher himself. It was all part of the dance—a classic game of cat and mouse.

The next offering was significantly slower and fluttered across the outside corner of home plate for a called strike. He grumbled a bit. Inside—outside. Inside—outside. He stepped out of the box and adjusted his helmet. His breath was hot.

"Come on, Boxcar," Murph yelled from the dugout, no longer able to sit still. "A little bingo. Come on now!"

The sound of his manager's voice quieted some of his frustration. He glared out at the pitcher, stepped back in, but backed out once more when an explosion of pigeons passed in front of the sun. They circled high overhead with a flutter and frenzy, casting a cold shadow that extended halfway across the diamond. Boxcar remained on the periphery of the chalk-lined rectangle alongside home plate, banging his cleats again. The pitcher shivered a little and pounded his glove while continuing to toe the rubber with an awkward restlessness. He released a venomous spray of tobacco juice in the batter's direction and cocked his head invitingly. Boxcar laughed. "Relax, Sporty," Boxcar said, staring playfully out at the tiny hill that lay some sixty feet in front of him. "I'll be your huckleberry."

He dug in once more. The congregation of birds dispersed fearfully and the darkness lifted, the sun revealed once more, fresh in a clear blue sky. Boxcar was certain he knew what was coming next. The Rangers catcher was set up prematurely on the inside half of the plate. It was a transparent ruse, a feeble attempt at making Boxcar believe they were going to bust him in again.

The pitcher took his sign. He placed his hands together and let them fall, slowly, methodically, until they came to rest momentarily at his waist. Then he lifted his leg and cocked his arm back behind his ear. Boxcar could hear the catcher shifting behind him to the outer half of the plate as the ball rolled effortlessly out of the pitcher's hand. The sun caught the tiny sphere as it traveled to the catcher, laces spinning like a carnival pinwheel. It reminded Boxcar of the tiny white butterflies he used to observe from time to time as a kid, skittish but graceful. The ball orbited on the gentle breeze momentarily, suspended precariously like a wayward dandelion seed, before beginning its descent for its final destination. Boxcar's eyes widened. The padded cowhide glove yawned patiently behind him, waiting to receive the tiny traveler. But Boxcar's bat interrupted the artful choreography and caught the ball square as it floated across the plate, sending it screeching toward the gap in left center field.

Murph was bent over the watercooler when he heard the thunderous explosion off Boxcar's bat. He turned quickly, eyes wide but incredulous, and saw the ball rolling inexorably toward the wall and his beleaguered Brewers circling the bases. Pee Wee scored first, followed closely by Jimmy Llamas. Murph was on the top step of the dugout, alongside Mickey. His moribund spirit took flight.

"Come on, Woody!" he screamed, arms flailing like a windmill, as Danvers rounded third base. "Get the damned piano off your back!"

Danvers hit the inside corner of the bag in full stride. His face was strained—two hungry eyes and a clenched jaw fully visible with the loss of his cap. His chest heaved and his spikes whirled like two rotors, unearthing large clumps of clay in his wake. He was halfway down the third-base line when the shortstop, standing impatiently on the lip of the outfield grass, received the cutoff throw. The ball was in his glove for a mere second before he whirled and fired a bullet toward home plate.

The crowd had worked itself into a dizzying fit of glorious expectation. Everyone was standing, willing Danvers to safety. The ball and the runner arrived at precisely the same time. The crowd gasped, then fell silent after a thunderous sound pierced the air. Both the catcher and Danvers crumpled helplessly to the ground, dazed and shaken by the violent collision. Danvers lay limp, balled up in a twisted heap stretched across home plate. His eyes glazed over and tiny beads of sweat and blood sat nervously on his dirt-stained cheeks, quivering curiously beneath the penetrating stare of the yellow sun. The catcher rested some five to six feet beyond the circular dirt cutout where he usually sat, flat on his back, pinned beneath the weight of his gear and the disappointment of having let the ball roll from his fingers following the vicious collision.

"Safe!" was the call, an exclamation that shattered the silence. The crowd exhaled, a collective wind that seemed to ruffle every flag in the ballpark. Everyone remained standing and roared with approval.

The Brewers took that one-run lead into the ninth inning. Murph had hoped to plate one or two more insurance runs, but it was not to be. Arky Fries went down looking, ending the Brewer rally prematurely. So Murph crossed himself, sighed wearily, and handed the ball back to Butch Sanders.

"Come on, Sandy," he implored, patting the pitcher on the shoulder. "I need this one. Bad. Let's sit 'em down, okay? One, two, three."

Sanders looked like a little boy who had just limped away from a street fight. His eyes, two fading stars, sank languidly into a face both red and awash with despair. He stumbled onto the field, shoulders rounded and dusty, and took his place on the hill. Tiny black flies flickered all about his cap, briny and askew, and a steady buzz from the crowd hopped on the frenetic air until finally settling directly above him. He exhaled. He knew he had nothing left.

He peered into Boxcar for the sign. His first delivery was feckless, a flat fastball that just glided across the middle of the plate. It was fired right back at him, narrowly missing his head, and scooted into center field.

"Mickey," Murph called, continuing to watch the desperate affectations of his wounded pitcher. "Run down to the pen with Matheson and Barker and loosen up."

The next batter caught a similar pitch right on the sweet spot of his bat, sending a frozen rope to third. The ball appeared destined for the left-field corner. But Woody Danvers, still riding the high of the previous half inning, lay out, full extension, and snared the smash in his web just at it passed by.

"Oh, Jesus!" Murph bawled. "Matheson? Matheson? Would you move your ass down there?" he yelled desperately. Sanders was out of gas. Murph knew it. The Rangers knew it. They were all licking their chops and swinging from their heels. Even the crowd knew it, and a smattering of boos and jeers began cascading onto the field. Murph stretched his glance to the bullpen. Matheson knew what he wanted and shook his head and held up five fingers. Murph cursed and crossed himself again.

The next batter sent two long foul balls soaring into the bleachers before lining a sharp single to left. That was followed by a scorcher to right. The runners each advanced one base, loading the bags for the Rangers' third- and fourth-place hitters.

Murph's heart sank. "Time!" he called. He hung his head and made the long walk to the mound. "Like some goddamned Abbott and Costello routine," he muttered under his breath.

He hated these trips to the mound more than anything. His spirit always labored, buckling beneath the weight of ruthless castigation that would come from the fans, the local press, and at times his own team.

"Left 'im in too long" or "Never should have started him to begin with" were only two of the comments he imagined being bandied about. And as if the concern over their words weren't enough, he lamented over what *he* was going to say—that desperate search for the pithy sentiment that would preserve the dignity of his pitcher and at the same time extricate himself from any further scrutiny or criticism over why he had stayed with him so long.

On the way out, he measured his gait, mindful of the myriad superstitions attached to stepping on the sacred lines of chalk. So, he would walk gingerly, methodically, like one who was negotiating the dimpled, slippery side of a fallen tree trunk stretched across a raging river. His focus was clear—just get to the other side. And although he tried to prevent it, his eyes always strayed from the intended destination, wound up flirting with the many faces in the crowd, rendering him lost amidst the kaleidoscope of images and the shrill, admonitory voices filtering through the fitful abstractions. It was then, at that moment, when he always felt the sweat beading on his back. Each step he took stoked the fires of vexation even further and seemed to amplify the discord raining down on him.

"You lousy bum! Go back where you came from! You stink so bad you could knock a crow off a shit wagon!"

These sounds and sights swirled turbulently and always seemed to him not simply the atmospheric conditions of a ballpark in flux but the rushing of the flames of hell. It never got any easier. He often mused that one day, when he arrived at the hill after conquering the proliferation of pitfalls that always accompanied a pitching change, the earth would laugh sardonically and just open up and swallow him whole.

"You gave it your best, kid," he said to Sanders, patting his back. "It's okay. Hit the showers." Sanders hung his head and departed without a word. Then Murph made a deft motion with his right arm, signaling to the bullpen.

Mickey bounded out from the pen to a faint, inquisitive buzz that insinuated itself into the ear of every person in the park. Murphy was at it again. Another reclamation project. He was the champion of the lost cause. A long list of misfits and has-beens trailed in Arthur's wake. He'd been quiet of late, stopped courting this quixotic pie-in-the-sky philosophy after his last effort ended so bitterly. Scooter Moran, the Athletics' young, talented third baseman who'd ascended the amateur ranks like a phoenix, was left for dead after he was beaned in the left eye by Grover Daniels.

"Never be the same," they all said. "Nobody ever is."

Murph thought differently. "I know the A's let Moran go. I know. But I'm telling you, Mr. Dennison, I can feel this one. Really. He's gonna be fine. Let's sign him." Scooter was grateful to Murph, but all the gratitude in the world could not resurrect his moribund career. He batted a meager .138 in his first twenty-one games with the Brewers. The nineteen-year-old phenom from Mississippi had felt the heat from both the fans and the press.

So did Murph. He had left the struggling third baseman in during some pivotal moments, and in each instance Scooter's failure translated into failure for all the rest of them. Dennison was just about to drop the hammer on both of them when Scooter disappeared. Just up and left. Cleared out his locker one night. Walked in with tears in his eyes and a bag draped over his shoulder. It took him less than ten minutes to pack his dreams into a tan gunnysack. Then he caught a train back home.

Murph was crushed. "Jesus Christ! This is the thanks I get? Not even a goddamned note? A thank-you?" It took a while for the sting of failure and disappointment to abate. Most thought for sure Murph had finally learned his lesson. But old habits die hard. So when the crowd saw Mickey entering the game, hat askew, jersey stretched uncomfortably across his preposterously large frame, they only gasped momentarily, then rolled their collective eyes and sighed.

A small, impromptu gathering took place at the mound underneath an uncertain sky: Murph, Boxcar, and now Mickey. Mickey took the ball and smiled, his fleshy cheeks dimpling. Murph raised his eyebrows and smiled back. Mickey's eyes looked directly into Murph's, so intensely, and with such fervor, that Murph could see the little dark flecks, illuminated by intermittent flashes of sunlight, in the colored part around the pupils. The boy was so pure. Inside Murph's head, a cyclone was at work. He wondered, as he had the previous three innings, if the time was right.

"Well, Mick, she's all yours. Just relax. Relax. Throw the ball right to Boxcar's glove."

"Uh-huh," Mickey replied, thinking thoughts about baseball and farmhouses and the anthill he had discovered only moments before.

"That's right, kid," Boxcar added. "Nothin' to it. Like shootin' fish in a barrel. Just listen to me—hit the targets, and we'll be fine. Got it?"

"Yup. Yup, Mickey can do that."

The fickle sun came out once again, this time for good, tinting the late-day sky a pinkish orange. Murph returned to the dugout, cyclone still raging, and Boxcar squatted behind the plate. Mickey stood on the rubber, feet dangling awkwardly over the dirty white stripe, and peered in at Boxcar.

"Okay, Mick!" he yelled. "Just give me a few warm-ups here."

Mickey nodded confidently as if he had been putting out fires like this all his life. He smiled again and pounded the ball into the pocket of his glove. But before he could release his first toss, his eyes wandered to the frenetic crowd, and a strange, hunted look fell across his face. Then came the nervous rocking, back and forth, back and forth, like a pendulum. Boxcar stood up.

"Mickey," he yelled, waving his arms over his head. "Here. Look here. Just here. At me. Come on now. Hit the glove. Toss me the ball. Right here."

Mickey blinked hard. His nostrils flared for a second and he ran his tongue across his lips. Then he moved his back foot off the rubber and arched his back, a spasmodic gesture punctuated by the peculiar rolling of his arms, and fired the ball at Boxcar. The ball popped in the catcher's glove like a pistol shot, reverberating through the stands. The report of Boxcar's glove silenced the bristling crowd, leaving them speechless and wide-eyed beneath the pall of improbability.

Pop! Pop! Pop!

The sound was deep and leaden, like heavy stones falling to earth.

Pop! Pop! Pop! Pop!

Seven tosses, each one drawn to Boxcar's glove with the accuracy of an archer's arrow. The sound engendered great interest among spectators and players alike. All eyes were fixed on the burly pitcher. Even the ushers and peanut hawkers suspended their business to take a gander at a most extraordinary event.

The next Ranger batter strode to the plate with a curiosity that supplanted his desire to tie the game. Who was this kid, swaying side to side, rolling his arms like some kind of vaudeville magician? How could this freakish farm boy who looked more like something that should be featured at a corner carnival than at a baseball game throw a ball with such velocity, such accuracy?

It was all picture-perfect. The young, unknown phenom, riding in on his white horse to save the day—all in front of an eager crowd. What could have been better?

Yes, it was all perfect, until the batter stepped to the plate, disrupting the harmony of the dream and diverting Mickey's attention from Boxcar's glove. There he was. Just him against the batter. It was strange, he thought, that he was out there alone. In his overwrought condition, it was more than he could handle. All at once he looked oddly uncomfortable, as if he had already digested what his senses and intellect could not yet grasp.

Mickey's first pitch was a dart that whistled by both the batter and the catcher, soaring about two feet above the intended target and coming to rest up against the backstop.

"Like a goddamned frog in a frying pan," Matheson cried. "Has the kid even pitched to a live batter yet?"

Murph cringed in the dugout, his hopes collapsing as the runner from third scampered home with the tying run. Boxcar retrieved the ball and walked it back out to Mickey. "Relax kid, okay? Relax.

Nice and easy. Just play catch. Warm-ups, remember? Just like that. Okay?"

"'Couched in his kennel, like a log, with paws of silver sleeps the dog,'" Mickey recited.

Boxcar's eyes narrowed. Mickey was withdrawing fast. His mind wandered to his mom and the farm and to the black, triangular spot just behind Oscar's right ear.

"Mickey? You okay?"

The boy was miles away.

"Come on now, Mickey. Take the ball."

Mickey was unresponsive. Boxcar looked into the dugout, in Murph's direction, but the manager's face was expressionless. Then the frustrated catcher raised his eyebrows and held up both palms to the sky. But Murph did nothing. Said nothing. He just stood there, shoulder propped awkwardly against the dugout wall, thinking about all the times his life had forked, and how each path he'd chosen had led to this sort of silent desperation.

"Murph!" Boxcar shouted from behind his mask. "What's up?"

The catcher stood on the mound, hands resting impatiently on his hips, waiting for a suggestion, some encouragement, or just a word or two on which he could hang his frustration. "Hey," he continued to shout. "What are we doing here?"

Murph saw Boxcar, perplexed, and the image became, all at once, mesmerizing and impenetrable. The longer he looked, the more unreal it became until he felt a sense of panic, as if he needed to shake himself out of some alien transfixion.

"Just, eh—just keep talking to him, Box," he yelled back, swallowing hard. "Keep talking to him."

Boxcar shook his head and frowned. He nourished a constant stream of encouraging thoughts in his head, ever mindful of the grave situation, but whenever he said any of them out loud, it just seemed forced and ineffectual. "Come on, Mickey," he implored again, this time placing the ball firmly in Mickey's glove. "Just throw the ball. You can do it. You are the best out here."

A slight buzz came from the stands, as if a hornets' nest had been disturbed, yet most of the people suspended any further action and ultimately fell still and silent, wetting their lips while studying the erratic behavior unfolding on the pitcher's mound.

After a lot of posturing and moving of dirt with restless spikes on the mound, the umpire broke up the exchange. "Let's go, fellas. Let's play ball."

Boxcar returned to the plate. Mickey moved some more dirt around in front of the rubber, then reluctantly placed his feet across the white stripe. He brought his hands together at his waist, rolled his arms, reared back, and fired. The pop of the catcher's glove resonated throughout the stands, followed by a collective gasp and then the umpire's call.

"Strike one!"

Boxcar grimaced and shook his left hand. He returned the ball to Mickey with his right. "Attaboy, big fella! Keep firing."

Mickey threw four more times, and although each delivery "popped" the catcher's glove, they all fell outside the strike zone.

"Oh, Jesus Christ!" Murph muttered under his breath. "Another walk. The bases are filled again."

Boxcar showered Mickey with all sorts of clichéd encouragement, and the young pitcher continued to roll his arms and deliver. But he could not place the ball where Boxcar wanted. Eight more balls out of the strike zone, and the Brewers found themselves down by two runs.

"Time!" Boxcar yelled. He flipped up his mask and began to make his way back to the mound, but was suddenly arrested by a stern admonition from the dugout.

"Boxcar, you get your sorry ass back behind the plate. Enough already. Let the kid alone. He'll be fine."

Boxcar sighed and pulled his mask down over his mouth. He crouched back down behind the plate, baking in the unrelenting heat. The day had been just too long. His knees hurt and his right elbow felt as if someone had taken a hammer to it. Sweat beaded on his upper lip, and one drop found its way into his mouth when his lips formed the words nobody could either see or hear.

"Goddamned asshole."

Mickey peered into the rounded glove. He licked his lips, rolled, and fired at the next batter.

"Strike one!" the umpire announced.

With the ball back in his glove almost instantly, Mickey rolled and fired again.

"Strike two!"

The crowd exploded in applause and whistles, intoxicated by the popping leather and the umpire's approval. Everything in the tiny ballpark clicked into slow motion, creating a dream state in which the secret thoughts and longings of all witnessing the spectacle were revealed. This wonderland blundered against familiar disappointments until, little by little, it again became a scene of real life, with people screaming and applauding with rabid expectation.

"Come on, Mickey!" some of them exhorted from the bleachers. "Go get 'em."

Mickey seemed unphased, unemotional as ever. He took the ball, banged it in his glove two times, rolled his arms, and fired.

"Ball one!"

The disappointment did nothing to thwart the crowd's excitement. They cheered and whistled and stamped their feet until the next pitch was thrown.

"Ball two!" screamed the umpire.

A palpable release of air all around the park was followed by a nervous whispering. Boxcar pumped his fist with dogged optimism; Murph paced and lamented to Matheson as the crowd watched through slightly parted fingers.

"Ball three!"

All the euphoria yielded suddenly to a cold probability. The Ranger batter stepped out of the box and smiled, banging his spikes, secure in the belief that something good was coming. Up two runs already; full count; bases loaded—he was sitting pretty. The entire Brewers team sagged a little, aware of the same reality. Woody Danvers was the first to approach the mound, followed by McGinty and then Boxcar. The threesome formed a half circle around the struggling pitcher. At close range their faces showed the tension.

"Come on now, Mickey," Danvers demanded. "This ain't no joke here. Stop screwing around."

"Back off, Woody," McGinty answered. "That ain't gonna help." Then he turned toward Mickey. "Come on now, buddy. Burn it down the pipe. He ain't swinging."

Boxcar was more guarded. He watched Mickey's eyes. They were glassy and skittish. The pitcher's stomach felt sick. Boxcar could see it. The other two went back to their positions, satisfied that their words had altered Mickey's spirits. Boxcar remained a moment longer. Then he offered some simple encouragement: "Mick. It's just a game."

The sky was filled with roiling clouds driven by a stiff wind that slipped into the stadium through concrete walkways, stirring up a storm of hot-dog wrappers and discarded box scores from the morning's sports section. Mickey, unnerved by the sudden squall, stepped off the rubber once or twice and swatted nervously at the heavy air.

"Okay, Mick," Boxcar yelled from behind the plate. "Come on now. Nice and easy."

Mickey paused for a long interval, trying to collect the varied thoughts germinating in his mind. *Three balls and two strikes; fire it in there; Murph's frowning; wind in my face; six rows of apples, five deep; what's Oscar doing; my stomach hurts.*

"Come on, Mick!" Boxcar yelled again. "Here we go."

Mickey stepped gingerly to the center of the rubber. His eyes caught the batter's arms, big and trunklike, hanging over the inside half of the plate. Mickey slid his feet along the white stripe, finally coming to rest some five or six inches left of his initial spot. He made a slight sound with his lips, as if he had just spit out a tiny fleck of dirt or a watermelon seed, then began his delivery. With arms in full motion, he leaned back, gave a violent push with his back leg, and fired the ball directly at Boxcar's mitt. The red laces sliced the air and hissed angrily as the ball rocketed toward the batter, Mickey's eyes wedded to its path like those of a mother bird who had just pushed her last baby from the nest. He followed its flight the entire way, willing it to its intended destination, blinking only when the white sphere disappeared in the soft, brown leather folds waiting patiently.

"Ball four!"

Mickey was motionless. The batter clapped his hands in approval as another run crossed the plate.

From the bench, Murph saw his dream begin to wane.

"What now, Skip?" Matheson asked, chewing on the end of a whittled piece of wood. "You want me to go get 'em? He's just spinning his wheels. Can't see the point of leaving him out there. He's about as much use now as a yard of pump water."

"Farley, what the hell are you saying? He's all we got now. I ain't going to Lefty. I can't burn another pitcher."

Matheson broke away with sudden uncharacteristic reticence before uttering his final shot.

"You're right," the sententious old man replied. "Be like closing the barn door after the horse already escaped."

The muscles in Murph's face stiffened. He couldn't understand what was happening out there. He was so sure it would work. That Mickey would succeed. Now the entire scene resembled nothing more than a fun-house mirror in which his own reflection was cast, distorted and grotesque. The kid still wanted the ball. But Matheson was right. Mickey was fried. Murph knew it, but had no choice but to go with him. He had all but decided to turn the reins over to Matheson and head for the showers himself, unable to stomach any more failure, when a line drive off the bat of the next batter found its way to McGinty's glove and an inning-ending sparkler turned in by Danvers stopped the bleeding.

The defensive gem kept Murph around, but his hopes were quickly dashed when the Brewers were retired one-two-three in their half of the ninth. He hung his head, kicked the watercooler, and cursed his rotten luck. Then he caught sight of McNally across the field, smirking, heading his way, wanting to hurt someone.

"Jesus Christ, Murphy," the opposing skipper gloated. "Is that your best? What kind of freak show are you running over there?"

Murph was just about to let loose on McNally when from the top step of the dugout he saw Dennison, motioning to him with a stone countenance and an impatient finger for a postgame meeting.

After the game, the Brewers' locker room morphed into a maelstrom of anger, disappointment, and frustration. Each player sat at his locker carping about Murph and how the old guy was getting kookier than Matheson.

"This ain't some friggin' sandlot league," Finster bawled across the room. "Christ, how many more games are we gonna have to lose before something changes? What the hell is he thinking?"

"He's losing it," Llamas responded loudly. He spit nervously. "The friggin' guy is desperate and he's killing us in the process. An overgrown clodhopper? That's his answer? Ain't things bad enough without this bullshit?"

A smattering of garbled commentary continued as the players got undressed. Mickey sat in front of his locker, next to Pee Wee, still in full uniform. He heard the acerbic banter and his eyes grew moist. He wiped them with one hand and brought the other to his stomach, where a pain throbbed deep within. He had all but suppressed the emotional explosion when Danvers happened by.

"Nice going, hayseed," he mocked, knocking the boy's cap off with a sharp blow to his head. "Way to blow the game, bumpkin."

Pee Wee retrieved the cap from the floor. An awkward silence was filled with the arrhythmic breathing of rising tempers.

"Back off, Woody," Pee Wee fired, fearful that the entire room was going to turn violent. "Your goddamned home run still counts."

"Yeah, defend the yokel, McGinty, you little turd," Faber shouted. "That idiot there's the best thing ever happened to you. For sure." Faber paused. "There's finally someone freakier than you."

Pee Wee stood up among titters of hysterical laughter.

"Anytime you want a piece, Faber, you know where to find it."

The entire room erupted into a frenzy of derisive hooting, stamping feet, and banging lockers. Boxcar, who had hoped to stay out of the fracas, stepped away from his locker and was just about to settle the room when Murph came in on his way to see Dennison. The ruckus ceased instantly.

"Don't let me spoil all the fun, fellas," Murph said, his face expressionless. He had heard the source of commotion with ears ablaze. It bothered him to be the object of their criticism and ire. It bothered him even more that he had dragged Mickey down with him. His heart constricted with a repulsion for himself so clear, so intense, that it almost took his breath away.

"Hey, Mick," he said, walking over to the sullen boy. "Everything good here?"

Mickey was surprisingly unmoved. He wanted to scream, to tell his manager how awful he felt. He wanted to tell him he wanted to go home but did not know the way. And that he didn't know what a hayseed was. But he didn't. Somehow, he knew better.

"I'm okay, Mr. Murphy," he answered mechanically. "Mickey is fine."

Warren Dennison's office was dimly lit by a whisper of light creeping in from behind cream-colored vinyl roller shades stretched awkwardly across varnished cherrywood window frames and the artificial glow from two bulbs burning modestly behind Victorian bowls of frosted glass. Dennison was seated behind his desk, arms folded, ankles twisted uncomfortably, while he fiddled with one of the pilot lamps on his radio.

"I just want to listen to a little Glen Miller," he complained. "Is that too much to ask? I can't see a goddamned thing on this dial." He threw his hands up in frustration and turned to Murph and began probing him with small eyes buoyed helplessly behind large, horn-rimmed glasses.

Murph hated these postgame debriefings. And he hated Dennison's chamber and all of its punitive connotations. Each visit was, to him, an exercise in mind-bending torture, tantamount to the merciless wood spoon his mother used to hammer across his knuckles whenever he transgressed as a boy.

"You know, Murph," the old man said, releasing a white, viscous cloud of cigar smoke into the stagnant air, "a lot of fellas got their eyes on this team. Cripe, you've got yourself a nice bunch of guys here. More than enough talent to win. Fans love 'em too. Yup, you sure are sitting in the catbird seat. Be a crying shame if, oh, I don't know, if one or two bad decisions messed things up for you."

"How's that?"

Dennison was staring directly at Murph, but his mind wandered to his youth, and to some of the fantastic stories he'd heard as a child, such as the ones his dad used to tell about his boyhood chum Brody McGinn, the great "Irish Warrior," who, as a boy of just twelve, combed the neighborhoods of south Chicago between Armour Street and Barberry Avenue with an anticipatory malevolence.

"Come on, Pop! Did he really bloody a whole group of wise guys with nothing more than an old two-by-four and a bad attitude?" Warren asked, wide-eyed and smiling. "Just because one of them stepped on his shoes?"

"Why certainly he did, Son. What's not to believe? It's a tough world out there. And someone's gotta be in charge."

Dennison grinned as he reminisced.

"Ah, sir," Murph interrupted. "You were saying?"

"Oh, yes. Yes. About the team. Say, did I ever tell you about Brody McGinn? There was this little Irish kid who—"

"Listen, Warren. With all due respect. Let's cut all the raba daba. Shall we? You got something to say to me? Huh? Then just say it. Cards on the table. Right now."

Dennison smiled awkwardly and wrapped one thumb around the other. "It's that boy of yours—Mickey. I am not running some kind of goddamned safe house or church charity, Murph. Ya hear? Now, hell, I don't know anything about this kid, except that he doesn't belong anywhere near a ball field."

Murph sighed and fidgeted in his chair. The darkness seemed to flow around him like a rushing tide. A familiar heat began to smolder at the back of his neck. The tiny embers took flight, creeping around to his face, flushing his cheeks while running down both arms, igniting his skin before finally settling in the tips of his fingers.

"Again, with all due respect, sir, I have to disagree. Sure, the kid's a little green. But I saw him, Warren. I know what he can do. He's gonna be golden for us. Just you wait."

"I pay you to manage the ball club, Mr. Murphy. I'm not interested in your prognostications. Let me spell it out for you—plain and simple. You are stepping on my shoes. It's getting uncomfortable. And I do not like to be uncomfortable. If you don't see your way to the postseason this year, I'm afraid I'll have to—well, let's just say I'll be forced to explore other options for this organization. You understand? Right? Just business. Nothing personal."

Murph looked around at the dim interior, at the suffocation spawning from Dennison's tomb. He was such a hump. Frustration stole his voice momentarily so that all he could expel was a mirthless laugh.

"Come on, Warren. How could I possibly think that? Personal? That just wouldn't be like you."

INDIANA AND BACK

The rooster's greeting of the new day had ceased and the sun had begun to dry the morning dew. The sound of a hammer pounding an anvil and the abrasive tenor of Clarence's voice screaming for Molly scattered the few barnyard dwellers who had been bold enough to feed near the cantankerous farmer, unleashing high-pitched squeals that reverberated throughout the countryside like an alarm.

The Tussler farm was sparse and severe and filled with harsh moments just like these. A distinct grayness attached to everything, a suffocating grimness that emanated from its proprietor and sullied everything in its wake. But for Mickey, it was home. The only thing he had ever known.

"A visit home might do you a world of good Mick," Murph announced as they pulled up to the battered mailbox. "Besides, I did promise your folks."

Their feet struggled on loose gravel as they moved with care and precision, careful not to announce their arrival prematurely. It was a somber morning. The only perceptible movement came from a trifling wind that bent the tall grass just to their side, exposing a beleaguered groundhog tending to his morning chores.

As they moved closer, they could hear Clarence in the barn, banging things around and cursing everything under the sun, and figured it best not to enter.

They had no sooner awakened the creaky boards on the front porch when the screen door groaned and out came Molly, washboard in hand.

"Mickey! Come here, boy. Give your mama a hug."

Arthur smiled and watched as two massive limbs swallowed the tiny woman.

"How are you, boy?" she asked. "Is everything good?"

Mickey's eyes were scanning the property.

"Mickey? Is everything good?"

"Yeah, Mama. Good. Mickey is good."

His eyes continued to rove. She smiled and ran her fingers over his shirtsleeve.

"Okay, sweetheart. I get it. Why don't you run and see if you can find that confounded pig of yours."

Mickey bounded off the porch, leaving Arthur and Molly to themselves. She looked different, he thought. Her eyes had a warmth, something soft and vibrant struggling to find the light. Even her hair looked different, possessed a radiance and silkiness that flourished in the emerging morning shine.

"He sure loves that pig," she said almost apologetically.

"Yup," Arthur replied. "Talks about him a lot."

"Would you like to come in, Mr. Murphy?"

"Arthur. Please call me Arthur."

She blushed a little and touched the hair at the back of her neck and then at the top of her head. She smiled genuinely, girlishly.

"Okay, Arthur. Would you like to come inside?"

"Your husband's still out back, right?"

She nodded, wishing she could stop the part of her mind where thoughts of Clarence and all of the hidden shame resided. If only it were all just outside her, a jigsaw puzzle perhaps, where she could simply reorder the pieces.

"Very well then," Arthur said, smiling. "Lead the way."

The house was quiet and still, but the familiar pungency remained. The inside was just as he remembered, dark and austere, although this time, the grave furnishings seemed to trouble her more than they did him.

"Please excuse the mess, Mr.—I mean, Arthur. Can't seem to ever keep up." She frowned at the pile of dirty clothes strewn across the floor.

"Well, this is a lot of work for a pretty lady to do all by herself," Arthur replied. "I think it's just fine."

She looked at him sideways through her hair. He was strong, not so much in a physical sense, although she could see the ripples in his biceps every time he moved his arms. He had an air of confidence, of righteousness, one that seemed to elevate him above any other man she had ever known. This was most apparent in his eyes, two brown pools that possessed a depth and understanding to which she was not accustomed.

"You know Mrs. Tussler—Molly—Mickey is doing well," he said, picking up the dusty clarinet resting on the mantel. "I don't want you to worry or anything. I brought him here just so he could visit. I thought you might like to see him."

"I miss him something awful. More than I thought. It's sort of empty in the house without him. You know? But, I'm glad he's gotten out of here. And I'm certainly happy he's with you."

"Well, we're all happy to have him."

"Has he been difficult? You know, sometimes he has these—well, episodes you can call them. Mostly when things get a little too much for him to handle."

"Nothing that we haven't been able to help him with. But now that you mentioned it, what can you tell me about that strange poem he recites sometimes? It is a little odd. Anything I should know?"

She laughed softly. "'Silver.' By Walter de la Mare. It's my favorite poem. I used to whisper it in Mickey's ear when he was small. Just when he was most upset. He'd get into my lap and I'd rock him in my chair and whisper it over and over until he calmed down. Then one day, years later, when he was maybe ten years old, Clarence upset him so. I wasn't around, and he just started reciting the words. All of them. It was amazing. He is not stupid, like some folks say."

"No ma'am, he is certainly not stupid." Murph smiled at her, clarinet still in hand. "Do you play?"

"I used to. A long time ago."

"I love music. Sure would love to hear a song." Looking at him, she knew he was sincere. It made her smile. Yet thoughts of Clarence and his disdain for any endeavor that fell beyond the limited scope of farmwork squelched any inclination to fulfill the request.

Her mind wandered back to the last time she'd held the instrument at her lips. They had only been married a little more than a year. It was a blustery, wet day in late fall. She was outside tending to the animals, struggling most of the day under November's gray dissolution and its dappled gloom. She had been at it for almost six straight hours. Her clothes were damp and her face cold and chaffed. Now, with night steadily approaching, she looked up at the distant trees arching spidery against the changing sky and felt a surging desire to be inside, warm by the fire.

When she reached the house, Clarence was still nowhere to be found. She breathed easily. Changing her clothes, she peeled the damp fibers from her skin, shuddering spasmodically when a cool wind caught her bare body. When she was dressed again, the chill lingered.

She wandered downstairs to the kitchen to prepare the evening meal. There were potatoes to peel and carrots to chop. She rummaged through a kitchen drawer, finally pulling out a serrated paring knife. She had just begun her assault on the vegetables when a chill slipped up her back, prompting her to set the knife down and seek the warmth of the fire in the adjacent room.

In the glow of the crackling fire, she sat on a chair with her knees drawn up to her chest, pulling them tight with her arms, fashioning a shelf on which to rest her head. She appeared anesthetized by the roiling flames, lost in a conflagration of images that, to her dismay, flitted before her with powerful vibrancy.

She could see, suspended somewhere just above the iridescent blaze of the logs, an airy, miragelike picture of a little girl dressed in a white, lacy cargo dress. In one hand she holds a yellow flower. In the other, a shiny black clarinet. The girl is smiling. Molly sagged.

The picture, vivid and familiar, stirred her deepest regrets. Gaunt and hollow-eyed, she gasped, driven full tilt to the mantel where the same instrument had lain for months, shrouded in dust.

With gentle breaths and delicate strokes of her fingers, she wiped clean the sooty instrument. It sparkled in her hands, magical. She licked her lips and drew the clarinet to her mouth slowly, deliberately. It tasted sweet. Her face melted into a radiant smile.

Then she played. One song after another, she played, each more passionate than the last. Her entire body was alive, tingling with ebullience, an electricity that flowed recklessly underneath her skin and into her fingers and toes. She was intoxicated, swept away by the enchantment until she heard the door bang open and felt a cold blast of air at her back.

"What the hell are ya doin', woman?" Clarence asked. "Why ain't ya in the kitchen, fixin' supper?"

She felt all at once small and exposed. "I'm sorry, Clarence. I was cold, and then I saw the clarinet, so I figured—"

"Oh, you done some figering now, did ya?" he said sarcastically. His mouth hung open and his hat crossed his forehead in a straight line, just above his half-opened eyes. He was looking around the room as if he were considering letting her go with just a stern admonition. Then, with a panting fury, he ripped a shotgun off the wall, aimed the barrel at a point just above her head, and pulled the trigger.

"There ain't no time on this here farm for no music playing, little Miss Molly. Ya hear? Don't let me catch you again, else my aim may not be so good next time."

The recollection was painful and strong.

"I don't think so, Arthur," she finally said. "I can't play. Not today."

"Aw, come on now. Don't be a party pooper. Just one song. What harm could it do? Come on. One song. What do ya say?"

"I can't explain it. It's just not a good idea."

"Is it him?"

She nodded and shared a little of the sordid history. He stood motionless and listened, his head cocked slightly to one side. She had tears in her eyes. He let her struggle through each reminiscence, then held the instrument in her direction. She looked at it, with curious uncertainty, her arms stretching and retreating in conflicted desire until finally Arthur placed the black object in her soft hands.

"That was a long time ago, Molly. Besides, he's outside and I'm here. I won't let anything happen to you. Go on. Take it. Please. It's okay. Just one song."

Molly cradled the instrument with maternal affection, as though she had been reunited with one born from her own being. The carved wood under her fingertips was electrifying and summoned a world long past, one replete with laughter, harmony, and artful deliberations. She smiled a brilliant smile, a smile so radiant, so lustrous, that it illuminated the dreary shadows that hung in every corner of the room—a smile so powerful, so dazzling, that it only ceased to shine when she brought the magic shoot to her lips.

With eyes closed and heart aflutter, she began to play. It was painful at first, as she struggled with the compulsion to yield to the calamity that had stripped her of something she loved so dearly. But Arthur prodded gently, and before long, there was music. Beautiful music.

The notes were soft and weightless. Her spirit took flight and her radiance seemed to wash across the homely little house, bathing the dust and dirt and dark-paneled walls in brilliant fire-lit hues.

Arthur began to sing softly. "'Here I slide again; about to take that ride again; starry eyed again—taking a chance on love.'"

She opened her eyes, and pulled the instrument from her lips. She stood silent, looking at him with childish amazement. "You know Benny Goodman?"

"Are you kidding? I love him."

The two shared a laugh and continued to play and sing. He marveled at the transformation as Molly's breath resurrected the exanimate instrument. It was magical—so magical that he even forgot, for the moment, those things that weighed heavily on *his* mind. Compelled by the unremitting melodiousness, he stood with eyes closed in joyful silence, swooning in the exactitude of the measured notes. It was all so beautiful.

But, the respite from the outside world was shattered when Clarence, roused by the unfamiliar sounds from his house, came roaring inside.

"What in tarnation are ya doing, woman?" he bellowed. "I thought I was clear about messing with such foolishness. And with a guest in the house?"

Molly withered, shoved back into grim wordlessness. Her head fell, and Arthur could see the light in her eyes surrender to the farmer's dominion.

"That's okay, Mr. Tussler," Arthur interjected. "It's no big deal. I don't mind."

"Well, I sure do!" Clarence roared back. "Listen, Molly, put that stupid thing away and go fetch Mickey and have him meet me by the shed out back in a short while. I got a job for him but I want to talk with Mr. Murphy a spell."

The two men walked uneasily toward the back of the property. Arthur lamented quietly having to spend even a second with Clarence. A peripheral glance showed the ornery simpleton picking his teeth with a screwdriver he had pulled from the front pouch of his soiled overalls.

Up ahead, just past two overgrown cornfields split by a narrow dirt path, was a fishing hole. The water, still and murky, was steaming in the morning sun. Arthur cringed from the smell.

"Look, maybe we should be getting back to the house," he suggested. "It's a might hot out here."

"Poppycock," Clarence snorted. "It's purty as a picture out here." He scratched his backside, belched loudly, and came to rest with a thunderous sigh on a rotting log. "Best damn fishin' spot in the county," he boasted, casting his line into the water. "Have a seat."

The worm at the end of the line landed gently on the water's surface, not too far from an old tire that was partially immersed. A perfect circle of ripples unfurled from the spot where the lure landed, forming a halo that framed the favored spot momentarily until both worm and frame vanished beneath the surface.

"You fish, Mr. Murphy?" Clarence pulled ever so slightly on the line.

"No, Mr. Tussler. Can't say that I do."

"Well now. That's a darn shame. Gotta respect a man who fishes. Fishin' is a real test of smarts."

Arthur's eyes rolled, then watched with mild interest as Clarence pulled in his line. "That may be the case, Mr. Tussler, but I'd like to think that despite my lack of fishing experience, I'm still a pretty shrewd fella."

Clarence cast the line again, this time with greater force. "You seem to have taken a real liking to my family, Mr. Murphy," he said, squaring his shoulders to the water. "That's a mighty curious nicety."

"You're lucky, Mr. Tussler. You have very special people in your life. It's easy to like 'em."

"Yeah, well, you don't live with 'em, now do ya?" Clarence turned to face Arthur.

Arthur was more than willing to hold Clarence's gaze and saw no *real* indication that he was looking to intimidate him.

"Look, exactly what is it that you want to talk to me about, Mr. Tussler? I really need to be heading back."

Bright, orange reflections of light spattered the water between long, spiking shadows. A faint redolence of manure and wet grass floated on a tired breeze, burning the inside of Arthur's nose.

"I was thinking, seeing you got my boy down there with you— and I miss him so—that maybe you could see to it that the little woman and I can git a little more money—you know, just to make up fer all the pain and suffering."

The smell of wet earth drying rose between them.

"Look, Mr. Tussler, Mickey is being looked after first-rate. There's nothing to worry about. I've gone out of my way to see he's okay—and will continue to do so. But you have to understand this is minor league baseball we're talking about. And not everyone's sold on him the way I am. I'm in no position at this point to give you any more money."

"That's crap! I know how you city boys work. I ain't just some big, stupid country bumpkin. I know about things too, like penicillin and that there Marshall Plan they's always talking about on the radio. So don't treat me like some yokel from the sticks. You can't come in here and throw around yer fancy words and ideas about music and whatnot and the way you reckon people should be living out here and expect all of us to jest sit up and holler." The farmer was bent over his boots, tugging on an errant piece of fishing line tangled in his laces. "It just don't work that way."

"Well, if that's the way you feel, I'm afraid I'll have to leave Mickey here—with you—and that the contract you signed will become void—uh, no good anymore. Of course, this means you'll have to give back the money you already received." With his announcement, Arthur stood up, stretched his arms, and made as if to leave.

"Now just hold yer horses there," Clarence cried. "Hold on. Nobody said nothing about leaving the boy here. He wants to play baseball. I'm a good father. I understand now. We both want what's best fer the boy, right? Well, then I'll make the sacrifice. Fer the boy."

"Now, that's more like it. Oh, and if you'd like, I *can* arrange for you and your wife to come down and see Mickey play. If it would help with all the suffering, I mean."

"Us? Come down there? To watch a retard play baseball? Are you off yer rocker?"

"Just something to consider. And if *you* don't want to come, maybe you could send your wife. I know she'd enjoy it."

Arthur walked with swift purpose back to the house, eager to rid himself of any more interminable exchanges with Clarence. His course was guided by the sound of rotten apples splattering against wood.

"Hey there, Mick. Ready to head back?"

"I reckon so, Mr. Murphy. Sure. Head back." Mickey looked down at the ground. "I just have to finish this last row."

Arthur watched, just as he had only weeks before, as Mickey fired, with alarming precision, each of the remaining apples into the turned barrel some one hundred feet away.

Thud. Thud. Thud, thud, thud.

Arthur's eyes, wide with wonder, battled against the improbability of such a spectacle. One hundred feet? And so accurate? Hell, the rubber was only sixty and change. It made him think. His thoughts bounced off each other like honeybees at work in a field of spotted jewelweed. In time, they ascended to the most fertile patch, and they buzzed feverishly until one broke free from the others. It flashed across Arthur, at that instant, that something could be done to help the boy. That all the disorder and Mickey's uneasiness on the field could be righted. Murph's face grew brilliant with pleasure. With eyebrows raised, and a boyish smile that could not be contained, he tucked away the revelation, said his good-byes, and walked to his car.

The ride back to Diamond Drive was cloying. Arthur was haunted by the memorable scent of anxiety, by all the things he should have said to the ignorant farmer. This was always his problem—the web of regret, and how to extricate himself from its sticky spirals before more damage was done. He had gotten better with time. Managed to muster the strength and resiliency most times to convey his feelings about things that rubbed him wrong. Yet he still found himself ill equipped to drop the hammer—to deliver the whole truth with a swift, punishing wallop.

The trip home was long. Mickey talked about everything from Oscar's feet to road signs to how many breaths he could take in a minute. Murph just locked his hands on the wheel and listened as Mickey continued to pepper him with all sorts of minutia.

"Mickey thinks tomato soup is my favorite," the boy said. "What about you Murph?"

"I don't know Mick. I'm not much of a soup guy."

"I just don't like it when there is anything floating on the top," Mickey continued. "Like crackers, or a piece of the tomato."

"Uh-huh."

"Do you think a tomato is rounder than an orange, Murph?"

"I don't know, Mick. I never really thought about it." He sighed helplessly. "And I have to tell you. It's been a long day already. I'm sorry Mick. But I really do not want to talk about tomatoes and oranges."

"Okay, Murph. But I think it is. Round." The boy paused, his eyes scanning the trees that rolled away just outside his window.

"Potatoes aren't round," Mickey continued in much softer tones. "They look sort of like —"

"Mickey, please! Enough!"

They rode on for several minutes in silence, the only audible sound a faint hum coming from deep within Mickey's throat that only ceased when he swallowed a piece of the licorice laces he had stuffed in one of his pockets.

"How much of that stuff do you have in there?" Murph asked.

Mickey frowned.

"I got's no more," he replied. "And Mickey is still hungry."

They stopped at a diner just up the road. Then they pulled the car onto the shoulder not long after so that Mickey could pee. Shortly thereafter, he was hungry again. They stopped repeatedly, each time to tend to either Mickey's insatiable hunger or to make use of the dense undergrowth along the road's shoulder in order to relieve themselves. Arthur was beginning to flip. This was the fourth stop in the last hour. He could feel the muscles in his neck tightening and his stomach beginning to churn violently, as if his whole body were trying to turn itself inside out. He thought he just might lose it right there. Start screaming at the kid about all the work he had ahead of him and how many hours they had lost farting around. But he burst into a nervous laugh instead as he watched Mickey surveying the cluster of gooseberry bushes for the perfect location to unzip his trousers. "Great thing about being a guy, eh Mick?" he laughed. "Don't really matter where you are. The possibilities are endless. Yup. When you're a guy, the whole world's your toilet." Mickey stopped what he was doing, stared at Murph blankly, and placed a handful of berries in his pocket with great care before proceeding to take care of his business.

Murph just rolled his eyes. He was definitely shot. They had gotten lost twice, spent way too many hours at roadside diners and had nearly suffered an unfortunate encounter with poison ivy on the previous two bathroom jaunts.

"Okay Mick," he warned. "That's it now. I wanted to be home hours ago. No more stopping. It'll be dark soon. But if we drive straight through, we'll be home in time for bed."

He drove with nervous urgency, Mickey seated quietly by his side, as if the falling of night might come down around on all sides, locking him in. Foolishly, he tried to outrun it, as if his efforts could stem the tide of nature's unyielding choreography. He fixed his gaze on the landscape ahead, wedded to the irrational quest, with all sorts of calculations lighting in his head. He knew, however, when the winding asphalt before him began to melt into the horizon's purplish yawn, that he was losing. His head drooped. And when the dark blanket had finally been lain across the countryside, and all he could see was the phantom outlines of cornstalks and fruit trees mocking his restlessness, he felt this profound sense of defeat.

The next night he was home, but the feeling continued. At the onset of evening, Arthur sat alone in his room, wrestling with the collection of discordant voices in his head. The restive dance of thought drove him from his chair to his bed, back to the chair, then finally to the window, where he stood momentarily, arms folded, before leaning out the tiny casement to close the shutters on a magnificent picture where white and salmon pear blossoms shimmered in the glowing twilight. The splendor of the scene struck him oddly and threw a spotlight on his misery. He sweated nervously and bemoaned with unexpected ferocity the misfortune that had dotted the last thirty-six hours. Dennison was an ass—a first-class scumbag whose manipulation and cold, calculating manner scraped the delicate fabric of Arthur's sound but sensitive core. All he wanted to do was give this kid a shot. And now his job was on the line. It hardly seemed fair.

Then there was Clarence Tussler, the most loathsome, repugnant excuse for a human being he had ever met. He recalled with an alarming vividness the harsh words expelled from the farmer's lips and the foul breath on which they floated. Mickey didn't stand a chance with him. And poor Molly. How could such a gentle creature survive under that viscous cloud of gloom? He spent the better part of the evening with Mickey, mostly chatting and getting things ready for the next day.

"Your dad's quite a guy, Mickey," Arthur said. "I had a chance to really talk to him."

"Uh-huh," Mickey answered, spilling the colored candy contents from a cardboard tube.

"It makes me wonder how you get along. You know, with each other?"

"I reckon I do okay." The boy sat engrossed in the curious ritual, separating the candies into rows by color. "Mickey does okay. But Oscar doesn't like all the noise."

"Is that right?"

"Sure. Pa's always screaming and all. It really bothers Oscar. Mickey can tell."

Murph watched with fascination as Mickey began placing the colored chocolates in his mouth.

"Those are real good, eh?" Murph asked, laughing. "Guy at the general store just got 'em in. Calls 'em M&M's."

Mickey never looked up. He just kept sliding the M&M's, one by one, row by row, across the table and into his mouth.

"What about your mom?"

"Mama's a nice woman."

"No, I mean, does your dad yell at your mom?"

A dead silence greeted Arthur's words. Then Mickey's gaze fixed on the fireflies that had gathered outside by the window. All of a sudden, Arthur could no longer see the value in going further with his inquisition, or in trying to figure out why things fell against each other the way they did. He knew that—especially regarding Molly. She was so lovely yet so fragile, so sad—a hummingbird feather beating nervously against a stiff, frigid squall. He tried to quantify her energy, the resiliency she needed to continue the struggle. At first he marveled at the chimerical nature of such an endeavor. Perhaps he could learn something from this timid, careworn creature. But ultimately, it just made him sad. Poor Molly. She was his last thought when his head hit the pillow.

He dozed, but it was a fitful sleep, punctuated by his whirling and turning in the tumult of fragmented images and restless thought. He hated nights like these, when all around him hung these menacing abstractions, waving to him wildly. He could feel his body, weak and skittish, turning away from the formlessness, but was always powerless to wake himself during these moments.

Mercifully, dawn ultimately swallowed the moon and stars and a yellow sun ushered in the smells and sounds of a new day. Everything seemed better to Arthur. The sky was a deep, royal blue, and the tender shoots of grass emerging timidly from the barren lawn he'd seeded last fall were a vibrant green. He heard the sounds of springtime in the air, as if for the first time—screen doors banging behind eager children, bicycle tires rolling on gravelly thoroughfares, and from high in the thickest boughs of the sycamores, twittering from the indigo buntings, a melodious serenade announcing their arrival. It all smelled better too. Floating tenderly on the warming puffs of air was the bouquet of lilac, wisteria, and honeysuckle, tickling his nose with an intoxicating redolence. He closed his eyes and filled his lungs. What a day.

He drove to the ballpark with the windows open, although this made conversation with Mickey a near impossibility. He rolled his window halfway up, then back down again, then up almost all the way, trying to find just the right formula that would allow him to enjoy the warm, fragrant air and still be able to hear his soft-spoken passenger.

Mickey was hunched close to the windshield, as if his propinquity to the front of the car would somehow expedite the voyage. He seemed uncomfortable, although he pointed now and again excitedly and made a glib comment or two when they passed some stray dogs and wayward children wandering alongside the road. The observations almost ignited some conversation, but Mickey remained, for the most part, distant and meditative. He was feeling a little un-comfortable in his own skin. Baseball was overwhelming. It had trapped him. Forced him to retreat into a labyrinth, and he was too young, too inexperienced, too awestruck by all the eye-opening hap-penings, on and off the field, to find his way out.

"What's the matter with you this morning, Mick?" Arthur probed. "Cat got your tongue?"

"Cat, Mr. Murphy? No, no cats. Oscar's a pig. I don't got no—"

Arthur steadied himself with a long, purposeful breath. "It's just an expression Mick. That's all."

They rode the rest of the way in relative silence. Arthur was ru-minating over everything that was just plain wrong. His anxiety be-came indissoluble. He lamented that he always seemed to submit to the feckless desires of others, especially of those for whom he held unmitigated disdain. He was always dancing around Dennison, fear-ful of castigation.

Be a crying shame if one or two bad decisions messed things up for you, he recalled bitterly. Dennison's words echoed in his ears. Christ, he was such a smug, pompous ass.

"Go screw yourself, Warren," he always wanted to say. Just once, so Dennison would know that he was aware of what a asshole he was. Those words, however, could never pass his lips. They always got stuck, it seemed, somewhere in his throat, where they struggled and burned and festered for a while before he chewed the inside of his cheek, hung his head, and simply swallowed them until the next time. He fantasized wildly that his message would be delivered through some other medium—so that these elusive words would never have to meet the air. He considered this as he looked to his right and saw Mickey.

They arrived at the ballpark in plenty of time. It was a beautiful day for baseball; temperate breezes pushed a smattering of cotton-like clouds across a pale blue canvas. The sun was playing hide-and-seek for most of the early day, splashing the field at intervals with warm wrinkles of happiness. All around the tiny stadium were the sounds of the pregame euphoria—tractors grinding, coaches hollering, reporters snooping, and turnstiles clicking. This frenzy of anticipation would build to the crescendo that came only by way of that magical incantation "Play ball!" Once those words punctuated the air, the place went still, as if placed beneath a glass bowl, and all that could be heard was the traditional hymn to America, played on a C melody saxophone, and the erratic breathing of eager worshippers.

Lefty took the ball for the Brewers. He had been sparkling in his last three outings—won all three contests, allowing just nine hits and four earned runs while fanning a mind-boggling thirty-two batters. His run of good stuff continued against the Tulsa Beavers, as he set down the first nine men to step to the plate, five on punch-outs. "I'm rolling, fellas," he boasted. "Everyone hitch your wagons." His bluster continued to soar after he fanned the next three Beavers, and in the Brewers' half of the fourth, Woody Danvers launched a three-run rocket over the left-field wall, giving the Brewers and Lefty what figured to be all they would need.

The weather, however, turned unexpectedly, and out of the frowning face of the sky, a light rain began to fall. Initially it made a whisper and then a soft murmur, like voices conversing in a closed room. It seemed to be a passing shower. But soon after, it began pounding the earth with thunderous blows, like a herd of self-indulgent colts charging through a clay pan canyon.

Arthur and the others watched from the dugout steps as the water hammered the infield dirt, creating syrupy, glasslike puddles that swelled and bubbled before sprawling across the entire diamond.

"Great Caesar's ghost!" Matheson lamented while scratching his head. "You better get comfortable, boys. Looks like we're gonna be here awhile."

During the rain delay, the players busied themselves with a variety of activities. The scene was like some sort of vaudeville spectacular gone wrong.

"Hey, guys," Jimmy Llamas announced proudly to his outfield cohorts, Buck Faber and Amos Ruffings. "Check this out." The quirky Llamas, known for his uproarious histrionics, produced from behind his back three rolled-up pairs of stirrups, which he held out ceremoniously, kissed, and then, with much fanfare and self-promotion, juggled to the delight of the others.

"Hot damn!" Faber roared. "He's a regular freak show."

On the other side of the clubhouse, Woody Danvers was dealing blackjack to lanky first baseman Clem Finster, Butch Sanders, and Larry, the equipment boy. It was just for fun, but tempers were high nonetheless.

"Hey, Danvers, that's the third blackjack you dealt yourself in the last five hands," Finster complained. "Lemme see that deck."

"Go to hell, Finny," Danvers fired back. "It's all good. Ain't my fault the gods are smiling on me and crapping on the rest of you losers."

"Enough. Let's play. But just make sure, Danvers, that those cards of yours ain't something you pulled from Pee Wee's bag of tricks," Sanders added. "I ain't no patsy, Woody."

Danvers just smiled.

Pee Wee McGinty had his own thing going. He was the team magician, always ready to entertain on a moment's notice. He loved these delays more than anyone. With a trainer's table doubling as his stage, he set up shop, littering the tabletop with all kinds of gadgets, bells, and whistles. Mickey and Arky Fries stopped banging out their cleats and pulled up to watch.

"Ladies and gentlemen!" the tiny, self-proclaimed wizard announced happily. "The Great McGinty will now amaze you by making this baseball glove disappear, right before your eyes." Mickey and Fries both smiled.

Boxcar looked up from his crossword puzzle just long enough to catch the bewildered look on Mickey's face. He made a face of his own, annoyed by McGinty's outburst, and exchanged a quick glance with Lefty, who was by himself in the far corner, working the callus on his pitching hand with a thin slab of brick that had broken free from the dugout wall. Eager to complete what he had started, Boxcar looked back at the paper on his lap but winced and sighed as the hard laughter from Faber and Ruffings slid into a dizzying coughing fit.

"Hey, shut up over there!" the ornery backstop thundered, frustrated by the eight-letter word he had yet to decipher. "I can't hear myself think." His mouth twitched a little. It slid to the left, then back over to the right. His stare narrowed, revealing with more detail the deep lines around his eyes. Then, tapping a pencil softly against his chin, he continued his assault on the puzzle, only to be thwarted once again.

"Hey, Box, got a minute?" Murph asked. "I think I have an idea."

Murph put his hand to his head and felt his hair, wet and sparse. He frowned, then pulled his cap over the damp mess, mumbling something about the way things used to be. He laughed at himself sometimes, a senseless mocking that vacillated between whimsy and self-loathing. What was he still doing in this game? Hadn't it all just passed him right by? He thought about farming, about all the opportunities he had passed up just to remain close to it all. For what? Corn and chickens were a tangible, hands-on validation of effort. At the end of the day, you could trace your steps and lie down easily, having tasted the fruits of your labor. After all, what exactly did he have? The rain, strong and steady against the clubhouse roof, shook him from the contemplation.

"Let me see your glove a minute," he finally asked.

With the passing of the final shower, and under a blazing sun that seemed to lift the deluge with impatient hands, the players, one by one, began filtering out of the clubhouse and onto the field like ants intoxicated with the expectation of picnic remnants. The ground sank beneath their eager feet, and a few of them groaned when some of the runoff found its way into their shoes.

"Christ!" Lefty complained. "You guys actually gonna play in this crap?" Then he spit tobacco juice from the space between his front teeth and shook his head. "Won't catch me out there. You know how many careers were ruined on days like today?"

The field was a mess—a quagmire of woeful turf bowed by the deluge and streaked here and there by intermittent tinges of ocher courtesy of the encroaching swirls of mud. It looked like a child's finger painting. The sun's hands, however, were fast at work, and after almost two hours, eleven bags of sand, and several artful strokes with some metal rakes, the diamond was asparkle again and ready for play.

"Hey, Larry," Arthur ordered. "Lefty is done. Been sitting too long to finish. Don't want that arm of his tightening up. Take Mickey down the right-field line and warm him up."

The players from both sides stretched and ran and played pepper, trying to shake off the ill effects of their idle endeavors. And when the final fungo was hit, and the few spectators who had braved the soaking showers settled back in their seats, a tiny roar could be heard as Mickey and the rest of the beloved Brew Crew took the field.

The sun, fully exposed once again in a pale blue sky, bathed the players in golden hues. Mickey stood tall on the mound, like a tiny mountain. The nervousness that had befallen him in his first outing was gone, replaced somehow by a quiet confidence that spilled out of his tattered jersey.

"Come on now, big boy!" Boxcar encouraged. "Just like warm-ups before. Put her right here." Nausea began to work in the catcher's stomach, an uneasiness for the hulking farm boy, as the first batter approached the plate, swung twice, and dug himself into the sandy muck that just hours before was the batter's box.

With the umpire crouched expectantly behind him, Boxcar set the target just as he always did—high and inside. It was his calling card—hard stuff in, junk away. The entire field knew his way, so they always made the defensive adjustments accordingly. They had watched Boxcar from their positions for years. But on this most unusual day, a curiosity emerged from the yawning cowhide—a bright red sphere of sorts imprinted right in the center of the pocket.

"What the hell is that?" Danvers whispered to McGinty, as both infielders peered in incredulously. "Is that a goddamned apple painted in his glove?"

Pee Wee liked Mickey and would have done anything to help the boy. But he questioned Murph's vision. He scowled, dimpling his smooth, ruddy cheeks. His eyes fluttered, and Danvers lamented under his breath about the "bush league" appearance the team had seemed to suddenly embrace, just as Mickey rolled his arms, reared back, and fired. The pop was thunderous and separated all of them from their cynical thoughts.

"Steerike one!" the umpire shrieked.

A spring wind, which carried on it a mixture of oohs and aahs, blew across the diamond. Boxcar smiled from behind his mask and returned the ball to Mickey. Then the enigmatic pitcher cupped the ball with his right hand, buried it inside his glove, rolled his arms, and fired once again.

"Two!" screamed the umpire. "On the corner."

The batter never even flinched. It was past him almost instantly. Perplexed, he stepped out of the box and banged his spikes with the knob of the bat, trying to figure out how it was possible to hear the ball behind him before ever really seeing it.

Mickey was cool. He caught Boxcar's toss and stepped back on the rubber, impervious to the gaping mouths and incredulous stares aimed at him. It was as if he were back on the farm, tossing apples. Everything around him seemed to just melt away, so that all he saw was the eleven-inch leather frame sixty feet away from him.

The batter returned to the batter's box. He held his right hand up behind him as he dug in with his back foot. Mickey just waited. Then, after a few practice passes with his Louisville Slugger, the batter was ready. Mickey rolled his arms again, uncorking a tiny white meteor whose trajectory was true. The batter grit his teeth. He was determined to make contact this time. As the ball streaked toward home plate, he began his swing, a violent, spasmodic explosion whose force buckled his knees and drove him to the ground in ignominious defeat.

"Steerike three!" the umpire thundered. The batter kicked the dirt and cursed his fate.

"Shake it off, Rumson," the Beavers' skipper screamed from the dugout. "He got lucky."

And then it happened again. And again, and again, and again. Mickey buzzed through the entire Beavers lineup, sitting down one discouraged batter after another. The crowd was electrified. All of their own hopes and dreams and wild aspirations rose to the surface, a molten energy that fixed itself to this episode so remote, so absurdly improbable. Something about the whole scene was supernatural—this misfit farm boy, with all his quirkiness, mowing down batter after batter. Just to be a part of it, even from a distance, was intoxicating. Upon the eradication of each batter, the crowd stood up, in unison, and saluted the unlikely icon by placing their right hands in their left and rolling their arms breathlessly, all the while chanting at fever pitch, "*Mickey! Mickey! Mickey!*"

"Have you ever seen anything like this?" Murph said to Matheson. Murph couldn't help but chuckle. Things never went this well for him. He, along with everyone else in the park, was swept away by what looked like the simultaneous spreading of wings by a frenzied flock of seagulls.

Not everyone was amused. Some took exception to all the attention.

"What the hell is Murph thinking?" Finster complained in between innings. "Is this a baseball game or some cheesy, two-bit publicity stunt?"

Buck Faber nodded. Something irreducibly human, or maybe just male, threatened the order of their world. "Something needs to be done, Finny," he said gravely. "This is crap."

The crowd, however, continued its celebration. With each strikeout, the Brewer faithful exploded from their seats like champagne, roared their approval, then lapsed into this bizarre choreography of rolling arms that spilled across each section of the stands like an ocean wave. Of the fifteen Beavers Mickey had faced, he'd fanned ten and retired the other five on weak ground balls to the infield.

When the final out was recorded, on a 2–2 fastball that shaved the inside corner, and a small group of Brewers, lead by Murph, charged the mound in celebration, Mickey was overwhelmed. Stampedes were never good. His first impulse was to run. Pee Wee saw the panic and thought he heard Mickey call for his mama as he darted in the other direction. But the shortstop was able to arrest Mickey's flight with what started as a bear hug but ended up looking more like a little boy hanging on to his father's leg.

"You done real good, Mickey," Murph said, smiling. "Real good."

"Like peaches and cream," Matheson added. "Peaches and cream."

Mickey was still unsettled but smiled back. The crowd remained on its feet, chanting Mickey's name and saluting him with the reverent impersonation of their newest hero's delivery.

"They love him, Murph," Boxcar said, as the three of them lingered on the field. "They ain't never seen anything like it before."

Murph looked up at the crowd one last time, animated by a new certainty. "You got that right, Box," he said, shedding any previous trepidation. "Things are sure looking up."

SUMMER—1948

News of Mickey's Herculean exploits vibrated in sweeping circles. It was all anyone could think about. In every barbershop, saloon, factory, and schoolyard, talk of the "fireballing phenom" insinuated itself into even the most banal conversations. Casual discourse that included such mundane topics as the Republican Party and the gross national product, and issues of a more whimsical nature, such as the latest weather patterns, dance music, or the recipe for Aunt Mabel's sweet-potato pie, somehow always made its way back to the local baseball scene. The fervor knew no boundaries. Young. Old. Male. Female. Sports enthusiast and occasional observer. It was of little consequence. Talk of Mickey and the Brewers was on everyone's lips.

Perhaps it was the fantastic headlines that adorned the local paper every fifth day:

"Brew Crew's Fireballer Brands Colts."

"Mickey Gases Rangers."

"Baby Bazooka Shoots Down Bears."

Of course, it could have been the mythological stories, turgid tales of superhuman physical feats that seemed to swell in proportion with every outing Mickey had.

"Hey, Pop," a little boy asked his father after having just seen Mickey pitch a game, "do you know that Mickey once threw a ball one hundred ten miles per hour? Threw it so hard that it tore the glove and three fingers right off the catcher's hand?"

"Don't be silly, Son," the father admonished, rubbing his son's head playfully. "One hundred ten miles per hour?" The man chuckled, brought his index finger to his temple, and scratched gently. "I don't think it could have been any more than one hundred. Don't believe everything you hear, boy." Then he smiled at his son's naïveté before continuing, "Besides, it was only one finger, not three."

Or maybe it was just a natural reaction to unnatural happenings, the universe's logical response when something spectacular suddenly lights up the gloomy face of the daily grind. Whatever it was, Mickey had created quite a stir.

Despite some of the rumblings, the entire team was inspired by all the attention. With the exception of Lefty, the long faces and slumping shoulders were replaced by laughter, unbridled enthusiasm, and boyish antics. Brewer baseball was fun again. Nothing screamed this enjoyment more than the off-the-field high jinks. They roared when someone filled Jimmy Llamas's jockstrap with liniment—and when Woody opened his locker only to discover that his favorite bat had been painted pink. Boxcar got a cap full of shaving cream, the fingers in Pee Wee's glove were stuffed with hot dogs, and Lefty received a hot foot that burned his spikes so badly it took three of them to put the fire out.

"You guys are a bunch of jackasses," he complained. "You know that? A bunch of friggin' jackasses."

"What's your problem, Lefty?" Boxcar teased. "I thought you loved smoking."

Boxcar's sarcasm sent Lefty's blood rushing to his temples. "Hilarious, Box," he fired back. "You're a regular Jack Benny. You don't screw with a pitcher's feet. Jesus, how goddamned stupid are you?" Then he looked around awkwardly and folded his arms close to his chest, trying to cradle his wounded ego. "You wouldn't do that to Mickey now, would you?"

Boxcar scratched his chin in mock rumination, his face now

hardened and grave. "Hell no! Do that to Mickey? No way. Now *that* would be stupid."

The pitcher did not appreciate Boxcar's flippancy. Lefty had a nasty temper and unreasonable resentments. He paced for hours afterward, trying to exercise muscles that had tightened in his jaw and all around his other joints. All he could think about was his career, and the disastrous course it had suddenly taken at the hands of this novelty act. He stretched and threw and ran but just couldn't shake the suffocation. He was still seething the next day.

"So Murph wants us to treat Mickey like one of the guys, huh?" he mumbled to Danvers. They both smiled. A swirl, a glimpse of sweet justice passed before them. "I think that can be arranged."

The next day, Lefty and Danvers stood outside Mickey's locker, like sharks drawn by the scent of blood in the water. Lefty beat his palm in gentle pantomime with the head of a hammer while his partner in crime rattled a box of tenpenny nails.

"This is perfect," Lefty said, grabbing the boy's cleats. "A real classic."

As Danvers handed him one nail at a time, Lefty drove each one through the inside of Mickey's cleats and into the floor.

"Looks real natural," Danvers said, laughing. "He'll never know the difference."

Hours later, as they all dressed for the game, Mickey took center stage. Lefty and Danvers could barely contain themselves, and a few of the others who were privy to the prank could not take their eyes off the hulking victim.

Mickey chatted softly with Pee Wee as he slipped his jersey over his head and pulled his pants up around his waist. He was in a fine mood, smiling and laughing easily with Pee Wee as the affable shortstop relayed a joke about a farmer, a dead donkey, and a town preacher. All eyes were glued to Mickey as he pulled up his stirrups and put on his cap, leaving only his cleats, which lay seemingly harmless on the floor in front of his locker.

At first the boy was just confused, tugging on the sides of the shoes with only mild frustration. Pee Wee didn't even notice any trouble. Then, like an electric shock, the uneasiness rocked Mickey's entire body. His chest heaved and sweat formed on the back of his neck. He let out a gasp, then looked up with pitiful gray eyes, wondering what was happening. Tears began to fall in his lap.

"Mick, everything all right?" Pee Wee asked.

The boy tugged harder at the cleats. "My shoes," he cried. "My shoes. Mickey can't move 'em."

Pee Wee reached over and yanked at the cleats. They did not budge. He looked up disgustedly and shook his head. "Which one of you asses did this? You know the rules. Anything permanent to equipment is off-limits." They all just looked at each other and shrugged.

Pee Wee continued to help, trying to wedge a small screwdriver underneath the cleats while Mickey pulled from the top. Kneeling there, Pee Wee thought with distaste of how this horrible moment was ripping Mickey apart. He tried to calm the boy, but the longer their efforts proved fruitless, the more he unraveled.

"Don't sweat it, Mick. We'll get it." McGinty was right there for him.

But Mickey was losing it. He began rocking nervously, and the tears flowed more steadily now. Lefty and Danvers looked on with twisted delight as Mickey, in a sudden burst of explosive energy, ripped the tops of the cleats clean off the soles, leaving just the skeletal remains nailed to the floor. Several others roared with laughter.

This made Mickey sob even louder. "Oh, Mickey broke his shoes!" the boy wailed. "They're broke." Then came the robotic recitation. "'Slowly, silently, now the moon, walks the night in her silver shoon . . .'" He paced back and forth and rolled both fists over his forehead.

"It's okay," Pee Wee assured. "It's not your fault, Mickey. One of the guys is just playing with you. That's all."

The commotion brought Murph in from his office. He took one look at Mickey and knew something was amiss. Then he looked around the room as the afternoon sun splashed light across all of the shiftless faces.

"What the hell is going on here?" he demanded, eyeballing the tattered cleats still in the boy's hands. "Mickey, is everything all right?"

Mickey's forehead became beady with sweat. He sat biting his lips, fists clenched. A great hollow of darkness sprung from his eyes. "Sure, Mr. Murphy. Everything's all right. All right. The fellas is just playing with me. Fun. Just playing. That's all." His voice was thin and brittle.

Murph looked incredulously at Pee Wee, who nodded in agreement.

"That's good," Murph said loud enough for all of them to hear. "Because if everything ain't all right, and I find out about it, they'll be hell to pay."

Out of fear and necessity, things eventually returned to normal. Things got better for Mickey as well, as most of the others grew to appreciate the unusual but likable character that he was. The pranks still continued, but most were of a more harmless nature. They were all a part of it. The ribbing. The practical jokes. Even Murph and Matheson felt the wave of jocularity sweeping the ball club. Jimmy Llamas made sure of that.

Llamas and his girl loved the town carnival. Llamas always made a point of playing the games there, especially those that afforded him the opportunity to show off his throwing. On their last night there, Llamas went crazy. Won all kinds of crap, stuffed bears and Kewpie dolls. He could barely carry it all home. Most of it wound up in the trash, except for a few special prizes. He found a most unusual use for one in particular.

"Okay," Murph announced that following morning. "Which one of you chuckleheads put the goldfish in the watercooler?"

This electricity found its way onto the field as well, appearing as dramatically as the gardenias outside the ball park that had burst into brilliant white. The tremendous energy flowed from player to player. Clem Finster, who swatted just nineteen home runs in his first two seasons with the Brewers, went on a tear, belting fourteen round-trippers in just eight games.

"I don't know what it is," he told Woody, who was busy talking to his own group about his latest run of good fortune. "It's like the ball is twice its size."

Boxcar, Arky Fries, Buck Faber, and Amos Ruffings also caught the bug, each delivering hits at epidemic proportions. Collectively, over that same eight-game stretch, they were batting .476 and accounted for 74 of the staggering 108 runs the Brewers scored. Even Pee Wee got into the act, producing several extra-base hits in addition to his usual repertoire of dying quails and Baltimore chops, including a game-winning, two-out, two-run triple to beat the Colts in extra innings.

"Holy Hannah, Matheson!" Murph cried as they rushed onto the field to join the others who had already begun forming the crew who would hoist Pee Wee on their shoulders in celebration. "It's raining hits."

The pitching was clicking too. Although Lefty was struggling a bit with his control and now found himself third in a five-man rotation, the others seemed to be rejuvenated by Mickey's stellar performances. Butch Sanders, Rube Winkler, and Gabby Hooper all caught fire at once, each reeling off consecutive victories while holding opponents at bay with an assortment of breaking balls and some well-placed hard stuff. They were painting corners and breaking bats as never before, seemingly inspired by the actions and simple words of their unlikely teammate.

"Say, Mick," Winkler had asked days before the unlikely streak began, as the whole group of pitchers farted around after one of their workouts. "Tell us. Please. How do you do it? Strike after strike? Christ, it's unbelievable."

The inquiry startled Mickey. He had been standing off to the side, shaking his legs nervously while gazing off at the ring of birds that had gathered in center field when they approached. He looked puzzled, as if he did not understand what he had been asked.

"Come on, big fella," Sanders prodded, rubbing his head. "Don't hold out on your brothers. What's your secret? How do you throw that ball exactly where you want it, almost every time?"

Mickey shrugged tentatively and looked down at his spikes, wincing at the torn grass that lay beneath them. "Mickey don't have no secrets, fellas. Honest. A secret's almost like a lie. And Mickey don't lie. I don't reckon I know how I does it. Mickey just looks at that there apple in Boxcar's glove and hits it."

Hit it he did, especially in the twin bill the Brewers had with the Youngstown Bisons. In game one, Mickey turned in a one-hit, complete-game shutout, disposing of the Bison hitters with an incomprehensibly low sixty-nine pitches. The game lasted just one hour and forty-five minutes. He was brilliant. Fanned thirteen batters, walked no one, and didn't allow a ball out of the infield. Mickey was so economical that it forced Murph to alter his plan for game two.

"Hey, kid," he said with a contemplative smile and sparkling eyes that appeared to be lit from within. "How would you like to go again? You know, pitch the second game?" Mickey opened his mouth to answer, but Murph rushed on. "Your pitch count was really low, and I feel that you're really on today, Mick. Besides, I can't remember the last time we took both ends of a doubleheader. So, what do ya say?"

Mickey shrugged his shoulders and held up his hands helplessly. "I don't know. Isn't it Lefty's turn this time? Lefty still has pitches left."

Murph wrinkled his nose. "What?"

"Lefty still has pitches left."

"What does that mean, son?" Murph asked, scratching his head.

Mickey turned his head to the side, as if he had no intention of answering the question. Then, in very certain terms, he said exactly what he meant. "Lefty Rogers threw seventy-six pitches last game. Seventy-six. Usually throws one hundred thirty, sometimes one hundred thirty-six. Yeah. That's right. One hundred thirty-six. He still has fifty-four pitches left. Maybe sixty."

Murph stared at Mickey, his lips parting slowly, until his mouth hung completely open. "How do you know that? You *counted* his pitches?"

The boy did not answer. Murph was speechless as well. It didn't make any sense. There was no perceptible logic in it. How could it be? Murph was just about to continue his efforts to get Mickey to pitch the second game when he looked at the boy almost sideways, as if a light switch had suddenly been thrown.

"Say, Mick, how many did Hooper throw *his* last game?"

"One hundred thirteen."

"What about Sanders?"

"One hundred six," Mickey answered instantly.

Murph folded his arms, laughed, and shook his head. "Well, I'll be damned," he said under his breath. "Amazing." He continued to stare at the boy with tremendous, fathomless, incredulous eyes.

"I'm just curious," he continued sheepishly. "How many strikes did you throw last—"

"Fifty-four," Mickey said before Murph could finish his thought. "Fifty-four strikes, fifteen balls."

Murph smiled. "That's great, Mick. Really. That's why I want you to—"

"Bison's pitcher threw sixty-six strikes. Sixty-six strikes, fifty-nine balls."

Murph was still in awe but was growing frustrated. His head began to swim. "Okay, okay, Mick. I get it, I get it. But I need you for this game. Right now. Please. It's okay. I'll take care of Lefty. You can borrow his fifty pitches, or whatever the hell it is you said, and you'll pay him back later. We do it all the time here."

Lefty was seated at his locker, stretching his stirrups and filing the nails on his pitching hand when Murph asked to speak to him. He saw the look on his manager's face, heavy and burdensome, and knew instantly he was not going to like what he heard.

"You're gonna sit this one out, Lefty. Mickey's getting the ball."

The words exploded in Lefty's ears. His eyes filled with gloom. Some plug in Lefty seemed to loosen, for he began kicking lockers and throwing baseballs all around the locker room, all the while glaring at Mickey.

"This is bullshit, Murph!" Lefty roared. "Bullshit!"

Mickey took the ball in game two and rewarded Murph's confidence in him with another gem. Even with a fastball that had diminished some in speed due to fatigue, he was still too overpowering for the opposing batters. It took him less than one hundred pitches to dispose of the Bisons for the second time in less than four hours.

"Well, I ain't seen anything close to this in quite some time," Murph said, beaming after the game, rubbing Mickey's head affectionately. "What a performance."

Mickey was overwhelmed again. Without moving his head or blinking an eye, he surveyed his surroundings. Raucous laughter. Jubilant smiles. It was certainly a far cry from the austere stare he was used to back home. He smiled hard too, unable to help himself.

"Yeah, Mick," Boxcar and a few of the others added. "You were something else."

"Thank you, guys," he finally said. "Mickey is really happy. I like baseball. Baseball is fun."

Every one of them laughed.

"Fun?" Jimmy Llamas repeated out loud. "Fun? Can you imagine that? Fun he says. Of course it's fun. I can just see the headlines in tomorrow's paper. 'Baby Bazooka Gets Twin Killing.' Unbelievable. And he's just having fun."

"Yeah, Llamas," Woody added. "And he'll probably get more girls tomorrow than you ever did too."

Llamas placed his hand on his chin in contemplative pantomime. "Can't say I'd blame 'im." He chuckled. "Even in my zoot suit, on my best night, I couldn't run with him. Hell, the way he throws, I have to admit, I find myself curiously aroused as well." They all laughed even harder.

The excitement and adulatory comments were not limited to the team. Some of the hysteria spilled over from the stands and into the locker room. "Murph, some people are here to see Mickey," Matheson bellowed. "Say it will only take but a minute." They were all still showering and changing. Murph crossed the floor, pausing only long enough to catch a glimpse of his own face, suddenly softer, in the trophy case against the wall. Then his eyes moved forward and discovered, standing by the gate, an elderly gentleman and a small boy, no more than ten years old. The man was tall, with a red face and thin wisps of silver arranged neatly across a balding head. The boy was quiet and held on to the man's leg as though he were in danger of falling through the floor.

"Walter Harrigan," the man said, extending his hand in Murph's direction. "*Governor* Walter Harrigan. And this is my grandson, Billy."

The man sat, with the boy now resting on his lap. He felt the need to speak—felt it rise within him uncomfortably, not like a pain but like a rushing tide that threatened to lift him back off the chair. He blinked at the line of shadows from which Murph had emerged and unfurled his story.

Billy had been born with a degenerative condition that had kept him confined to a wheelchair his entire life. Polio was the initial diagnosis, although the doctors were never quite certain. Walter spoke about all kinds of tests and treatments he had procured for the boy after his mother passed away suddenly and his father ran off with a cocktail waitress. "I am responsible for the boy now," he explained grimly. "Not something I planned on—certainly not at my age. It hasn't been easy. I tell you—I had all but given up any hope when your young phenom here—Mickey—came along."

The man swallowed hard. Tears formed behind his eyes but he did not cry. His face was strangely lit from the window to his side as he detailed the miraculous events surrounding the boy's implausible recovery.

"It must have been Mickey's second or third game," he explained. "We were sitting right behind home plate. Close enough to smell the pine tar and cowhide. Billy was entranced by Mickey. The warm-ups. The popping of the catcher's glove. Everything. He did not take his eyes off him the entire game."

Later that day, hours after the game, Billy disappeared. Walter had just lain down to take a nap and left Billy as he always did—in his wheelchair outside on the porch. When he awoke, a short while later, he discovered to his horror an empty chair and no sign of the boy anywhere. He panicked—raced around his property frantically, calling out the boy's name, besieged by the thought of how easy it was for a man to destroy his entire existence with just one careless act. His heart pounded as he darted from place to place until finally his flight was arrested by the sight of Billy at the edge of a grassy slope—standing erect with a baseball in his hand while rolling his arms in lionizing mimicry of his hero.

"It's a miracle I tell you," the governor said, his eyes now fully wet with emotion. "An absolute miracle. We just needed to come down here and thank you. That's all."

Murph smiled. He waited a minute, looking down at the boy whose eyes were lit like two birthday candles. Then he called to Mickey and watched as the governor and his grandson shook hands with Mickey and told him how thankful they were for all he had done.

"You are a very special young man," the governor said. "I will never forget what you have done for my boy. Never."

Mickey smiled, his face a subtle blend of aloofness and asceticism, then was a little confused when the governor handed him a brand-new baseball and a pen.

"Just one more thing, if we may. Would you mind doing us the honor?"

Mickey, trying to conceal his uneasiness, stood absently.

"He wants you to sign your name, Mick," Murph explained. "On the ball. You're a celebrity now. Famous. It's what famous people do sometimes."

"Okay, Mr. Murphy. Mickey will do it."

The legend grew. It did not take long for newspapers to catch wind of this miraculous development. It was more fodder for sales; another feel-good story, replete with the kind of emotion that would capture the heart and imagination of everyone who read.

"Brewers' Mickey Heals Governor's Grandson."

Talk of the miraculous headline grew like bananas in bunches, replacing the unflagging criticism of not too long ago. A confident surge of cheers and whistles attended just about every discussion of the Brew Crew. All was magical in Brewer Land. A little success can lighten even the darkest doldrums.

But something was amiss. Lefty, who had remained aloof in the shadows of the postgame activities, faded even further, like a child's ball that has gradually been losing air through some slow, invisible leak. He busied himself for as long as he could at his locker, folding his uniform pants and cleaning dirt from his spikes with a tongue depressor, but he found the fawning over Mickey intolerable. He was being replaced by this mystical kid and was growing more desperate by the minute.

Practice was earlier than usual the next day. Unable to sleep the night before, Lefty was the first to arrive. He came in quietly, went straight to his locker, and noticed with some alarm that someone had been there before him. His spikes had been moved, and something odd was sticking out from the slats in the top of the locker.

The cryptic note, a soiled cocktail napkin smeared with several ink blotches that had bled together unceremoniously, was barely legible. The pitcher removed his cap and scratched the top of his head while deciphering the message.

> *Meet me at The Bucket. Back room.*
> *10:00 pm. Don't be late.*
>
> > > C.M.

He read deliberately, lost in the mystery of the strange request. What could it mean? Whom was it from? He thought a lot about the past few weeks—how he was outside himself, a stranger drifting helplessly through what had formally been a pretty good life. Now he was afflicted with this strange antagonism, his taste for life vanquished by the arrival of Mickey. He thought some more and was certain that he was about to make some sense of it all, when all at once he felt a flowering uneasiness that came in the form of voices from around the corner. It was Murph, and maybe Boxcar and Woody. He folded the note away, conscious somehow that discretion was in order.

At approximately three minutes before ten, Lefty pushed open the back door of the local watering hole, frequented most often by a few of the more downtrodden locals, and was greeted almost instantly by a stagnant odor, aggressive puffs of musty air laced with whiskey and cigar smoke. He stepped inside, his feet moving gingerly across the tacky floor, and saw nothing at all. The only light came from a single brass lamp with marble-swirl glass, which illuminated little more than the mahogany, bow-fronted table on which it sat.

As he moved cautiously toward the light, he finally saw him, standing in the farthest corner, his back to the center of the black room, hunched slightly, and bathed in lurid reflections.

"Come in George" came a voice from the shadows. "Can I call you George, or do you prefer Lefty?"

"Coach McNally?" the anxious pitcher asked. "Is that you?"

There was no immediate response. Lefty strained his eyes and his mouth grew set, a thin, severe line. He shook himself as though to free the seizing darkness, trying to rid himself of the specter of impending danger that shrouded his brain.

"Yes, why, yes, it's me," McNally finally replied, turning ever so slightly in Lefty's direction. A splash of light threw itself across a face awash with calamity. "How are things Lefty? Team's doing good, huh?"

"Yeah. We're doing okay."

"Okay?" McNally snapped. "Okay? I'd say you're doing better than okay. Christ, eight wins in your last ten games? That's downright impressive."

"Yeah, I guess so."

McNally shifted his shoulders and moved to the center of the room, and with the lamp now directly at his back, Lefty viewed him in silhouette.

"Tell me, Lefty," he continued purposefully. "For a guy on the hottest team around, you sure don't seem all that happy now." He paused, as if hatching something else of great importance, then picked at his two front teeth with the end of the penknife he pulled from his trousers. "I wonder about that."

"What do you mean? What are you talking about?"

"It's okay now, boy. You don't have to mince words with me. I know what it's like to be underappreciated. To take a backseat to some two-bit hayseed when it's you who ought to be doing the driving yourself. You follow?"

Lefty sighed. His face grayed with anger and resentment. It was as if the coach had located the bruise on his forearm and was stepping on it with all his weight.

"I don't know what you're talking about," Lefty insisted. "I ain't got no problem with Mickey."

"Listen, boy." McNally placed his damp hand on Lefty's shoulder. "It's only natural. Who could blame you? You're a stud. Probably the top prospect in the whole damned league. Hell, I know if you was wearing my uniform, you wouldn't be playing second fiddle to some circus retard. That's for damn sure."

Behind one of the threadbare walls, a man's muffled laugh was suddenly muted by footsteps. Lefty's gaze slid around the room. His stomach protested and he could feel his saliva bubbling, hot and acidic, at the back of his throat.

"Look, Mr. McNally, if it's all the same, I'd like to get going. Do you want to tell me what it is you want from me? Why did you ask me here?"

McNally threw his head back and laughed. In his diabolical cynicism lay the difference between men like him and most others.

"It appears to me, Lefty, that you and I have a similar problem. Life doesn't always give you what you want—or deserve. But there are always options. You know, ways of helping your cause along, so to speak. This Mickey poses a very large problem for the both of us. So, I was thinking that, uh, I don't know, that maybe we could do just that—take charge of our destinies—and in the process, help each other too."

McNally snickered and rolled his arms in bitter mockery. Lefty winced at the prospect attached to McNally's declaration. He had not expected anything like that. But somehow, it sounded a whole lot better than what Murph had been saying to him lately. He steadied, considered, and decided.

"Okay," he finally said, folding his arms while resting his bottom on the corner of the table. "What did you have in mind?"

JULY

Molly caught her reflection, a distorted image cast unexpectedly in the soapy water of a washbasin. She stopped scrubbing, as if startled by a stranger, brought her wrinkled fingers to her face, and touched deliberately, trying to substantiate what her eyes had just revealed. Her skin, damp with an early evening humidity, seemed to wither beneath her touch, a gradual fading that alarmed her as never before. She dropped her head and wept openly.

Her heart felt as though it were precariously resting between two stone walls drawing closer and closer, inches away from pressing together. She had survived all these years by not focusing on the vast parameters of the world at large but on what was immediately around her. It usually worked. She could lose herself in the mixing of animal feed or the husking of corn. She knew just how to wash a cow's udder—a warm cloth and gentle strokes—so as not to alarm the animal prior to milking. She could even spend a whole afternoon bottle-feeding the lambs. But occasionally, this vapid existence preyed upon her more tender sensibilities, awakened now and again by glimpses of what could have been, and she cried out in painful protest for the life she really desired but had yet to cultivate.

Over fading heartbeats, she heard Clarence's voice, cold and vituperative. "Molly!" he bellowed from inside the barn. "I can't find my goddamned penknife." His voice scraped at her soul and pressed those walls even closer, suffocating what little breath she managed to hold. Where were the moments she'd read about in all those tantalizing romance novels? The horseback rides and careless walks through wildflower meadows? The taste of strawberry ice cream cones while swaying gently on a porch swing? Or the sound of violins or clarinets floating on a cool summer breeze?

Life just seemed to make its pattern around her. She cooked and cleaned, and on most days, like today, she washed. She made all of Clarence's meals, ordered his socks and underwear, and watched dutifully from the kitchen window each evening for when he was finished in the field, then prepared his pipe so that he could smoke while listening to the radio. Then night would arrive outside their window, with its pinching air and silent darkness, and she would prepare to retire next to him, holding only a gas lamp to light their way and stabbing thoughts of yet another day's drudgery.

There was, however, on occasion, some conversation. Not the exchange of pithy observations she'd prefer, but it passed the time. She always marveled at how her depth of feeling and emotion could co-exist with his absence of imagination. It became a game of sorts to her—retaining her sensitivity and passion while navigating the stagnant waters of their relationship.

"Say, Molly, have ya had a look-see at Oscar lately?" Clarence asked, picking his teeth with the tip of a rusty piece of chicken wire. "Moping around, like he's done lost his best friend. I swear to Christ, if I didn't know no better, I'd get to thinking that little porker sort of misses that boy." He laughed sardonically as he packed up the feed pails for the day.

"We all miss him, Clarence," Molly replied. "Makes perfect sense, doesn't it?"

Clarence chewed the inside of his cheek and said nothing. Molly frowned. She could smell his sweat. She saw herself being watched by him—with those dark, ulcerous eyes—and shuddered at the realization that there was no longer a visible beginning or end to how they were tangled together. Her spirit sagged with a palpable heaviness. But she refused to vanish, to disappear beneath its uncompromising weight. She took a deep breath and composed herself.

"You know, Clarence, now that you brought it up, don't you think it's about time we went and visited the boy? Mr. Murphy says he's doing real fine."

The sun, in its steady descent, caught the broken clouds. The day's light dimmed on Clarence, but not enough to mask the bilious imp that had suddenly seized his soul.

"Hush up your mouth, woman!" he chided, making a deft motion as if to backhand her. "Do ya hear me? Are you plum out of yer cotton-picking mind? Wanting to go all the way to Milwaukee, or wherever it is, just to watch some good-fer-nothing game? Hell, you must be stupider than that retard of yours."

"Clarence, I just—"

"Clarence nothing, goddamn you!" he ranted. He picked up a plate and fired it through one of the kitchen windows.

"You shut your trap, little Miss Molly, ya hear? I've had enough of this foolishness. So help me, if it don't stop, I swear to the Almighty you'll feel me."

Molly felt, listening to his harangue, a pain and desperation so deep that she could scarcely fathom how a person could feel it and still remain a part of this world. But there she was, still making her way. Surviving. She was certain, however, that this resiliency would one day fail and the pain would kill her. She'd end up dying right here, in this hellhole, right next to the man she abhorred.

"And another thing," he screamed, slamming the end of a tarnished flail in between the slanting boards of the kitchen floor. "If all this Mr. Murphy talk continues to be something, I reckon I'll have to learn you proper. And then once I've done that, I will just git rid of the problem altogether—like you know I can, Molly, same way I got rid of that fox in the henhouse." He raised his hand again. Molly winced and curled her toes in fear. "Am I understood, little Miss Molly?"

Mickey was also struggling. He missed Molly and would have loved to have seen her. He did okay on most days, but still found himself thinking of her a lot. Being with Pee Wee helped a little. As the early season spilled into summer, the two of them began spending a good amount of time together, mostly at Lucy's, the local diner just minutes from the ballpark.

The place smelled like animal fat and cigarette smoke and was sort of dark, with only errant light slipping through the turbid glass squares that ran asymmetrically along the front of the tiny structure—errant light that once inside fell oddly on the few seated figures, casting each in ghostly shadow. The two of them sat facing each other across the gray Formica tabletop, exchanging bits of information between mouthfuls of cheeseburgers and apple pie.

"You have much family back home, Mick?" Pee Wee asked. "You know, brothers and sisters?"

"Nope. Mickey just got a ma and Oscar, my pig." He paused deliberately, as if weighing something of great importance, while moving some potatoes around on his plate. "And I got a pa. I got a pa."

"I don't have one of those. I mean a pa."

Mickey's hands worked nervously, moving the food on his plate around in small, tight circles. "What about a pig? Do you got a pig, Pee Wee?" Mickey asked, looking up from his plate.

"Ain't too many pigs in Chicago. But we had a kitten once, my sister and I, but he ran away. Broke her heart, poor kid. His name was Ziggy."

They sat there traveling for a moment through early recollections. They were suddenly nostalgic and maudlin as each pushed back the imaginary walls of time.

"Did your daddy teach you to play ball?" Pee Wee asked. "You know—catch and all that? That's how I always picture me with my dad—if things had been different."

"Naw, my daddy don't know nothing about that sort of thing."

"You guys close? I mean, do ya do other things, like hunting or fishing?"

Mickey's posture and voice were full of resignation. "Nope. Nothing like that."

Pee Wee moved in closer. He was near enough now to see some

of the scars on Mickey's face. "Well, then, besides work, what is it that you all do on that farm of yours?"

"Nothing. We don't do nothing. Mickey's always stirring up trouble. It makes my pa holler a lot. He gets real sore."

"Well, that don't seem right now, does it? Don't it bother you? You know, all the yelling?"

"It's okay. It's okay. Mickey's used to it."

Pee Wee felt a pressing need to turn the conversation elsewhere. He crossed his arms tightly and sighed. "Are you having a good time with the fellas and all, Mick? I mean, I know that some of the guys are giving you the business and whatnot."

Mickey's eyes wandered to a poster tacked up sloppily on a bulletin board behind the counter. It looked as though he were measuring it with his eyes.

"That's Rosie the Riveter," Pee Wee explained. "She's sort of an icon. You know, from the war and all. It's no big deal. Her face has been around for years. I guess you've never seen her before. Christ, the way you're staring at it, you'd think it was a Picasso or something."

"She looks like my ma. The handkerchief in her hair. That's just like my ma. When she scrubs the floor."

"I guess you miss her and all, especially when the fellas get on you the way they do."

"Mickey's having an okay time, Pee Wee. Okay. It's okay I guess."

"You know, Mick, you can help yourself sometimes. Like when they ask you questions and then laugh at your answers. They do that stuff on purpose. You don't have to answer them. Just lie—make up a story to shut them up."

"Mickey don't make up stories, Pee Wee. On account of there's so many to choose from."

"What does that have to do with anything? Just pick one. Any one. Don't give them what they want."

Mickey brought his palms to the sides of his face and held them there, as if steadying the surging thoughts inside his head. "Let's say someone asks me what I ate here at Lucy's. Mickey had a hamburger. That's what I would say. But supposing I don't want to say that, 'cause the guys will laugh, and I want to say sweet-potato pie instead. But I can't say sweet-potato pie because before I can get the words out, I would want to say bacon and eggs, or meat loaf, or macaroni and cheese. Or maybe I'd just start naming sweet things, like chocolate pudding or sugar cookies. I don't know. Things get all bunched up sometimes. So you see, Mickey don't tell stories. It hurts my head. It's just easier to say hamburger."

With this glimpse into the workings of the boy's mind, Pee Wee smiled, because he now felt a little closer to Mickey than before. "Well, I have to say, that no matter what anyone says or does, including you, Mick, we're all mighty glad you're here. All of us. Cripe, since you got here, the team's been playing better than I've ever seen."

Outside, it was humid and all at once dark. Claps of thunder alternated with flashes of lightning. Then the rain came hard. Pee Wee and Mickey watched, through the cloudy window, as some of the locals scampered frantically through puddles that were already ankle deep. Pee Wee chuckled. Mickey dipped his finger in some ketchup and brought it to his lips. He opened his mouth, let his finger slide inside, and sucked it clean. His gaze was fixed off in the distance. The weathered wood fence that edged the road just outside conjured more images of the farm back home. He had begun to feel pangs of loneliness, a sort of bottomless anxiety, when a clanging of pots and pans from the kitchen jolted him from his thoughts.

"So if it weren't your daddy who taught you, where'd you learn to pitch like that, Mick?" Pee Wee asked. "Sure is the most goddarned thing I've ever seen."

"I don't reckon I ever did. Too busy with the farm."

"How's that?"

"Why, it were Mr. Murphy showed me how to pitch. Shoot, I ain't never even seen a baseball until Mr. Murphy put one in my hand."

Pee Wee paused, rolled his two fists in his eyes, then asked with sudden resolution, "Are you trying to tell me that you never pitched before? Or even played baseball?"

Mickey nodded.

"Nothing? Not even a catch or a pickup game?"

"Nope. Most I ever done was throw some crab apples into a wine barrel for Oscar's slop."

Pee Wee smiled and let his forehead fall quickly into his open palm. "This is too much. Here we are going out on a six-game road trip, fighting for first place, and our star pitcher is some hayseed who got his training from a pig."

A look of sudden amusement passed between them. Mickey abandoned his pursuit of a trapped fly that was frenetically bouncing against the window and smiled. They sat a little longer, each piecing together the difference between the polluted past and the near future burgeoning with opportunity.

The road trip began against the Mudcats. The stands were packed. At the ballpark, with the smell of cowhide and freshly cut grass in your nose and the taste of hot dogs dancing on your tongue, your vision of the world adjusted, narrowing to a snapshot of life as it should be—ordered, playful, and limitless in possibility. Each enchanted game shows you the glory and breathless exhilaration that lies somewhere out there, just within your grasp, there for the taking should you ever decide to finally reach.

On this day, the atmosphere was particularly electric. The Brewers, who traditionally generated little interest outside their immediate geographic region, had suddenly become a draw, due mostly to the hype surrounding their newest pitching sensation. Although Mickey was not slated to pitch until midweek, the crowd caught a glimpse of the "new look" Brewers anyway when Woody Danvers drilled a 2–2 fastball over the center-field wall in the top of the ninth inning to sink the hometown heroes and lift the Brew Crew into second place, just three games behind the rival Rangers of Spokane.

Their winning ways continued that week, including convincing victories over the Indians and the Sidewinders. Murph called on Lefty

next; he had been showing signs lately of snapping out of his prolonged doldrums. Lefty was sharp. He made it through the seventh,
bottling up the Spartans with a blazing fastball and a twelve-to-six
hook that was, by all accounts, "dropping off the table." But the
Brewers' potent offense had stalled, providing Lefty with nothing
more than two infield hits for support. The anemic attack drew the
ire of the irascible southpaw.

"Un-friggin'-believable!" he ranted, firing his glove against the
dugout wall.

Boxcar put on his inscrutable face. "What's your problem now,
Rogers? Hell, you're throwing better today than you have in a
dog's age."

Lefty's thoughts zigzagged. Several of the others stopped what
they were doing and fixed their eyes on the two men.

"Oh, nothing is wrong, nothing at all," Lefty shot back, launching into a diatribe that resonated throughout the dugout. "Everyone
else gets runs. That's all. Sanders, Mickey. I bet even Larry would
get a few runs on the board if he took the hill. It's crap. There's always plenty of scoring for everyone else. Not me. No, sir. Not Lefty.
Lefty has to do it all by himself." He walked off in a clumsy daze.
"Bunch of bull!"

Matheson had been watching the entire episode. He spat out a
wad of chew on the dugout floor and doddered over to the cantankerous pitcher.

"Come on now, Lefty my boy," the old man cajoled. "We need
this one. Bad. You sulking and carrying on like this, all full of piss
and vinegar, don't do no good. You gotta shake it. Or we is done.
Hell, for want of a nail, the entire shoe could be lost."

Lefty turned his head slowly toward Matheson, then exhaled in
thunderous, absolutely unbearable exasperation. "What the hell
does that even mean?" he wailed. "I can't listen to this drivel anymore. Do me a favor, you babbling old fool. Just go away. Pick up
your sagging mess of a body and get the hell away from me."

As the game went on, Lefty crumbled beneath the weight of his
discontent. In the eighth, he walked the leadoff batter on four

straight balls, which prompted the Spartans' skipper to play for one run. The next batter squared and dropped a beautiful bunt that hugged the chalk as it crawled up the third-base line. In his haste to cut down the lead runner, Lefty fired wildly to Arky Fries at second, sailing the ball over his head and into center field. Both runners advanced. Lefty sweated heavily and cursed his misfortune once again. Murph folded his arms and glared out at him from the dugout steps.

Things only got worse. The next Spartan batter took advantage of another mistake—a hanging slider—and laced a single back through the originator, scoring both runners. This was followed by a frozen rope that split Jimmy Llamas and Buck Faber, and a round-tripper off the bat of the Spartan cleanup hitter, Buzz Billings—a prodigious blast that seemed to climb higher and higher until finally slamming into the scoreboard some four hundred feet away. When Murph took the ball from Lefty, the pitcher scowled like a wounded animal. Under his cap, his brow sweated with humiliation.

"Hit the showers, kid," Murph instructed. "Enough for one day."

Lefty could feel himself slipping out of the manager's favor, feel the space he had left, a space undoubtedly now occupied by another. The realization stung.

Murph turned the reins over to Butch Filocomo, who, after walking the first man he faced, induced a 6–4–3 double play before fanning the next batter to stop the bleeding.

Clem Finster led off the ninth for the Brewers with a sharp single to left. A walk to Amos Ruffings and a push bunt by Pee Wee loaded the sacks for the big boppers. In the wake of the Brewers' threat, a murmur went up from the restless crowd. The Spartans, mired in last place, were notorious for squandering leads late in the game. All too often, the Spartan faithful were brought to the brink of victory, only to have their hopes dashed unmercifully by an errant throw or misplayed ball.

"They'll break your heart, boys," the old men in the bleachers always grumbled to each other. "Just like a cheap tramp."

Jimmy Llamas smiled as he dug in for his at bat. With the bags juiced, he was sitting dead red—pipe fastball, first pitch. He got it and smashed a searing line drive to left center. He was halfway between first and second when he heard the ball thump in the glove of the Spartan center fielder, thwarting Llamas' quest for late-game heroics. The stellar play seemed to deflate the entire team. Danvers followed Llamas' liner with a weak foul-out to the catcher, and Boxcar, who usually thrived on opportunities like these, proved he was indeed human, taking a called third strike to end the game. It was the team's first loss in more than two weeks, and it left the upstart Brew Crew tied with the Rangers for first place, setting the stage for a classic showdown between the rivals the following day.

The Rangers sent their ace, Bucky Vardiman, to the hill under a gray sky that threatened to dump rain on them at any minute. Despite a heavy, whistling wind and a dampness that hung over them with ominous patience, Vardiman was on, setting down the Brewers one, two, three.

"Come on, fellas," Murph implored desperately. "We can't keep doing this. We need the bats."

Mickey trotted out to the mound in the bottom half of the inning, looking to silence what was already a hostile crowd. A commotion started in the lower seats behind first base. A man with a grizzled beard and paint-stained overalls was doing his best to incite the others around him.

"Hey, freak show!" he screamed to Mickey, looking back at the others for approval. "Look at me!" He mimicked Mickey's unusual delivery. "Look at me, funny boy! I'm a ballplayer." Mickey heard him and was conscious of being watched, but continued to roll his arms and fire his warm-up pitches. He wondered, as he delivered each toss, why the ornery man was taunting him. Having no tangible answer, he mistook the man's ignorance for his own shortcomings. For a brief moment, he thought of Clarence. The recollection made him wince and shudder, altering his mechanics so drastically that the frazzled hurler sailed the next two tosses clear over Boxcar's head, much to the delight of the raucous crowd.

"Come on now, Mick," Pee Wee said, trotting in from his position at short. "Forget everyone else. Just you and Boxcar. Right? That's all. Come on now. You can do this—just like tossing crab apples, right?"

Mickey, still absorbed in thoughts of his father, pounded the ball in his glove.

"Hey, Mick," Pee Wee persisted, placing his hand over Mickey's glove. "Come on now. Nobody's better than you. Nobody."

Mickey said nothing, just stood there, sucking his teeth and staring moodily into the stands. He made out one or two faces, including the slovenly, loudmouthed grumbler, but after some time, each visage just melted into the next, like gray shapes in the darkness.

When Mickey had seen enough, his eyes, hot and watery, turned to Boxcar's glove; then he rolled his arms, leaned back, lifted his leg, and fired two more warm-ups—this time strong and accurate.

The half inning began on the umpire's call. The Rangers' leadoff man, Kiki Delaney, bounded to the plate. He was a rabbit. He was only a .260 hitter, but he could go from home to first in just over four seconds. Delaney was also a terror on the bases, swiping a league leading seventy-six bags each of the last two seasons. Everyone in the league knew that he was the catalyst for the Ranger offense. So, the scouting report that Murph gave to Mickey and Boxcar was simple: keep Delaney off the bases.

Mickey missed up and away with his first offering, then evened the count with a fastball right down the pipe. Delaney stepped out of the box, tapped his spikes with the barrel of his bat, and checked the third-base coach for signs. After studying a series of frenetic gestures that looked something like a full-blown seizure, he eased back into the box, slowly, methodically, then laid his bat out flat just in time to deaden Mickey's next offering. The ball wheezed and stumbled, staggering past the mound and out of the reach of a charging Clem Finster before dying just before Arky Fries could get a handle on it. By the time Fries picked it up, Delaney was standing on first base, laughing. "Let 'em play small ball all day long, Mick," Danvers shouted. "They can't touch ya."

Mickey's first pitch to the next batter allowed the speedster to steal second. After the next delivery, he was standing on third. Delaney was putting on a clinic. The Ranger bench erupted in jubilant approval. Mickey groaned. A maudlin urgency filled him. He could see the entire Ranger bench, knees bent, eyes squeezed tight and mouths agape, laughter exploding from every uniform. He could hear them too.

"Baby Bazooka?" They laughed, some doubled over in a desperate search for air. "Are they kidding us? More like Kiddie Cork Gun!"

Mickey heard the jeers. His whole body slumped.

"Shake that off, Mickey," Murph yelled from the dugout, his eyes on McNally and the others. "Come on, big fella, just work the batter."

Mickey opened his mouth and licked his lips. They were dry, except for two gummy, white bits of saliva resting in the corners. His stomach ached and he felt a distinct throbbing at his temples. He was close to caving. Then, under the cover of a dark gray sky, Mickey found the tiny red target in Boxcar's glove and the oppression lifted.

"Strike one. . . . Strike two. . . . Strike three!" the umpire shouted in succession. The batter sat down. Three pitches later, another batter fell victim. Then another. The raucous heckling and hissing from the Ranger dugout eased to a series of sighing complaints, and from all around the stands, dim rows of pale faces fired deep-throated, guttural invectives not at Mickey but at their own beloved boys of summer, chastising them for their poor performance against what they deemed a less than worthy opponent.

Vardiman and Mickey continued to put up zeros on the board, silencing the crowd with a good old-fashioned pitchers' duel. It was definitely a day for the cerebral baseball enthusiast, one who could appreciate the understated excitement of nibbling corners and purpose pitches. While those enamored with the long ball and barn-burning baseball lamented the "stinker" of a game, the baseball purists delighted in the classic repartee between hurlers, a skillful jousting that left them on the edge of their seats.

With the game was still scoreless with two outs in the top of the ninth, Danvers strode to the plate. He had fanned his first three times up. Vardiman had made him look bad, mixing his pitches and changing speeds with the precision of an artist. Danvers was frustrated. In truth, he never hit Vardiman well. In twenty-one career at bats against the Ranger ace, he was batting a pitiful .048 with sixteen strikeouts. Danvers was always at a loss to explain it.

"I'll be goddamned!" he would say after facing his nemesis. "This son of a bitch is toying with me." The others always laughed and rode him about it. Usually, Danvers just moped and sulked. But on this day, he was downright angry. Vengeful. He walked through the dugout spouting off about pride and retribution and how they were all masters of their own destinies. He stood at the dish this fourth time, sinewy and loose, knees bent, shoulders square to the pitcher. He grit his teeth and waved his bat over his head in willful defiance, determined to expiate not just the day's disappointments but every one of his previous failures as well.

Vardiman began the sequence with a tight slider for a called strike. Danvers shook his head and readied himself for the next offering. Vardiman peered in at the catcher. He shook off the first few suggestions before nodding at the last. He reared back, cocking the ball behind his ear, and let fly a two-seam fastball. Danvers swung wildly as the ball buzzed through the air, leaving the befuddled hitter a tangled, crumpled mess. Strike two. Vardiman took the ball back. He positioned himself on the rubber. Danvers stepped out to collect himself. His face, already contorted with frustration, hardened even further when he saw Vardiman laughing behind his glove.

As he glowered at the smug pitcher, Danvers suddenly relaxed. He felt beyond everything, especially his recent failures, as if he were all at once in the hands of something extraordinarily larger than himself—as if the universe had reached down and embraced him, determined to replace his sickly spirit with a restorative smile. This feeling warmed his stomach and sharpened his senses, allowing him to see the next pitch leave Vardiman's hand as if it were delivered in suspended animation. The laces spun toward him, orbiting dutifully through the damp, viscous air. All the natural impulses and baseball reactions that had lain dormant in the wake of his history with Vardiman surged up inside him; he lifted his foot, placed it down again with purposeful vigor, and whipped the bat head through the hitting zone with blinding speed. The golden lumber found the ball, caught the tiny orb where the bat was fattest, and sent it sailing over the center-field wall. Danvers blinked hard and leaped with joy, circling the bases with spirited gestures.

Murph was smiling too. The way Mickey was throwing, one run was all they needed. Mickey retired the first two batters in the Rangers' half of the ninth with little protest. His team's malaise, coupled with the thought of dropping the game to his mortal enemy, sent McNally into a dizzying fit of petulance. It was intolerable to him that he should be dominated by Arthur Murphy and his twisted reclamation project. Most times, McNally could find a dead space amidst all that bothered him and rest inside, numb to the festering disappointments that scraped at him like tiny shovels. But on occasion, he would get caught in the tide of circumstance, dragged to the shore, and the sun would sting his eyes and shine brightly on all his failures, and he would see everything for just what it really was.

"Time!" he called, stepping out of the dugout with festering antagonism. Everyone watched curiously as he walked deliberately toward home plate. His eyes were small and dangerous.

"Hey, ump." He pointed to Boxcar. "Is that glove he's using there to code? I mean, I sure ain't ever seen nothing like that before."

"What's wrong with it, Chip?" the umpire replied curtly, eager to resume play.

McNally was posturing behind Boxcar, hands on hips, sights set on reprimand. "Have him take it off his hand," McNally instructed. "Have a look in the pocket."

The umpire removed his mask and tapped Boxcar on the shoulder. As he questioned the catcher and examined his glove, Murph came flying out of the dugout like a mother bear protecting one of her cubs.

"What's all the commotion, Box?" he asked breathlessly.

"Relax, Murphy," McNally snapped back. "Just making sure everything's legal, that's all."

"Sherlock Holmes here wants to look at my glove, Skip," Boxcar explained. "Says it's no good."

Murph cut his eyes in McNally's direction. "What kind of horse crap are you trying to pull, McNally? That glove's as straight as the pointy nose on your face and you know it."

The three of them looked on as the umpire turned the glove over in his hands, deliberating. Murph stared at the trio of fine lines stretching across the ump's forehead, outraged at the absurdity unfolding before him. The umpire continued to contemplate, and McNally tapped his foot in thoughtful expectation.

"Chip's right, Murph," the umpire finally concluded. "This ain't regulation."

"Come on now," Murph pleaded. "There isn't anything in the rule book that says a player can't have a little paint on his glove. This prick is just trying to get in my pitcher's head."

"I'm sorry, Murph, but I'm at a loss here. Truth is, I don't really know what to do. You may be right. But be that as it may, I have to take the glove out of play. I'll let the guys who make the rules decide later on."

"Are you kiddin' me!" Murph exploded. "Is this really happening? What kind of a goddamned circus is this?"

"Come on, Murph. I don't make the rules, I just follow them."

"Yeah, Murphy. Give the guy a break, would ya?" McNally gloated. "That's the only fair thing to do." His eyes were off to the side, and he was trying to pretend the outcome was not his intended purpose. "Rules are rules."

Murph's face flushed.

"So that's it?" Boxcar complained, looking to Murph for help. "I'm just supposed to hand over my glove—just like that?"

"Just give 'im the glove, Box," Murph said, shaking his head as he walked toward the mound. "You can use the extra one."

Mickey was given a few warm-up tosses in light of the delay. Murph stood behind him and watched. Mickey was clearly agitated. He turned to Murph several times and asked for the old glove—the one with the painted apple—but Murph just shook his head and stood behind the mound and watched him struggle with the new one. He cringed as each of the five tosses sailed clear over Boxcar's head. The wildness was followed by the faint recitation of the now all-too-familiar de la Mare poem.

"Hey, now that's the farm boy I remember!" McNally taunted from the bench. "Hot damn!"

Murph walked around the dirt circle and faced Mickey. The boy was staring down at his spikes, defeated.

"Listen, Mick, there ain't nothing to this," Murph encouraged. "Really. A glove's a glove. Just pretend that big old mitt is a barrel, filled with apples. Nothing to it. Come on now. Remember— nobody's better than you."

The walk back to the dugout was perhaps the longest Murph had ever taken. God he wanted this game. It had been so long since the Brewers had seen first place. And McNally was such an ass. He wondered, as he resumed his familiar stance atop the dugout steps, just how he would be able to stomach this sort of loss.

Mickey's feet struggled to find their spot on the rubber. He looked like a baby deer who had just gotten its legs. He was awkward, spastic, and his clumsiness only fueled further the derision coming from the Ranger dugout.

"Why me?" Murph whispered to himself. "Why?"

The frazzled hurler faced the third batter of the inning. Ozzy Newcomb was the ninth-place hitter—an offensive threat by no means. But Mickey looked wild, and Newcomb was up there to work a walk. He set his feet in the batter's box, crouched, and cut the air with a few practice hacks, mostly for effect. Mickey rolled his arms, reared back, and let fly a fastball, up and away.

"Ball one!"

"Attaboy, Oz!" McNally yelled from the bench. "Walk's a hit."

Mickey regrouped. He sighed heavily and peered in at Boxcar. The catcher was smiling through his mask as he traced with his right forefinger the outline of an apple in the pocket of his glove.

"Come on now, big Mick," he called. "Come on now. Toss that apple!"

Mickey looked lost, confused by Boxcar's zany antics. He squinted and scrunched his nose, trying unsuccessfully to ascertain some hidden meaning behind his catcher's behavior. But somehow, either the phantom picture or the mere mention of the word *apple* refocused the young phenom, and like the lightning that had just split the stormy sky, he was back. He rolled, reared, and fired a blazing fastball dead center. The pop of the glove was deafening.

"Steeerike one!"

The cry was followed by a distant clap of thunder and two more flashes of white light. Mickey got right back on the rubber and delivered again.

"Twooo!"

McNally scratched his head and cursed the sky. Through the inclement air came the weary groan of the crowd, a song of discontent that struck a chord that vibrated deep within him. All of these flurried failures and eliminations made his mind a barren, echoing place where the voices of detractors resonated with an unrelenting fury. Losing was such a tough nut to swallow. Always was.

He could still remember the very first sting of defeat. He was only eight. It came at the hands of Roger Forester while they sat around a dusty marble ring etched in the schoolyard dirt. Young McNally was the marble champion. Nobody at Thomas Jefferson Elementary was better. Except on that day. On that day, Forester could not miss. One by one, he sent every one of McNally's marbles—green ones, red ones, yellow ones—careening out of the circle.

"Oh my God, Chip!" his friends ridiculed. "How could you lose to Forester?"

He felt so naked, so vulnerable. And all he could think was to run and hide. That's just what he did. But that luxury had yielded with the passage of time. Now he had to face the music.

Through the intermittent lightning and thin veil of rain, Mickey looked ghostlike and menacing. His prodigious presence was never more pronounced than at that moment when his arms rolled and fired one final time, a blurred, gleaming line of white rocketing through the misty air past a sagging stick and into Boxcar's glove for strike three.

Within seconds of the umpire's call, the Brewers' bench erupted onto the field, each player, including Danvers and the other dissenters, loping frantically to join the celebration on the mound. There were hugs and handshakes and slaps on the behind for everyone. It was only one game, and they still had quite a stretch of schedule to navigate, but as Murph said while watching the team hoist Mickey on their shoulders and carry him around the field victoriously, it was "the start of something really special."

He lingered and watched, savoring the taste of sweet victory. It was glorious. The perfect ending to a perfect day. He held his breath and let the feeling wash over him. His thoughts were varied, ranging from his early days as a rookie to just minutes ago, when McNally tried to sabotage his glory. Then they took a capricious turn, wandering inexplicably to Molly and the farm. It felt weird at first—just snuck up on him and hung on the air for a moment before dissolving into an aura of something warm and familiar. He wondered what Molly was doing, if she was okay, and wished that somehow she could be here to share the moment with them.

But as special as the scene was, Murph could not help but notice that Lefty's contributions to the celebration were perfunctory. He was less than enthusiastic, with forced smiles and contrived exultation. He fooled most of them, but Murph continued to watch. Believing he was free from public scrutiny, Lefty finally abandoned the façade. His mouth morphed into a grimace and his lids blinked maliciously. Murph, preparing to welcome each of his players back into the dugout, thought it was one of the ugliest things he had ever seen.

It was late afternoon, and the entire field was now bathed in long, dark, stormy shadows. Murph greeted each of his boys with warm, appreciative hands.

Lefty was the last one off. His walk from the field back to the dugout was interminable. With narrow eyes that looked past Murph's and strayed momentarily to the Ranger dugout, Lefty watched the sinking sun, dying in a purple sky, ensconced in a halo of ignominy.

MIDSEASON

In a dark office with a picture of Shoeless Joe Jackson over the fireplace and rows of books in leather covers of varying shades of brown tucked neatly in mahogany cases, several men sat around, smoking and talking in hushed tones. There was Scotty, a stocky, muscle-bound, impatient man in his late thirties who looked like an amateur boxer; Quinton, a polished gentleman with a waxed mustache and an expensive suit, and two other men wearing baseball caps and of dire expressions.

"This freak show is killing me," the first of the two men muttered from beneath his cap. "I can't have it anymore. I *can*not—I *will* not lose to Arthur Murphy again."

Quinton sat with a rigid back suggesting some correlation between physical and moral probity. Stiff and robotic, he altered his posture only briefly to jot something down in a folder next to him. Then he inhaled deeply several times through flared nostrils.

"You better not," he responded curtly, tapping the end of his pipe on his chin. "Have you seen the standings today? You've dropped six straight since the Brewer debacle. Seven games is a lot of ground to make up in six weeks. You don't get paid to finish second."

The attacked man sat up straight and cleared his throat. "That's why I wanted to meet," he said nervously. "So that we'd all be on the same page here." He hesitated a moment longer, then looked in the direction of the second man, receiving only an obligatory nod.

"Say, let's lay da cawds on da table," Scotty ejaculated, running his fingertips across a slip of paper as if he were reading by touch. "It says here that you mugs want a little help with settin' up a little—uh, what we in the business refer to as an unfortunate event. Am I right?"

"Well, we don't want anything too drastic," the first man said cautiously. "We just want to put a little scare into him. Nothing full-blown. It should be easy. My friend here even has some people who are willing to assist us in carrying out the plan."

Scotty's full, chinless face contorted into something fierce and menacing. "Well, then why you guys wastin' my time here?" he barked. "I'm a busy guy."

The hardness in Scotty's voice sent a faint chill of doubt over all of them.

"What he means to say," Quinton interjected, "is that we would like you—need you—to assist us in the particulars. More specifically, to provide the muscle to go along with the method."

The stocky man stomped around the room, his short, burly legs rattling the trinkets and decorative objects that adorned the furniture pieces that somehow kept getting in his way.

"This is not my usual gig," he said peremptorily. "It's kinda small potatoes. But, I'll tell you what I'm gonna do." He scribbled a crude drawing on a cocktail napkin he pulled from his pocket. "This is the bar—this mark is me. This other one is your boy." Then he drew a series of lines and slashes until the napkin was filled with ink. "That's how it will work. See?"

Quinton and the two other men surveyed the rudimentary drawing. It appeared to their liking, although Quinton pressed the first man for approval. "Well," he said, poking the man's shoulder with his index finger. "What do you think?"

"I don't know," he answered, saddled with overwhelming responsibility. "I've never done this sort of thing before."

They all just stared at each other blankly, paralyzed by a cloud of indecision.

"All right, I've heard enough. This meeting is over." Scotty reached for his drawing and had it halfway into his pocket when the second man made his move.

He turned, looked at all of them anxiously, then approached Scotty with yielding, catlike steps. "No, it's fine. Don't leave. Really. The plan is perfect. We'll take it. I know just what to do. It will work out just fine."

Scotty's anger melted momentarily. He plunged both hands into his pockets and jingled the coins inside. The other two men nodded to each other, and the glimmer of optimism widened. Scotty turned toward the group , his face now expressionless. "Okay now, fellas," he said with a half-closed mouth. "Let's talk turkey."

In shadows cast by crystal lamps, a brown envelope exchanged hands. The sound of banter and light laughter was heard and the air thinned significantly. The troubles of the day, once grave and insurmountable, seemed to reconcile, arrange themselves in healing formation.

The Brew Crew was riding high, basking in the glow of a seven-game lead over the second-place Rangers. The team was reveling in the uncharted waters of what appeared to be limitless success. They were, as Matheson said gleefully, "a well-oiled machine." Any fractiousness spawned by the anxiety and ignorance linked to Mickey's arrival had been quelled by the boy's affable nature and his incalculable contributions to the team's improbable rise to the baseball penthouse. Only Lefty remained bitter and critical.

"Yo, Lefty, he ain't so bad," Danvers explained, trying to sway the belligerent pitcher. "Yeah, he's a little off. But, hell, think about what he's done for all of us—for this team."

"What he's done for us?" Lefty asked. "What has he done for me? Except maybe become a gnawing, goddamned pain in my ass."

Danvers shook his head wearily. "You need to let it go, Rogers. Really. You still have an important role on this team. It don't have to be you or him. There's room for both of you."

"Don't give me any more of your damned sentimental crap,

Woody, okay? You're full of it. If that retard played the hot corner instead of pitcher, you'd be singing a different tune and you know it!"

The team continued to win. And their confidence grew with every victory. The rest of the league watched enviously as this group of ragtag personalities blossomed into a brash, haughty juggernaut known for its overbearing back-patting and raucous on-field displays celebrating their newfound prowess.

These on-field celebrations, which seemed to be happening more and more frequently, found their way into the clubhouse and frequently extended to after hours as well. There were card games, hunting trips, and drinking. Plenty of drinking. One night, this feel-good camaraderie carried them to The Bucket. They were all there, laughing and carousing, tying one on as if there were no tomorrow. And to everyone's surprise, it was Lefty's idea.

"Come on now, guys," he'd said earlier that day. "Let's go get pie-eyed—all of us. As a team. Best thing for comradeship. You know what they say—a team that chugs together, slugs together!"

"Who says that?" Pee Wee questioned.

"Don't be such a pansy, McGinty!" Lefty chided. "Loosen up a little bit. Just 'cause you look like a schoolboy don't mean you have to act like one. And bring Mickey. It's about time the big fella got a little taste of the nightlife."

Murph was elated when he heard about Lefty's reversal. He and Matheson had been discussing, with no luck, avenues to squelch the dissension emanating from every pore of the disgruntled pitcher. Murph was just about at the end of his rope when he caught wind of it. The news was heaven-sent—a direct response to his prayers. Lefty was finally embracing the new kid. It was just what he had hoped for. His mind floated vaguely on the awesome thought that his team was gelling at just the right time.

"It sounds like exactly what we need," Murph said. "Just do me a favor, Pee Wee. Mickey can stay at your place tonight. That would be fine. But don't overdue it with him. He's still kind of green. And be back at a reasonable hour. We have early BP tomorrow."

"No sweat, Murph," Pee Wee said. "Sure you don't want to join us? Not too often all the fellas are together like this."

"No thanks." Murph's mouth expanded into a full-blown yawn. "I think I'll sit this one out. I got a date with a couple of tumblers of whiskey and Jack Benny tonight."

The Bucket was hopping with all sorts of personalities. Pee Wee and Mickey were the first to come in. Pee Wee's plan was to arrive early and then make an equally early departure. They were instantly greeted by a raucous din and the smell of stale beer. Uncomfortable almost immediately, they made their way to the end of the bar, where they sat on rickety stools talking and watching through a smoke-filled haze these drunken silhouettes colliding with each other.

"Ever been to a watering hole?" Pee Wee asked.

Mickey was twisting a thin plastic straw between his massive fingers. "A what?"

"A saloon. Bar. You know, where guys drink and horse around?"

"Nope, never Pee Wee." Mickey looked up suddenly and surveyed the place. "It is very loud. Why is it so loud?"

Pee Wee laughed.

Danvers, Arky Fries, Boxcar, and Jimmy Llamas arrived next. Danvers and Llamas had been arguing the whole way over and were still at it.

"There is no way you have a better arm than me," Llamas protested loudly. "You got a screw loose or something."

"Listen here, you ugly, liver-lipped mess," Danvers shot back. "Not only do I have a better arm, I can drink your sorry ass under the table, puke my guts up, and still walk out of here with something better than the heifers you usually take home."

Boxcar rolled his eyes and stepped in between them. He had been listening to their inane bantering for almost an hour and could not stand another minute. "Hey, why don't you two lovebirds do something useful with your mouths," he commanded, ordering each of them a beer. Then he waved to Pee Wee and Mickey and sent two more down their way.

Little by little, the rest of the team straggled in. They formed a tight circle around the bar and talked about everything under the sun, including what Clem Finster liked to call the three "basic Bs"—baseball, boobs, and booze.

Lefty was the last to arrive. He entered with a girl wearing bib overalls and a tight, white T-shirt against which her large chest strained. He whispered something to her, then he went one way, she the other.

The girl was gap-toothed, buxom, and sociable. Her hair was a thin, platinum-blond, strands of flaxen wheat that framed cheeks both sunken and made-up. She walked through the bar on thin legs that seemed to protest beneath hips and a derrière better suited for a much larger girl.

Lefty's eyes combed the faces at the bar, resting at last on Pee Wee and Mickey. He announced his arrival to the others, then swaggered over to the end of the bar with a big, stupid grin.

"Hey, the kindergarten's here!" he joked, slapping both men on the back. "Glad you guys could make it." Pee Wee felt something fracture in his chest. He really hated Lefty. Lefty was the only guy he had ever played with who refused to acknowledge his baseball prowess and his remarkable ascension to this level. And he just loved himself a little too much for Pee Wee's taste.

"Make it?" he answered quickly. "What are you spouting off about? We were the first ones here."

Lefty scowled. He checked his watch, then folded his arms as if to restrain himself. Then he pivoted oddly, frowning at the full glasses of beer sitting undisturbed in front of his two staid teammates and motioned to the bartender.

"Barkeep," he snapped. "Two whiskeys for my good friends here. The beer's just not cutting it."

Pee Wee held his hands up defiantly. "What are you trying to pull, Lefty? You want to buy *us* drinks? Who am I, the village idiot? I don't think so."

"Come on, McGinty, that really hurts. Can't a guy say he's sorry? Jesus, I'm just trying to bury the hatchet, that's all. When did you get

THE LEGEND OF MICKEY TUSSLER

so damned cynical? I know I've been a little rough on some of you guys. Especially Mickey. But it was all in good fun. Really. Now I'm just trying to make amends."

The two men faced each other. Pee Wee looked at Lefty with myriad misgivings. Lefty was just a horse's ass, incapable of anything even remotely altruistic. He had had too many experiences with the guy to think anything else was possible. But somewhere in the back of his head, Pee Wee heard Murph, and he was suddenly mindful of the manger's contention that things with Lefty had turned the corner. Who was he to stand in the way?

"Okay, Lefty," he said begrudgingly, fingering the tiny glass that was placed in front of him. "We accept—but just know that I'll be getting the next one."

"Hey, we're all friends here, right?" Lefty went on. "My money, your money. What's the difference, right?"

Pee Wee forced a smile and the three of them toasted their new alliance. Pee Wee brought the glass to his lips, nodded to Mickey that it was okay, then poured the mordant elixir down his throat.

"Yee ha!" Lefty cackled, juiced by the spirit of the moment.

Things seemed to get even better with time. Three rounds of whiskey later, all of them were feeling pretty good. Danvers and Llamas had joined them and were delighting in showing the prudent Mickey the art of doing shots.

"Hell's bells!" Llamas screeched, watching as Mickey put down one drink after another. "This boy can really pound!"

With all the commotion surrounding Mickey's drinking exhibition, nobody noticed that the young woman who had been hovering near them had slithered into the group and now occupied the seat right next to Mickey. She sat coquettishly, her eyes flashing with curious desire. She flipped her yellow hair provocatively and smiled playfully, revealing a small space between her front teeth.

"Say, fellas," she said, placing her hand on Mickey's shoulder and squeezing gently. "What's a girl gotta do around here to get noticed?"

Danvers hooted and slapped his knee. "Hot damn!" he screamed wildly. "Now it's a party."

Jimmy Llamas was equally impressed. He began fixing his hair with a damp palm, all the while staring transfixed with eyes that twinkled like a Christmas tree. With visions of some interlude dancing through his mind, he made his way over to the wanton woman.

"James Borelli, ma'am," he said politely. "At your service."

The woman yawned and tapped her cigarette case anxiously on the edge of the bar. "No thanks, honey," she said pointedly. "I got my eye on this big boy, right here." She licked her lips and, in the next moment, was sitting in Mickey's lap.

Danvers loved the action. This unexpected circumstance overwhelmed him; he could barely breathe, he was laughing so hard.

"Aw, go to hell, Woody," Llamas said bitterly. "She ain't my type anyway."

"Not your type?" Danvers roared. "Are you kidding me? What's wrong? Are you confused because she ain't walking around on all fours, chewing her cud?"

"Back off, Danvers, all right? It's not that funny."

Danvers just couldn't stop laughing. "I told you, Llamas," he cried, holding his sides. "I called it. Even Mickey gets more tail than you."

The other guys, with the exception of Pee Wee, enjoyed the show as well. He loved riding Llamas too, but seeing Mickey in this sort of situation worried him.

"Hey, guys," he said, "maybe this ain't such a good idea. I mean Mickey and all. Maybe we should step in."

"Do it and I'll break your arm!" Boxcar said, joining the fracas. "Mickey deserves a little fun."

"Come on, Box, I'm sort of in charge of—"

"Relax, Pee Wee," Lefty said, handing him another drink. "Nothing's happening. This ain't Ava Gardner in *The Killers* for Christ sake. It's all cool."

From a safe distance, they all watched as the woman, still seated squarely on Mickey's lap, whispered in the boy's ear, "My name is Laney Juris, tiger. What's yours?"

Mickey smiled nervously. To all their amazement, he was able to engage the woman in conversation.

"Michael's my name, but folks most always call me Mickey." Laney and Mickey continued to exchange pleasantries at close range, pausing only now and again to consume the drinks that Lefty kept sending over. The others just sat with their drinks and watched.

"What the hell can they possibly be talking about?" Llamas lamented. His head fell helplessly into his open palms. "This has got to be the lowest point of my miserable life."

Nobody said a word. They were all too engrossed in the spectacle unfolding before them to give Llamas a second thought. This irked him even more.

"So that's it, huh?" he began to rant crazily. "A guy bears his soul, and nobody can even say a goddamned word? Not even you, Woody?"

Danvers didn't hear a word he said. His fingers drummed the edge of the bar while he stared incredulously at the blond woman making time with Mickey.

"Hey, I was only kidding around, Woody," Llamas finally said. "You don't have to get all weird on me now. What's the hell's the matter?"

"Nothing. Nothing's wrong," Woody answered. "I could swear I know her—that I've seen her before. The girl, with Mickey. I know I have. God, it's driving me nuts."

Jimmy Llamas shrugged and Boxcar just drank his beer and watched as Mickey and the blond bombshell continued to enjoy each other.

Pee Wee petered out quickly. He had been in saloons before and imbibed and shared in the jocularity of such gatherings. But it always seemed to end the same way—with him sitting on a barstool staring catatonically at one image until it seemed to blur into kaleidoscopic splashes against a foreign canvas. The dart board on the wall; empty glasses piled precariously behind the bar; rings of cigar smoke hovering all around like demons; two men with beards, armwrestling for their day's wages; Laney's hand, soft on the side of

Mickey's face. It was all there, a time-warped, twisted patchwork of desultory snapshots that left him weak and stupid.

Not Lefty. The entire night, he appeared to be strangely fulfilled, deriving some perverse, vicarious thrill from the improbable happenings. He made a feeble effort to look disinterested, absent of thought, but he could not, on several occasions, help smiling in brilliant approval. He was just settling back in his seat after a quick run to the bathroom when Danvers's inquisition into the girl's identity reached his ears.

"Hey, Lefty. That girl over there. The one with Mickey? Don't we know her?"

A long, dark, oblong shadow detached itself suddenly from the darkness inside the bar and fell across Lefty's eyes. "Well, I think I'm gonna call it a night, boys," he announced suddenly. "I'm bushed."

He settled his tab and was just about to the door when Danvers's voice forced him back. "Hey, Lefty," he called to him. "Come on. I know we know her from somewhere. What is it?"

Lefty walked back into the room anxiously, his head tilting with some queer trepidation when Danvers's eyes suddenly lit up with a fleeting thought.

"Isn't that dame over there with Mickey the one you used to get with from time to time? I know you know who I mean. The one a few miles up the road, with the two sheepdogs?"

Lefty stiffened. He jerked upright, as if an electric current had been shot through his extremities. His brow furrowed and his lips parted, releasing words that were strained and delayed in coming.

"Her? Naw, that was another broad I was with. Looked nothing like this one."

The two of them stood there momentarily, in awkward silence, as Danvers turned the woman's face over and over in his mind's eye.

"It's the darndest thing," he kept repeating. "I guess I must have her mixed up with someone else."

"Yeah, I'm sure that's it. Don't matter much. You know what they say anyway, Woody. They all look the same in the dark."

Outside, the full moon shone in a black sky, its glow softened by the humidity lingering in the air. The night was advancing steadily toward the new day, and Pee Wee was feeling that he needed to collect his responsibility and head home. They were supposed to be at practice in less than five hours.

Pee Wee made his rounds, shaking hands and saying good-night to everyone. He was tired, enervated by an evening of drunken banter and sophomoric antics. But he felt good about the night. He couldn't remember the last time all of them had laughed as they did. It had been too long. But he was still having some trouble reconciling that it was Lefty, of all people, who had finally changed things.

His legs buckled and strained as he made his way to Mickey's end of the bar. Through the sea of inebriated faces, he struggled to catch a glimpse of him. It took some doing, but after some artful bobbing and weaving, he finally extricated himself from the crowd, only to discover that Mickey was gone.

Lefty was the first to feel his panic, arresting Pee Wee's frantic flight. "Relax, McGinty," he consoled. "It's fine. Mickey's cool. He's just out back under the moonlight with his special friend." He checked his watch again. "Yup, I'd say right about now, he's probably knocking at heaven's gate."

"Oh, holy Christ, are you serious?" Pee Wee lamented. "What's with this girl? How the hell am I supposed to go back there now?"

"Afraid you really can't. That'd be really awkward. And Mickey deserves the full treatment. Boxcar said so."

"Yeah, but I gotta get going. I just can't stay here any longer." Pee Wee fidgeted and turned away exhausted. He felt as though he had been struggling for hours up a steep escarpment, and now, having reached the summit, his hold had given way.

"Hey, it's no problem. I'll drop him off at your place once he's done. Shouldn't be too much longer. Our boy's still a rookie—remember?"

Pee Wee struggled with the pull of impulses both strong and mottled. "Are you sure it's okay?" he asked, having already decided his immediate course.

He watched as Lefty broke into an interminable grin that flushed his cheeks with a curious vitality. A faint pang of uneasiness gripped Pee Wee momentarily, and he thought he might just wait it out. But then the notion yielded quietly to his utter fatigue.

"Don't worry about it, Pee Wee," Lefty promised, "I got it covered."

SUMMER SWOON

Across a desk littered with depth charts and scouting reports, Dennison's face burned with wrath. "What the hell do you mean he's missing!" he ranted. "How can he be missing?"

Murph's face was grim, his eyes both dark and red. "I don't know what to say, Warren," he offered painfully. "Pee Wee was supposed to—"

"You don't know what to say!" Dennison roared, his voice clashing in Murph's ears like a collision of cymbals. "Are you kidding me, Murphy!"

With hand trembling, Murph dabbed the beads of sweat on his forehead. The light from Dennison's lamp magnified his growing consternation. "We better notify the sheriff."

Dennison got up and stood motionless, galled by the staggering absurdity of the misfortune. He had been so patient with this team—and Murph. Three losing seasons, promises of "can't miss" prospects that became nothing more than flashes in the pan, a dwindling fan base that had eroded his finances, and countless missed opportunities to move on to bigger and more prestigious endeavors because of this exaggerated sense of commitment to the unfinished project. And now this, just when it was starting to look as if he was finally going to bring the elusive chalice to his lips and sip the sacred nectar of the baseball gods. It vexed him that his life should be going on in the old way when he had done so much of late to alter that familiar trend. He idled in silent agitation, gnashing his teeth before unleashing a maelstrom that scattered the entire contents of the desktop.

"How stupid are you, Murphy!" he cried, telephone in hand. "You let him go to a bar? I swear to God, it's like you just can't stand being successful for once. Aren't you tired of being a disappointment, Murph? Just another washed-out, insufferable loser?"

Murph winced, seized by an unutterable horror. Dennison was right. What had he done? He could scarcely imagine the previous life in which he had existed, tiresome, without this charmed excitement.

"I really don't know what else to say," he mumbled. "I'm hoping he just wandered off—and that he'll turn up sometime this morning." Murph struggled with the overwhelming pall of misfortune. The cost of success, he realized, was always this moment when kismet waned and that familiar state of steady decline returned.

"I don't give a rat's ass what happened, or even *how* it happened," Dennison said, wringing his hands until the knuckles turned white. "I don't even care where he was all night. Just find him, you hear? Find him Murphy, or I swear, you'll be back in A ball, riding broken-down buses and eating your dinner from a foil plate."

In the fresh cool of early morning, with the melodious call of waking osprey off in the distance, Murph held a team meeting, an impromptu gathering in lieu of the scheduled workout. He stood in front of his players, a shell of his former ebullient self, growing more and more uncomfortable as he stared out at a sea of blank faces that matched the meaninglessness of the wide, white sky.

The clubhouse seemed dim, tinged with a somber voicelessness that belied the swirling undertow of accusatory anger. Murph glanced anxiously at his watch—it was almost eight o'clock, and although a couple of the guys had yet to arrive, the chain of thoughts that rattled in his head could no longer be contained.

"Uh, I guess by now all of you have heard the unfortunate news about Mickey," he began with great difficulty. "All of us need to pitch in today, before tomorrow's game, and help see if we can make this awful thing right again."

Nobody said a word. At the locker next to Mickey's, Pee Wee sat wearing a look of exaggerated grief. He had fallen into an agonizing dwelling on all he had done wrong the previous night—the whiskey, that brazen girl Laney, and worst of all, getting duped by that bastard Lefty. How could he have been so stupid? He went over it all in his head, time and time again, only hearing fragments of what Murph was saying about the hours leading up to Mickey's disappearance.

"So, he was last seen outside The Bucket with a young lady who he had been drinking with." Murph paused for a short interval, allowing the gravity of what he was saying to sink in. "Lefty, I am correct in saying that, right?"

The mention of his name startled Lefty, for he was busy concentrating on the blister that had formed on his left index finger. "Uh, yup, that's about right. And when I saw him, he looked to be having a grand old time too."

Irritation rose up in Pee Wee, like sleepy eyes adjusting to the glare of dawn. He was thinking about that stupid grin that Lefty had slapped to his face as Pee Wee walked out of the bar.

"So you just left him there?" Pee Wee screamed. "He was having a good time, so you just left him—with that bimbo—after promising me that you'd bring him home?"

Lefty sharpened his focus. The fire that had been awakened in him was desperate and strong. "Go to hell, sissy boy!" he fired back. "If you weren't such a candy ass, *you* could have taken him yourself."

"Are you kiddin' me, Rogers? Who the hell do you think you're fooling here? Everyone knows how you feel about him. Mickey was in your way—a big, talented thorn in your side. You couldn't wait to get rid of him. So you turned your back the first chance you could."

The others just watched in silent discomfort. Lefty was also still, Pee Wee's diatribe having touched a nerve someplace deep within the pitcher's iron heart.

"What about all the other crap?" Pee Wee continued. "You know, the invitation, the drinks, the Mr. Nice Guy routine? Huh? What about all that? Was that just part of your little plan? Jesus Christ, Rogers—you're so transparent. You're just bent out of shape because a 'retard' has been kicking your ass."

"Screw you, McGinty, and the white horse you rode in on. He left by himself, *after* I saw him—and you know it. I was gonna take him home, but he split. What did you expect me to do? That's it. Now you take back all that malarkey that you've been spewing in here, you little pissant, or I'll put you through that goddamned wall!"

Lefty rushed toward Pee Wee. His face was red with a violence that exploded once Pee Wee started swinging wildly at him, heat radiating like light from his clothes.

"You left him in there, you stupid ass!" Pee Wee bawled, struggling to break free from Boxcar, who had stepped in between them. "Christ, what kind of scumbag are you?"

"Relax, both of you," the burly catcher commanded, each fist filled with a shirt collar. "This doesn't solve anything. You heard what Murph said. We have to work together. We have to help each other find out what happened to Mickey. The rest of it—blame, whose fault it is—that's all wasted energy."

The skirmish now diffused, Murph proceeded with his speech, although he was having a difficult time dismissing the new thoughts in his head that had blossomed in the wake of Pee Wee's accusations.

"So we'll spend today searching the immediate area and surrounding towns. Ask anyone you see if they have seen him. Christ, it shouldn't be too hard to find him."

"What about tomorrow, Murph?" Danvers asked. "How are we supposed to play?"

Murph wondered the same thing, but his mind did not allow him to shape the words. He knew what his answer had to be. "Well, the game goes on, Woody. You know that. Baseball waits for no man. It's part of what is so glorious about the game. But hopefully, by tomorrow, he'll be back, and this will all become nothing more than a bad dream." Murph sighed as he surveyed the room. "Any more questions, fellas?"

Silent stares provided the response.

Boxcar sat at his locker, gripping his bat, and playing over in his head like a newsreel everything that had happened the previous night at The Bucket. He was testing the possibilities, but sitting there, struggling against this urgent need to know, it all became this jumbled mess inside his head. He looked over at Pee Wee, miffed at him for bringing Mickey to a place like that. God, it was just plain stupid. He wanted to put his hands on his shoulders and shake him. Make him realize how none of this would ever have happened had it not been for his poor judgment. But Boxcar, like everyone else, saw that the man was in emotional ruins. What good would stepping on him do now?

Of course, Boxcar was angry at himself as well, for playing the role of enabler. So many times that night he could have stepped in — should have stepped in — but for some reason, he had not seen the need. The whiskey, the girl, the predatory crowd. It was so clear a day later. Mickey had no business rubbing elbows with the motley crew at The Bucket. And Mickey should never have accepted anything from Lefty. Boxcar knew he'd screwed up.

Sitting there that morning, twisting the bat handle in his massive hands, Boxcar turned his attention to the self-interested pitcher who sat there that morning, unlike the others, seemingly impervious to the tragedy that had befallen them. While the rest of them were making preparations for a day of frantic searching, Lefty malingered at his locker, folding his stirrups and working some smudges off the tops of his spikes. Boxcar's eyes narrowed and his face burned. He got up, placed his bat in his locker, grabbed his bag, and headed for the door, stopping just long enough to whisper in Lefty's ear. "You better not have had anything to do with this, you scurvy little bastard."

The boy awoke in a crumpled heap that morning when the sun's fingers poked mercilessly at his eyes and the metal trash-can cover had become too painful to remain underneath his head. His clothes were torn and smelled bad. His stomach hurt and his mouth was dry, as if he had stuffed inside his cheeks too many spoonfuls of his aunt Marcy's homemade sponge cake. And his right hand really hurt. But worse than all of that was why. *Why?* That bothered him most, until the word *where* popped into his head. Where was he? He recalled very little. He vaguely remembered a girl named Laney. Where was she now? And little glasses. He remembered little glasses—fourteen in all—with dark liquid that burned his stomach. He sat up, with some difficulty, and looked down at his hand. It was bloody. And the fingers did not line up the way they always had. His heart thumped loudly. He began to think that he was reading about someone else—that all of this "jumble" as he sometimes called it was not happening to him. He had all but convinced himself when his hand really started to hurt. Then he knew it wasn't someone else; it was him.

He looked hard at everything around him. He was not sure that he had ever seen his current surroundings, much less belonged in them, and feared that he would continue for an unnamed time in a state in which he was simply a solitary puzzle piece, wayward, discarded, in an unknown, hostile geography.

His thoughts began to boil over. *Where was Laney? Baseball practice starts at eight. Why are my fingers all twisted? Oscar needs to be fed. The smell of my clothes is burning my nose. There is garbage everywhere. Where am I?* The thoughts just kept coming, wave after wave, and filled his head until he could no longer house all of them at once. He pulled his knees in close to his chest and began to rock.

"'Slowly, silently, now the moon, walks the night in her silver shoon . . .'"

Miles away, life on the Tussler farm kept moving forward in laborious ritual. Molly had lulled herself into a tired, dreamlike numbness, in which she felt nothing but the tiny wisps of grass stirring restlessly at her ankles. Emptying the slop buckets, her mind floated vaguely on the unfulfilled adage that *good things come to those who wait.* How much longer would it be? And would it arrive before death? She felt the bewildering sensation that somehow she had already died. Her body, though, as cruel as it seemed, was forced to live on. She ate, what little she could, and slept, some nights better than others. And of course, she rose each morning to face yet another day of toiling on the farm. This "life" of hers just went on. But despite the living, she felt this prevailing sense of disassociation, connected to nothing but feelings of exposure and alarm. The only thing that came close to bending her scowl into a smile was the thought of Mickey, free from the stifling world behind their wooden fences. It was as if a part of her had broken free, which is why when she received the call from Murph and thought that she had lost the only thing in her life that mattered, she prayed that death would be swift and reward her for her patience.

"Please, Molly, please do not panic," he said, trying to console her. "Don't talk crazy. Mickey needs you. I know we'll find him. It's nothing. Really. I just thought you should know."

When the sun rose the next day, Murph awoke at last from his fitful sleep. His eyes opened and surveyed from his bed the oblong splashes pressed against the wall, but his vision remained locked inside. For a fleeting moment, he thought that it had perhaps all been some hellish dream, that Mickey would be sitting at the breakfast table as usual, fully dressed, spikes and all, eating apple buttermilk coffee cake with a grapefruit spoon. The idea germinated only briefly, then died with the unmistakable sounds outside his window—reverberations of a new day, one without Mickey.

He suddenly felt an emptiness in his stomach. This longing grew from deep within him, an unremitting craving, like the need of a famished man for food and drink.

He rose from his bed and stumbled to the bathroom, dragging his feet across a floor already warm with a seasonal August heat. The water in the shower was cool but somehow bothersome, beating hard against his skin like tiny hammers chipping away at a crumbling edifice. He rolled his shoulders in mild protest, then adjusted the temperature and stood there, languishing now in a rising cloud of steam, wondering what the hell he was going to do.

He thought of Molly, and how the news had seized her. He marveled at how he could feel her anguish so many miles away. She was so beaten, seemingly beyond repair, and expressed not only this acute desperation but a pressing fear should Clarence find out. As she conveyed this feeling to him, she realized herself that she wasn't sure what frightened her more—Clarence's wrath, which she knew all too well could take many forms, or his likely indifference. Her words echoed in Murph's ears and bounced off the tiled walls as if they had just been spoken. He knew he had to see her as soon as possible.

The day was miserable. The field looked to be sick, frying under the oppressive sun. Murph blundered across the diamond, which seemed now to be starkly barren, and into the clubhouse, where he took refuge in his office. On the shelf behind his desk was a picture of him from his playing days, yellow and dog-eared, sandwiched between several books. He picked up the photograph, smiling faintly at some of the more pleasant reminiscences—Rookie of the Year, 1924—Batting Title, 1925—pennant-clinching home run that same year. God, things were good. He could still hear the crowd. He ran through every other memorable thing that had happened to him and actually began to feel a little relief, until McNally and the bitter specter of how it all ended slipped into his consciousness and dashed the nostalgic jaunt.

He had half hoped that he would arrive at the ballpark to discover that Boxcar or Pee Wee or one of the other guys had found Mickey, or that the sheriff had pulled some strings and uncovered where he was. No luck. He was to be alone with his thoughts, with only the faint sound of Matheson puttering around in the equipment closet for company. Murph stared around the room out of strange, black eyes, trying to fill the daunting minutes.

He busied himself with all the usual game-day duties—pitching charts, lineup cards, game balls—but he struggled as this impregnable emptiness pursued him. Behind a cluttered desk that matched the disorder of his thoughts, he tried to picture what Mickey was doing—if he was hurt, or lost, or God forbid worse. The boy was so pure, so simple. How could he ever survive?

And then, like a bolt from the blue, the ordeal was over. Sheriff Rosco shuffled in, Mickey by his side, and everything was right again. The boy was worn. His eyes were barely open and his breathing was quiet. His left arm dangled lifelessly by his side, and the other was crumpled at a right angle, pressed tightly against his chest.

"Found him in an alley, just off to the side of the road, 'bout three miles from The Bucket. He was just sitting there, talking to himself. The same thing, over and over. Not quite sure what it all means. But it looks as though he took a pretty good beating."

Murph stood dumbfounded, his eyes blinking randomly. "Did you catch the guys who did it? I mean, what the hell happened?"

"Don't reckon I know," Rosco said. "He won't say nothing I can make sense of."

Murph walked over toward Mickey. His spirits, which had risen dramatically with Mickey's appearance, fell markedly when Murph noticed the boy's right hand, bloodied and mangled.

"Oh, Mickey," Murph gasped. "I'm sorry. Jesus, boy, what happened to you?"

Mickey just stood there absently. Under the steadying influence of Murph's hand on his shoulder, Mickey struggled to form words that would just not come. He stood, inanimate as the big, moldy poles in the locker room, his eyes clouded windows to some peculiar expression, silent and far away, before he finally spoke.

"'And moveless fish in the water gleam, by silver reeds in a silver stream.'"

Murph got up and paced nervously, sat back down, got up again, then sat once more.

"We've got to get him to a doctor, Sheriff," Murph said. "I want him looked at."

"Whatever you like," Rosco replied. "Let's go."

Matheson, who had been observing the entire scene quietly, said suddenly, "I'll go with the kid Murph. You stay. Without you here, the rest of the guys don't have a row to hoe."

With Mickey on his way, Murph's thoughts turned to more pressing issues. *The Giants*, he thought to himself. *How are we going to play the Giants today?* He put his hands on the great stacks of papers towering across his desk and shuffled through, not in search of anything in particular, but just to satisfy his nervous appetite. He had just decided to check to see if Larry had outfitted the lockers the day before when Boxcar came in.

Murph hardly recognized him. He was standing in the doorway with his palm to his head, his glassy eyes fixed on a spot on the floor in front of him. His hair was messed, and he looked like only half of the inebriation of two nights prior had worn off.

"He's back, Box." A nervous chill climbed Murph's body.

"Mickey? He's back? When? How?"

Murph blew his nose and discarded the tissue basketball-style in the wastebasket just across the way. "Pull up a chair. I'll tell you what I know."

They sat together in Murph's office, talking casually between intermittent silences, trying to mend the fractured face of things.

"I should have been there, Murph," Boxcar said, hanging his head in utter dejection. "I saw the whole thing happening—and should have known he was in over his head."

"Don't," Murph said. "Don't do that to yourself. All of us played a role, Box."

"But I'm the captain, Murph. I was there. These guys rely on me. I know that sounds boastful, but it's true."

It *was* true, and Murph knew it too. He was so thankful for Boxcar. Boxcar was the closest thing he had to a real assistant coach. Sure, Matheson was a good baseball man. Nobody had been around the game longer. But age had stolen his effectiveness, leaving Murph to work essentially alone. So he really valued Boxcar's passion, experience, and equanimity. On so many occasions, Murph had deferred to the veteran catcher when unforeseen circumstances had rattled his cage and clouded his vision. Boxcar just had a way about him. All the guys respected him. Sometimes, when the situation necessitated it, he sat them down and lectured; on other occasions, when rational discourse fell on deaf ears, he took a more physical approach, allowing them to feel what he was saying; he could even resolve some problems with nothing more than a stare. True, his skills had diminished some with age, and he was beginning to tire a bit, but Raymond "Boxcar" Miller was still a presence, and even though he knew it was asking a lot, Murph was going to need him now more than ever.

The Brewers took the field in front of a stunned crowd that had been devastated by the early-morning headline: "Baby Bazooka Beaten!" They sat, in languorous waiting, united in this circle of suffering. Most fans that afternoon wore the news like a black veil through which no words could be voiced. No ballpark had ever fallen this silent. Others articulated their horror in writing, on banners and placards professing their adoration for the missing hero: WE LOVE YOU, MICKEY—GET WELL SOON!

The players were also limp, mired in listlessness. They took the field, trotting out to their positions with a sense of heartless obligation. They shagged fly balls, fielded grounders, and, when the cry of "Play ball" went up, held up their chins and readied themselves for battle as best they could.

Gabby Hooper took the ball in Mickey's stead. He was used by Murph almost exclusively as a mop-up guy, but with Lefty's blister and a twin bill on the docket for the following day, they needed everyone to take his game to the next level.

The Giants' leadoff batter opened the game with a sharp grounder to Danvers, but his backhand was tardy, and the ball deflected off the heel of his glove, kicking into foul territory and down the third-base line for a two-base error. The next batter took Hooper's first pitch and sent a weak two-hopper to Fries, who corralled it, pumped twice, then sailed the throw into the first row of seats behind first base.

"Jesus Christ, Frenchy," Finster screamed. "I'm standing right here!"

The third-, fourth-, and fifth-place hitters all singled hard to the outfield, scoring two runs and loading the bases while setting the table for what looked like a brutal inning. After a walk to the next batter, and a dying quail that fell between Pee Wee and Amos Ruffings, the eighth-place hitter turned on a fat, flat fastball, depositing the mistake deep into the Giant bullpen for a grand slam. Fifteen minutes into the game, the Brewers were reeling, facing an eight-run deficit.

Murph watched with weary, puzzled curiosity. Even in their worst slump, they had never played so poorly. Maybe it was to be expected. After all, they were embroiled in an ordeal. All around them floated this airy disquiet, something stale and deleterious hanging on the oppressive August air. It would take a little time, he thought, for them to shake the doldrums. He sat down on the end of the bench, palms set together and pressed gently to his lips, as if lost in thoughtful prayer.

The day grew hotter, with no breeze to cool the stifling humidity. The Brewers had allowed six more runs after the first-inning barrage and trailed now by fourteen. The Giants' pitcher, Red Meadows, had hung up seven straight goose eggs, crippling the Brewers' hitters with a knuckleball that was dancing like a moth around a hanging lantern. In the seventh, Arky Fries fouled out to the catcher, but Pee Wee and Jimmy Llamas reached consecutive bases on balls. Clem Finster ran his count full before swinging wildly at a ball in the dirt. With two outs, Woody drew the third walk of the inning, loading the bases for Boxcar.

"Finally," Murph said to Lefty, who looked as if he was struggling to stay awake. "This is just what we need."

The crowd, which had been silenced all day by the news about Mickey and the abysmal play of its team, recognized the possibilities too and began to stir.

Meadows had never had any luck against Boxcar, until that day. In his first two at bats, Boxcar had been retired on a weak comebacker and had struck out swinging. Meadows had been using knucklers all day to keep the Brewer catcher off-balance, so he decided to start him off with some good old-fashioned high cheese. Surprised by the selection, Boxcar took the pitch for a called strike one. It got him thinking, just enough so that when Meadows delivered again, Boxcar's bat was way ahead of the ball as it danced across the plate. Now in the hole 0–2, he knew he had to shorten up his stroke to protect against any further chicanery. With his hands now two inches higher on the handle, he caught the next floater just before it drifted by him, serving the offering the other way into the gap. The ball split the outfielders cleanly and rolled all the way to the wall. The runners scampered around the bases with little difficulty. They were fleet of foot, each crossing home plate by the time Boxcar approached second base.

Boxcar was moving full tilt, as fast as his damaged knees could carry him. His face was tight and his thoughts were somewhere else, someplace only he knew. Despite the lopsided score, and the protestations coming from the bench and players alike, Boxcar hit the bag in full stride, put his head down, and rounded for third. He just kept running. The Giant right fielder scooped up the ball with his bare hand. Then, out of a crow hop so forceful it threw him right to the ground, he released a missile, a tracer that never got more than four feet off the ground, right to the third-base bag to peg Boxcar by a healthy margin.

"Oh, crap!" Danvers groaned. "Now I've seen everything."

The little momentum that had begun to simmer vanished instantly like a rush of air expelled from a burst balloon.

The Giants capitalized on the sudden shift of momentum, pounding out eight more hits and plating seven more runs. When the massacre was complete, the stands resembled a ghost town, with only wrappers and peanut shells and other vague remnants of life riding on an unexpected wind, drifting carelessly by a scoreboard that marked the final damage: Giants 21, Brewers 3.

The next day featured a twi-night double dip against the Colts. Butch Sanders and Rube Winkler were awarded the pitching duties. Murph was optimistic that his team could put all of the distractions aside and go out and play the game as they had prior to the incident with Mickey.

The crowd was a good one, but many were still anxious about the ongoing saga surrounding Mickey and expressed that concern with more banners indicating their heartfelt uneasiness.

Sanders just didn't have it. His fastball was flat and he was throwing helicopters for curveballs. The Colts pounded him early and hard, batting around twice in just the first four frames. The home team answered back with runs in three consecutive innings, but the Colt onslaught kept coming, pummeling Brewer pitching for twelve runs on seventeen hits to double up the beleaguered Brew Crew, 12–6.

The nightcap was a little better, but the result the same. The Brewers jumped out to an early 3–0 lead on Clem Finster's long home run to left. Winkler, who hadn't started a game in over a year, was doing a fine job, dancing through raindrops inning after inning. He had allowed two hits in each of the first five frames, but managed to pitch his way out each time. Even in the sixth, when he walked the first two hitters, he maintained his composure, getting the next two batters on called strikes. But then the wheels started coming off. It began with a ground ball to Finster that sneaked through the five hole. That was followed by a can of corn to Buck Faber in right that, for some inexplicable reason, landed three feet to his left.

"Come on, fellas," Murph screamed from the bench. "Get your heads out of your asses!"

His plea did little to arrest the juggernaut of blunders. Pee Wee dropped a pop-up, Danvers booted a dribbler, and two runners scored when Boxcar's pickoff attempt at second base landed somewhere between Jimmy Llamas and the center-field wall.

Murph placed his hand over his eyes and groaned. "It's a circus," he lamented. "A goddamned circus."

The Brewers committed a staggering eight errors and ended the day on a sour note, a 13–5 humiliation.

The fans were starting to voice their displeasure, and the newspapers only fueled their fire. With the skid at three games, the headlines were prognosticating Armageddon, suggesting that the Brewer's lethargy and all the miscues were cause to be afraid: " 'Boo Crew' Nothing Without Mickey."

Murph was at a loss to stem the tide. He tried insulating his players from public scrutiny, issuing an edict that nobody talk to the press until the ship had righted itself. The sportswriters and announcers, however, were dogged in their pursuit, and with each miscue the team made on the field, the inspection intensified.

His blister fully healed, Lefty got the call the following day. The scene was ugly. The team took the field to a chorus of boos and jeers, and to a proliferation of cigar stubs, hot dogs, and rotten-fruit rinds that rained down on them like a summer storm.

"Go back inside, you lousy bums!" many of the discontented fans screamed. "We want real ballplayers!"

In the wake of the team's pitiful performance, the crowd's concern for Mickey converted to anger, each fan's frustration bubbling with a rapacious fury that begged for satisfaction.

They were facing the Bears, a team against which they matched up well. They just seemed to have their number, defeating them in five of the first six contests. Lefty set them down in order in the first inning, striking out the side with just twelve pitches and silencing, at least for the moment, some of the more vocal naysayers.

In the home half of the first, the grumbling continued after Arky Fries fouled out and Clem Finster and Woody Danvers tantalized the starving crowd with well-struck balls that died quietly on the warning track. But for the moment, the defensive part of their game was back. Lefty retired the next fifteen Bears to come to the plate, amassing a staggering thirteen strikeouts in the first six innings. The crowd, desperate for something to grab hold of, embraced the surly southpaw and showered him with applause and the celebratory chant of "Lefty! Lefty! Lefty!" The rejuvenated hurler stood on the mound to begin the seventh inning and his spirit soared. For the first time in months, he felt the warmth of the sun on his shoulders. His imagination brimmed with images of making a brilliant impression. As he toed the rubber, his mind's eye wandered to little children clamoring for autographs, young girls swooning at his every move, sportswriters and photographers fighting for his attention—and of course, he saw so clearly the bright lights of the major league city fortunate enough to capture his fancy. Suddenly, without notice, without warning, the disconsolation of weeks prior was gone.

The Brewers finally manufactured a run in their half of the seventh. After leading off the inning with a walk, Buck Faber was sacrificed to second on a perfect bunt off the bat of Pee Wee and took third on a wild pitch. Murph's wheels turned swiftly. He pulled Arky Fries out of the on-deck circle and whispered something in the ear of Nat Rudigan before sending him in to pinch-hit.

Rudigan made a couple of passes over the dirt at home plate with his front foot, dug himself a nice hole with the other, then windmilled his bat with gritty determination. Faber led off the bag in foul ground, clapped his hands, and chanted Rudigan's name, drawing the ire of the Bears' pitcher. He stepped off the rubber and motioned to third as if a pickoff throw were coming. Faber scampered back, then danced right back out when the pitcher resumed his position. It was all part of the dance. The pitcher collected his thoughts, got his sign, released a thin stream of spit to the ground, and with Faber hopping around in his peripheral vision swung his arms over his head, kicked his leg, and delivered. The ball appeared to be inside, but broke back over the middle of the plate for a called strike. Rudigan looked behind him in mild protest. The catcher chuckled under his mask at the umpire's indifference, then returned the ball to the mound. With ball in hand again, the Bears' hurler checked Faber at third again. He bluffed once, then again, before getting back on the rubber. Faber's lead was a little more brazen this time, and his eyes possessed a clear and present purpose. The pitcher gave one final glance over Faber's way, then rocked back, arched his leg, and fired. The minute the ball was released, Faber took off as if shot from a cannon. He lowered his head and pumped his arms feverishly, leaving behind him, with every powerful step, a confetti storm of dirt and grass.

Rudigan's timing was perfect as well. With the ball just about halfway home, he rotated his hips, slid his hand up the barrel, and pinched the bat between his thumb and forefinger. The delivery was true this time, a fastball right up the gut. Rudigan's bat caught the ball cleanly, deadening it in the no-man's-land between pitcher and catcher. It was a perfect suicide squeeze.

Lefty made the one run stand up. He breezed through the final two innings, racking up three more strikeouts, to finish the day with a sweet sixteen. It was by far his best outing all year. He walked off the field with a goofy grin, delighting in the crowd's revival of the earlier chant of "Lefty! Lefty! Lefty!"

The postgame milieu was frenetic and circuslike. Lefty preened about in front of the procession of reporters like a rooster in a hen-house, basking in the boisterous luster. He bent his green eyes to the retinue of writers, signaling with his finger that he would only address one question at a time.

"Hey, Lefty, does this mean the slump is over?" the first man asked.

"What slump?" Lefty replied curtly. "I was hurt, not in a slump."

"I'm not sure if that's true or not," the reporter continued, "but I was talking about the team."

Lefty shrugged and turned his head the other way.

"Lefty, how did it feel today?" another asked. "What made you so effective out there?"

Lefty stood there, without conscious thoughts, lost in his rapture. "Someone had to step up—for the team, you know? That's what the ace of a staff does."

"Has Arthur Murphy made that official? I mean, just until Mickey gets back?"

"I think the focus should be on what is happening now," Lefty said. "And right now, Mickey is not a factor."

"Yeah, but once the Baby Bazooka gets back, don't you think—"

"Listen, is this a postgame conference, or what?" Lefty's nostrils flared and his brow descended hard, forming lines in the shape of a tiny V. A sudden restiveness possessed him, and for a moment his outrage had him anxious and tongue-tied.

"Uh, you know what, that's enough," he finally said. "You wanna talk strikeouts, I'm game. You wanna know why my curveball was unhittable, I'm all yours. But this nonsense with Mickey—it has to stop. I won't do it. I'm a baseball player, not some goddamned social worker. You wanna know about Mickey, the manager's office is just around the corner."

When the interest in Lefty waned, most of the writers took the advice and spent some time with Murph. He was his usual affable self, fielding each question with that inimitable blend of candor and wit. Truth was, he felt a modicum of relief. The monkey was off his back, at least for now. But he was battling much larger issues. In between games, he had more important questions to answer. The local sheriff had been conducting interviews with all the players to gain insight into Mickey's situation.

John Rosco was a big, stolid man in his early fifties, with a salt-and-pepper handlebar mustache, a throaty voice, and deep, penetrating eyes that gave him an air of dignified mystery. He had been sheriff for twenty-two years and had never seen a situation like this before.

One week into the investigation, he had gotten nowhere. He began by questioning Murph and Pee Wee and worked his way through several other players before sitting down with Lefty.

"So, Mr. Rogers, the fellas tell me that you were the last one to see Mickey," he began.

"Is that right?"

"Yup."

"And he was with a young lady outside The Bucket?"

"That's right."

"Do you know that girl? Ever seen her before?"

"Nope."

"What time was that, Mr. Rogers?" Rosco scratched something on the white pad of paper in front of him.

"Don't know that I remember. Two, maybe three."

"Any indication of trouble? You know, a quarrel, anything like that?"

"Nope."

"Nothing at all?"

"Nothing."

"You sure now?"

"That's what I said."

Rosco put down his pencil and took off his hat and laid it on the desk. Some nuance in the pitcher's deportment struck him hard and sparked a notion in his mind.

"Saw the game earlier today, Mr. Rogers," he said, shifting gears. "Pretty impressive."

Lefty nodded indifferently. The fan on Murph's desk blew a hot wind across the side of his face.

"Must be pretty hard for all of you lately," Rosco continued. "I mean, with Mickey being on the shelf and all."

"We're okay." Lefty paused, thinking about the damaging implication of his response. He looked down at the desk and said he was sorry about what had happened to Mickey.

Rosco folded his arms and leaned back in his chair. "Yeah, but I'm willing to bet that a pitching performance like that, with all those people yelling your name, and everyone taking your picture and all—I bet that goes a long way in curing the hurt."

"I don't know," Lefty answered with all the emotion of a stone wall. "I guess so."

Rosco frowned, measuring the real meaning behind Lefty's terse replies. He found the pitcher to be an odd character. It was no single thing, he thought, but rather a combination of many. He sat there staring at the side of Lefty's head while many obscure misgivings passed over him.

"Well, now that Mickey is out of the picture, so to speak, it sort of leaves you in the catbird seat, doesn't it?"

Lefty flushed and moved uncomfortably in his chair. His brain spun wildly, then rested on a single thought. "What is it exactly you want from me, Sheriff Rosco?" Lefty felt a stabbing pain at the pit of his stomach.

"I'm just asking a few questions, Mr. Rogers. That's all. Just doing my job."

Lefty froze, paralyzed by the awkward silence that followed.

Rosco drummed his fingers a few times on the desk. Then he picked up his hat, met Lefty's steely eyes with a neutral gaze of his own, and in a strong, clear voice said, "Thanks for your time, Mr. Rogers. Good luck holding off those Rangers. I'll be in touch."

Murph's team failed to build on the momentum generated by the victory over the Bears, dropping each of the next three games. Murph was beside himself, powerless to combat the insidious contagion of losing that had gripped his entire squad. They lost games in every conceivable way. They could not hit, the pitching had become batting practice for opposing hitters, and the fielding had degenerated into a sorry comedy of errors. Even the mental part of the game had gone south, resulting in a late-inning loss to the Mud Hens when Ruffings, with one out in the ninth and the winning run standing just ninety feet away, caught a fly ball in right and unwittingly flipped it to a young fan sitting in the first row, certain that the game was over.

Dennison lambasted Murph for the team's deplorable performance, screaming and yelling about feeling as if someone had a hand on his throat and how he was tired of being fodder for the newspapers.

"You better think of something!" he warned. "Think of something, and fast!"

Murph took it home with him every night. He slept for a little while, or maybe he didn't. He never could tell, for it seemed as though he hovered torturously between the realms of dozing and waking, never quite crossing over into either. But one thing was for sure — not long after he was under the covers, he found himself on the edge of the bed, coiled up in a fetal ball.

He lay there, listening as the sounds of nighttime mocked his restlessness. A unexpected wind blew against the window, and in his thoughts a cast of amateur actors bumped into each other carelessly on a darkened stage. He directed, trying to order the chaos, but the players just executed their own will, vibrating in a mêlée of impromptu performances. All night long he blinked, trying to drop the curtain and bring the act to a close, but the show went on in painful perpetuity.

The only one seemingly impervious to the skid was Lefty, who got the ball the next day and turned in another stellar performance: nine more innings, twelve strikeouts, and just one unearned run. He was definitely in the zone.

His star had gloriously risen from the wreckage. The newspapers grabbed hold of his exploits and lionized him, using such words as *savior* and such expressions as *the cavalry* and *knight in shining armor*. It seemed, as a natural defense to the intolerable hurt, people became desensitized to the Mickey saga; it was just easier to leave that painful chapter behind for the moment and focus on something positive. Consequently, George Lefty Rogers became the talk of the town, the lone bright spot, the port in a season-threatening storm. He was, all at once, the town darling, capturing the hearts of an entire city, especially the younger female followers.

He began receiving flowers, candy, and other small tokens of affection, including perfume-laden love letters, a fistful of telephone numbers, and invitations to all sorts of social engagements. After one game, he even received a lacy brassiere from one of his more ardent admirers.

"Do you believe this crap?" Boxcar complained to Danvers as they watched while a throng of teenyboppers attacked the newly ordained king of Brewer baseball on his way to his car. "Does nothing make sense anymore?"

Danvers's mind was noticeably absent.

"Woody, I'm talking to you," Boxcar grumbled. "What's eating you tonight?"

"Nothing," he replied tremulously. "I just now remembered something that's been bothering me since that night at The Bucket. That's all."

They both stood stiff in the darkness, shaking their heads, as the senseless fawning unfurling before Lefty perverted his vision with sparkles of specious glory.

TUSSLER FARM—AUGUST

Though the day was not that warm, Molly sweated nervously. It was that time of the month when Clarence washed up and took the piglets that had reached sale weight into town. It was usually an all-day affair, which left Molly with the curious feeling of blood beginning to circulate again. And this day was unlike any other; it was extra special, for it coincided with a much needed day off for the beleaguered Brew Crew. Murph had some free time and was going to make good on that promise he'd made to himself.

He reached the farm just as the changing light of dawn splashed across the sky, creating a brilliant blending of purple, pink, and orange. With a full bouquet of wildflowers in hand, he started to walk up the gravel drive, and on a pile of stacked logs next to one of the food bins, he saw her sitting. She had on a beautiful blue house-dress, and her hair was pulled back off her face, braided in the back with a tiny matching bow.

As he approached, he was struck by her nervous demeanor; she sat there, hands folded, feet tapping, like an actress awaiting her cue. As he saw her drooping profile and considered turning back, certain he would never find the right words to say, his foot found a brittle twig and snapped it in two. She turned and looked at him.

"Good morning, Molly," he called, walking toward her gingerly. "Am I too early?"

She got to her feet, smoothed her dress with both hands, and blushed at the sight of the flowers. "No, no. It's fine. Just like we said."

They sat inside across from each other, her nervous, him looking into her beautifully sad eyes, light blue stones with lashes that burst open from them like the flower petals in his hand.

"I brought these for you," he said. "They're not much, but I thought they would cheer you up a little."

"Thank you, Mr. Murphy—Arthur."

He smiled at her. "Your eyes. They match your dress."

She smiled back, a short, quick smile, and then after some vain effort to be cavalier, she began to shiver and cry uncontrollably.

"What's happened, Arthur?" she asked through desperate sobs. "Is he okay?"

He came close to her. Her hand was warm and soft. She sat helplessly, staring at Arthur and the light that lit his face.

"He's fine, Molly," he whispered. "Really. I'm so sorry to have worried you like this. It was stupid. Never should have happened."

Molly breathed in some of the heavy air and wiped her eyes. She was tired. Languidly, she looked around, struggling for words. She brought the bouquet to her nose—it smelled sweet, and simple. She touched the purple, yellow, and white ruffles and was reminded, with painful memory, of how soft and gentle life could be.

There was no noise anywhere. He could smell coffee brewing in the kitchen, but did not want to ask for any. He looked at her. She was broken. A lump rose in his throat as he waited breathlessly for her to speak.

She was beautiful—a blossom that had somehow grown, lovely and fragrant, amidst a cluster of weeds. What, he wondered, was she doing here? With her hair pulled back, her face was winsome, soft and sculptured. In the burn of the morning light, she reminded him of the porcelain dolls his mother collected and displayed when he was a boy.

"Why, Arthur?" she finally said. "Why *Mickey*?"

"I don't know what to say Molly. The guys all love him. Truly.

They had this idea that they wanted to take him out—to a bar—and it just didn't work out." He lowered his head, wading through the unfortunate recollection while picking away nervously at the skin around his thumb. "We all figured that—"

"You knew about this? Before it happened?"

She stood up sharply and turned her back to him. He could no longer see her face, but imagined, based on the severity of her posture, that it had hardened considerably.

"I'm sorry, Molly. Really. I know it was stupid. I just wanted so badly for all of the guys—especially Mickey—to spend some time together, so that they felt like they were part of something." His mouth was dry. He stopped for a moment, unable to complete his thought without moistening his lips. "I don't know. It's hard to explain. Baseball is funny. You can have all the talent in the world, but if you're not a team, it's all for naught."

His words pierced her like a blade. She was crying softly. Her head had drooped and he could see the spasmodic rising and falling of her shoulders. All at once he was seized by an overwhelming ambivalence. One minute he was pleased, even surprised, at his ability to reach her—in the next, he had the distinct sense of being an intruder.

"So my baby was in a bar, drinking, when this all happened?" she asked through suffocating lungs. "Nobody was watching out for him?"

She touched her mouth, perspiration breaking out all over her face and across the nape of her neck. She turned and stared at him, in a catatonic stupor, through eyes both distant and glazed.

"He has a very good friend on the team—he was supposed to look after him, but something went wrong. Believe me, Molly, I never intended this to happen."

"Well, be that as it may, it really doesn't help me much, now does it?"

Her words tore at him and blurred to a raspy mumble.

"And what's being done, Arthur?" she said tearfully. "About the men who did this? I mean, is this it?"

"The sheriff is doing an investigation, Molly. And we have a few ideas of our own. We'll get 'em. And Doc says Mickey will be back with us, in full swing, in no time. So don't worry. It will all be resolved."

By late morning, the room was filled with sunshine. They had talked all they were going to talk about Mickey. Her anxiety had softened, yielding to the sheer joy of Arthur's presence and his delightful attentiveness.

They sat together, this time side by side, feeling their way to each other. Murph was thinking that he was, once again, no longer an intruder, although he still struggled with a vague uneasiness. His soul was reaching out to her, in its own blind, clumsy way, only to find that she was mostly unavailable. He felt an emptiness and grew unsettled and restless, uncertain how he could bridge the invisible gap between them. Mindful of the clock, and this feeling of utter frustration, he spoke to her teasingly, selflessly, as if she were a child.

"Seems to me, the last time I was here, I heard some very beautiful clarinet music," he said sheepishly. "Now I don't suppose I'm in line for another performance?"

She laughed uncomfortably. Then, as if his comment had melted her glacial emotional reserve, she began talking about her music. There was, for her, the most intense pleasure in talking about playing the clarinet, particularly since she was forbidden by Clarence to do so. Murph listened as her eyes scintillated and her blood ran wildly, her creative energy bucking and dashing like a gelding that had just broken free from its fetters.

"You know," she said, removing the instrument from its tomb atop the fireplace, "when I was a little girl, I dreamed of playing in front of people."

Murph held up his hands in mock exasperation. "Well, you're very good, Molly. There's no reason why you still can't."

She frowned, then a curious serenity seemed drawn from some secret source, and she brought the clarinet to her lips and played.

When it was time for him to leave, they were both struck by this impending sense of gloom, a hopelessness that neither wanted to admit. Molly felt a dependence on him, which she hated because she could not control it. She hated these feelings for him because they had grown too strong and because there was no place for them. He was just as drawn to her; she was a haven in the blizzard of a cold, unpredictable world that had left him, at every turn, empty and disillusioned.

"I'm sorry I didn't have more news for you about Mickey," he said, standing before her brokenly. "But know he's fine. And I will call you the minute I hear anything."

"It's okay, Arthur," she said softly. "Thank you for the flowers. And for everything else."

They stood for a short while facing each other, struggling beneath the weight of unspoken desire, uncertain how they should conclude their visit. The movement of his right hand slowly, steadily forward suggested he was content with just taking her palm in his. But during each of his first two attempts, after drawing Molly's hand away from her side, he hesitated and awkwardly, stupidly, pulled back. They both laughed nervously each time, until finally, after joining hands, he moved closer and kissed her forehead. She closed her eyes and smiled. His fingers lingered on her shoulder after the kiss, then rose to her face. Slowly, rhythmically, he caressed her cheek and traced the tiny bone in her nose. Her eyes fluttered, then closed once more, and he passed a finger gently over her lids and down her cheek again before coming to rest on her lips. They were soft, wet, and inviting. He leaned in closer; she could feel his approach, and though she wanted to dive into him, to lose herself in his strong, safe arms, an image of Clarence filled her head and polluted the moment, causing her to open her eyes with a frightful jump.

"I'm sorry, Arthur. I can't."

"It's okay, Molly, I—"

"Please. Please don't say anything else."

He nodded. Then, deciding to leave well enough alone, he grabbed his hat and walked away.

DOG DAYS

The Brewers only played .500 ball over the next two weeks. By the close of August, their once healthy lead had evaporated and they found themselves clinging to a one-game advantage over the surging Rangers. Murph had suggested to all of them that they come out to the ballpark earlier than usual, to shag fly balls, take grounders, and get in some extra batting practice. He was a staunch believer in working out the kinks.

"Muscle memory, boys!" he liked to say. "You will play the way you practice."

He also tried borrowing some inspiration from one of the parent club's aces, who was in town visiting family.

"Fellas, there's someone here who I'd like you to meet."

From the shadows of the clubhouse corner emerged a handsome gentleman, six feet tall and 175 pounds, wearing a stone look of determination and a gray Boston Braves T-shirt. There was a long silence as the visitor approached the group.

"A sore arm or a bum leg or even a slump is like a headache or a toothache, gentlemen," he began. "It can make you feel bad. Real bad. But if you just forget about it and do what you have to do, it will go away."

They stood there listening like little boys, their faces furiously impatient, as the gentleman spoke passionately about the value of grit, hard work, and determination. Once or twice an exhausted sigh escaped from the group, followed by some yawns and eye rolling. Then slowly, as one player after another recognized the surprise stranger, a bristling energy shook the entire room.

"Christ, Woody," Lefty whispered. "Do you know who that is?"

"I know who it is, for Christ sakes. Don't be such an ass, Rogers. Who do you think I am—numb nuts over there in the corner?"

"This is unreal," Lefty continued. "The Invincible One. Good old number twenty-one. I can't believe this."

Woody shook his head. "Yeah, it's pretty cool. But what the hell is Warren Spahn doing here? With *us*?"

The Braves ace continued to fire up the troops with stories about miraculous comebacks and glory seasons past and explained how Murph had told him how the team was struggling. "I'm here as a show of support. To let you all know it's normal. What you're going through."

But the main reason he was there—a reason only he and Murph knew—was to see Mickey. He just had to see for himself what all the fuss was about. All the hype surrounding the young prodigy was irresistible, even for one of the major leagues' top pitchers.

"Well, Murph," Spahn said after finishing his address to the team. "Where is this whiz kid anyway?"

Murph laughed. "He's the one in the corner, over by his locker. Arranging the baseballs from that bucket in rows."

Spahn shot Murph an odd look, then walked with him over to the boy. This couldn't be the phenom, he thought. Not possible. The guy he'd heard about was a killer. A chiseled mass of destruction and hellfire. "You're kidding me, Murph, right? That's him?"

"Hold your horses, Spahney."

Murph placed his hand on Mickey's shoulder. The boy continued to set the last few baseballs in place, oblivious of the two men. Then, as if the placement of the final ball had turned on a flashlight of sorts, Mickey turned suddenly to face his greeter.

"Twenty baseballs, Murph. Twenty. There are really twenty-one." Mickey produced an extra from his pocket. "This one don't fit."

"That's great, Mick," Murph said, taking the ball from him. "Not a problem." He plunged the ball into his own pocket. "I'd like you to meet a friend of mine, Mick. His name is Warren Spahn."

Spahn held out his hand.

Mickey reached for it and shook it vigorously. "Michael James Tussler. Folks just call me Mickey."

"Good to meet you, Mickey. You can call me Warren."

With shifty eyes, Lefty watched the scene unfold. There was his idol, the best southpaw the league had ever seen, fawning over some dim-witted hayseed who didn't know the first thing about him.

"Do you play ball too, Warren?" Mickey asked.

Spahn smiled. "Do I play ball?" He could hear the others, who were straining to listen in on the exchange, laughing in the background. "Yeah, I play a little."

"Mickey is a pitcher. But my hand is hurt now."

"I know. I heard all about you. Pitching's great. What better challenge can there be than the one between the pitcher and the hitter?" Spahn stood for a moment, looking at the boy in disbelief, trying to envision this awkward stray dominating on the hill. "It sure is a shame you can't toss that ball around. Would have loved to have seen it."

Murph glanced at the legend, and Spahn caught his gaze before checking his watch. Murph knew Spahn had to be going shortly.

"You know, Mick, Warren here pitches a little bit too. For the Braves. Maybe we'll go to his place one day and see him play."

Mickey smiled. "Okay, Murph." The boy paused. "Does Warren have a farm? With pigs?"

Murph's effort to shake the team from its doldrums began to produce some results. They were still missing the swagger, that intangible buoyancy that they had had when Mickey was in the lineup, but the hits started coming and the fielding improved considerably; Murph wasn't thrilled, but realized it could have been a lot worse. They had weathered what Murph hoped was the worst of the storm and, despite Mickey's absence, still had a shot down the stretch.

Much of the recent success was due to Boxcar, who had essentially put all of them on his back and carried them for almost twenty straight days. Murph was in his office the day before the tide had turned, computing batting averages and ERAs in a marble notebook after one of their particularly difficult losses, when Boxcar came in. He had not yet showered. He was a mess. One eye was partially swollen shut, and blood and dirt covered his face. He touched the side of his head awkwardly, searching for the source of the red trail. His fingers worked the hair at his temple, revealing a tiny hole that had only just begun to close.

"You look like hell," Murph said.

"Right," Boxcar answered glibly.

"You gonna get that checked out?"

Boxcar scowled. He was already thinking of something else. "I'm done, Murph," he said with a clear note of finality.

"Come again?" Murph asked, his face now several shades whiter than before.

"Done. With this bull. With losing. With getting my ass kicked every goddamned time we step foot on that field. It's enough. No more. I will not just lie down like some lily-livered chicken and lick my wounds. I'm telling ya. Tomorrow will be different, or I'm packing my bags."

Boxcar's announcement was prophetic; the beleaguered backstop was either flirting with clairvoyance or had suddenly discovered the power to will his desires into being. The next day, with the score knotted at six apiece, Finster lead off the Brewers' half of the ninth with a clean single to left. Jimmy Llamas followed with a single of his own, breaking a personal 0-for-23 drought. He stood at first base spitting tobacco juice through his two front teeth and firing his invisible six-shooters in celebration.

With Danvers due up next, Murph swallowed the bunt sign and green-lighted the power-hitting third baseman. Murph was going for it. He knew that all the percentages called for the sacrifice. But he had a hunch.

Danvers was overanxious. He had been pressing all day, leaving five men in scoring position during his first three at bats. He was shocked that Murph was allowing him to hit away and wanted desperately to reward the manager for showing such confidence in him. He was also struggling with the weight of his latest discovery, and what it would mean to the team if he exposed Lefty. How could they possibly win with their two best pitchers out of the lineup? How would that help any of them, including Mickey? He decided he would swallow what he knew, but it remained stuck in his throat.

The Spartans' pitcher began with a breaking ball in the dirt. Danvers swung wildly and missed. He swung and missed again at the next offering, a fastball letter high. Down 0–2, Danvers knew he had to protect the plate. He needed to look fastball and adjust to anything off-speed.

The Spartan pitcher peered in and got his sign. He nodded once, brought his hands high over his head, placed them together, then brought them to rest slowly at his waist. He gave Finster a quick look at second, glanced furtively over at first, then turned again to face Danvers, who was whirling his bat feverishly with wild anticipation. After refocusing on the catcher's target, and licking his lips, the pitcher let the ball spin out of his hands.

It was a poorly executed delivery. His elbow sagged, and he short-stepped his follow-through, causing the curveball to hang invitingly over the center of the plate. It was a classic mistake. An 0–2 cookie. Danvers recognized the blunder almost immediately. His eyes lit up, and he strained mightily to hold himself back.

With visions of a game-winning three-run homer filtering through his head, Danvers swung with reckless fury, pulling his head, stepping in the bucket, and leaving his shoes. There was a great wind, then a loud thump that echoed throughout the entire park. The bat missed the ball by a good two feet.

Mickey, seated next to Pee Wee, watched from the bench as Danvers fired his helmet against the dugout wall and slammed his bat back into the rack. The struggling man swore and kicked at the loose baseballs Mickey had lined up neatly on the floor. "A goddamned hanger, for Christ sakes! A hanger. How the hell did I miss a goddamned hanger?"

Mickey felt an odd lift of his heart, as if maybe he could help. The thought was uncertain, but far preferable to the uselessness he had been struggling with.

"It's okay, Woody," Mickey offered. "It was a nice try."

"What did you say? Are you talking to me?"

"Mickey said you made a nice try. Nice try." Then Mickey started for the scattered balls.

Danvers, with pale, cold, humorless eyes, lurched at the boy, who seemed to sink beneath the slugger's bluster. "Listen, farm boy," Danvers carped before storming off. "I don't need no dumb-ass, good-for-nothing yokel with a bum hand telling me nothing about hitting. See? You just sit there, doing whatever it is you do now, and shut your damned hole!"

Pee Wee could hear Mickey's heart thumping. The boy sat dumbfounded, his eyes wet, nose running.

"It's okay, Mick," Pee Wee said. "Really. It's not you. He's just an asshole when he's not hitting."

Mickey was somber, impenetrable, lost in the sudden imbroglio with Danvers. He was drowning in this sea of mockery. "They ripped the buttons off Mickey's jersey," he said, recalling a recent incident. "They cut the bottoms of my socks, hid my glove, and today they pissed in my cap." He paused and sat motionless, perfectly flat. "Mickey makes everyone mad."

"Are you kidding me?" Pee Wee replied. "Come on now, Mick. Jesus, the guys are just razzing you. That's all. You're still an important part of this team. Injury or not. It shouldn't be too much longer before the hand is all better and you're back in action. You'll feel like yourself again. Just hang in there."

The two of them focused their attention back on the game. Boxcar was up next. He'd already had a great day—three for three with a walk, three RBIs, and two runs scored. He was feeling it—that competitive fire that would just not submit, under any circumstances. He got just what he was looking for immediately—a first-ball fastball—and laced it back through the middle. The ball exploded off his bat, narrowly missing both the pitcher and Finster as he took his lead from second. The ball was through the infield and in the hands of the center fielder in seconds, preventing Finster, who had had to hit the dirt to avoid being decapitated by the sizzling liner, from advancing beyond third.

Murph was faced with another managerial decision. With one out, and the bases filled with Brewers, the specter of an inning-ending, rally-killing double play loomed large. Buck Faber, who was hitting the ball with authority of late, was due up. Murph pondered deeply, then grabbed Faber before he left the on-deck circle. "How do you feel about a squeeze?"

Faber frowned. "I'm not too good with the bunting, Murph. Besides, I can hit this guy."

Murph nodded. He let himself drift somewhere below the surface of his usual thoughts. So what? he considered. What was the worst that could happen? It was not as if they hadn't faced adversity before. Let it ride, he told himself. Just go for it.

"Okay, Bucky," he said, tapping him on the fanny. "Hit away."

Faber took the first pitch for ball one. The second offering missed as well. He was in the driver's seat. Bases juiced, winning run on third, and no place to put him. "Hitter's hard-on" they liked to call it. Sheer ecstasy. No one in that ballpark had any doubt—he was going to get a cripple pitch.

It came made to order. Four-seam fastball, straight as an arrow, right down Broadway. Faber jumped on it, struck it well, but only the top half. The ball appeared destined for the hole between the hot corner and short, but the third baseman stabbed it and began what looked like a tailor-made 5–4–3, around-the-horn double play. But none of the Spartans realized that Boxcar was tired of losing. He got a terrific jump off first and was in full flight just as the third baseman released the ball. The trajectory was true, a perfect throw, headed right for the bag. The second baseman straddled the base, hands ready to make the quick exchange. But the ball and the runner arrived at the same time. The ball barely had enough time to make an impression in the glove before Boxcar came in the way his name suggested, like a freight train, and separated the ball from the middle infielder and his shoulder from its socket. In the skirmish, and the frantic dash for the ball by the shortstop, Finster scampered home with the game-winning run.

Boxcar won a few games for them the more conventional way as well. He buried the Colts with a towering, game-winning homer; he neutralized the prolific running game of the Giants by gunning down seven would-be base stealers; and with the game on the line, he dashed the hopes of the Tigers when he dove headlong into the stands, snaring a foul pop that should have landed safely three rows back. Everyone—fans, opponents, sportswriters—watched in amazement, and all agreed that it was the most incredible stretch of dominating baseball they had ever seen one person play.

But, despite the superhuman exploits of Boxcar, the Brewers still lost another game in the standings to the red-hot Rangers. While the Brewers were struggling just to keep their collective heads above water, the Rangers had gone on a 15–4 run, beginning about the time Mickey was sidelined, and had completely erased the Brewers' commanding lead.

On the upside, the Brewers still had Lefty. He took the hill against the Sidewinders, with the Brewers in a deadlock with the Rangers for first place. Aside from Boxcar, Lefty was the only Brewer who had actually thrived in the absence of Mickey. He was just about unhittable in his last five starts and was throwing the baseball with a command and artfulness that hadn't been seen since his rookie year. His burgeoning strikeout total and domination of opposing batters had captured the imagination of the Brewer fans and lifted them out of their late-summer swoon. After weeks of hapless and hopeless play, they finally had something to believe in.

It was a Friday night, and after a long week of dairy farming, tool and die making, and other labor-intensive endeavors, the crowd was ready to unwind. They had come to cheer on the home team, carrying with them expressions of anticipation as well as placards, confetti, cowbells, and an eclectic assortment of other implements of merriment.

Lefty wasted no time, stoking the celebratory fires with a strikeout of the Sidewinders' leadoff man. The "bleacher creatures," self-professed Brewer diehards who had come about during the Brewers' earlier domination, roared with approval, clapping their hands, stamping their feet, whistling, and finally, after dancing what looked like some tribal rumba, hanging a rubber snake in recognition of the first killing of the night. Lefty loved it. He stepped off the mound and watched as the boisterous celebration that began in the bleachers erupted into a wave of frenetic movement that washed across the entire park, ending with a raucous chanting of his name. Life was beautiful.

The game was scoreless at the end of the fifth inning. Lefty's dominating performance, coupled with the Brewers' inept offense, made for a quick, uneventful game, another pitcher's duel. On the Sidewinders' half of the scoreboard, just below the word *hits*, stood the number 0. Across from that, on the same line on the Brewers' side, was the number 2. Ten rubber snakes hung from a metal bar that ran along the first row of bleacher seats.

The lack of offensive support dampened Lefty's spirits. He sat on the end of the bench brooding, leaning forward, head down between his knees. He was convinced that yet another of his great efforts would die the same death as so many others, until Clem Finster got a hanging slider in the bottom of the seventh and drilled it out of the yard.

The minute Lefty heard the crowd howl, he sprang from his seat. "Oh, yeah, Finny!" he yelled, pumping his fist in the air. "That's right. That's what I'm talking about. That's just what I needed!"

Boxcar and Murph exchanged a look. Then Murph glowered. The push of blood in his head seemed to cease unexpectedly, removing him momentarily from what he was watching. Winning was sweet. Christ, it meant everything to him, now more than ever. But Lefty's narcissism was intolerable. "Friggin' guy," Murph mumbled out loud. "Unbelievable."

Lefty continued to throw darts, insulated in a cocoon of self-absorption, and the bleacher creatures continued to hang snakes—fourteen of them through eight innings. Despite the excitement, a peculiar hush seemed to fall across the crowd, like calming air moments before a late-afternoon thunderstorm. Something special was about to unfold, and the entire ballpark could sense its steady approach. With just three outs to go, Lefty had yet to yield a hit and was standing toe-to-toe with baseball immortality.

Under the silent flicker of lights that glowed like stars set in a sleepy sky, the Sidewinders took their final shot at Lefty. Their leadoff man, Buzz Stuber, looked sick, like a little boy on his first day of school. He came to the plate, eyes wide, his whole body shaking as if he were operating an invisible jackhammer. Lefty had punched him out three times already, all swinging, and now Stuber was facing a dubious date with the golden sombrero.

"Okay now, Stubey!" the Sidewinders bench yelled to him. "Come on now. It only takes one."

The frustrated batter locked and loaded, the bat sliding around ever so slightly in his sweaty palms. Boxcar put down one finger. Lefty nodded, then lifted his right leg and whipped his arm around. The ball was swift and painted the black of the plate for strike one. Stuber's spirit sagged even further. He shook his head dejectedly, kicked the dirt, and blew a long puff of air out of his mouth. He malingered a bit outside the box, tapping his spikes and fiddling with his belt buckle, procrastinating with this and that until the umpire admonished him. "Let's go, fella. Play ball."

Stuber stepped back in. His hands were a little steadier now and his knees had stopped knocking. Lefty grinned with confidence as he stared him down, and wild expectation filtered through his head, including the postgame hoopla that would undoubtedly accompany his first career no-no.

Lefty delivered a fastball, inside half of the plate. Stuber never flinched. He rotated his hips, went down almost all the way to one knee, held the bat out flat with a slight tilt to the left, and dropped a picture-perfect bunt down the third-base line. Danvers was caught flat-footed behind the bag. He charged frantically, trying to compensate for his poor positioning, but in his haste to barehand the ball, it rolled up his palm and off his wrist, coming to rest at last just to the right of his foot.

The miscue sent Lefty into orbit. He stormed around the infield, hands on hips, swearing and spitting, looking to the heavens in tortured disbelief. Then he glared over in Danvers's direction, picked up the rosin bag from behind the mound, and fired it to the ground, barking about stone hands and bush-league play. The fit continued for another minute or so, with everyone watching in disbelief, before finally subsiding after the official scorer ruled the play an error. Then, and only then, did Lefty's vitriol soften enough to allow him to continue.

Boxcar, however, had seen enough. "Time!" he called, motioning for the infielders to join him in the center of the infield. He flipped up his mask and walked out to the mound, fists clenched, biting his lip. His gait was deliberate, purposeful, and his face sweaty and crimson. Reaching the mound, he stood for some seconds and did not move. A great hollow of darkness appeared to be facing him. There was so much he wanted to say, to do, that for a brief moment it paralyzed him. Everyone just stood around waiting. The silence was interminable. Then, as if a light switch had suddenly been thrown, Boxcar was back.

"Hey!" he began through clenched teeth, poking Lefty's shoulder and motioning over to Danvers. "You got a problem with Woody? Do ya?"

Lefty said nothing, just stood there quietly, frazzled in front of the penetrating gaze of the assembled company.

"What about Pee Wee? Or Fries? Or maybe it's Finster? Are they doing it for you today?"

Lefty grinned nervously. The outward show of disrespect lit a fuse somewhere deep inside the fiery catcher.

"Listen, you selfish piece of crap," he threatened, grabbing him by the throat. "We've been down this road before. I won't do it again, you hear? These guys—all these guys—play for Murph, and the team. Not you. You understand? Screw your goddamned no-hitter. It don't mean crap."

Boxcar let him go. Lefty's face was remote, still voiceless. His eyes swept momentarily across his teammates, then shifted above Boxcar's shoulder to the crowd, then fell again on the disdainful visage directly in front of him.

"Hey, you listening to me, Rogers? You getting me? Don't you ever show up another teammate again—not on my time."

"Yeah, yeah," Lefty answered. "I got you, tough guy. You can stop putting on the show. Everyone saw you."

Lefty retired the next three batters in order. When the final pitch landed safely in Boxcar's glove, the no-hitter was complete. Lefty threw his arms up in exultation and jumped around on the mound like a little boy, waiting to be mobbed by his jubilant team-mates. It never happened. They just left him frolicking in a queru-lous bonfire of self-idolatry. Only some of the fans were with him—the few who were not estranged by the odd on-field exhibi-tion just moments before. This tiny faction stood and applauded the effort, lost in a frenzy of vicarious exhilaration that blinded them to the real drama unfolding. Lefty's teammates' behavior told the real story. Led by Boxcar's example, they simply refused to feed Lefty's swelling ego, offering only brief, perfunctory expressions of acknowledgment before walking silently off the field. It was the quietest no-hitter ever pitched.

Lefty celebrated quietly as well—that night, at The Bucket, with just a few of his more ardent female admirers. He had drawn the attention of some of the local baseball groupies, young girls with wanton ways, determined to hitch their wagon to what they believed was a rising star.

They sat all around him, a coterie of pandering floozies, fawn-ing and drinking and feeding his ravenous ego.

"Oh, Lefty, you were spectacular out there," one of the girls said. "Like a gladiator. It just made me tingle all over watching you."

The others giggled coquettishly and added saccharine comments of their own. Lefty ate them up. Every last one.

He had been there awhile, trying to decide which one of them he would take home with him, when another girl came up from behind and tapped him on the shoulder. Unlike the others, her face was severe and offered no outward show of affection for the star pitcher. She seemed bitter. All the misery in the tortured girl's life was present in her dark eyes. She swayed slightly, nervously, from side to side, her head half-tilted.

"We need to talk," she said, her voice cold and raspy. Now."

A sort of dullness settled on him. He was tired and drunk and did not really care to engage the girl. He turned only slightly on the barstool, just enough to catch her eyes. "I told you," he whispered through clenched teeth, "never to come here." He dismissed her with an abrupt turn of his head.

She did not leave. "George, you promised." She grabbed his shoulder. "You said if I helped—"

He flared at her. She was slow of wit. Her dimness made his blood boil. "I said not to bother me here," he ordered. "Now, turn around and go away."

She crumbled. Laney Juris had met Lefty the first week he was with the Brewers. She was standing outside the train station, waiting for a distant relation from the East who never showed. He had just gotten off his train and was fumbling with his bags.

An enormous orange sun was staring at him from the tips of the distant trees. He stood looking at it. Then he saw her. She was smiling. Although her face was covered by a shadow cast by her hat, he could see the ends of her mouth, bent up toward her eyes. "Beautiful sun," he said to her, struggling to manage the load in his hands. "Gonna be a hot one tomorrow."

"It's sure starting to feel that way," she answered playfully.

The two of them walked for a while alongside the tracks, watching the horizon slowly swallow the big orange ball. She told him all about herself, how she lived alone, and that her mother had died years ago.

"Tuberculosis," she said. "She was sick a long time."

"What about your father?"

She answered in a low, even voice, without emotion or tears. "Haven't seen him in years."

"That's rough. I know a little bit about being on your own. Baseball can be a pretty lonely life."

Her feet threw up dirt and loose gravel. She looked down at the roadside, and at the stones lying in desultory patterns against the metal rail, as if the scene were some sort of portrait of her life.

"Oh, you're a ballplayer?" she said eagerly. "Who for?"

"Brewers. Today's actually my first day with the club."

"I love baseball. The players are pretty okay too."

They talked some more, then sat down on a redwood bench beneath a Victorian gaslamp and watched the trains pass by.

"What's your name?" he asked.

"Laney. Laney Juris."

"Laney. That's mighty pretty."

"Thank you. Do you have one? A name?"

"George Rogers. Nothing too pretty about that, although I do have a nickname."

She wrinkled her nose, pretending to be formulating a guess. "Are you gonna tell me, or do I have to figure it out by myself?"

"Lefty. Guys on the team call me Lefty, on account of me being a southpaw and all."

"Well, that's not very original." She laughed.

"Maybe so, but it works for me."

Then he put that arm around her, placed his other palm gently on her cheek, and kissed her. A deep passion flooded her.

"You know," he told her, "some people say that life's a casting off—that we have to find happiness whenever we can. You ever hear that?"

She nodded and placed her hand on his knee. He leaned forward, took the hand in his, and kissed each finger, one at a time. She saw him, muscular and firm, as if he had emerged, godlike, from the setting sun.

"You ever make it with a ballplayer, Laney?"

The crudeness of the question startled her. Her eyes blinked twice, as if she had come suddenly from a dark room into the bright sunshine. For a moment, all her feelings were conflicted. She was intrigued, and wonderfully excited, yet suddenly on guard. She had been here before. The memory halted her passion, but then yielded to a more recent recollection, the one of a lonely girl in a single room eating tuna by candlelight.

"No," she said, the faint cloud around her eyes lifting. "But if someone were to ask me tomorrow, I may have a different answer."

The days that followed were good. But Lefty was a ballplayer. And many girls like Laney were out there, which reduced her over time to just an occasional diversion whenever the churlish pitcher was bored or horny. This left poor Laney feeling cheap, and vulnerable. She existed in silent, unfulfilled yearning, bitterness, fettered to this man's capricious interest in her. Each time they were together, she promised herself it would be the last. She knew, somewhere in her fractured soul, that she deserved better. But the loneliness was brutal, enveloped her until she could scarcely breathe. He was all she had. So when Lefty came calling, as he did a few times each month, every fiber in her body wanted to say no, screamed to her to just get up and walk away. She heard the call, but could not bring herself to do it; she stayed and made the promise again.

Now, many months later, she was embroiled even further. Lefty had made a promise to her, too. He had never done that before. She believed him. Trusted him. She had expunged all of the heartache and disappointment, all of the regret and bitterness, all in exchange for a vision of something real and lasting. Now she wanted what was hers.

"I will not leave, George," she insisted, demanding his attention. She grabbed his arm and began tugging at him. "I helped you. You promised me things would be different if I helped."

He looked at her and started to say something and then stopped, anger raging beneath his skin. She appeared to him to be this alien presence, secreted suddenly from months of silent brooding. He wanted to hit her, to take his hand and strike her hard, right in the mouth. But the girls were around. So he filled his lungs, unclenched his fists, and then, through tight teeth, finally whispered, "What did you really do, Laney? Huh? Talk to some cowpunching retard? Drink some free liquor? Please. You gotta be kidding me now."

"Don't you say that to me, you bastard! The plan would not have worked without *me*! Remember, George? That boy is out of your way for a while because of *me*! And now the sheriff is talking to me. Okay? So, what about us? Huh? What about that promise you made? I've been waiting, George."

Lefty sighed with vexing exasperation. "Meet me outside, in back. And leave after me, so nobody sees."

The moon, through thick clouds, was vague and ominous. The air was cool and bothered the sweat on her forehead. She found him out back, leaning against a trash receptacle.

"Look, George, I know you told me never to come here again, but you don't return my calls and I have been—"

"Shut up!" he screamed. "Just shut your mouth, you little tramp. I don't owe you nothing. Nothing, you hear? That promise don't mean a hill of crap. Seems to me I already paid for that, long time ago. I kept you around longer than I should have. There's nothing happening here. Got it? I have a lot of people to see. I don't have no time for some alley cat. It's over. That's it. Now get your stuff together and don't ever show your face again."

She felt dizzy and her helplessness raged anew. "What are you saying?" she screamed. "Why, George? Tell me why."

He had no answer for her.

She cried. She cried a lot. She just stood there before him, and cried. And then it happened. Laney saw deep into him, as if his eyes had somehow become portholes to his blackened soul. She shuddered and gasped, and in that one instant, her loneliness and misguided affection for the man turned to loathing.

"You asshole!" she screamed. "You friggin' asshole! I am not some worthless piece of crap. Do you hear me? Don't you walk away from me! Do you hear me? You will respect me! You will respect me!"

The words fell softly on Lefty's back.

WARMING IN THE PEN

Quinton Harrington and Chip McNally sat in the dim light of Quinton's office and toasted their recent good fortune. A lamp resting precariously on a teetering pile of binders threw a flat, yellow beam across the room, forming a circle that expanded to include Quinton's tight jaw, his manicured fingers wrapped carefully around a clear, beveled glass containing a brown liquid, and some stray papers placed errantly in front of him.

"Here's to sweet victory," he announced, lifting his glass in the direction of the ceiling. "And to a well-executed plan."

McNally also raised his glass and smiled. Then he pulled out the sports section of the morning paper. "And to a two-game lead in the standings," he added, "with just fifteen to go."

It made them both smile. The Rangers had made up an incomprehensible amount of ground in such a short time and were on the brink of eliminating the Brewers and clinching a postseason appearance.

As time went on, the yellow beam seemed to expand, extending farther to reveal the dark circles under McNally's eyes. He had spent all night working on his lineup, aware that the next game, a pivotal matchup against the Brewers, could prove to be the final nail in their coffin. What little sleep he managed to get was punctuated by broken dreams, a peculiar patchwork of episodic exchanges between

Murph and him. In the most haunting of the series, he is young again, the fleet-footed number nine, dashing through the outfield in pursuit of a fly ball. His eyes are focused on the ball; his mind wedded to that vision of a game-saving catch. He is there, just about to snare the ball in his glove, when he is run down by another outfielder—Arthur Murphy. So there's no catch. No glory. Nobody screams his name, ever again. It's all gone, in one, fleeting moment. Gone. All that's left is a busted knee and broken dreams that spill out all over that outfield.

In the confines of the dusky office, with the smell of leather and new carpet perfuming the air, the residue of that dream lingered. He could still hear the sound of the collision; his knee still throbbed. They were both painful reminders. But alcohol was good—it dulled the senses. Helped him forget. As for so many others, the bottle was McNally's good friend—the great equalizer, the momentary panacea for many a shattered baseball career.

The two men continued to drink their whiskey and light cigars, then resumed their discussion.

"I think tomorrow should be the knockout blow," McNally said cheerfully. "Murphy is reeling over there—poor bastard. They're really down. One more loss, they'll fold their tents."

Quinton stood there, pouring whiskey down his throat, his mind clicking fitfully like some tired contraption. "I'd like to believe that's the case. It sure would be nice. I know Mickey's still on the shelf. But are you sure that Rogers is not available? I don't need any flies in the ointment."

McNally jiggled the ice cubes in his glass and smiled. "I am positive." He held up two fingers on each hand and clicked down as if to type quotation marks on the stale air. "Sore arm."

Across town, a different kind of meeting was taking place, one laced with anger and vitriolic exchanges.

"Mr. Murphy, have you seen the morning paper?" Dennison asked bitterly.

The question sort of floated, lingered for a while like a dandelion seed caught on a spring breeze. Both men sat quietly in the veiled light of Dennison's lair, staring at each other. The reproachful silence angered Murph. His spirit writhed with exposure and shame, not because of Dennison's remark, but because of his own inability to ameliorate the disaster left in the wake of Mickey's injury.

"Yes, Warren, I have seen it."

"Two games Arthur—two. With only fifteen left on the damned schedule. Do you understand what that means? My God, how could you blow such a big lead?" Dennison struggled with the brutal misfortune that had befallen them. "Look, I am the first one to admit that I was not in favor of this kid joining our team. I was wrong. He's the best thing that ever happened to us. I get that losing him was quite a blow. But, Arthur, for Christ sake, that was a month and a half ago. When are you going to get yourself together? What is it that you are doing about this?"

Dennison's condemnation was a logical consequence of the team's subpar performance; but the bilious owner's incessant attempts to belittle him, to impugn his character as a baseball man and manager, irritated him, scraped against his grain to the point of complete exasperation.

"You know something, Warren? I'm dealing with a mountain of crap here. Are you aware of that? I lost my best pitcher, whom I still feel personally responsible for. My other stud is a friggin' head case, who the rest of the team wants to string up by his balls. And now this whole investigation that Rosco wants to conduct has everyone feeling sick and out of sorts. So you know what? I don't need your crap also. All things considered, I think I've done a pretty damn good job holding this thing together."

Dennison sat back in his chair, rolled his shoulders as if to shake off the ill effects of a blindside, and glanced out the window. The sun was going down with a riotous swirl of brilliant color, varying shades of pink, orange, and sea-foam green. He looked on, with vague interest, then shook his head. He had always had a vision of Murph as someone who would, someday, take the disappointment of unfulfilled promise and convert its turbulent energy into sweet, vindicating success. It's the reason why he'd given Murph the job.

"I believe you're hungry," he told him that very first day. "Hunger is good. It's the key."

But some years later, Dennison had yet to see that hunger yield anything more than mediocrity, which led him to believe that what he had perceived as hunger really was, at best, a whimpering vacuity.

"Let's go about this thing a little differently, shall we, Arthur?" Dennison said in forced conciliatory tones. "Because I'm at the end of my rope here. Maybe I have not expressed myself clearly enough." He wrinkled his nose. For a moment, it was all too much for him. He tossed around a cluster of ideas that resonated in his head like a roomful of people all chattering at once. Some were soft, and understated, while others possessed an earsplitting energy that threatened to suffocate those less inclined to promote themselves vaingloriously. He entertained all of them for a while, then just let them go and went with his gut instead.

"It seems to me, Arthur, that there comes a time in every man's life when he is tested—really tested—when fate grabs him by the balls and forces him to look inside himself and see what he's made of. You know, to really take stock. I really believe that. And fair or not, ready or not, goddammit, this is your time."

The room grew tight and oppressive. Arthur's mouth opened, but he didn't have any words ready. Dennison sensed his distress and took out a cigar from his top desk drawer, lit the end with a silver Dunhill lighter, and blew a perfect ring of smoke into the heavy air.

Arthur's mouth quirked in annoyance. His lips pressed tightly together to hold the anger. Who the hell was Warren Dennison, a guy who had never played an out of professional baseball, to question him? What the hell did he know about pitching woes, defensive lapses, and hitters with trained eyes who were all of a sudden swinging wildly at 2–2 sliders in the dirt? How could he know what it was like to manage such a combination of divergent personalities, to give each the room to grow and play safely? And what about game day—game management? The X's and O's. Sacrifice or swing away?

Hit-and-run or straight steal? Leave the pitcher in or go to the pen? Infield up or play for two? What the hell did Dennison know about any of it? Arthur knew the answer—it was there all along. Always was. Dennison didn't know jack. So the anger boiled. And like magma bubbling beneath the earth's crust, it sought some release.

"Do you think it's easy to manage a ball club, Warren?" he finally said. "To throw nine guys out there who will execute the plan the way it's drawn up? Do you? Do you even have a clue? Maybe you haven't noticed, but I don't have the '27 Yankees out there. I work with what I'm given. And sometimes, well, to be perfectly honest, it ain't enough. You've heard it before, Warren. Matheson's famous line? You can't make chicken salad out of chicken shit. And then I bring you Mickey, this phenom sent straight from God. Someone who can improve the quality of the entire team. And you balk. Tell me I'm crazy. Question my ability to scout. But he does exactly what I knew he would. And you just admitted that yourself, but you still don't give me one ounce of credit, even though that kid put us back on the map. But I still say nothing. I just suck it up and keep winning games. And life is good. Then he's taken from me, and everyone else can see the giant hole it created except you. I cannot fill that hole. We patch it now and again. But the hole is the hole. It's there and it's real. I am playing shorthanded. So don't call me in here and give me some lame crap about me finding myself, and don't lay this whole goddamned thing at my feet. I will not listen to you drag my name through the mud any longer."

Two Victorian bowls of frosted glass set neatly on the wall to the left of the desk held flickering bulbs that had previously bathed the room with the soothing mimicry of candlelight; now, however, instead of that peaceful glow, the constant spattering of light hit Dennison's eyes hard, making him wince as if his retinas were somehow detaching. He glared at Murph with a red, swollen face, suffocating now that he had not only been questioned, but challenged so irreverently.

"You may be in charge of the on-field duties, Mr. Murphy, but that is only the case for as long as I say so," Dennison fired back.

"The fact that you may know a little bit more about the nuances of the game than I do does not preclude my need for you to be successful." He spoke with a heightened purpose, his face still red and swollen. "And, at any point you demonstrate that you are incapable of doing so, and I trust you are aware of what I'm about to say, then I will have no alternative but to find someone—and I will—who can."

Murph did not get up at once. Even after Dennison excused himself, Murph just sat there, staring at the flickering lights, his heartbeat matching the erratic cadence of the mechanical flames. He was drained, his resiliency recoiling from sheer exhaustion. He would have to get up, sooner or later; he knew that. But the thought was daunting, for sitting there, with his vitality and will to fight draining from him, he could not imagine facing a world turned suddenly to furious, unpredictable motion.

TUSSLER FARM—LATE AUGUST

The honey tint of the early-morning sky was a mirror of the bright, awakening earth. Molly was up prematurely, having been bothered all night by the curious feeling of a current of water flowing though her body, swiftly, inexorably, into nothingness.

Arthur Murphy's visit had gotten her to thinking and had created a heightened sensitivity to everything. She was suddenly aware, for instance, of this sound, a faint rattling that she was previously incapable of understanding—a sound that she had been hearing all along but was unable to put a name to. Standing there, her hands blistering from the plunger she pushed through a threadbare butter churn, she thought that perhaps she finally knew.

Near the edge of the property, by the gray, weathered fence, she saw Clarence walking dumbly beside Oscar, who had wandered out to the road to wallow in a shallow puddle just inside the gate. She watched as this man whom she viewed more and more with an unaffected scorn teased the porker, rolling a turnip between his fingers, in sight of the pig, then pretending with a sharp, deft motion to throw the delicacy into the puddle next to him, rendering the animal confused and agitated. Clarence repeated the torture, laughing louder and louder each time, stopping only when Molly, who had seen enough, called to him.

"Hold yer horses, woman!" he bellowed. "I'm a coming."

Clarence faked three more throws before tucking the turnip in his pocket and heading back up. With the sun having ascended, she saw him in full, reflectionless light and heard that rattling again, this time louder.

"That pig's dumber than a stump," Clarence said as he approached. He laughed and turned his head to her in righteous declaration. "Just like the boy."

She hated that expression, ever since the first day he'd used it. Mickey must have been five, maybe six years old, and Clarence had just shown him how to get water from the well. He was standing back, arms folded, watching as the child attempted to replicate the procedure he was just taught.

"Go on now, boy," Clarence instructed. "Fetch us some water."

Mickey was cautious, moving with great trepidation, fearful no doubt of drawing his father's ire should he fail to please him. His steps were measured and small, buckling under the tremendous weight of Clarence's stare. He stopped several times, his face awash with fear. It seemed the young boy was infinitely weary of just contemplating another step. His stomach burned, and behind his eyes, a throbbing pain knocked mercilessly. His feet froze. All he wanted to do was lie down, right there in the grass, and go to sleep.

"Go on, boy!" Clarence repeated impatiently. "Do as your told."

Mickey took a few more steps. Once at the well, he placed his hand on the crank and, looking at his father, began releasing the coiled rope from its spool, lowering the metal bucket into the black hole. With each crank, the winch creaked and more rope unfurled. It was all going according to plan, until Mickey was seized by an overwhelming dread attached to the swaying of the bucket. Why was it shaking so? Surely he was doing something wrong. His face contorted and he groaned in protest. Then, in desperation, he reversed the process, cranking the bucket back to its original position. Clarence just rolled his eyes.

After hiding his face in his hands for fear of being judged insolent, Mickey made another pass. He placed his hand back on the crank and tried again. But each time the rope was lowered, the bucket swayed uncontrollably to the side. He must have started over seven or eight times before Clarence finally flipped.

"What the hell in tarnation are ya doing, boy!" he hollered.

The young boy quaked. "The bucket," he tried to explain. "Mickey can't get the bucket to stop moving."

Clarence opened his palm and covered his eyes. His head dropped helplessly for a moment, before his temper reared its ugliness.

"The bloomin' bucket is *supposed* to move, you imbecile!" Clarence screamed. "Holy Christ, this can't be happening. You are dumber than a stump."

Clarence's abuse of Oscar had taken Molly right back to that day. She had never forgotten those words, or the crestfallen expression on her little boy's face.

"Let's go inside, Clarence," she said now, blinking her eyes wildly in an attempt to erase the painful recollection. "I'll fix your breakfast."

Molly and Clarence ate by the sun's yellow light with cool, damp winds blowing through the open windows that suggested an afternoon rain. The smell of freshly baked bread, strudel, and ham steaks belied the discomfort of the moment.

Clarence cut his food vigorously and slurped his coffee. Molly watched quietly as little scraps of food flew from his mouth and into his beard and onto his shirt and the table in front of him. Repugnancy had grabbed her by the throat and was tightening its grip. She strove terribly to speak.

"So, were you able to fix the bucket on the corn planter?"

"Sure was," he said. "Darn thing just needed a little elbow grease, that's all." He finished his coffee and wiped his mouth on the sleeve of his shirt. "What about you, little Miss Molly? You were up a mite early today. What's got you all bushy-tailed?"

"Nothing particular now. Just figured we could use some fresh butter, that's all."

"What fer, woman? Today a holiday I don't know about?"

"No, no holiday, Clarence. I just thought I'd do some baking. That's all."

Clarence shot her a look that went through her like a pin that paralyzed her momentarily. "You plan on doin' some baking, do ya? Why's that? Are we expectin' someone?"

"Uh, no, Clarence. Who would we be expecting? That's crazy. You know how I just like to bake."

"Don't get short with me now, woman. I won't tolerate none of yer sass. I was just a wonderin', that's all."

"Well, I suppose I *could* cut down a bit on what I've been making. I mean, with Mickey gone—I mean, not home anymore. No sense wasting food."

"Yer darn tootin'. I tell ya what. That boy may have a brain the size of a rabbit pellet, but that's one retard who can put away the grub."

His words wrung her heart like burly hands. "Enough!" she blurted out, unable to restrain her disgust. "Can you please stop talking about him that way? He's not a retard!"

Clarence sat back and smiled, eyebrows raised in curious amusement. "Relax, little Miss Molly," he said condescendingly. "I was just foolin', woman."

"Those things are not funny to me—they never have been. I'm sick and tired of it. I will not listen to it anymore. I just can't listen to it anymore."

Some unfamiliar passion in the phrasing of her request ignited a fire deep within him, altering his visage.

"Come again? Are you talking to me?" A ravaging wildness seized him. He shoved his plate away, splashing a pitcher of milk across the table. Uttering a strained, guttural sound, something that rose up from the depths of his soul, he lunged at her. She dodged, leaning to one side, and knocked the chair out from beneath her. She tried to move beyond the table, but his large paw grabbed her at the elbow and spun her around. Disoriented, she did not at first feel the glancing blow to the side of her face.

"You just better hush your mouth, woman. Hush it now, you good-fer-nothin', stupid cow, or you'll feel me again."

She stood silent in her blue-and-white apron, staring as Clarence stormed outside. As she watched him stomp across the field, she set her mind to some chores in the kitchen. Now that she had finally spoken her mind, she thought that she had perhaps made a mistake; maybe it would have been better to just bury the silent desperation, the way she had for years, keep it hidden where nobody, not even Clarence, could step all over it.

As she washed out a dirty saucepan, she looked at her hands. They were old, chaffed and calloused. All the tender, pink skin she remembered was gone, buried beneath the hardened layers of her labors. What had happened? she wondered. Why had this life of hers succumbed to this suffocation? Nothing was right. Standing there, with her hands immersed in a basin of turbid water, and her right cheek still stinging from Clarence's attack, she felt as though she could not go on. Clarence made each day's existence a living misery. He was a martinet—selfish, belligerent, and unpredictable. He stalked around the farm like an army general on a mission to subdue everything and everyone in his path. It was brutal. But then the stormy skies would part, for a little while, and the meager rays of sunshine that sneaked through were welcomed and embraced with such a rapacity that all the previous torment was overlooked. It made it tolerable. But it was a wicked cycle. And now, even those rare moments had been vanquished by some dark, evil energy. The hopelessness enveloped her. She dried her hands and undid her apron strings. Then she sat back down at the messy table and cried.

She tried to forget. It had worked in the past. There had to be a way of leaving it all outside. Separation was key. But the drama, it seemed, had morphed into something insidious, a masterful force with a life all its own. She could see it all in the distance, despite her best efforts to bury it: Clarence, Mickey, her lack of fulfillment. It was all there—misery at arm's length. But the problem was worse than that. She also felt it inside; the separation was gone. It was in her heavy legs, her tight throat, and her heaving chest. It was in her pout and the grayness in her eyes. There was no denying it. She bawled at the idea that she had become one with it.

All at once the room was filled with this dreadful sense of waiting. So much of her recent awareness had come in the wake of Mickey's leaving and then Arthur's news that he had been attacked. She missed Mickey something awful. With Clarence gone for a few hours, she picked up the telephone and sought counsel in the only place she could think of.

"Arthur, it's Molly. Molly Tussler. Can we talk?"

He was home, getting ready for the much anticipated showdown with the Rangers. He had spent all night, and the better part of the early morning, shuffling his lineup and figuring out who was going to get the ball. With Mickey out, and Lefty having suddenly announced that his arm was sore, he was struggling to find the right combination. He had penciled in four different starters and had still not come up with something that looked good to him.

"Is everything okay?" he asked her. "You don't sound so good."

"How is Mickey? Do they know anything more about how it happened?"

"He's right here, Molly, with me. He's sitting at the table, doing some kind of number puzzle. You want to speak to him?"

"No, no, that's okay. If he's happy, that's fine. I really wanted to talk to you. I was hoping you had some more news for me."

"God, Molly, I wish I had something more to tell you. You know I do. But it's like I said. Mickey's good. He's fine. The sheriff's department is still investigating, and I check in with them every day. But I'm afraid that there's nothing new to report."

She fell silent. All he could hear on the other end was the sound of her erratic breathing. He thought about her desperate questions and put aside his own struggles for the moment, recognizing the torment that eddied in her voice.

"Did something happen there? It's not like you to call."

"I'm just having one of those days," she said brokenly. "Some moments just seem to be harder than others."

He wasn't sure what she meant exactly, but he was startled by his own unconscious thoughts. "Is it Clarence? You haven't told him what happened, have you?"

"No, he still has no idea."

"How have you managed to keep it from him?"

"Are you kidding? He hasn't even asked."

"What do you mean?"

"Just what I said," she lamented, tears brimming in her eyes. "This is what I live with, Arthur. Not just now, but always. I don't know. I'm not sure I can do it anymore."

Arthur struggled with the storm about to burst inside him, his head resonating with the voices of Dennison and Molly and, on some subconscious plane, McNally as well. He knew it was futile and counterproductive, but he couldn't help but think, as Molly continued to express her utter disconsolation, that all of his own problems would be nil if only he hadn't let Mickey go out that night.

"Listen, Molly, you have to hang in there," he said, half trying to convince himself of what he was saying. "Don't talk with such gloom. Mickey is going to be all right. He's great. So are you. I know it. You have to believe, Molly. Believe in something."

"Thank you, Arthur, really. I know what you are trying to do. And talking to you helps. It does. But I've been through a lot. Seen a lot. And after all that, I don't really believe in anything anymore."

Before hanging up, Arthur promised he would call her soon. He did not know what else to say, how he could possibly extricate her from this eternal night that she was passing through. He wanted to offer so much more, out of both a deep affection for her and a profound sense of responsibility. But he was tired and had his own problems to deal with.

His words did help her. She felt better just having spoken to him. She exhaled a deep, cleansing breath and looked out the window at the world before her. The sunset was mesmerizing, the most beautiful part of a long and lifeless day. Just as the fiery ball touched the rim of the horizon, it all at once exploded in colorful display, filling the air with brilliant flecks of violet, orange, and red jewels set in the crown of the early-evening sky. It made her smile, but at the same time question how such beauty could coexist in her world of longing and misery.

Some minutes passed, and all the color faded to black. Clarence lumbered through the door, sat down at the kitchen table, removed his boots, and pulled over a plate of warm biscuits and gravy. The room was warm and filled with the redolence of an entire day's cooking.

"Sure smells good, Molly." He slammed a biscuit into his mouth, licked his fingers, and swallowed. "I guess it'll make up fer your lip this morning."

She frowned, her eyes full of pain and fire. It was more than she could stand. She returned a frying pan hard to the countertop and disappeared up the stairs.

Outside her window, the moon had risen above a bank of clouds, taking the place of the tired sun. She watched silently as a dark shadow, fast and birdlike, flashed across the face of the shining wafer. It was followed by another, then several more, until all had completed their passage. Brimming with envy, she wondered where they were going.

Before she could get too far in her ruminations, Clarence stomped up the stairs. He stood behind her, voiceless. She did not turn around, but knew he was there; she could hear his uneven breathing and smell his stale, sharp breath.

"I don't remember hearing you say you was sorry fer gitting me all upset this mornin'," he finally said.

She jumped a little. His words were spoken in such a measured way that she knew he was going somewhere. But she could not bear to look at him. She remained facing the window, swaying slightly.

"I didn't," she answered blankly. She stood, her arms dangling straight down, fingers limp, shoulders slumped. She couldn't move, just stood there swaying from side to side, waiting for Clarence to make his next move.

"You know, little Miss Molly," he said, his clumsy feet moving loudly across the oak floor. "That's all right. I understand. There's more than one way you can say yer sorry."

With that, he stole up behind her and placed his hands on her shoulders and squeezed gently. She cringed, her entire body protesting his touch and his lurid reflection cast in the glass before her face. She wanted to run, or to fly like those migratory birds outside her window. She froze instead, as she always did.

Clarence was oblivious to her repugnance. He put his chapped lips on her neck and reached around her back to fondle her breasts. She closed her eyes, dizzy and breathless from the constant sickness gnawing at her heart. She could feel his hardness against her back and braced herself for the inevitable ugliness that was about to follow.

"Come on over here, woman," he instructed, grabbing her hand and leading her to the bed. "Show me how sorry you are."

As she had so many times before, she acquiesced. Just shut her eyes tightly and tried with unwavering desperation to leave her body as Clarence climbed on top of her. She knew she could not stop him from invading her, but her mind, her mind was all hers. Even Clarence, with his brutish, hulking strength, could not penetrate the impregnable walls of her imagination.

The next few minutes passed in a dream. She was somewhere else, where lush green lawns rolled away from beautiful country villas under a sky as resplendent as the one she had just seen an hour before—and where men, despite their rural upbringing, grew from their dull, feckless state to become attentive, engaging creatures, mindful of a lady's tenderness and appreciative of such frivolities as music and poetry. It was a picture of life as she often imagined it should be, and it lasted for the duration of the sexual incarceration, bursting suddenly like a cloud of rain once Clarence had finished.

When he finally released her, buckled his pants, and went downstairs, she breathed again. She balanced her head and came back slowly, her thoughts returning with a practical approach to her daily grind. She thought about the laundry, and fixing Clarence's pipe for him. But somehow, it was different this time. It felt as if the dream state had suddenly, accidentally spilled into the conscious world and had, without warning, erased the line of demarcation, capturing her and demanding in no uncertain terms to be heard.

PENNANT RACE

The Brewer locker room was enveloped in somber distress, an anxious silence punctuated by an air of intense listening, as if the reticence would somehow, any minute, break apart and bring forth a voice of reassurance and hope. Their recent slide had all of them miserable and searching for answers. Even Boxcar, the last bastion of unbridled optimism, was stoic. When Murph came in and taped the lineup card on the wall, he stopped, scrunched up his nose, and barked loudly and plaintively about the eerie hush that had stifled his team.

"This ain't some kind of funeral, ya know! The season's not over, ladies. We're on in less than two hours. Don't even think about dragging your emotional bullshit or whatever it is on that field. You hear? If it's too much for you, and any of you pansies want to skip today and maybe go get your hair done, or pick out a prom dress, I'm paying."

His admonitory oration now complete, Murph exited quietly. They all just sat for a while, staring blankly at each other, with barely a word passing between them. Danvers was the first to stir. He got up off the bench, wrapped a towel around his waist, and walked over to check out Murph's plan for the day. He wasn't in front of the card more than a second or two when he exploded.

"Is he kidding me?" he roared. "Seventh? He dropped me to seventh?" With pride pulsing through his head, he screamed in violent protest, "How can he do this? Today, of all days, with Whitey Buzzo in the stands. It just figures. Two, maybe three times a year, the most notable scout for the big club comes down, and where am I? I'm in the goddamned seven hole. It's crap!"

Danvers's tirade diverted Lefty's attention from his work on his glove. The words *Whitey Buzzo* seemed to linger in a curious and uncanny manner, for the minute Danvers was out of sight, Lefty slipped away from his locker in search of Murph.

Thoughts of finally making it to the show filled the pitcher's head, leaving little room for anything else, including the agreement he had struck with McNally. This was no day for a "sore arm." Lefty found Murph in his office, at his desk slumped over behind a pile of equipment catalogs and old newspapers. His head rested neatly in his palms, with each of his fingers buried somewhere in the graying strands atop his head.

"What the hell is it, Rogers?" he said, barely looking up. "I'm real busy here."

"I, Murph," Lefty replied eagerly. "Actually, I think I may be able to help. Uh, my arm. I was just stretching it out—did some practice tosses. It feels pretty good. I think I can go."

Murph lifted his head and stopped what he was doing. "Listen, Rogers, if you're kiddin' me—"

"No, I mean it, Murph. I know the team is down. Hooper isn't ready to go against the Rangers. They'll chew him up and spit him out. Same with Winkler. But I got them. I can win today. Really, I'd like to help pick us up."

Murph looked at his watch. It was almost noon, one hour before game time. Not a season had passed where he had not fallen short of expectations, unable to pull something out of his bag of tricks. It always seemed he was a dollar short and a day late when it came to miracles on the diamond. Lefty's announcement lifted his spirits considerably. It was a bolt from the blue. The game wasn't do or die, but they needed a win badly. And Lefty Rogers gave them the best chance at that.

"Okay, Rogers. If you're sure you're up to it, I'll make the change. Now go get ready."

Lefty bristled with optimism. The situation could not have been any better. With Mickey injured, and the Brewers struggling for their postseason lives, the stage was set for fairy-tale heroics. The only hitch was McNally, who would probably crap himself once he saw him on the hill. But Lefty was certain that he could convince Mc-Nally that the one game was meaningless, particularly since the Brewers were spiraling out of control anyway. There was no way they could catch the Rangers—not the way things were going. What did it really matter? And with another good outing, he could very well be on the next train to Boston, sharing a locker room with good old number 21, and all of the minor league drama would become just a fading memory.

The day was perfect. Warm sunlight; temperate breezes; a stadium filled with growing expectation. And of course, there was the thought of Whitey Buzzo, sitting somewhere in the ballpark with a pen and clipboard. Yes, it was surely perfect. But Lefty was right about McNally. The minute Rogers came out of the dugout and stepped across the chalk line onto the grass to begin his warm-up tosses, the opposing manger lost it. "What the hell is that stupid ass doing out there?" he whispered to one of his coaches. "He's supposed to be on the shelf."

McNally paced nervously. His concern was not the actual game as much as it was Quinton, who would certainly chastise him and make him responsible once he discovered the transgression. Just the thought of it burned his stomach.

McNally stepped out of the dugout like a frightened child and turned his head furtively in the direction of the stands, where Quinton usually sat. He had yet to arrive. McNally breathed a little easier, thankful for the momentary reprieve, but knew he didn't have much time to minimize the damage.

Once or twice he caught Lefty's eyes wandering from Boxcar's glove over to the Ranger dugout, and at least one of those times their eyes locked and McNally glared at him, grabbing his left arm and grimacing, only to be rebuked by the subtle shrugging of the pitcher's shoulders and the mouthed words *Sorry — game on.*

Lefty inhaled the blue sky and the carnival of expectation swirling in the stands. He scanned the crowd quickly, examining each man he thought could be Buzzo — someone middle-aged, with a gray suit, fedora, and of course that clipboard. But there were so many faces, and not nearly enough time to dissect each one.

Once on the rubber, Lefty narrowed his focus. It was all about the batter. In and out. Change speeds. Mix in the breaking ball. Location, location, location. He had all of it, right there, fresh in his mind. He went over the plan in his head one last time. Then he took a deep breath, licked his lips, and waited for the umpire's right arm to fall to his side, listening ever so carefully for the traditional call to arms, the familiar cry of "Play ball!"

His first pitch was a strike, up and in. The next also found the zone, this time on the outer half. Then, after wasting one in the dirt, he followed up with a seed on the inside corner for a called third strike. It was just the kind of start he had hoped for. He was sharp, popping Boxcar's glove harder than he had all year. He stood on the mound like a man possessed, his confidence soaring even higher as he set down the Rangers in order.

Quinton arrived just in time to see his third-place hitter whiff on three straight curveballs. He never touched his seat — just stormed down to just outside the Ranger dugout.

"McNally, get your ass over here," he ordered through clenched teeth. "What the hell is going on?"

"I don't know, sir," he answered blankly.

"You told me, in very certain terms, not to worry. Remember? That he was under control. 'Sore arm,' remember?"

"I know, I know."

"Well, what the hell?"

"I said I don't know. Hell, I'm just as surprised as you are."

Quinton and McNally continued to volley concerns, the owner gesticulating wildly with each objection he fired. He was hot across his neck and chest. McNally's cavalier attitude unhinged what little patience Quinton had left.

"You listen here, McNally, goddammit. We will talk about this after the game, regardless of the outcome. This is outlandish. Who does this guy think he is, anyway? Something needs to be done. And I mean *now*. I do not take kindly to being made a fool of."

The thought of Quinton's retribution unnerved McNally, climbed up his spine and settled like a swelling at the base of his skull. "Of course, sir. We'll meet right after the game."

During the game, Mickey and Matheson shared the end of the bench, exchanging words that no one else cared to hear. Mickey was the only who would sit next to Matheson, for he was the only one able to block out the relentless prattle. Today was no different. The boy was swimming, lost in a flurry of varied thoughts that glazed his eyes, while the elderly coach's glib discourse revealed the ill effects of his dotage.

"Water don't run uphill, kid," he said, staring blankly out at the sun-drenched diamond. "Know what I mean?"

Mickey sat idly, unresponsive.

"Yup, married me a pretty little filly years ago, on a day just like this. Sun shining. Sweet smell of honeysuckle in the air. Married her right on the ball field. Imagine? Right there. Married at twelve noon and then played a twin bill right after that. Won both ends too. God, she was pretty. Those were some mighty good days." Matheson paused momentarily, shaking his head with burgeoning sadness. "You know, it's true what they say, kid. You never miss the water till the well runs dry."

Mickey's head was still swimming.

"Bah, these young Turks can't tell their ass from a hole in the ground. "Look at 'em. They don't know what it takes to be *real* ballplayers. My uncle—now, there was a ballplayer. And a man. Yes, sir."

Mickey reached for a baseball and began picking at the stitches.

The sententious old coot rolled his eyes skyward, then furrowed his brow, as though he had forgotten where he was. "Did I tell you how pretty my girl was? Yup. She was a beauty. Aw, but everything's changed. These guys don't know nothing. It's a goddamned country club. My uncle could build a shed in just two hours. Two hours. Can you imagine that? That was a man. Remember, kid. And never forget. You reap what you sow, and what goes up sure as hell comes right back down."

Mickey dropped the ball and then busied himself with the dirt in his cleats, seemingly impervious to Matheson's delirium.

"Hey, boy," the coach complained, jolting Mickey from his stupor with an unsympathetic hand on the shoulder. "You hearing me?"

"You know, we got a donkey fenced up right next to a big lilac bush," Mickey said, looking up at Matheson while swatting at a ring of swirling mosquitoes. "We call him Homer."

"What on earth—"

"Homer likes the smell. He sure does."

Matheson leaned back, his confusion yielding to yet another of his desultory thoughts. "Homer, huh?" he reminisced. "Used to play with a fella from Oklahoma. Name was Homer Reddington. Kid could hit the fastball a country mile. Never seen anything like it. But the son of a bitch couldn't touch Uncle Charlie. Yeah, he didn't last very long."

Mickey was bemused. "Did your uncle Charlie play ball too, Coach?"

"Did *who* do *what?*" Matheson fired back. "Damn, boy, you really did just fall off the turnip truck. Uncle Charlie ain't my uncle. His name was Fred. Uncle Charlie's what we here call a curveball. You know. Yellow hammer. Hook. Bender. Yacker."

"I don't know nothing about hitting no curveball," Mickey said. "Mickey can chop wood pretty good though. When my daddy lets me."

"How's that?"

"Mickey's gotta ask to use tools. On account of me being slow. If I don't ask, I could catch a pretty good whupping."

Matheson listened as Mickey detailed how Clarence had tied

Mickey's hands behind his back with chicken wire until they bled the last time Mickey touched Clarence's ball-peen hammer without permission.

"How is that big paw of yours anyway?" Matheson asked, frowning in the direction of Mickey's right hand. "You almost ready, son?"

Mickey flexed the hand, curling his fingers into a fist as if to test the veracity of Matheson's idea. "Mickey reckons it should be good soon," he said resolutely. "Yeah, good soon."

The game unfolded in the Brewers' favor. After four innings, Murph's team had a 2–0 lead courtesy of back-to-back jacks off the bats of Finster and Boxcar. Murph couldn't help but smile, his first in days. He was thrilled by his team's sharp play, and by the way they had responded to his little reprimand in the locker room. He was so moved by the collective effort that he even felt a twinge of respect for Lefty, a seed of esteem that grew steadily that day until he heard Lefty spouting off in between innings.

Lefty believed, from the first pitch, that he would be able to conceal his selfish motives behind the admirable façade of teamwork and impassioned competition. He had done a pretty good job through the first part of the game, duping the guys into believing he had sacrificed his health to help the team avoid falling any further behind the Rangers. But his eye was forever in the stands, searching for the one man who was his ticket to the big time. He had yet to see him or hear of his whereabouts. The frustration of not knowing if the risk he had taken was worth it finally mastered him.

"Has anyone seen Whitey Buzzo?" he asked, pacing up and down the bench. "Buzzo? You know, the Braves' head scout? Wasn't he supposed to be here today?"

Everyone in the dugout just stopped and stared, eyes wide and appraising, as if someone had just thrown a light switch. So much for selflessness and team dedication. In this new light, Lefty's popularity waned. The ugliness was out there. It tossed about in the clear brightness of the changing air associated with early September, air that whispered the steady approach of fall, air that brought with it undercurrents of summer's longings and disappointments, as well as hints of new beginnings and fresh starts. It was the kind of air that pinched your cheeks and filled your lungs, malaise-awakening, senses-sharpening air.

"Does Buzzo's rumored appearance today have anything to do with your miraculous recovery?" Murph asked, walking over to Lefty with grim expectation.

There was suddenly something odd in Lefty's face. He just stood there with vacant eyes.

"Unbelievable," Murph said, shaking his head. Then, standing beside Lefty in the thick gloom that had once again befallen them, Murph surrendered, threw up his hands, and walked away.

"What?" Lefty called after him. "I don't get it."

Everyone stopped what they were doing. Conversations ended. Warm-ups ceased. Even the on-deck batter stepped out of the circle and stopped his pre-at-bat ritual. It was eerie, as if a cone of silence had been dropped across the entire scene, freezing everything for the moment. There was nothing but silent stares.

Lefty cowered a bit under the painful glare of all the others. "What's the big deal?" he called after Murph, who had just about disappeared from sight. "I mean, who cares? We're winning, ain't we?"

The next inning began with Danvers booting a routine grounder. That was followed by a blooper off the tip of Pee Wee's glove and a tailor-made double-play ball to Finster that slipped through the wickets into right field, loading the bases with nobody out. It was the ugliest baseball they had played in quite some time. Lefty just closed his eyes and hung his head.

The disparity in their play from the first four innings to the present was surreal. Each labored at his position, as if a wave of disillusionment had washed over them, carrying away with it all the energy, spirit, and momentum that had taken so long to muster.

Then the all-too-familiar pattern emerged. Lefty started to come undone, squirming and straining under the cloud of misplays. He glared at all of them with contemptuous eyes, as if they had all conspired against him in some twisted, elaborate plan. He was out-raged, and as was usually the case, he lost his focus.

He walked the next batter on four straight pitches, forcing in a run. The next batter took a grooved fastball and lined it to left, plat-ing two more Rangers. Lefty unraveled. No matter how hard he grit his teeth, the onslaught just kept coming, including four more sin-gles, two walks, a hit batsman, another error, two stand-up triples, a ground-rule double, and two gopher balls. The entire ballpark was stunned, like a punch-drunk boxer. In just minutes, the Brewers were looking at a seventeen-run deficit.

Lefty was inconsolable, like a fretful, half-soothed child at bed-time. After each individual assault, he took the ball back and looked into the dugout at Murph with souring eyes, waiting for the manager to yank him. It was no matter to Murph; he just let him go.

On the other side of the field, McNally laughed sardonically. It was sweet justice; the proverbial two birds with one stone. His team had further reduced the play-off chances of his archrival's squad, and Lefty, whose overt disrespect and blatant lie had alienated Quinton, had shown his true hand for nothing. Things were looking good. McNally was sure that Quinton would go much easier on him now that it looked as though the Rangers would cruise to the pennant.

The Rangers tacked on five more runs before Murph finally de-cided that Lefty had had enough. Murph lingered on the top step of the dugout for a minute, motioned to Boxcar to meet him at the mound, then called time and stepped out onto the field. It was one of those long, dreadful walks, a painful jaunt through a firestorm of boos and second guesses. He knew how bad it looked. Nobody except the team would understand. God, he hated losing to McNally— especially this way. And the thought of being raked over the coals by the sportswriters and fans didn't sit too well either. But sometimes things order themselves by importance. Lefty Rogers was out of con-trol and needed to be taught a lesson. And it just could not wait.

"What the hell are you thinking, Murph?" Lefty complained. He was angry, ashamed, humiliated, and for the first time in a long time, he felt the full ignominy of personal failure. "Did you not see what the hell was going on out here? Jesus Christ, are you trying to ruin me or something?"

Murph and Boxcar shared a silent exchange. It was good, Murph thought, to have him out there. His fiery countenance fueled Murph's resolve.

"Give me the goddamned ball, Rogers," he told him. "We've all seen enough."

"Take your friggin' ball. What a goddamned disgrace, I tell you. Your whole team threw this game. Rolled over and took it up the tailpipe. And what did you do? Big, tough manager with the dime-a-dozen minor-league sob story? Nothing. That's what. You just sat there on your fat ass and watched the whole thing happen. Pathetic."

Indignant, Lefty slammed the ball in Murph's palm. He was off to the showers, but before he could get far, Boxcar stepped in front of him. Lefty returned the fire in Boxcar's eyes and for a second felt as though he were onstage, and the curtain was coming down. The final act. Lights out. It was the beginning of the end or of something new, although of exactly what, Lefty was not sure. He looked long and hard into the stone face of the Brewers' field general with absolute loathing, something that activated the catcher's only words.

"Don't let me catch you in the locker room after the game."

Quinton's office was lit like the town's fair, sparkling in the afterglow of victory. It looked as though the Rangers were going to cruise to the pennant and their first postseason berth in years.

"Not a bad day," McNally said.

Quinton raised his eyebrows and smiled wickedly in acknowledgment with great satisfaction and a tinge of camaraderie. "Not bad?" He laughed. "I'd say things worked out masterfully." He paused, smitten with the pleasure engendered by his successful machinations. "But, alas, there's still work to be done."

"What do you mean?"

"It's time to drop the hammer."

"What?"

"Jesus, McNally. Do I have to spell out everything for you?" Quinton stared curiously at the picture of Shoeless Joe hanging over the fireplace. "The seed was planted and we got what we wanted. Now it's time to get out before we get burned. And what better way to do it than to have that ungrateful little bastard Rogers take the fall. He's practically asking for it. It's genius."

"What are you saying? Are you going to turn him in?"

"Well, I believe it is our civic duty to do the right thing," Quinton said, smiling. "I mean, assault is a serious offense. It should not be taken lightly. I think the sheriff would be most appreciative if we helped him bring his investigation to a close."

"But won't Lefty—"

"He has no proof. It would be mere hearsay. His word against ours. Besides, his fingerprints are all over this thing."

McNally stood rocking a little, side to side, his hands shoved deep into his pockets. He was alert, intent, his breath faint so as not to interfere with his understanding of Quinton's plan.

"What don't you get, McNally?" Quinton asked almost belligerently. "It's pretty black-and-white."

"Are you sure this whole thing won't backfire on us?"

"Come on, use your head a minute." Quinton scowled. "The retarded boy wonder will be coming back soon. So, with Lefty in the can, at least for that duration, their pitching will still be short. It's a brilliant plan. Absolutely flawless." He paused momentarily and stroked the stubble on his chin. "But, I guess you do have a point here. Maybe, just to satisfy your anxiety, we can wait a little while."

McNally was breathing harder now. Aware of this, he tried desperately to convince himself that it was excitement and grand expectation, not fear or guilt or uncertainty. The culmination of months of planning had all at once risen up and presented itself like a peeled onion, each layer thicker and more acerbic than the one before. He had some unexpected difficulty facing it. At a loss for what to do, he shut his eyes and just stood there quietly.

Outside, it was dark, except for a blurred glow from stadium lights that had yet to be cut. Murph was tired, and his mind worked in random rumination. He stood before his team, eyes fixed on their fallen faces, needing to say something but unable to formulate the appropriate words. He had asked them all back—a team meeting he called it—an eleventh-hour attempt at rallying the troops before the final countdown. Naturally, his chief concern was his own immediate future. Where would he go? What would he do? Baseball was in his blood; it's all he really knew. The thought of existing outside the game frightened him like nothing else.

Then there were his players. So many, such as Boxcar and Pee Wee, who just poured their hearts and souls into the team and wanted nothing more than to raise a championship flag high above Borchert Field. It had been a season filled with such excitement and promise—a once-in-a-lifetime opportunity that just turned on a dime. It seemed like another life, another world.

And what about Mickey? It had been too long. He had hoped beyond hope that it would all have a happy ending. That the boy would come back and still be able to pitch. He had said it so many times, to everyone, that he himself had begun to believe it. But now even he feared the worst. It was awful. He hadn't even begun to think of how he would tell Molly if the kid was washed up with them.

"Uh, I called you all here tonight so that we could talk about some things," he finally said. "But I'll be perfectly honest with you guys—I'm sort of at a loss as to what to say."

"It's okay, Murph," Boxcar said, trying to mitigate the manager's turmoil. "We all understand."

For a minute, it was difficult to swallow, and Murph's eyes welled with water. Then he composed himself, and his soul's passion directed his words.

BAKER'S WOODS

Nine miles off the road, just beyond a low ridge of hemlocks, and across thickets littered with tumbled conifers, stood a small, dilapidated cabin, an abandoned shanty with weathered wood shingles and a rusty tin roof. With its partially boarded windows and a front door that was locked crudely from the outside by an iron spike angled just below the knob, it resembled more of a prison than a country dwelling.

It was Pee Wee's getaway—in the heart of the tangled mess all the locals called Baker's Woods—the place he went to fish during the off-season and when the busy schedule permitted. It was the first place he thought of when Murph suggested to him that he organize some sort of "bonding activity" to help everyone relax while at the same time get to know Mickey a little better.

"Just throw him together with a few of the fellas," Murph suggested. "Shoot the bull for a while. We need this now. It's our only shot. Once they get to know him like we do, they'll understand. They'll feel better, and he will too."

Through those partially boarded windows slanted rays of light fell across a dusty floor and over a group of wet, hungry guys sitting on wooden crates as they bantered about the day's events. The place was a shambles. The windows were cracked and clouded, the broken sills filmed with a greenish soot. Flaps of splintered wood and viscous cobwebs hung loosely from the sagging ceiling. Walls that had been erected with little attention to the basic laws of geometry and physics now signaled a slow, steady protest.

"This place is a dump, McGinty," Danvers complained. "This is the best you could do for us?"

Pee Wee shrugged. "It ain't the Taj Mahal, pretty boy, but the fishing sure is sweet."

"Yeah, not bad for only a few hours of casting," Finster commented, looking at the score of fish dangling from a string in Pee Wee's hand. "Too bad you can't hit as good."

Danvers finally laughed. "We all did pretty good. Enough to have us a good old-fashioned cookout."

The three men surveyed the room with jocularity until their eyes fell on Mickey, who had failed to even get a nibble. He was just sitting there, sullen. He appeared so distant, so far away, that Pee Wee was tempted to view him through the binoculars he wore around his neck. Pee Wee shuffled his feet nervously as he watched the spirited mood he had tried to engender begin to wane.

"Jesus, Mickey," he said, laughing, trying desperately to infuse some levity into the room. "How is it that you grew up on a farm, with a father who's a fisherman, and you do not know a blessed thing about fishing?"

Finster and Danvers sat quietly with their faces wrinkled, frozen in bemused amazement. They had grown to tolerate their most unusual teammate, but still found him odd and for the most part unapproachable.

"I reckon Mickey fished no more than a couple of times," the boy replied. "Couple, two or three."

"How is that possible?" Pee Wee persisted. "You told me your pa was always fishing in back of your place."

Mickey just stared at all of them blankly. "I kept getting my hook caught on the bushes, sometimes in the trees. I tried, but Mickey just couldn't help it." He paused reflectively. A single tear formed in the corner of one of his eyes. "Last time was real bad. Real bad. Pa broke my fishing pole across my back and threw it into the water. Told me that a fishing hole ain't no place for a numskull."

Danvers, busy opening a can of chew, looked up at the boy. "So that's it? He says you can't fish no more, and that's it?"

Mickey frowned and sat rocking gently on his crate, staring at the little silver can in Danvers's hand. "It ain't no bother. Fish don't deserve to be treated that way anyhow."

"Why do you listen to something like that?" Danvers said. "Christ, if my daddy pulled that horse crap with me, I'd bust him one in the mouth."

Mickey blushed. His thoughts were suspended somewhere between Clarence and the little silver can in Danvers's hand.

"You want to try some?" Danvers asked, mindful of the boy's gaze. He pinched off a piece of tobacco and handed it to Mickey. The boy looked at it quizzically before sliding it into his mouth.

"It ain't that simple," Pee Wee interjected. "It's not like any other relationship you may know. Mickey's daddy ain't such a nice fella."

"That don't make no difference," Finster said. "You gotta look after yourself. Be a man. Maybe that's what we should be teaching our boy here."

Pee Wee looked at Mickey, who was packing the chew against his cheek awkwardly with his tongue.

"Well, Finny's got a point," Danvers agreed. "That certainly would have helped that night at the Bucket. If our boy here knew how to fight, then maybe we wouldn't be in the mess we're in right now."

"I don't think that would have mattered none," Pee Wee shot back. "You know that Woody. Ease up, will ya."

"I ain't saying nothing that ain't true," Danvers said with a glint of protest in his eye. "I just mean to say that a man—no matter what type of man he is—has gotta know how to defend himself."

"Against three guys?" Pee Wee lashed out. "Three of them? You're telling me you could handle *three* guys?"

Both Danvers and Finster rolled their eyes and slowly, quietly looked away.

"Tell 'em what happened that night, Mick," Pee Wee insisted. "Go on. Tell 'em. I want you to tell them everything you've told me."

For a while, Mickey said nothing—just sat languidly, arms folded against his chest. The skin across his face tightened, and his eyes, lit only by a few errant rods of sunlight that had infiltrated the dilapidated structure, darkened even further.

Twice he tried to speak but failed. The air seemed to thicken. He sat uncomfortably, rocking and blinking his eyes, his right cheek now distended. Then he exhaled mightily and pushed out a few words.

"It were bad," he said timorously, struggling to keep the wad of chew in place.

They all watched as Mickey explained how it all had seemed so wonderful. A beautiful girl, caressing his back, kissing his face with soft, full lips, whispering wonderful things in his ear.

"You are just the cutest ballplayer I have ever seen, Mickey," she'd said. "Just adorable. Do *you* want to see how cute *I* am? Hmm? Or maybe you'd rather just feel for yourself."

It all happened so fast. She had told him that she wanted to take a walk with him, in the cool night air. They strolled for a while, hand in hand, eyes fastened to the full, glowing moon and the glinting constellations all around.

"Ever just sit, Mickey, and look up at the stars?"

He shook his head, too busy with the joy of her presence to answer.

"My mama, she and I would sit outside, on an old blanket sometimes, and just stare at the stars for hours," she said brokenly. "I used to be able to spot 'em all. Andromeda, Orion, the Big Dipper. I knew them all."

"Why?"

"Why? What do you mean why, silly? Because they're there."

"We never spent no time watching stars," he said absently. "I don't suppose my pa would like it very much."

Her body gave a nervous jerk. Through the chilly summer air, she heard a faint, faraway sound that quickly died.

"That's a shame, Mickey. My mama used to say that God's promises were like the stars—the darker the night, the brighter they shine. I think about that sometimes."

A mild buzzing was in his ears, something nervous and uncontrolled. He turned his head and swallowed hard. She looked as if she was going to cry. Face-to-face with an unannounced emotion, she had no words of any kind. She breathed in the night air and shook her head as if to rattle the troubled thoughts from her mind. Then she grabbed his arm and pulled him behind a service station.

"Enough with the stars. I think we would have more fun back here." Then she grabbed his other arm, slid her hand over his, and brought his fingers to her breast. It was soft, he thought, and he marveled at how the tiny nipple rose up beneath her shirt to welcome his advance. It was a glorious feeling, exciting and energizing, like electricity flowing under his skin. He wanted to touch her everywhere, with his hands and mouth, to explore the contours of her curvaceous frame with the reckless abandon surging through his body. It felt familiar to him, although he did not know why. He thought of his first hayride, and the first time he jumped into a stream without his clothes. He remembered the rush, the breathless flow of energy and the thumping of his heart.

Now, it was happening again. And this time, that feeling had traveled to other parts of his body as well. He smiled uncontrollably and was just about to take her other breast in his hand when the moon disappeared. One minute he was lost in the rapture of his first romantic interlude, and the next, he was holding his head, struggling to get up off the ground.

"So did you get any?" Finster asked as Mickey struggled through the memory. "You know, before you were clocked?"

"Get any what?" Mickey asked quizzically. Then he swallowed hard, his face exploding into a full-scale grimace.

They all smiled. "You're supposed to spit the juice *out*, Mick," Pee Wee reminded him. Danvers and Finster laughed. They watched like patrons at some vaudeville act as Mickey crumbled to his knees and grunted, enveloped in a wave of dry heaves.

"Christ!" Finster howled, slapping his knee with perverse delight. "The boy's gonna blow!" The laughter rose slowly to the surface like tiny bubbles before building to a raucous crescendo.

"Go get it, big fella!" Danvers roared. "Let it all out, brother! It's okay! It's all part of the baptism!"

The whimsical moment lifted the tension, preoccupying their thoughts for a while until they all just sat around effortlessly bantering with Mickey.

"What'd they hit you with anyway?" Danvers asked.

Mickey shrugged and held his stomach gingerly, still feeling the effects of the violent outburst only moments before. "I don't reckon I know," he finally said, moving his hand to his head and rubbing it as if the injury had just occurred. "But it sure did hurt."

They all laughed again. Something pure and simple and likable about the boy could not be denied. Mickey was pleased that they were laughing and joined in before continuing his sordid tale.

His head ached and his nerves were frayed. He sat on his crate with an occasional birdsong and the approaching night wind for accompaniment, sunk in the dark recollection.

"She smelled good." His lids fluttered wildly. "But Mickey never made sex before. I was scared."

Danvers looked at Finster and smiled. The two of them shook their heads in glorious astonishment.

"Yeah, the first experience with the fairer sex is an amazing moment," Pee Wee reminisced. "I still remember mine."

"Of course you do, McGinty, you little turd pie." Danvers laughed. "It was only just last week." He spit out some tobacco juice while the others roared with approval. "But then again, I'm not sure if your mama really counts."

Mickey was dizzy with happiness over his true involvement in the banter. "Mickey doesn't know many girls," he continued. "But I know Laney. She really smelled good."

"How do you like that?" Finster mused. "That's awesome. Our little boy's growing up, guys. Sounds to me like our young friend here just may have had a chubby in his pants."

Mickey spoke about the stars that night and about the sweet air, and went carefully through the pantomime of the moment, slowly, methodically, as if his audience required meticulous, laborious repetition to grasp what he was trying to impart. "So I get knocked here, right in the head." He simulated what he believed the blow must have looked like. "Then while I was getting up, another guy kicked me in the gut, and then someone else stomped on my hand. Then the sheriff was driving me to the ballpark. That's all I really remember."

"What about that girl, Mick?" Finster asked. "You ever see her again?"

"Nope," Mickey said, checking the buttons on the front of his shirt. "But I think she really liked me."

Danvers tapped the little silver can with his finger and stuffed a wad of chew inside his cheek. "Of course she did, big fella," he said, his eyes noticeably softer. "Of course she did. What's not to like?"

MILWAUKEE—SEPTEMBER

In the still of the early-morning air, news of Mickey's imminent return to the Brewers' lineup spread around town like a wave of ground fog filtering through a sleepy valley, fueled by the improbable headline in the *Daily Gazette:* "Baby Bazooka Close to Return; Rogers Held for Questioning." As the sun climbed higher and became a small fire lodged high and bright in between gathering clouds, people everywhere were unfolding their newspapers and gasping at the sudden turn of events that had breathed life into a dying dream.

For Murph and the Brewers, the elation over the startling announcement was energizing but a bit premature. Mickey would not be "game ready" for a little while. However, when the players heard the news being bandied about, many of them spoke of karma, and how those printed words just hours before could, quite possibly, trigger some sort of self-fulfilling prophecy or enlist some sort of divine intervention.

"You know, I think somehow Murph knew, that son of a gun," Boxcar said to Matheson. "He must have just known somehow. That it wasn't over. And now I feel it too. It's bigger than all of us. We're gonna make it. Somehow, we're gonna make it."

Matheson chuckled and scratched his chin. "Well, you know what they say, Raymond. God gives us a little garden in which to walk, but an immensity in which to dream."

Boxcar smiled, marveling at how the old man had actually become a parody of himself. "Who exactly is *they*?" he asked, tongue in cheek.

The others heard Boxcar's prognostication and sensed it too. They felt oddly outside of themselves, as if some higher power were moving them inexorably along, like chess pieces, toward some magical prize. Naturally, the loathing they felt toward Lefty was real and difficult to corral. Word was out that George "Lefty" Rogers had had a hand in the vicious attack on Mickey and that the police were building quite a compelling case against the suspended pitcher. The revelation was devastating, but they managed to set it aside and look to their unfinished business.

It was not as though they felt Mickey would be some sort of panacea. They had all been around too long to believe that, and each understood that the young gun was still not ready to jump back in. The doctor told Murph that it could still be as long as two weeks. But somehow just having him close had them all juiced.

The clubhouse was quite a scene, something right out of a Frank Capra film. Only a few days ago their backs were against the wall, and they were staring into the fires of ignominious defeat. Now, seemingly every opportunity had been given back to them.

In other places, however, the feel-good story generated little more than obligatory acknowledgment. Quinton and McNally found all the hoopla a tad overbearing and uproariously humorous.

"Do you know who that was?" Quinton asked McNally, placing the receiver of the telephone down gently. "Sheriff Rosco. He wanted to thank me for my help with the investigation." Quinton's modest grin broke into a full-blown nefarious smile. He looked over his shoulder at the picture of Shoeless Joe, some indefinable feeling of invincibility coming over him. "He also wanted to tell me that all of Rogers's accusations against me and the team are being dismissed as unfounded," he continued, rolling his cigar from one side of his mouth to the other.

A wave of calm passed between them. It felt like standing on the railroad tracks with the train coming—lights flashing, whistle blowing—and having nowhere to go. And just when the train is close enough so that you can feel its power and smell its smoky breath, the railroad operator engages the switch and sends the locomotive speeding off in a different direction. The ecstasy of relief is intoxicating.

"Do you know what the rest of 'em are saying?" McNally said, laughing. "I mean their team? They're actually talking like they have a chance now. After all this. Can you believe it? It's sad. Really pathetic. Even if the missing link comes back in time for half of the games and plays well, it would still take a miracle for them to even get close to us."

Quinton's lips tightened around his cigar. "That's quite all right. Let them go on believing that. They pose no threat. The minute they lose their next game, they'll realize that all of this pomp and circumstance was meaningless. Let them talk. But do not engage them. I want to keep them focused on themselves rather than us. And once they've worked themselves up into this fairy-tale frenzy, the final defeat will be that much more painful for them—and that much sweeter for us."

"I'd say it's pretty damn sweet already," McNally boasted. "The view from the penthouse is a hell of a lot better than the one we may have had if it weren't for our self-absorbed, hotheaded friend."

Quinton agreed, then held up his ceramic pencil case in mock invocation. "Well then, here's to Mr. Rogers," he toasted. "May his mattress be firm, his cockroaches friendly, and his bread and water clean and plentiful."

"And to Ms. Laney Juris," McNally added, "and the other unknown source who fingered our careless friend."

A prison cell is no place for a ballplayer. Baseball players are built for life under a vast, blue ceiling, with clouds for company and warming bolts of sunshine to light their way. They are made for the great outdoors, creatures of the fresh green earth, delighting in the redolence of newly cut grass, wet unslacked lime, leather, and pine tar. They are designed to run and throw and move freely, like willful stars in a galaxy, their energies and aspirations gliding in some sort of cosmic, celestial dance. That is why for George Rogers, gifted south-paw for the Milwaukee Brewers, four stone walls and cold, iron bars were an all-out assault.

With the moon bright on the outside window and slanted shadows that stretched across the concrete floor mocking his restlessness, Lefty sat on the edge of his rickety mattress, springs squealing plain-tively each time he moved. His chin was in his hands and his elbows rested uncomfortably on his knees as he lamented the wicked twist his fortunes had taken. The last thing he recalled with any clarity was sitting at the Bucket, his sorrows soaking in a bottle of Jack Daniel's. Then Sheriff Rosco and his deputy had their hands all over him, and with barely a warning, he was facedown, kissing the dirty floor.

"Let's go hotshot," Rosco mocked. "You're needed in the pen."

They dragged him out, hands pinioned behind his back. It was humiliating. A star of his magnitude, being yanked away in front of scores of eyes, two of which he recognized immediately; eyes that did not want to look but could not turn away; eyes that were green in sunken cheeks. Laney's eyes. They were eyes that held a story that needed to be told but could not be, a story of hurt and broken prom-ises, one of regret and recrimination.

Once at the station, Lefty sobered up and sulked, all of his indis-cretions and their consequences resonating in his head like falling timber in a gloomy forest. A thrumming began in his chest as he digested Rosco's biting words:

"Seems like you're in it up to your neck, Rogers."

"That's crap," Lefty replied. "I don't know what the hell you're talking about."

"Is that right? Tell me more."

In the dankness of a tiny, malodorous holding cell, Lefty spoke freely, his focus narrow. He had always been a creature of the mo-ment. A one-strike-at-a-time kind of guy. It was always all about him. He saw everything only in terms of how it impacted him, at that very point in time. His insufferable self-absorption had rendered him a victim of a kind of egomaniacal myopia, a deficiency that left him open to the predatory ways of others.

"They came to me, told me they needed help getting Mickey out of the way. I told them to take a walk. Hell, he's my teammate."

"Is that right?"

"Sure, that's all I know."

"And who's *they*?"

"Coach McNally, of the Rangers. And some other stuffed shirt. I think he is the owner."

The sheriff turned his head away, looking at nothing, thinking of nothing, save the course of the present interrogation. With one hand on his head, and the other awkwardly at his hip, he resumed his questioning.

"And exactly why did they want him removed?"

"Because he was winning. Why else? He was getting our squad all sorts of attention. The Rangers were second fiddle. You can see why they would want him gone, can't you?"

"I don't know, Mr. Rogers. That's why I'm asking."

"Well, why aren't *they* here? Why aren't you asking them anything?"

Rosco chewed on the butt of his unlit cigar. "I got nothing that says they were part of it. And the motive is thin. Lots of guys in the league play well. They're never attacked. It ain't like it's open season on baseball players. Besides, there are no witnesses. No one saw what you have described. For all I know, you're just blowing a whole lot of smoke."

"Look, I am telling you *they* are the ones who came to *me*! You got nothing on me."

Rosco had the sense to let him go for a while. He sat back in his chair, rolling his cigar in between his teeth, his left hand busy it seemed with repairs to his shirt. "Interesting," he continued, fingering the tiny lint balls attached to his shirtsleeve. "I seem to have a different version of the story. I got me a teammate of yours who can link a certain young lady to you. And that young lady, while she defended you as best she could, hung you out to dry, my friend."

Lefty scoffed. "So what? It's their word against mine. Right? Like you said, no witnesses. Who's to say how it really happened?"

Rosco, struck by the smugness of the statement, reached into a cardboard box resting by his feet. "Ever seen this before?"

"Can't say that I have. Looks like a regular baseball glove, but I ain't never seen it before."

"We found it in your locker. Along with some other personal items. And, as luck would have it, they all belong to Mickey."

Lefty straightened up and pounded his fist on the table in front of him. "That's impossible. I never seen any of that stuff before. Can't you see what's happening here? It's a setup, I tell you. I had nothing to do with what happened to Mickey. You got the wrong guy here."

Lefty sat there resting, almost blank-minded, except for an involuntary picture of McNally that formed in his mind's eye. He was slowly realizing that he had been played.

"That's rather curious, because a Miss Laney Juris, your girlfriend, seems to think otherwise."

"Girlfriend? This is bullshit. I'm being set up here. I don't have a girlfriend."

Rosco laughed. "Well, not anymore I presume. I mean, hell, you can't have a girl grab you by the onions and squeeze and still call her sweetheart. Right? Come on now. What kind of guy would you be? But then again, you wouldn't care about that, now would you. Because you dumped her, right after you used her of course for your little plan. And, despite this twisted love she still has for you, she decided to get even."

Rosco placed his hand on Lefty's shoulder and leaned in real close, so that he could smell the pitcher's fear. "You were sloppy, Mr. Rogers. That was a mistake. A real mistake. Even a dope like you should be familiar with that old saying: 'Hell hath no fury like a woman scorned.' Is all this sounding about right?"

"She's a lying bitch," Lefty screamed. "Just some psycho boot licker that I poked once or twice. Now she won't leave me alone. She made up this fantastic story 'cause she wants a piece of me, on account of me telling her to hit the bricks."

Rosco stood up, stretched his arms, rolled his shoulders, and let out a raucous yawn.

"And I want to know which teammate of mine is in on this. It's that self-righteous bastard Miller, isn't it?"

Rosco put his finger to his lips, then spoke deliberately. "What it looks like here to me, Mr. Rogers, is that this here country boy blew into town and became a thorn in your side. Was cramping your style. He stole your thunder. So you and your girl, this poor, desperate waif from the other side of the tracks, cooked up this plan to get rid of him, clearing the way for you to be the hero. Almost worked too, except someone remembered she was your girl. Then your head got a little too big for your cap, you dumped your little lady friend, and she blew the whistle. Case closed. Now you could be looking at some hard time for aggravated assault."

Lefty sagged. At first, he refused to believe it was happening. It was not that he was a stranger to these harsh vicissitudes; he had had his share of misfortune of late—a sack of calamity he carried around with him wherever he went. But the dreamlike quality of the unfolding debacle was hard to grasp.

He moved now across the dirty prison floor to the window, in the direction of the plaintive wailing of a stray dog and the discordant melody of night creatures that seemed to linger in the oppressive air. Then he sat again and slumped, thinking for a second that this is what it must feel like to drown in the ocean. The waves just continue to swell and keep coming, taller and faster, and although you manage to dive under a few, they continue to roll over you, beat you down, until you stare hypnotically at the last, knowing that it's the final one, and coming bigger and stronger. But you don't move, can't move, because your spirit has been broken and you're tired of fighting, and because some small part of you, deep inside your soul, is relieved, almost elated, that the struggle is finally over.

THE RACE TIGHTENS

The Brewers played their next game under a bright moon, a glowing candle set in the soft sky.

Mickey was not available to pitch and wouldn't be for another few days, but his presence was definitely felt. All around the ballpark, signs and banners expressing love for the unlikely hero who had captured the fans' hearts rippled and waved in the cool night breeze. A restless energy had been excited by the likelihood of Mickey's returning to pitch for the Brew Crew during the stretch run. Everything just seemed better. The balls were whiter and the grass a more vibrant shade of green; the dirt felt softer, the crack of the bat was louder, the players' legs were lighter, and the air smelled sweeter. Even the hot dogs tasted better.

The players all sat cross-legged before the game, watching from the dugout as the exuberance of both children and adults spilled out of the stands and rolled across the field. It was magical, like a small child who for the first time discovers the flight of a butterfly or the trail of light left behind a shooting star.

"Would you just look at this place?" Pee Wee said, wide-eyed and breathless. "What a frenzy."

"That's good old-fashioned electricity," Finster said, swaying histrionically to the rhythmic cadence of the "Let's go Brew Crew" chant. "Can you feel the energy?"

"Amazing," Danvers marveled. "Just amazing."

Under that bright moon, and a coal black sky dotted here and there with glinting diamonds, the Brewers took the field dreamily. Despite having only started three games before in his brief career, Rube Winkler got the ball. He was not the best choice for such a weighty assignment. His chewed fingernails and sweaty forehead were clear indicators of his nervousness. He was the first to arrive at the ballpark and the last to walk onto the field, fettered to the dugout rail by a fear of failure.

"Come on now, Ruby," Matheson cajoled at the behest of Murph. "This is your night. Nice and easy now. Steady as she goes. Remember—little strokes fell great oaks."

Both Murph and Matheson had to practically throw Winkler out of the dugout. It was ugly. But once his feet hit the turf, it was as if all the energy in that stadium rose up from the ground and shot through his legs and into his arms and spread to the rest of his body too. As quickly as it had come, his fear was gone and he strutted around the mound with a quiet intensity.

With the raucous crowd shouting and clapping and stomping their feet, Winkler delivered the game's first pitch. It was a jam job, a two-seam heater that sawed the Bison batter's bat in two. The barrel went sailing down to Danvers at third, while the handle remained safely in the grip of the batter. He shook his hands as he walked back to the dugout, trying to drain the bee sting from his throbbing fingers. Then, with a new piece of lumber in hand, the Bisons' table setter prepared for Winkler's next delivery. This time, Winkler dropped a wicked yellow hammer right into the hitting zone, buckling the knees of the batter, who had been geared up for another fastball.

Boxcar pounded his glove in approval. "Attaboy, Ruby!" he yelled from behind the dish. "Way ahead now. Be smart."

Mickey sat stoically on the bench between Murph and Matheson. All he would be on this day was an observer, safely ensconced between the Brewer brain trust.

"Mickey sure would like to toss the ball around out there," he said with partially suppressed excitement. "Sounds fun out there, like the summer carnival my ma always takes me to every July."

Matheson groaned, his mouth sliding slightly to the side while his feet dangled helplessly beneath the bench. "This ain't no roadside cavalcade, young fella," he admonished. "No, sir. This here's Murph's livelihood. His life's blood. Ain't nothing carnival about that. Enough kids' stuff. You best heal yourself but fast and be ready to put your keister on the line when you're called."

Matheson's words ricocheted across the dugout and seemed to repeat themselves over and over to Murph, who sat with folded arms, his face still calm but his voice a pitch higher.

"Relax, Farley," Murph said, patting the old man's knee. "It's okay. He's excited. He just wants to play."

Winkler was excited too. An irrepressible grin exposed the joy he was feeling over his early command. He worked quickly, eager to maintain his rhythm. Before each batter even had time to get set, Winkler was in midstride, his arm arched back like a stretched bow, his toe pointing in the direction of his next shot.

He was cruising when the most feared of all the Bisons' hitters strode to the plate. Winkler postured and adjusted his cap. His first impulse was to retreat rather than face the music. But he fought valiantly against the surging anxiety. He drew a breath into his lungs and wiped his hands across his chest, which was rumbling like a volcano. He looked as if he could blow at any second. But then, somehow, the gases settled and the ball came out of his hand effortlessly. It traveled toward the batter true and strong, although its trajectory deviated some from that intended. Boxcar, who had been set up on the outside corner, about an inch from the dish, reached back over the plate to snag the ball as it sliced through the hitting zone, dead center. He would close his glove just as the ball arrived, but before that, the batter unfurled his bat and tagged the cardinal sin right on the screws, sending a low drive up the middle. It was most certainly a clean single to center. But Pee Wee had been shading the batter that way and got a great jump on the ball. With just two quick steps, he closed the gap between himself and the ball to almost nothing.

The velocity of the drive, however, was tough to gauge, and at the last second, realizing that he was going to come up a little short, the crafty shortstop lay out full, his body completely horizontal, and snared the ball on one hop just as it was going by. He sprang to his feet, cocked his arm, and fired a strike to Finster, nipping the runner on a bang-bang play at first. Winkler, realizing that Pee Wee had bailed him out, pumped his fist feverishly and pointed his finger at the shortstop in admiration. Then he retired the next two batters uneventfully.

Pee Wee's stellar play set the tone for the entire game. Every time one of them faltered, another was right there to pick him up. When both Danvers and Boxcar failed to knock in Pee Wee from third with less than two outs, Finster delivered a clutch two-out single that ignited a four-run inning. After Arky Fries made back-to-back errors in the top half of the fourth inning, creating a real jam for Winkler, the snakebitten pitcher reached back for a little something extra and fanned the next two batters to squelch the threat. Jimmy Llamas got into the act as well, turning in a circus catch at the base of the wall with the bags full of Bisons who had reached safely courtesy of a walk, a throwing miscue, and a hit batsman. The entire ballpark seemed to catch fire while watching Llamas fire his invisible six-shooters in the air as he jogged in toward the dugout. The scene that day was indeed magical; all logic and reason dissolved into brilliantly detailed fiction.

The remarkable Brewer victory, coupled with a late-inning loss by the Rangers to the lowly Mud Hens, had Dennison dreaming of future glory.

"You know, Arthur, I just may owe you a slight apology," he began.

"Why's that?" Murph questioned.

Dennison was seated behind his desk, hands folded neatly on a pile of old newspapers. "I believe that this farm boy of yours, the one I called a reclamation project some months ago, is some sort of a talisman. I hate to admit it, gosh darn it, but just the mere mention of his name and the whole yard becomes some sort of enchanted holy land, like something out of the *Arabian Nights*."

Moving soundlessly, he rose from his chair, walked to the window, and glanced out at the distant lights that glowed faintly in the thick night air like fireflies on a freshening breeze.

"We picked up a whole game tonight, Arthur," he continued, turning around to face Murph. "One full game. We're only two behind with nine left. And the last one, I'm sure I don't have to tell you, is just what we want—head-to-head against that pompous ass Quinton and his little bitch McNally. This is good. This is real good."

Murph was quiet. It was difficult for him to be totally receptive to Dennison's overture. The man was so erratic, so irascible, and too many things could go wrong in nine games that could spoil the premature celebration.

"Listen, Warren, I appreciate the sentiment," Murph began, "but we are still looking at an uphill battle. We are still shorthanded here. Our pitching is a huge question mark. I really don't want you to expect too much."

"Come on, Murphy, loosen up a little for Christ sakes. It ain't so bad. Winkler tossed a gem tonight. And you still have Sanders and Hooper. And, let us not forget our ace in the hole, returned to us by the baseball gods, just in time."

"We may not have Mickey at all, Warren. I told you that."

"I'm not asking you for miracles, Arthur. That was already done for us when the doctor said Mickey could be ready for the stretch. No, I'm not asking for anything miraculous here. All I'm asking is for you to keep us close enough, in striking distance, until Mickey returns."

Looking at Dennison, Arthur saw on his face a curious expression of tranquil pride. He hated these proclamations of Dennison's and stood there in hopeless agitation, his hands opening and closing below the frayed cuffs of his sweatshirt.

"Well, we'll do our best, certainly, but you've been around this game long enough to know that things happen, Warren. Bad hop. Dropped third strike. Blown call at home. Stuff happens, and there's no way of knowing or preventing it."

Dennison opened his eyes wider and stared at Murph. He smiled and gestured to the championship pictures on the walls all around as if to say, *Can't you just see us up there with the rest of them?*

"I will do my best, Warren. Really. I think we have a decent shot here. But no promises. I just can't do that."

Dennison sat back down, tucking his feet as far back under his chair as they would go. Arthur saw the owner in a stark, uncompromising light just as he had always been—unwavering and impossible to please.

"Just get us to that last game, with Mickey and a chance. Just a chance. That's all I want."

Realizing the improbability of that scene, Murph restrained himself and smiled at Dennison, as if he were impervious to the incessant badgering. However, his mind was elsewhere—on a field somewhere, wondering what the next two weeks held for all of them.

SEPTEMBER 9, 1948

In the early light of dawn, just as the sun hit the dew-laden tips of the vaulting evergreens off in the distance, lighting them up like splintered crystals, thoughts of Mickey, safe and on the mend, filled Molly's head. She breathed easier, with a tranquillity of spirit washing through her veins.

But as she tended to her morning chores, looking all around her with a critical eye, she felt again that same ineffable longing—a curious gnawing that reminded her of the illogical hunger she sometimes felt after having eaten heartily. Why had she never done anything about it? Or at least said something. Today, more than usual, it bothered her. Suddenly, she caught herself driven to some decisive action. The torment of years of silent surrender had now rendered her weak and vulnerable—had broken down her resolve, allowing her lofty visions to take full possession of her. Just knowing her boy was okay was no longer enough; she wanted to see him—to touch him. She thought for a second, before she shook the thought from her consciousness, that she felt the same way about Arthur too.

Her hunger was real. She had grown more than she had previously cared to recognize. Grown, just like the many rows of corn, seemingly tall and heavy overnight. She thought of the times and places and dreams she had cultivated in her mind, never thinking for a second that they would come to startling fruition, towering, insatiable visions that dwarfed even the tallest of those green-and-brown stalks.

Now she was a paradox, the wife of a small-town farmer saddled with the sensibility and imagination of someone far more cosmopolitan. She was sick with this contradiction. Could not stomach another day of quiet desperation, of doing Clarence's bidding instead of her own.

That morning, just as Clarence was setting out for the field with a sack full of chicken feed and a monkey wrench sticking out of the back of his overalls, she stopped him.

"What's eatin' at ya, woman," he barked, moving impatiently past her touch. "Ya look like somethin' the cat done drug in."

Molly winced a little, her face pale and extinguished. "I need to talk to you, Clarence. Now."

"A farm don't run on no talkin', little Miss Molly," he snapped back. "I done told ya plenty of times, woman, that I don't have no time fer such foolishness."

He made a sudden, deft attempt to pass by her, but she slid her feet across the floor ever so slightly, obstructing his path.

"I mean it this time, Clarence. I will not be silenced like some child."

On most occasions, a declarative statement of this sort would have resulted in a full-scale haranguing about honor, duty, and obedience. But for some odd reason, today Clarence was game.

"Okay now, missy," he relented. "I suppose I can listen fer a spell. Now what's got yer unmentionables all in an uproar?"

She stood uneasily in his shadow, her eyes welling up. "I want to see Mickey," she blurted, as if any delay would have suffocated the thought forever.

Clarence laughed. "Not this again, woman. I thought you said it were something important."

Frustration propelled more feelings to the surface. "And another thing. Seeing as we are talking and all, I like the clarinet. It's something that's mine. For me, Clarence. I want to start playing again. You know, around the house and all."

Clarence's face distorted. The mere mention of anything outside his pedestrian parameters caused it to assume a hideous, menacing presence.

"Woman, yer plum out of yer gourd, you know that? Where's all this malarkey comin' from? Ain't I done by you right? Don't I give ya everything ya need?"

She could not answer. She folded her arms, turned her back to him, and listened as his boots trampled over the floor, scraping toward the door. He was grumbling under his breath. Then, with tears in her eyes, and scarcely a thought of the fallout, she fired her final salvo.

"I'm going, Clarence, with or without you."

She remained still, her back to him, listening to the irregular cadence of his asthmatic breathing. He was now just as engrossed in the topic as she was and, with her peremptory tone, just as affected.

"You listen here, woman. I just about had enough of yer lip. Now you shut yer mouth and git yer apron on and start acting like a woman, or you just may feel me."

With her back still to him and her head slumped so that her chin rested softly against her chest, she cried quietly. He brought up a wad of phlegm from his throat with alarming force, spitting it into a tin can next to the counter. Then he struck a match on his heel, lit a cigar, and walked away.

"Going by yourself," he mocked, placing his hand on the doorknob, his laughter dying away slowly with every step he took until the closing of the door extinguished the sound for good.

With a little broken sob in her throat, Molly sat for a moment, weak and trembling. The strength that had risen up just minutes before was gone, escaped like air from an open balloon. The cycle of emotion was turning. She had spoken her mind, unburdened her heart, but there she still sat, miserable and alone.

Murph was home, eating breakfast and listening to the air hum with the sound of water moving through the pipes, when the phone rang. It was her.

"I didn't know what else to do," she sobbed, her words barely audible. "I just needed to talk."

"It's okay, Molly. I told you to call anytime." Murph felt that at any cost he had to keep her with him, had to allow her to see that she was not in the helpless situation she thought she was. "What happened, Molly? Did he hurt you?"

"No, he didn't hurt me. Not really."

"You know, you don't have to stay there. I know how you feel about doing what's proper, Molly. But for Christ sake, is it proper or good or right for you to suffer like you do?"

"I'll be okay, Arthur. I probably shouldn't have called. I just needed to talk to someone who would listen."

He *was* listening. And thinking. The cutting division between right and wrong, honest and dishonest, and honorable and the opposite had left little room for the unforeseen.

"You know, Molly, you could come here."

"What?"

"Here. You could come here. Visit Mickey. Stay as long as you like. Maybe some time away would put things in perspective a little."

"I can't, Arthur," she said, her voice small and fading. "It just wouldn't be right."

"I'm not suggesting anything like *that*, Molly. I just think that maybe you need a change of scenery. That's all."

For a while, all that was audible was the faint hum in both ends of the phone, until she broke the silence. "How's my boy?" she asked, diverting the discussion to a far more comfortable topic. "Is he still doing well?"

"Terrific. He's terrific. Doing fine. He should be back in the lineup in just a couple more days."

"Does he look okay, Arthur? Is he eating?"

"He's fine, Molly. Really. He's doing great. I'm telling you, if you were to come, you'd see that for yourself. And you'd feel a whole lot better."

She twirled the phone cord in circles, wrapping it around her fingers in tight coils that matched the ones squeezing her insides.

"What about you, Arthur? How are *you?*"

"Me? I'm okay I guess. Same as usual."

"How's the team doing? Are you still winning?"

"We're doing okay. Hanging in there. The guys have really missed Mickey, and you already know about George Rogers being let go. It's been a rough few weeks. No pitching. It's tough to win with no pitching. But I think we're back on course."

He said the words with only a hint of conviction, with no real attempt to mask his undeniable uncertainty. His whole life smelled of failure, and of the shame and restlessness that attaches itself to such failure over time. These collapses of promised success seemed to him to be frequent and numerous, and in no way limited to the baseball diamond. He could recall bitterly how difficult it had always been for him to cultivate relationships with women. Life as a baseball man was more often than not a barrier, something that did not lend itself to conventional, long-term affairs with the fairer sex. He often lamented over some of his missed opportunities and was even more embittered by the couple of relationships that actually did flower, only to wither beneath the oppressive demands of life as a professional athlete.

He was remembering clearly three women. One was the daughter of the wealthiest man in town. He was just twenty-one at the time, a young, wide-eyed stallion who had the baseball world on a string. He met her at a dinner party given by his mother. She was wearing a light blue, lacy cocktail dress, way too fancy for a house party. Her skin was perfect, a creamy white that just beckoned to be touched and caressed. He noticed her immediately—the angelic face, flowing hair, round breasts—but she paid him no mind, until her mother mentioned who he was and what everyone was saying about him. He suddenly found himself the object of her undivided attention.

"Do they really call you the next Ty Cobb?" she said, batting her lashes while tilting her head ever so slightly to the side.

"You know baseball?"

"I know enough."

They were together for several weeks. She attended all of his games, and they spent just about every evening with each other, attending various functions for her father and other prominent people who traveled in his circle. It appeared, to everyone who saw them, that they were destined for the altar. They were perfect. The budding superstar and the wealthy debutante. But then McNally ran him down in the outfield one afternoon and everything changed.

"It's nothing personal, Artie," she explained. "I just need someone who's a little more high profile."

Then there was the woman whom he met at the ballpark after one of the last games he played. She was a soft-spoken, petite beauty with a perceptible spark behind her blue eyes.

"Would you sign this baseball for my younger brother?" she asked, offering her hand to him as he exited from the back gate. He remembered thinking how tiny yet perfect her fingers were. Like angel's hands. He signed the ball and handed it to her, and she gave him her name and number. It all seemed good. They dated for a while. But that softness, the demure fragility that he found so goddamned appealing, belied some terrible longings she held on to. Over the time they were together, she became needy and demanding, almost despotic in her requests to have him by her side. He explained at every turn the demands of life as a baseball player, and that he was doing his best, but she would not entertain his words. He ended the romance after just two months.

The third woman, the most haunting of all, perhaps hurt him the worst. Samantha was everything he ever dreamed of. Blond hair, electric smile, hourglass curves, and a baseball fan besides. He was completely smitten. The love he felt for her was unlike any other he had ever experienced—it was intoxicatingly oppressive and uncompromising, way too intense for him. He felt almost paralyzed by her, suspended in her sweet smell and in constant thoughts of holding her so close that he could feel the blood running through her body. He knew it was unhealthy, this obsession, but he couldn't help himself. He was the moth, she the irresistible flame.

The only comfort came in his belief that she returned the feeling, until that night at the monthly church dance. He had been on the road with his team for two weeks. It was only his second trip as a manager. He had made every effort to limit his attention to just baseball, but somehow, thoughts of her burrowed into his resolve and he found himself dividing his thoughts between the field and sweet Samantha.

As they danced that night, he shared with her this feeling of desire that had plagued him for two solid weeks. She nodded and looked away. She was stiff in his arms, and sweating a little, smelling of powder or flowers and soft, young feminine mystique. He tried to engage the girl, but each time he pulled back slightly to look into her eyes, she buried her head in his chest.

Later that evening, he kissed her, with soft lips and gentle tongue—the way he always did. She accepted the kiss, but did not return the overture—just tolerated the intrusion, her mouth flat and uninvolved. Her aloofness filled him with a vague doom.

"What's wrong, Samantha? Is everything okay?"

She looked at him, finally, with vacant eyes. "Nothing is wrong, Arthur. Really."

He never forgot the way she looked at that moment, or the way she looked later that same night, the last time they made love. She told him to go to the bathroom while she got ready. It struck him as odd; he had seen her undress before, many times. He wanted to press her for an explanation. But he humored her instead and waited until she called to him.

When he came out, minutes later, she was lying on the bed, naked. It startled him. He saw only her beauty—was blinded by it. She had the most beautiful body he had ever seen. It was perfect in its size, curvature, and proportion, like a carefully crafted sculpture. He stood there, tingling with virulent arousal, unable to move or speak, his eyes fixed on her long, smooth legs and her perfectly round breasts, two creamy bags of luscious flesh, adorned with deep pink circles, full and hard. He remained at a distance for some time, drinking in her angelic pose, amazed that God could create such a perfect being, and even more astounded that of all the guys she could have had, she chose him.

He moved toward the bed in glorious anticipation, a noticeable swelling hot against his leg. She was even more breathtaking up close, and he could smell her scent, musky and strong. But then he saw her face, riddled with desperation, a pleading of sorts, as if she were suffering some unknown calamity. It stopped him cold. Her big, dark eyes were fixed on him as she lay there distantly, as if she had just given herself up to sacrifice. Her body was there for the taking, but the look behind her eyes arrested him—his blood ran cold and the swelling in his shorts withered.

"Samantha, are you sure you want to do this?"

She never did answer. She just lay there, her thoughts somewhere else.

Only after they were through did the cold shadow of doubt fall fully on him. They lay next to each other for many minutes, struggling beneath the suffocating weight of the silence, each wanting desperately to say something but unable to form the words. He could feel her warm body next to his. He wanted to reach over to her, with his hand or foot, just to feel some connection to her, but he did not; she was not there, and he knew it. So he lay there quietly, listening to her breathe until finally the words came to her, words that resonated in his ears like mortar shells.

"Arthur, I think we should talk."

He could remember nothing else about that year except the hunger, and the lonely meals in his room that did little to fill him. He was plagued by this emptiness, his inability to satisfy those incessant pangs no matter how hard he tried. He thought he could short-circuit the longing, cut it at its source by replacing it with something else. Baseball seemed like the logical choice. It's all he had, and so much went on every day. But it's hard to wrap your arms around a late-inning loss or the feeling you get after winding up on the short end of a barn burner. He felt that same sort of hunger now as he and Molly continued their telephone conversation.

"I have some wash to do, Arthur," Molly said, her voice soft and fading. "I should really go."

"Okay, Molly, I understand. Just think about what I said. I'll be in touch. It would be great for everyone if you would come."

He closed his eyes as a tendrilous anxiety squeezed him; it made him feel worse. In the darkness of his mind, everything seemed more menacing. When he opened his eyes again, he tried to focus on something concrete, but everything he stared at was marred by optical imperfections, as if each of the failures in his life had suddenly risen up and taken the form of tiny specks that floated now unmercifully in his field of vision. He blinked nervously, trying to expunge these painful reminders from his sight, but there was no denying them. All he could do was numb the pain.

He poured a glass of whiskey and gulped at it greedily. Standing by the window, gazing stupidly at the patches of dandelions invading his lawn, he realized how perishable all the moments of his life really were, and how as he aged, this life was now begging him to be lived.

MID-SEPTEMBER

The Brewers reeled off consecutive wins against the Colts and the Giants, but gained no ground, remaining two games back with just seven to play, as the Rangers took a pair from the Senators.

McNally was feeling pretty good about his team's chances. They were playing well, well enough to possibly run the table and capture the pennant regardless of what the Brewers did. But when a freak accident during practice took out his best pitcher for the rest of the season, McNally went straight to Quinton with a moonstruck idea.

"You still have that lawyer friend? You know, the one who helped you out a couple of years back?"

"What's on your mind, McNally?"

"Well, do you? Is he still around?"

"Bradley Winston? Sure. I mean, I still see him now and again. Actually, I just spoke to him last week. Our wives are getting together for some country-club thing. So what?"

McNally laughed. "What if, by chance, our friend Mr. George Rogers were to post bond—you know, if some munificent soul were to offer some financial assistance. Wouldn't that free him up for another team, perhaps one in need of some pitching down the stretch?"

"Rogers can't play, Chip, if he's awaiting trial."

"But what if he's *not* awaiting trial? What if he's acquitted on a technicality? You know, there were a few things that Rosco and his deputy did that could be construed as a little suspect. Nobody knows that better than us. I was just thinking how a shrewd lawyer could really work that, if he were inclined to do so."

Quinton said nothing, but his eyes flashed with the light of sudden possibility. He was stunned by McNally's suggestion, not because he thought his manager incapable of such chicanery, but because he himself had failed to see it first.

"You know, McNally," he finally said, biting the end off a cigar with some deliberation. "It's taken a little while, but I have to say, I'm really starting to like your style."

McNally arrived at the jailhouse early in the morning and was directed to an austere cell.

"This is my room," Lefty said to the coach from the shadows of the farthest corner. "Nice, right? Sorry I haven't had the time to write and thank you."

McNally caught sight of the cockroaches on the broken toilet seat and the dilapidated cot on which Lefty had been sleeping and knew he would have no problem selling the pitcher on his proposal.

"Listen, Ace, how would you like to get out of here—leave this place and come pitch for me?"

"Haven't I had to deal with enough of your bullshit already? Just how stupid do you think I am?"

McNally looked at him and laughed soundlessly. "Listen, I can understand you being upset and all, Lefty, but I—"

"Upset? I ought to tear your head off, you backstabbing piece of crap."

McNally felt he had to placate Lefty at any cost. The guy was desperate, sure, but McNally needed him more than Rogers knew. So he let him rant until Lefty finally tired, like a boxer who had just emptied his load in the first round of a title match. Then McNally took over again.

"Come on now, Lefty, we're your only real friends here. Wasn't us who turned you in. That was your own team that did that. It's terrible. Just terrible. I mean, we certainly could have. After all, you did break our agreement. Sore arm, remember? Anyway, that's not why I'm here. I think you're gonna like what I came here for. So I think, Mr. Rogers, that it would be in your best interest to control your anger and listen to what I have to say."

A thaw was in the air as the two men discussed the possibility of Mr. Winston taking on Lefty's case.

"Money talks, Lefty. We'll get you out today, on bail, and then Winston will begin working on some of the legal issues. He's good. He'll have you cleared of charges in a jiffy. And the best part about it, for you anyway, is that it won't cost you a goddamned dime—just a few innings." McNally sighed and then smiled. "Well, Ace, what do you say?"

Mickey returned to the lineup the same day Lefty was released to the Rangers. Both teams had not played in days because of torrential downpours that had flooded the entire region. The hiatus provided by Mother Nature helped both squads, for each could now send its best hurler to the mound for the next game.

The water was still pretty high in most of Borchert Field, but small parts it of were dry enough for practice. Murph divided up the guys. The infielders took the right-field line and played pepper; the outfielders worked on cutoff throws in the opposite corner; the pitchers, including Mickey, threw lightly from a makeshift mound just at the edge of the center-field grass.

"Did you hear about Rogers?" Murph asked Boxcar as they watched the pitchers loosening up.

"Yeah, Danvers just told me. Didn't take him long. Christ, Dennison just let him go a few days ago. Scumbag. He should feel right at home with the rest of them. Does Mickey know?"

"Don't think so," Murph said.

"Are you gonna tell him? I mean, before he finds out himself?"

"I really don't know. Seems to me that I should hold off as long as possible. Why upset him any more than he is already. Besides, I don't know how he'll ever understand it all anyway. I barely do.

Illegal search and seizure. Police brutality. It's all crap. The god-damned guy's guilty."

Each of them realized just how elementary their principles had always been. Right was right, and wrong just wrong. It always seemed simple. Logical. Now, facing the unspeakable human vileness that had touched all of them so profoundly, they were at a loss to make any sense of it. Ultimately, though, they let it go, realizing they had bigger issues directly at hand.

Once Mickey had loosened up enough, Murph marked off with his feet the proper distance, sixty feet six inches, and called Mickey over. With Mickey back, Murph was a new man. The churning of uncertainty that always settled in his stomach waned. His appetite returned and he was sleeping again. He even looked better. His eyes were focused, his ashen face was restored to a healthy rose, and he appeared to be standing straighter, his shoulders square and strong.

"Okay, Mick," he said, tossing a ball in his direction. "Let's see if ya still got it."

Boxcar squatted, and under waves of sunshine that had only just begun to sponge the puddled earth, Mickey tossed his first pitch in almost two months. The windup was still the same—that inimitable fist in the glove, followed by the rolling of the arms—but the delivery was off. Way off. The ball leaped from his hand and sailed a good two feet to the left of Boxcar's glove and splashed to a stop off to the side.

"Relax, Mick," Murph said assuredly, pulling out a new baseball from his jacket pocket. "The ball was probably wet. Try this one."

Mickey took the ball, wound up once more, and fired. The ball missed the mark again.

Murph tried to buffer the flutter of anxiety that was rising from deep within his gut. Mickey's eyes glazed over and he was mumbling incoherent thoughts adorned with rhyming couplets.

"Take it easy, big fella," Murph said, looking at Boxcar, his alarm now rampant. "Just try again."

Mickey continued to fire baseballs all over the place. His control had never been so erratic. Murph felt, as he watched the debacle unfold, a growing irritation that bordered on something far worse.

The grass behind Boxcar must have been littered with a dozen base-balls before Murph couldn't stand it anymore.

"Box, where's the other glove?" Murph screamed impatiently. "You know, the one we used last time?"

"Right here." Boxcar reached into his bag and pulled out the special glove, the one with the red paint in the pocket. He put it on his hand and pounded it hard, then squatted back down and set the target. Mickey smiled, recognizing the familiar sight.

The results, however, were no different. Mickey just could not find Boxcar's target. High, in the dirt, wide left, then right. He was all over the place. Murph sighed. His luck, he lamented silently, was curdling again. Time was waning, and he needed Mickey badly. His stomach burned, and he could barely breathe. He brought his fist to his chest and let out a belch, then motioned to Boxcar to stand up.

"This is not working," Murph complained. "We need to try something else."

Everything blurred before his eyes. He could not decide what to do. There would never again in his life be another moment like this—where every decision held the potential to either bathe him in champagne showers or lead him back to the pit of ignominy.

Boxcar saw Mickey sitting Indian-style on the damp grass a few feet away, the boy's thoughts miles away, and said, "Come on, Murph, this is unreal. I really don't know what to say. I'm sure it will be fine. But I have to say, I never saw someone have so much trouble tossing the old apple."

Murph took off his cap and wiped his brow. Suddenly, his eyes lit, as if someone had just thrown a switch. "What did you just say?"

"I just can't believe how much trouble he's having throwing."

"Yeah," Murph said with curious alacrity. "Trouble throwing the old apple."

Murph and Mickey left the park immediately. They walked quietly by a small brick schoolhouse and down past a defunct dairy farm, spotted here and there with weeping stacks of hay ravaged by blister beetles. Mickey wanted to stop, his gaze suspended somewhere beyond the chicken-wire boundary, but Murph trudged on, carrying with him an empty burlap sack, a piece of coal, and a half-baked idea of how he was going to fix Mickey's problem.

Mickey's eyes strayed though he followed Murph's every step. Just around the bend, past an irregular lake, was Blaney Grove, seventy acres of the best-tasting apples around. The grounds were pristine, a brilliant canvas of seasonal colors, the trees all nestled in perfect rows on a rolling, green lakeside slope.

Murph stopped momentarily and took a quick look all around. Then they hopped over the weather-beaten post-and-rail barrier and made their way across the grassy expanse, a pale green meadow littered here and there with random trees and some premature fruits of the season. They walked purposefully, Mickey stepping through some undergrowth, holding back branches and ducking his head, while Murph bent down now and again and loaded some of the damaged ground fruit into his sack, his eye ever watchful for the proprietor.

They walked quite a ways before this prairielike parcel finally gave way to some of the countless rows of pregnant trees. Where several of these rows intersected to form an empty triangular sector, Murph set down his sack and rested. "This is perfect," he said, smiling. "Just what the doctor ordered."

From the middle of the open space, he eyed one of the trees—a tall one with a large girth.

"Wait here, Mick," Murph instructed. He jogged over to the mammoth tree, removing some of the loose, fragmented bits of bark from the ancient trunk with his hands before pulling out the piece of coal from his pocket. Carefully, he fashioned a black circle, eighteen inches in diameter. When he finished, he cocked his head to the side slightly, observing his handiwork. He smiled. Then he placed his feet together and precisely marked off the distance back to Mickey—sixty feet six inches.

"Okay, big fella," he said with childlike exuberance, producing an apple from the sack. "Let's see if you can get this thing right in that circle over there."

Mickey nodded, although he was not quite certain what Murph meant. Confusion abounded in the slow lowering of his eyes.

"Come on, Mick," Murph prodded, mindful of the young man's hesitation. "Just like on the farm—back home. Pretend that circle over there is a big old barrel, lying on its side. Don't think about anything else. Just let it fly."

Mickey stood for a moment longer in the thickening afternoon, his eyes now glued to the primitive drawing some sixty feet away. The vision conjured by Murph's words roused a host of other associations. He fingered the apple in his hand nervously, the rest of his body paralyzed by the poignant reminiscence.

"It's okay, Mickey. Take your time. No rush. You can do this. I know you can. Come on, smash that apple, right in the circle. Oscar's hungry, and you know how he loves apples."

Mickey's face softened as if Murph had pulled a plug, releasing all of the uncertainty and angst, sending it rushing through Mickey's pores and extremities and into the ground. All at once the boy felt liberated. He brought the hand holding the apple into the other. Then, with the afternoon air heavy with the song of cicadas, he rolled his arms, reared back, and hurled the fruit at the tree.

The apple whizzed through the air like a meteor, a flash of red and green. Murph laughed out loud and pumped his fist in the air in relief when the apple hit the circle dead center, bursting into a thousand fragments that rained down like confetti all around the roots knotted at the tree's bottom. "Yee ha!" he screamed, arms stretched to the heavens in unbridled exultation. He was smiling harder than he had in months.

"Here, Mick," he said impatiently. "Try it again."

Mickey took another apple from Murph. He stood there, scratching the backs of his hands with his fingernails, pondering the meaning behind Murph's reaction, an explosion of emotion so powerful that it had now crossed over into his world. Buoyed, Mickey launched into his prepitch ritual and fired once more at the tree.

Splat.

The wormy fruit struck the tree in the exact same spot. Murph gushed with satisfaction, then emptied the sack and had Mickey throw again and again, just to make sure.

Splat. Splat. Splat.

It was the most melodious sound Murph had ever heard—the triumphant song of the bull's-eye. A million thoughts flooded his mind but never made it past his lips.

The sun had begun to dip below the distant treetops, bathing the orchard in oblongs of rich shadows. Short of declaring right then and there that Mickey was "back," there was absolutely nothing to say. They remained in the grove only a few more minutes, enjoying the cool beneath the tree's lowest bough, chatting in between sampling some of the orchard's offerings.

"Sure is pretty as a picture," Murph commented, then bit into the sweet flesh of a burgundy indulgence. "Nothing like good old country living, huh, Mick?"

"Uh-huh," he answered, his words garbled by cheeks distended with hunks of apple.

"I tell you what, Mick. You look good. Real good. I feel like you're ready. You know, for the games coming up? Nothing too crazy. Maybe a few innings to start. We'll play it by ear. What do ya say?"

Mickey heard the groaning of a passing freight train off in the distance, running heavy and slow, the laborious clatter of metal cars ringing, vacant and timeworn. He wondered what the train was carrying, where it was headed, and if, with its crawling speed, it would ever arrive at all.

"Mick? What do you say?"

"What do I say? What do you mean, Mr. Murphy?"

"Pitching. Tomorrow. Do you want to pitch for me tomorrow?"

The *clickety-clack* of the train's wheels grew distant, a fading echo that wheezed and gasped before finally dying in the cool air of late afternoon.

"Yup," Mickey said, his right arm raised in the direction of the train's final timbre. "Mickey will pitch tomorrow, Mr. Murphy."

Tomorrow came fast. The clouds hung low and thick, suffocating a hot sun that pushed against the steel gray curtain with little success.

The Sidewinders arrived at Borchert Field to find the modest arena transformed by festive ornamentation and breathless pandemonium. Throngs of ebullient fans spilled into the ballpark like a sea swell, cramming the stands with zip and vinegar, waving banners fashioned with love and fastidious care while stamping their feet and screaming, at fever pitch, Mickey's name.

"We want Mickey!" *Boom, boom, boom boom boom.* "We want Mickey!" *Boom, boom, boom boom boom.*

"Do you believe this place?" one of the opposing players remarked, staring out incredulously at the raging energy. "It's like the World's Fair in here."

Homespun signs and banners fashioned from bedsheets and paints rippled in the breeze. In one corner, the words BABY BAZOOKA BACK AT LAST. In another, IN MICK WE TRUST hung as a testimony to the phenom's importance to the team. And in dead center field, draped over the railing for all to see, was the most heartfelt sentiment of all: WELCOME BACK MICKEY—WE LOVE YOU.

The fans' frenzy lasted all through warm-ups, rising and falling, until reaching a crescendo when the object of their unadulterated affection stepped onto the field with the rest of the hometown heroes. All rose in joyful adulation, saluting Mickey with raucous cheers and undulating arms all rocking in unison. Mickey wanted to exclaim that he did not know what he did to deserve all of this, but Boxcar was calling for warm-up tosses.

With the announcement of the Sidewinders' first batter, the roar of the crowd dulled to a restless murmur. Mickey stood on the hill, a prodigious wall of bone and muscle. He was calm, composed, staring in at Boxcar's glove with stolid eyes cast in what appeared to be a pasteboard mask. The call of his name, popping in and out like an erratic heartbeat, found his ears. He tried to remain composed but couldn't help but smile. It was good to be back. Buoyed by the overwhelming outpouring of affection, he rolled his arms, rocked back, lifted his leg, and fired. The fervor in the stands swelled again, strong and constant.

"Strike one," the umpire called, his voice straining to be heard over the commotion.

The hooting and stamping grew stronger with the second strike and even stronger with the third. The little ballpark rocked beneath the zealous feet of rabid Brewer faithful. Their ace was back, and they were loving every minute of it. He was sharp and showed no signs of his prolonged absence, disposing of the Sidwewinders in routine fashion, one, two, three.

The air had a cool edge to it, a subtle hint that postseason baseball would be arriving in the blink of an eye.

Murph wanted to draw first blood, so he sent Pee Wee up to bunt, hoping to push across an early run. The Brewers' leadoff man, however, bunted through the first two offerings. Ripples of displeasure reverberated softly through the energized crowd. Pee Wee stepped out of the box and blew on his hands. His head throbbed at one temple. He considered, for a fleeting moment, attempting it again, figuring nobody would be expecting it, but the specter of a bunted third strike stopped him. He eased his way back in and backed off the plate a hair, convinced that he was about to see a little 0–2 chin music. But instead he was greeted by a twelve-six hook that buckled his legs, ringing him up for the first out. Instantly, the boobirds were off their roost, questioning Murph's conservative strategy to open the game.

Mickey rolled on though, providing the fans with plenty to cheer about. He was perfect through the first four innings, with the exception of a second-inning walk and a hit batsman in the third. He was not the Mickey of old, not yet anyway—the guy who mowed down opposing batters with pitiless balls of fire. To the contrary, he never looked more human. Of the first twelve outs, only two were recorded by strikeout. The Sidewinders had put the ball in play all afternoon, but not with any sort of authority. Danvers, Pee Wee, and Arky Fries were called on several times each to corral routine grounders that sputtered weakly to their yawning gloves, and once or twice a Sidewinder bat found the bottom half of the ball and sent it airborne, launching cans of corn that fell harmlessly into the leather webbing of one of the outfielders. The only real challenge came with two outs in the fourth, when Mickey sawed off a bat with a hard two-seamer that cut the lumber in two, sending the splintered barrel spinning at Danvers's head just as the ball approached.

"Holy hell," the startled third baseman exclaimed. "Some mighty big mosquitoes buzzing around today."

Mickey was as good as gold. But as the day wore on, he tired. His legs labored and the muscles in his shoulder and biceps atrophied, rendering his usually potent arm ineffectual. It was a troubling sight. Six innings of intense hurling brought to light his diminished stamina and left the standout pitcher merely a shell of his former self.

He began the seventh inning by walking the first batter on balls that were up and well out of the strike zone. It was a sure sign that he was tiring, something that Murph had not anticipated—especially the way Mickey had cruised through the first six. But in a heartbeat, the team's fortunes had changed. Murph saw his chances slipping away, and was alarmed over his lack of remedy.

"Hooper," he screamed desperately. "Start getting loose."

While Gabby Hooper trotted down to the pen, the Sidewinders began hitting Mickey hard. Lumber was cracking like logs on a raging fire. First a single. Next came a ringing double off the base of the center-field wall. Then another single. Another walk moved the runners from one station to another. The merry-go-round was in full swing.

Mickey was pale, with dark shadows under his eyes. He looked around, desperate and forlorn, mopping his sweating face on his sleeve. His lips moved deliberately, forming words that nobody could really hear or understand.

"'A harvest mouse goes scampering by, with silver claws, and a silver eye.'"

Murph recognized with alarm the boy's withdrawal. "Time," he called, emerging from the dugout for the long trip to the mound. He had hoped that Mickey would be able to get through the inning—that he would not have to yank him prematurely—but trailing 4–0 late in the game, he was left with little choice.

"You did good, Mick," he said, holding his hand out for the ball.

"Really. You kept us in this thing. Gave the fans a real thrill. It just wasn't meant to be today."

Mickey's head sagged. He had all but collapsed.

"Hey, don't sweat it, Mickey," Boxcar added, joining the conference on the mound. "You did good for your first time back."

The wounded pitcher chewed the inside of his cheek and balanced idly on the edge of the rubber. "Gee, I'm sorry, Mr. Murphy," he said, erupting in tears that shimmered in the glow of the late-afternoon sun. "Honest. Mickey is real sorry."

Murph's face was pained as well. "You got nothing to be sorry about, boy." Murph waved a finger before Mickey's face. "You did just fine. Fine, ya hear? And if you don't believe me, listen to the crowd when you walk off this field." With that, Murph took the ball from Mickey's sweaty palm and nudged him off the mound. Mickey's first steps were tentative, like those of a foal venturing from its mother's protective gaze for the first time. He was moodily silent, his cleats scarring across the green carpet.

Somewhere between the mound and the dugout steps, however, the thunderous, rhythmic rumble of the crowd pierced his impenetrable veneer, reaching into his bones and jolting him from his stupor.

"Mickey! Mickey! Mickey!"

The entire ballpark was on its feet, clapping and chanting for him. He walked a little lighter now, the sound gloriously potent; it carried him all the way to the dugout, where he found a seat on the bench and watched, his heart much lighter now, as Gabby Hooper took the reins.

But Murph was still distraught. He had rolled the dice starting Mickey, and they had come up snake eyes. It was a long shot, he told himself, a dream he was ill-advised to entertain. How could he have expected anything more from Mickey? After what he had gone through? And Murph himself? That story was already written. He was always going to come up short. That's just the way his stars aligned. He sighed and shook his head, the reality of yet another failure sinking in his stomach like a lead ball.

Hooper did, however, get out of the seventh with no more damage and escaped the eighth and ninth unscathed. He had stopped the bleeding, but as the Brewers faced their final three outs, they found themselves trailing 4–0 and teetering precariously on the precipice of postseason extinction.

Pee Wee's name was announced to begin the last of the ninth. The words echoed loudly, as if having been uttered in a hollow canyon. The crowd had capitulated, resigned to the grim recognition that Murph and the beloved Brew Crew had made a valiant effort but had regrettably come up, once again, short.

Pee Wee served the first pitch he saw softly to right field for a leadoff single. However, half of the disillusioned crowd had all but reached the exits just as Arky Fries stepped in the box. The first pitch to the Brewer second baseman was in the dirt, a sharp slider that rattled off the catcher's shin guards, skipping off to the side. Pee Wee advanced to second with little trouble. The next three pitches missed the mark as well, putting Fries on first and arresting the flight of the rest of the crowd, at least temporarily.

With the first two men on base, and the heart of the order looming, ripples of guarded expectation slithered through the ballpark. It began as a murmur, faint but audible, then swelled in strength after a sharp single to left off the bat of Woody Danvers, loading the bases with nobody out.

Murph leaned against the dugout wall, stomach burning, wondering how much of what was transpiring he should believe. It was the strange thing about baseball. You just never knew. Fickle fortunes he called them, each moment flickering like a candle in the wind. A bad hop. Windblown double. A line drive that just tickles the chalk. The proverbial game of inches. So many great ones before him had tried in vain to figure it out. It was all so inscrutable. What looked like a certain victory often melted into a pool of defeat, seemingly willed by a higher power, while many a loss was averted by that very same force just as the crushing jaws of setback were ready to close. Fickle fortune could certainly humble you.

Clem Finster strode to the plate with a chance to do some real damage. Murph watched as the power-hitting first baseman lined up his knuckles and cocked the bat behind his head. The anxious manager entertained all sorts of scenarios in his head. A sharp single to drive in two. A bases-clearing gapper. A grand salami to tie the game. God, his imagination was ravenous. What an opportunity. He tried to supplant the urge to count the runs before they had even crossed the plate. He had been seduced far too many times before. But, hell, bases juiced with nobody out. Surely they would come away with something. The odds were with him. Unless of course Finster buckled under the pressure and whiffed. Or worse still, hit into a double play. That would certainly kill the rally. Goddamned baseball. The game could tear your heart out.

Murph chewed his fingers as the Sidewinders' right-hander delivered ball one. He exhaled loudly and spit out fragments of fingernail and skin. The next pitch was a sweeping curveball that broke around the plate for ball two. Finster stepped out, reveling in the advantageous count.

"Hey, now, Finny," Murph called out, unable to suppress the nervous energy bubbling in his stomach. "Hitter's count. Selective now. Be selective. Zone up in there. Aggressive, but smart. No help now. Selective. Here we go, Finny."

Finster nodded in the direction of Murph's voice, then set himself deep in the box. He was trying hard not to smile, certain that he was in the catbird seat, sitting on a fat fastball. There was no way the pitcher wanted to go 3–0. And he knew it. What a glorious spot. It was every little boy's dream—to be up in the big spot, game on the line. He closed his eyes for a moment and remembered.

He was so lost in the fantasy that he never even saw the pitcher release the ball. As it traveled toward the plate, Finster caught sight of the white flash at the last second and shivered with pleasure. He swung from his heels, whirling the bat through the hitting zone like a sword. The ball broke a good three inches off the plate and skipped with one hop into the catcher's glove. The bat caught nothing but air, leaving Finster in a crumpled heap next to home plate.

"Finster, goddammit!" Murph roared from the top step. "What

the hell kind of swing is that on two and oh? Jesus Christ! What did we just say?" Finster stepped out and tried to regroup, arching his neck back and rolling his shoulders. He rolled his eyes in disgust.

"Remember now, Finny," Murph screamed. "No help here. Wait for your pitch!"

His zealousness slightly dulled, Finster watched as another fast-ball in the dirt made the count 3–1. He breathed a little easier now. He licked his lips in anticipation, mindful that the pitcher had crippled himself once again and would have to deal something right down the chute. This was it. With Murph screaming something about "zoning up," he dug in and watched dutifully as the Sidewinders' hurler came set, raised his leg, and fired. The ball's trajectory was perfect—a flat fastball heading right for the heart of the plate. His eyes widened. Bathed in sweat, and with a rush of adrenaline coursing through his body, his hands hitched and his front foot rose in simultaneous choreography. Everything was in sync. As he began to move the bat head through the hitting zone, the flight of the ball betrayed him, rising up and away, missing the mark completely.

"Ball four! Take your base."

Finster flung the bat away with gnawing ambivalence and trotted to first base while the crowd screamed wildly as Pee Wee crossed home plate with the Brewers' first run of the game.

Boxcar was next. His walk from the on-deck circle to the batter's box was greeted with more screaming and thunderous applause. Mickey notwithstanding, the veteran catcher remained the crowd favorite. So many times in the past they'd watched as the brawny warrior put the entire team on his back and carried them. Now here he was again, with another opportunity to pull them from the brink of disaster.

The Sidewinders' pitcher was rattled. Boxcar's was the last face he wanted to see; it was a nightmarish visage, complete with square jaw and furrowed brow seemingly chiseled out of stone. The man was all business—a baseball machine. But the pitcher had no place to put him. There was only one chance—he had to outthink him. He had missed with four of the last five balls. Boxcar was smart. He would be taking the first one. If the pitcher could slip a fastball by him to start, then he could go to the breaking ball, perhaps get him out in front and induce a double play to kill the rally. That was his last thought as he unleashed a four-seam bullet right down Broadway.

The one pitch was all Boxcar would see. It seemed that the pitcher's ruminations, as calculated and deliberate as they were, somehow echoed in Boxcar's mind. *He's gonna try and get ahead*, he told himself. *First-ball fastball.*

Boxcar strode into the pitch and plastered the ball. With the crack of the bat, everything seemed to grind to a series of slow-motion frames. The pitcher winced, then hung his head. Boxcar glanced to the heavens, laid his bat down quietly, and admired the flight of his handiwork. All around the ballpark, eyes widened and mouths hung open vacantly, void of sound. Murph removed his cap and jumped up on the dugout's top step for a better look, the imp of expectation leaping from his heart. Each fan was also pushed into motion, springing from his seat as the little white sphere rose high in the sky like a midsummer sun. The ball soared higher and higher, a prodigious blast that seemed to scrape the clouds before touching down somewhere beyond the light stanchions in center field.

Then, Borchert Field erupted into a mêleé. Waves of ardent fans spilled over the railings and rushed onto the field to join their team in the riotous celebration at home plate—a head-rubbing, back-patting fracas that lasted long after the game had ended, fueled in part by news of the Rangers' loss, which placed the Brewers just one game behind the leaders with six left to play.

STILL RACING

Several days had passed since the last telephone conversation between Molly and Murph. Looking out his bedroom window, he thought about what he had told her and remembered her pointed reaction. There wasn't much he could do. She would have to decide for herself if she wanted to change her life. Slowly, helplessly, he dropped his eyes from the tops of the distant pines, down, way down, until they came to rest upon a tiny patch of ground at the foot of his lamppost.

From the morning shadows up the road, a large, steady figure emerged and passed into the lamplight in front of his house, then turned its boots up the narrow gravel walkway and onto his front porch. Murph watched from the window as the figure stood silently in front of the door, its hurried breath clouding the unseasonably cool air, until it finally formed a tight fist and dealt the paneled wood a series of short, hard blows.

"Boxcar, what brings you around so early?" Murph asked, wrinkling his nose at the morning chill. "Everything okay?"

"Everything's fine," Boxcar answered, stepping inside. "Is it a good time?"

"Sure." Murph pointed to the kitchen. "I was just about to pour myself a cup of joe and have some breakfast. I'll set another place."

Boxcar pulled a chair out, sat, and stretched his legs. "Mickey up yet?" he asked quietly.

"Nope. Still sleeping. We didn't hit the hay until late last night."

"He feeling okay?"

"Sure. I mean, I guess he is." Murph took out a glass plate with an assortment of confections. "You like doughnuts?" he asked, sliding the plate in front of Boxcar.

"Love 'em," the ravenous catcher said, groping for one of the white-powdered circles.

Murph filled Boxcar's cup, then his own. He sat across from his catcher, vaguely disquieted by the unexpected visit. "So what's wrong, Box? I've known you a long time. You ain't exactly the visiting kind."

Boxcar sat uneasily on his chair, squeezing an invisible ball in his right hand while the distant sounds of waking birds punctuated the morning air. "Nothing's wrong Murph," Boxcar said, rolling the edges of a napkin between his fingers. "I was just doing a lot of thinking last night."

A brisk wind coming through the window over the sink slipped up Murph's back and made him shudder. He looked at Boxcar with a long, penetrating stare, clasping and unclasping his hands nervously.

"Don't try to fool me, Box," he said, raising his eyebrows. "If nothing's wrong, then why are you here?"

Boxcar felt a knocking in his gut. He dismissed it as just the coffee and the heaviness of the doughnut expanding in his stomach. He stood up and moved away from his chair, trying to escape from the tightening of his middle. Then, blushing a little, he looked at Murph sitting there unchanged.

"Look, Murph, I don't want to make waves or anything. I don't. But I think we have a chance—a *real* chance to win this thing."

"Yeah, I think we do too," Murph said, smiling. "I guess now would be the appropriate time to thank you for yesterday. You were clutch, as always."

"That's not what I'm looking for. The thing of it is, I don't know how many more shots I'm gonna get, Murph. Look at me. Failing knees. Graying temples. It takes me almost a whole goddamned hour every morning just to straighten up. I ain't getting any younger."

Murph scratched his head and folded his arms tightly to his chest. "What are you trying to say, Box?" Murph asked with a palpable abruptness. "Quit beating the devil around the stump and just spit it out."

The sky outside grew overcast and a vast, discouraging light poured down onto the dirt road and gravel walkway and into the kitchen.

"It's Mickey, Murph. I don't know. The kid's been through a lot, ya know? Maybe this is all just too much to handle. I mean, he's done okay since he's been back. But you saw him out there. He wasn't himself. I'm not suggesting we cut him loose or anything like that. Hell, I love the kid. We all do. But maybe we need to rethink just how much a part of these next six games he should be."

Had this been the week before, even a few days before, Murph would have been inclined to agree. The kid really seemed to be struggling and was of no use to them on the field. But now—now it all felt different. There was something there. He could feel it. And it wasn't just a romantic delusion, colored by his personal feelings for both the boy and Molly.

"That kid, Boxcar, is the main reason why we're even able to have this conversation. He's our heart and soul. Look at how this place has changed since he's been here. All he has to do is show up and the whole place is ignited. The fans, our guys, the whole godforsaken town, for Christ sakes. Now you can't sit there and tell me that you don't know that."

Boxcar shook his head ambivalently. "I know all of that, Murph," he pleaded. "But that excitement you're talking about—that energy— all that only works to our benefit *if* Mickey succeeds. That's the rush."

Murph fiddled with the top button on his shirt. Anxiety arrived in one sudden thrust. "What are you saying here, Box?"

Boxcar's eyes dilated with trepidation. "Just think how devastating it would be, for all of us, if Mickey started one of these pivotal games and went into the tank. Emotionally? Psychologically? It would be a friggin' disaster. We would never recover."

Murph scowled. All of a sudden he was a man with two minds. With one, he was right there. Focused on the moment. With the other, he was someplace else. Only when Boxcar moved closer to him and apologized for questioning his plan did Murph become one again.

"Listen, Box. None of us knows for sure what the future holds. Immediate or otherwise. God knows, I'm living proof of that. But every baseball man must live and die by a credo. You know, a philosophy by which he makes those impossible decisions. It's the only way. For me, it's always been simple. Not the results, naturally. But the decision. You dance with the girl you brought to the prom. It's the only way. That's it, Box. That's me. Understand? All of you, together, are what make us who we are. *All* of you. That includes Mickey. He is our guy. The spark in our engine. The wind in our sail. So, win or lose, for better or worse, we do this thing together— with him. Same way we've been doing all year."

Boxcar sat quietly, digesting the morsels of wisdom. For an instant, some filament, light and ethereal, spun itself out between his soul and Murph's, so that both of their lives, at that moment, were kindred, a part of each other, and the contention and angst about them vanished.

"I hear ya, Murph. I do. I just wish there was something we could do to help him relax a little."

"What exactly do you mean by relax?"

"You know, he seems a little jumpy. On edge. He's not himself at all. Do you know the other day he tore the door off Llamas's locker, just because Jimmy took a few peanuts from his bag. Said he was saving them for the squirrels. I thought he was gonna throttle him. It was a little scary. That ain't like him, Murph."

Murph sat as inanimate as the dish towels hanging on a bar just below the sink. "I know he's not right, Box. Who can blame him? But he's still the best we got."

"Well, isn't there something we can do? Something we can give him, to soften the trouble he's going through?"

The catcher's words chased Murph's thoughts back to Molly. "I think I have just the thing. As it turns out, I was working on just that very thing before you got here."

Murph's initial impulse was to pick up the phone and call her again. He was thinking that news of Mickey's successful return to the team would lift her moribund spirits and spur her to some sort of action. He could still feel the charm of the previous day—the improbable success that had transported the team and an entire crowd of doubters into the stratosphere. He wanted her to know—for Mickey's sake, and selfishly, his own. The bitter residue of rejection, however, from their last conversation directed his sensibility to a safer means.

Dear Molly,

Forgive me for not calling, but I do not want to pressure you any more than you already are. Besides, I remember you saying something about Clarence not being able to read, so I figured that this would be the safest way. I certainly do not want to place you in harm's way.

Anyhow, Mickey is doing well. He pitched the other day for us. You should have seen the crowd. They love him, Molly. Every time I think that maybe I made a mistake taking him from you, I am reminded of just how appreciated he is. It is really something.

Even though he is doing well, I think he would really love to see you. I think he's sort of homesick. A familiar face would do him some good. Besides, I wouldn't mind seeing you as well. I haven't heard any clarinet music in a while!

You can call, or write, to let me know what you are planning. The season ends in nine days. Then it's on to the play-offs! It would be awesome if you could be here to watch your boy do his thing.

Be well, Molly. Should you need any help—with anything— please let me know. I would be happy to assist you.

With warm regards,
Arthur

What was to be? he wondered, running his tongue gently across the preglued flap of the envelope. He saw the entire universe only through his eyes and concluded that it was all disordered. Unhappy marriages. Unscrupulous people free to spread their cancer with apparent impunity. The diabolical preying upon the weak and hardworking Joes. Where was the sense in it all? He wasn't young anymore, his vision colored by nice thoughts and childlike dreams. Those days were gone, having fallen victim to the disillusionment of too many bad days. All he could do now was talk to the baseball angels, or whoever or whatever it was that decided the fates of people like himself, and hope for the best.

MILWAUKEE—LATE SEPTEMBER

The Brewers continued to apply pressure on McNally's Rangers, winning their next three games in convincing fashion. It appeared that they were peaking at just the right time. Clutch hitting, quality pitching, and stellar defense had all of them believing that they could just not be beat.

Of course, winning would not be enough. Trailing the Rangers by one game, they would need some help—for some team to play spoiler and knock the league leader down, at least once, setting up a one-game showdown on the final day of the season.

And as if the hope had traveled directly from the team's mouth to God's ears, it happened. If there is such a thing as baseball angels, then they most certainly heard Murph's prayers, for the very next night, beneath a coverlet of thick clouds that veiled a glossy moon, the lowly Colts defeated the Rangers on a suicide squeeze bunt in the bottom of the ninth, knotting up the standings in a dead tie with just two games left on the schedule.

The sudden turn of events sent Quinton into orbit. Immediately following the game, he summoned McNally to his office.

"This is unacceptable, Mr. McNally!" the petulant owner barked. "Do you want to tell me how the hell we are tied with those goddamned Brewers, after all that's happened? After all this? How in God's name is that possible?"

Something felt small and tight inside McNally. His heart was stilled. "I don't know how to explain it, sir. It, uh, just sort of happened."

"You don't know how to explain it? Is that what you said? Well, isn't that just great. That's just great. Maybe you can explain how I'm supposed to feel about the matchup in three days—Rogers versus that fireballing freak show—should we even be lucky enough to get there. How should I feel about that now that our team—*your* team—is playing like a bunch of schoolgirls?" Quinton paused for effect. "Maybe we need a new manager, Chip—someone who *can* explain why things are the way they are—someone who can get the job done."

"Don't worry, Quinton," McNally insisted. "I'll handle it. We will get there. And we will win this thing. There's not a doubt in my mind."

"Your assurance is charming, McNally, really, but I cannot afford to take that chance. We need some insurance. Something to make me sleep a little easier at night." Quinton raised his eyebrows. His imagination, left to itself, began to bristle with evil machinations. McNally watched as a nervous shadow fell across the face of Quinton, who now looked to be possessed by an unnatural spirit.

"Oh, I know what you're thinking," McNally said tremulously. "And I don't like it, Quinton. Not one bit. We've been down this road before, not too long ago. It was almost a disaster the first time, and I really—"

"I'm not talking about anything like *that*, for Christ sakes. Hell, what am I, an imbecile? There are other ways, Mr. McNally— understated ways—to accomplish what we need to do." Quinton walked over to the frazzled manager, sat down across from him, folded his hands, and began to pontificate.

Murph's preparation was much less diabolical. He sat at home after practice, with a bottle of Irish whiskey at arm's length, charting out the strategy for the next two games—two games in three days—two games to decide who would move on to the postseason. The first of several sheets of paper strewn across the kitchen table was devoted to game one. Operating under the assumption that the Rangers would defeat the Bisons, he knew the game was a must. You couldn't get to the dance without a ticket. He toyed with multiple permutations of batting orders and pitching rotations, mindful that should they advance past the first game and meet the Rangers, he was going to need the right people light and rested. He had all but hammered out things for game one against the Giants—a configuration that would leave Mickey fresh for the final game—when a gentle tapping on the door interrupted his deliberations.

He could not believe his eyes. There she was, just as he had remembered. Her hair was pulled back from her face, revealing the light cheeks and bare shoulders bathed in a soft, creamy white. She smiled, a flowering smile with lips finely made of a deep red satin.

"Did someone call for a clarinet player?" she asked, her eyes warm and delicately sentimental.

"Molly Tussler," he said with the readiness of a small child on Christmas morning. "Ain't you a sight for sore eyes."

Her arrival brightened everything around him. The air was filled with the perfume scent of spring blossoms and the mellifluous tone of her angelic voice.

"How on earth did you get here?"

"My brother-in-law was coming up this way anyhow. I just tagged along."

He reached down next to her for her bag, which was stuffed with assorted articles of clothing, toiletries, and a sopranino clarinet sticking out of the small pouch in which it was stuffed. He grabbed the handle of the bag and brought it inside.

"Is this all you brought with you?"

"Yes, that's it," she said quickly. "Well, I mean, that's almost it. I also brought something for Mickey." Standing in the doorway, she motioned to the truck still parked outside. A man got out, walked around the vehicle to the passenger side, and opened the door. Then, without as much as a grunt or a gratuitous oink, out popped a portly, black-and-white pig that walked languidly up the path, stopping here and there to smell the cooling air and to nibble the wilted dandelions that dotted the edges of the walkway.

"Come on, Oscar," she called, "here boy." Her eyes jockeyed between the indolent porker and Murph's bewildered face. "I hope it's all right. You said Mickey could use some familiar faces. I thought this one would really do the trick."

"No, that's fine. Fine. No problem. We can set up a place for him out back."

"Is Mickey around? I can't wait to see him."

"Yeah, he's inside washing up. Boy, is he gonna flip when he sees you."

Her face relaxed into a smile. "Thank you, Arthur."

The afternoon passed quickly, with the two of them talking and marveling at the joyful reunion between Mickey and Oscar. Arthur realized that he had never really seen the boy smile.

"He's so happy, Arthur," Molly said. "Thank you. God, it's so good to see."

"Don't thank me, Molly. It's all you. This really completes the picture. He needs to have you—uh, and Oscar—around."

She stood still, arrested by a scene of perfect wonder.

"What about you?" he asked. "How are things with *you?*"

"I'm okay," she replied a little tearfully. "This is not easy, as you know. I'll have some decisions to make. But for now, I'm all right."

Murph found himself falling away from the moment as the thought of both their lives entered him.

"You know, Molly," he said, removing her clarinet and fingering the keys. "This may sound a little corny. Heck, a lot corny. But life is a lot like baseball. Fair or foul. Base to base. Win and lose. And there's always another at bat. A chance to redeem yourself. You could be washed-up one day, and a hero the next. Truly. Nobody is tied to their fate."

"It's okay, Arthur." She placed her hand gently on his knee. "You don't have to try so hard. It's okay. Really. I know what I have to do."

Murph gripped the sides of his chair, his heart brimming with a blind tenderness. "You know, Molly, I've thought about you. Often."

She smiled uncomfortably. "I know, Arthur. I know. I've thought about you too."

A silent energy passed between them and stole their voices. In the dying light of the afternoon, they sat staring at each other noncommittally—struggling with an odd amalgam of both shame and confusion. There was so much to be said—so much emotion bubbling just beneath the surface—yet they sat quietly, neither daring to tear at the veil between them for fear of unleashing the many delights and wonders that would no doubt overpower them.

The next day at Borchert Field, a steel-colored cloud slowly spread across the sky, producing a glasslike effect that hung above the ballpark like a transparent cover. The stands were filled to capacity, with fans standing in the aisles and up against the interior walls. The place looked like a carnival, with decorative bunting and colored streamers undulating in a crisp September breeze. The Brewers gave everyone, including their own Gabby Hooper, something to cheer about early, staking the starter to a four-run cushion in the bottom half of the first inning. But the lead, and the good feelings that accompanied it, were short-lived, as a plethora of errors and well-struck hits in the top half of the next inning resulted in five runs for the Giants.

Undaunted, and playing with an urgent sense of purpose, the Brewers fought back in the third, stringing together consecutive hits by Danvers, Boxcar, Finster, and Jimmy Llamas. With two runs already in, Buck Faber launched a 2–2 curveball into the first row of bleachers in left, putting the Brewers ahead, 9–5.

"Yeah, Bucky!" Murph yelled from the dugout as the ball disappeared over the wall. "That's huge! Huge!" Murph paced nervously in front of the bench, unable to corral the excitement and uncertainty pumping through his veins. "Come on now, fellas," he continued to rant, walking back and forth. "We got 'em. No letting up now. Come on. This is our time. Right here. Right now."

He continued to pace, tapping each of them on the back as he passed by, before coming to rest on the bench next to Hooper. The pitcher had his right arm wrapped in a towel, and he was chewing the nails on his other hand.

"How ya feeling, Hoops? You okay?"

"Yeah, Murph. I'm good."

"Don't be a hero here. This is no time for false bravado. Tell me the truth. We got a four-run lead again, and I want this one to stick."

"I said I'm good."

"All right. But any trouble, I have to yank you. Without this one, there may be no tomorrow."

Hooper was built like his mother, lanky and slight. His legs and arms looked like pipe cleaners—four skeletal limbs emanating from a scraggy trunk that was also lean and sparse. It was always the knock on him throughout his career—that he lacked the strength and stamina to go deep into games. This year, however, he had silenced many of his critics, logging the most innings pitched on the team. It was the main reason why on this most important day, he got the nod over Sanders and Winkler. Still, when he ran into trouble and an inning was prolonged, his physical size became an issue.

The top of the fourth began innocently enough, with the Giants leadoff batter tapping a comebacker to Hooper for an easy 1–3 putout. But disaster was not far off. The next batter lined a base hit to right, followed by a push-bunt single and a four-pitch walk. Hooper looked dazed. He rolled his shoulders, as if trying to summon some additional strength from somewhere inside his body, his breath trembling through distended cheeks. Murph saw all the signs of alarm but let him go another batter, trying to buy Winkler a little more time to get loose, only to regret that decision when the next Giant batter cleared the bases with a triple off the glove of a diving Ruffings.

"You better get him outta there, Murph," Matheson droned dryly. "A tree don't move none unless there's wind."

Murph scowled. "Time," he called, storming to the mound in a fit of self-loathing. God, why had he left him in? His body was wilted and sick with hurt. The thought of squandering another lead ate away at him with ravenous fury.

"You did fine, Hoops," he said mechanically, placing his hand on the back of Hooper's neck. "Some days, it just doesn't fly."

Murph gave the ball to Rube Winkler, whose first few pitches had the effect of gasoline on a fire. Each of the four batters he faced reached safely, and three runners crossed the plate, putting the Giants ahead again, 11–9. The crowd rumbled and roared, littering the field with apple cores, banana peels, and soda bottles. Murph heard the cries of the disgruntled and felt all the angry faces in the crowd swivel in his direction. Standing on the top step of the dugout, he felt like an idiot and vowed he would not be burned twice by indecisiveness. He stepped onto the field again and with a hiss of dismay yanked Winkler immediately.

Butch Sanders was next in the rotation for the day, leaving just Enos Willard, a young left-hander with little game experience, and Mickey, whom Murph was saving for the last contest against their nemesis. Sanders was sharp, allowing just one inherited runner to score, and shut down the Giant attack for the next two innings. His effectiveness lifted the spirits of the disheartened crowd and became a catalyst for the offense, which exploded for five runs in the home half of the sixth, lifting the Brew Crew to a 14–12 advantage over the pesky Giants.

Murph was pleased, but his optimism remained guarded. When Sanders took the hill in the seventh, Murph had the young Willard get up in the pen. The sun had split the thick cloud cover, spilling onto the field in long, slanted rays. Murph leaned against the exterior dugout wall as if he were trying to balance himself. He glanced to the skies once or twice, in half prayer, half demand, pleading for something good. Nine outs. That's all he needed. Nine stinkin' outs. After all he'd been through, he did not think it was too much to ask.

Sanders whiffed the first batter and retired the next on a foul out that was corralled by Boxcar just before it landed in the seats behind home plate. With two quick outs, and Sanders pitching with a full tank, things were looking up. The crowd, sensing that their team was closing in on what would be a monumental victory, began to stir. Everyone in attendance stood anxiously, some stomping their feet in a frenzied effort to release the coiled tension, while others placed their hands together over their mouths in silent prayer.

Sanders stood on the hill, his chest puffed out, as he stared down at the Giants' pinch hitter. Sammy Bouton was a slick-fielding utility man, a skilled defensive player who could play anywhere in the field. But each time he stepped to the plate, he elicited derisive comments from other players, including his own teammates, such as "He couldn't hit water if he fell out of a boat" and "I've seen better swings in the park." Sanders couldn't help but smirk a little. The inning was all but in the books.

Sanders painted the black of the outside corner for strike one. The inept Bouton grimaced and rolled his eyes. The crowd's animation echoed in his ears, as did the acerbic taunts from the opposing dugout. He watched the second pitch go by as well, a fastball that shaved the inner half of the plate for strike two. Bouton choked up on the bat handle and gritted his teeth, vowing that if he had to go down again, it would be swinging.

Sanders peered in at Boxcar, who was slightly out of his crouch, his mitt elevated around the letters to provide Sanders a guide for his waste pitch. The self-possessed pitcher, however, shook his head doggedly until Boxcar, visibly annoyed, reset the target lower. *Waste a pitch? On this pineapple? No way.* Sanders was determined to finish him off immediately.

With a deft, windmill-like motion, the Brewer pitcher released what was sure to be the final pitch of the inning, a fastball that was targeted for the outer portion of the plate. The ball, however, drifted unexpectedly back toward the middle. Bouton swung his bat like an ax, chopping at the ball with a blind vengeance that somehow, some way, caught most of the ball as it crossed the plate, spitting it back past Sanders and on through the middle of the diamond. The Giants bench erupted in a rash of celebratory hoots and gestures.

Sanders scowled, banging his fist in the pocket of his glove. He cursed himself. Danvers trotted in from third to mitigate the pitcher's frustration. Too much was riding on every pitch. But Sanders was in no mood for pep talks or condolence pats on the back.

"Just turn around, Woody," he barked. "Keep your rah-rah babble to yourself and just play third base."

Sanders lost all control. He began unraveling like a spool of yarn in the grasp of a playful kitten. The next batter drew a walk. That was followed by a sharp single, then a booming double that emptied the bags. The boos began to rain down on Borchert Field again.

Sanders was inconsolable. He fired his cap to the ground and stomped around on the grass behind the mound, muttering venomous commentary about the injustice of his fate. Murph saw the wild look in his eye and sprang out of the dugout without delay, gazing out at the bullpen and pointing to his left arm the whole way out to the mound.

"If we lose this thing, Sanders, we'll do it with pride," Murph admonished. "Not whining, like some two-bit bush leaguers kicking around the sandlots. Now pick your goddamn head up and sit your ass on that bench and support this team."

Willard bounded out of the pen like a frisky colt, buoyed by the opportunity to showcase his stuff. His cap was pulled snugly over his brow, hiding the delirium in his eyes, but his explosive smile and full, baby-smooth cheeks were visible.

"We got ourselves a good old-fashioned barn burner, young fella," Murph said, his arm draped affectionately over the rookie's shoulder. The young pitcher edged closer to Murph, his eyes wobbly with anticipation. "We're down fifteen to fourteen. Just give me strikes here, kid. Nothing fancy now, ya hear? Just stop the bleeding. Finger in the dike. Ya got it?"

Willard licked his lips and nodded. "Sure, Murph. You got it."

Murph trotted back to the dugout, nursing a roiling knot in the pit of his stomach. He watched nervously as Willard peered in to get his sign from Boxcar. Then, with a rush of adrenaline coursing through the young hurler's body, he retired the next Giant to step to the plate on just one pitch—a blazing fastball that burst into the hitter's kitchen and caromed weakly off the bat handle, rolling harmlessly to Arky Fries for an inning-ending groundout.

The Brewers went quickly and quietly in their half of the seventh. A pop-up, a foul-out, and a caught-looking had them back on the field just as Willard pulled his jacket over his arm and sat down to catch his breath. The Giants, however, were more resilient, continuing to chip away at the Brewer's resolve, pushing across an unearned run in the eighth and an insurance tally in the ninth, leaving the Brewers trailing 17–14.

With their season hanging in the balance, and a throng of nervous fans storming the heavens for a miracle, the Brewers began their final at bat. Murph leaned stoically against the dugout railing, his attitude almost peaceful, a kind of abject meditation. He would have to deal with the fallout of this latest failure—he knew that. It was all part of the cycle, just like all life, consisting of this continuous undulation of expectation and result.

He was not totally disconsolate, however, and did not feel the full force of paralyzing dread that usually accompanied such egregious disappointments. Maybe it was Molly. Just her presence could have been enough. He didn't know. He had seen her in the stands, watching him, and once or twice their eyes connected and she smiled at him. Maybe her softness was just what he needed to mitigate his chronic heartache—to provide some perspective. He didn't know. Whatever it was, as he stood there while his entire season slipped slowly away, it merely seemed to him that this latest chapter was just another in the same continuing saga. There was no need for alarm. Once again, it appeared, time and events had conspired against him. He was being played with, manipulated by a capricious wind blowing him everywhere but nowhere in particular.

Pee Wee would be the first to try to stem the tide. He wasn't having a particularly productive afternoon, having reached base just once in five at bats. Now, more than ever, they needed base runners.

"See a strike, McGinty, will ya?" Murph whispered to him on his way out of the dugout. "Let's make this guy work a little bit."

"You bet, Murph. I got him."

Pee Wee did just as he was told, working the count to 2–2, but his eagerness got the best of him, and on the next pitch he tapped a weak roller to short. The ball, slowed by the thick tufts of infield grass in need of manicuring, rolled harmlessly into the glove of the Giant shortstop, who reached in and grabbed it across the laces and fired it across the diamond. Pee Wee never looked. He ran, head down, arms pumping, eyes fixed longingly on the bag. As his strides brought him closer to the base, he heard the desperate cries of his teammates imploring him to run harder. He glanced up briefly and saw the eyes of the first baseman widen and his arm extend in the direction of the ball. The moment was at hand. Like a projectile being flung from a slingshot, Pee Wee lunged desperately for the base, his front foot clipping the corner just as the ball popped the glove.

"Safe!"

The crowd roared its approval as the Giant first baseman whirled around and assailed the umpire, pleading his case to no avail.

With his leadoff man aboard, Murph's wheels began to turn. He watched dutifully as the Giants pinched their corners, trying to eliminate any chance of an opportunistic Brewer laying down a bunt. His eyes glued to their defensive alignment, he flashed a series of signs to Arky Fries, who stood outside the batter's box, staring intently into the dugout at Murph before finally tapping his helmet in acknowledgment.

The pitcher brought his hands to his waist and came set. The sky swirled now with roiling clouds. He drew a cleansing breath and expelled a thin stream of tobacco juice from the side of his mouth. Then, after several spastic nods of his head and a couple of furtive glances in the direction of the leading McGinty, he delivered.

With the ball in midflight, Fries turned and squared, laying the bat flat in front of him. Both Giant corners jumped. The bold attempt alarmed them, made them breathless, and they rushed the batter with urgency. Fries saw them coming and held the bat still for just one more second, drawing them closer, then pulled it back unexpectedly. "Butcher boy!" the Giant bench screamed frantically, recognizing at once the stratagem. But it was too late. With a deft chopping motion, Fries fired the bat through the hitting zone and slapped the ball past the charging fielders, allowing Pee Wee to scamper all the way around to third. Hot freshets of adrenaline sprang up in Murph's blood.

"Attaboy, Frenchy!" he exploded, clapping his hands wildly. "Yeah! Yeah! That's what I'm talking about!"

The crowd was awash with elation, stamping its feet and howling with skittish resolution. The decibels rose steadily as Woody strode to the plate with a golden opportunity. Had anyone else, with the exception of maybe Boxcar, been placed in this situation, expectation would have been nil. But this was Danvers. He had been clutch all year, leading the team in late-inning RBIs. He was cool, unflappable, and definitely had a flare for the dramatic.

He stood tall, confidently, wielding his bat, but fell behind after taking a sharp curveball for strike one. He stepped out and shot the umpire an incredulous look, aware, just as the sun broke free from the clouds, of the swirling angst that had enveloped the park.

He resumed his stance in the box, his mouth hot and slightly ajar. Bursts of discordant voices exploded in his ears, and his eyes began to betray him. He gazed out at the sun-drenched diamond and blinked, struggling with distortion, and had all but cleared his hazy lenses when the pitcher dropped another hammer on him. He stepped out again, shaking his head vigorously.

Curveball. He's coming curveball again, he told himself.

Danvers filled his lungs, dug his back foot firmly into the soft earth, and tucked his chin on his left shoulder. Then, with the rumble of the crowd echoing in his ears, he narrowed his eyes and set his sights on the pitcher's hand.

The third and final pitch of the at bat came like a lightning bolt, quick and explosive. He saw it as a blur—recognizing it too late. His hands were slow—too slow—and the ball was on him and past him before he could swing.

The crowd fell mute, deflated by Danvers's failure, as if they had all been betrayed by a fault in the universe, some heinous injustice that should have been corrected before they were forced to witness it. That same expression was tattooed on Murph's face as he stood, anxious, against the dugout rail, arms folded, his face furiously impatient.

"Okay, Box," he called, trying to suppress the feeling of impending doom as the battle-scarred catcher got ready to take his turn. "Do your thing now."

Boxcar's chest was scalding inside. This was it—most likely his last chance for glory. One last chance at redemption. He approached the plate, his eyes shining, like a hungry man seated before a grand repast he has yet to sample. He thought of all he had done in baseball—the times he was the goat as well as the hero. So many moments—just like this. It had been a good career. He could not complain. But no matter what had occurred in the past, he knew that this would be the one they would all remember.

The pitcher's first offering was met with exuberance; the ball had no sooner broken the plane of the plate when Boxcar threw the bat head out and whistled a long, arching fly ball that climbed the sky steadily, scraping the underside of the one gauzy cloud that was still dozing overhead. The entire crowd rose to its feet in unison, their heads craning desperately to follow the majestic trajectory. It was a beautiful flight, until it hooked to the side, inches in front of the left-field foul pole. The Ruthian blow was nothing more than just a long strike.

"Son of a bitch!" Murph lamented loudly, slamming his foot against the watercooler. "That close."

Boxcar was unfazed. He reloaded, his sights set on late-inning theater, and tagged the next delivery on the screws, sending it screaming into the left-center-field gap and all the way to the wall. Pee Wee scored easily, and Fries was not too far behind. It was just what they needed. The tiny ballpark rocked with merriment as Boxcar gimped into second with the biggest hit of the season.

Trailing now by just one, with the tying run on second and two shots to get him in, the crowd could sense something magical. Clem Finster validated that sensation instantly, shooting an outside fastball down the first-base line. The ball skipped off the façade of the stands and rattled around in the corner, eluding momentarily the eager hands of the right fielder. Boxcar had gotten a good jump, but still lumbered clumsily around the bases, knees laboring under the full weight of his brawny frame. He was really pushing himself. His mouth twisted open and to the side, as if it were about to become entirely unhinged, as he rounded third. With chest heaving and eyes firmly fixed on the catcher's chest as though it were a bull's-eye at some roadside carnival, Boxcar prepared for landing.

The Giant catcher, set in the direction of the throw, heard the massive tremors coming down the baseline and flinched, his eyes darting for a moment that way in an attempt to gauge the probable collision. His concentration diverted, the ball skipped off the heel of his glove while Boxcar slid safely under the would-be tag with the tying run.

A faint, late-afternoon breeze began to stir as the sun crept lower. Murph's eyes found the grandstand and the myriad faces scrutinizing the diamond drama. He looked wearily as these faces appeared to him, first one, then another, then one beyond the next, seemingly out of thin air, each one mumbling over the hammering of his heart. Then he saw Molly as he flashed his signs to Finster at third. Molly—standing angelically among the bristling throng, the drowsing sun at her back. Her arms were folded gently across a white, lacy blouse, just below her breasts. She was smiling, and in the full glare of the sun, everything else seemed to vanish.

You're gonna do it, she mouthed.

The sky was crossed with thin rungs of red and orange and purple, and behind them flashed the fading sun, moving downward slowly as if descending a colorful ladder.

Jimmy Llamas emerged from the dugout holding his bat, a surging pressure building in his arms and legs. He too took a sign from Murph, then stepped into the batter's box to a chorus of raucous cheers.

Finster inched off the bag at third. The Giant pitcher, uneasy about the size of the lead, stepped off the rubber. Finster snickered and retreated playfully. The two of them repeated this a couple more times, lost in the impromptu contest of cat and mouse, much to the loathing of the impatient crowd. Only after the pitcher realized that he was powerless to alter Finster's position, did he turn his attention back to Llamas.

Llamas's face was tight with anticipation. He looked a little sick. The thought came to him that this moment was his—all his—and with that thought came a vague heaviness. The glory would taste so sweet, no doubt. But what if he failed?

The pitcher took his sign as Llamas wrestled with the opposing forces. He breathed deeply, pulling in air from both his nose and mouth, licked his lips, and readied himself for the ball. What he saw first was the pitcher's foot, suspended in the air, dangling in the crosshairs. His cleat was torn and muddy. Then Llamas's eyes found the arm, followed by the hand as it moved swiftly past the pitcher's ear and into full view. He was entranced, as if he were staring into a crystal ball, in which images of his immediate future were being cast.

Next came the ball, released from the curled fingers like a caged dove. It took flight and commanded Llamas's full attention. Finster was watching too and had broken into a full sprint upon the ball's discharge.

"Squeeze!"

The admonition rang out across the field and the entire Giant infield rushed the plate, where Llamas stood, his hands and body rotating to face the pitcher in an artful attempt to catch the ball with his bat.

Llamas followed the spinning white sphere all the way in. His expression was hardened, as if etched in stone. His hips swiveled and his knees bent, and after sliding his top hand up the barrel, his bat lay at a forty-five degree angle, in perfect line with the ball.

Perfect it was. The lucky lumber deadened the pitch instantly, sending it whimpering back out toward the pitcher's mound, where a frantic race for the ball ensued as Finster dashed madly down the line. With eyes puddling and hearts aflutter, the Brewer faithful watched the drama unfold.

The Giant pitcher was the first to get to the ball. He looked like small child chasing a windblown dandelion seed. He could hear the catcher's urgent cry for the ball, and through his peripheral lens he could see Finster just steps away from the promised land. But he still had time. He still had plenty of time.

His thin, determined face was lit with hope as his bare hand tickled the laces—a hope that disappeared when, to his dismay, the perfidious ball danced out of his palm and off to the side, clearing the way for Finster and opening up the celebratory gates through which both players and fans poured.

It was pandemonium. But Murph said nothing. Did nothing. He stood there on the dugout steps, watching the celebration, as if he were viewing it through a distant lens. What had just transpired appeared to come slowly to him, as if it had to penetrate some fog in his head. Was it real? Was it really happening? To him? He did not move, for fear of disrupting the dreamlike harmony, but gradually his incredulous expression began to clear, draining off every doubtful line until nothing was left save a look of utter satisfaction. Then his eyes found Molly in the crowd, and he raised a finger in her direction. She brought her hand to her heart, tapped gently, and smiled.

The three of them—Murph, Molly, and Mickey—sat at the kitchen table that evening, a family of the most unlikely making, sharing a meal of Molly's making while discussing the details of the afternoon's excitement.

"Well, Arthur," Molly said, dabbing the corners of her mouth delicately with a cloth napkin, "I have to tell you, honestly, that I have never seen, in all my life, something so thrilling. I had goose bumps the whole time. Honestly, I just cannot stop thinking about it."

Murph turned to face her. She looked young, with beautiful, soft hair and so many layers of intimacy behind her soft, rosy cheeks. But her mouth still sank a little, closed after every hint of hopefulness with a stirring sense of disillusion. She had an odd look on her face, as though she had just seen something wonderful that she knew would never be hers. He beat against it with all his soul.

"You sure brought us some luck, Molly," he said through a toothy grin. "Ain't that right, Mickey? You were like an angel today, on our shoulders. Things don't usually go that way for us. I imagine folks around here will want you to stay for a while."

The boy was ordering the food on his plate and never looked up, but responded nonetheless. "I reckon all those people jumping on the field was the darndest thing Mickey ever saw. I stepped on a few of them. Didn't mean to though. Just sorta happened." He used his fork as a shovel, plowing the contents of his plate back and forth before dropping the implement on the table in favor of his bare hand. "Do you reckon I can give these to Oscar?" He lifted his head and held out two boiled potatoes.

"Sure, Mick," Murph said, grinning. "Why don't you go out back and see what he's doing."

Later that evening, Molly and Murph were alone. It felt good to Murph, safe and familiar. They chatted about all sorts of things — where she grew up, her parents, the clarinet, and of course, Clarence. Molly, however, was not experiencing the same level of comfort as he was and altered the direction of the discourse.

"Big game in two days," she said, shifting the emphasis away from herself. "Should be exciting." She stood up suddenly, awkwardly. Unable to handle the emerging feelings stirring between the two of them, she began busying herself with the dishes.

He followed her to the sink and stood behind her. He wanted to slip his hands around her waist—to touch her hair, maybe kiss the back of her neck. It seemed that what little had already transpired between them had been leading to this moment. That it would be the end of one story and quite possibly the beginning of another. But he too felt the stranglehold of circumstance and opted for a much safer route.

"I never did apologize, directly that is, for what happened to Mickey," he said, standing next to her. "I hope you're not angry with me."

"Don't be silly, Arthur. I know it wasn't your fault. You have done so much for him. Given him opportunities that he never would have had. Really. You have been so good to him. Like a guardian angel. I can't wait to see him play."

Later that night, despite a tangible awkwardness, he kissed her. He held her closely, so that he could feel his blood mix with hers, and kissed her softly on the lips. No one else was around, except Orion and the Seven Sisters, winking from above with silent approbation.

They had ventured outside, to gaze at the moon, and maybe walk in the cool night air. It was not supposed to happen. She was talking about how time had just slipped away from her, and how there was so much of life she had yet to experience, when their faces sort of became tangled in each other. At first, their lips and their eyes trembled as they gazed at each other, questioning but understanding. That's when it happened.

"Arthur, this has to go slow," she said, the moon's glow reflected in her eyes.

His heart flooded with passion. Hearing her say those words was more than enough—more than he'd expected. He was leaning, warm and quivering, his back up against the top rail of a wooden fence. The night was glorious. Something electric. Standing there, he could swear he felt his life changing all around him.

"There's nothing to worry about, Molly," he whispered. He stepped way from the fence and cleared some errant strands of hair from her eyes. "There's no rush. It's okay. Some things—the things that are most important—they tend to just happen all on their own." He stopped momentarily, wiping his mouth with the back of his hand. "And those are the things always worth waiting for."

LAST STAND

An eery, dreamlike dusk fell on Lefty as he moved stealthily toward Murph's place. With his car safely ensconced in the sweeping canopy of a weeping-willow grove just a half mile up the road, he ventured out on foot, his boots dusty from the parched soil in the roadbed.

As he walked, Lefty let his eyes wander, something he often did when his mind was filled with myriad things to weigh. Life was a continuous learning curve, just like baseball. Throw an 0–2 fastball down the middle and get burned, it never happens again. Easy enough. Why then, he lamented silently, hadn't the same principle applied to his life outside the lines? In his dizzy state, he was not able to ascertain what he had gained, if anything, from his previous dealings with Quinton and McNally. If he had gained a new maturity, self-awareness, or inner strength from his past troubles, he could hardly feel it now as he walked toward the house so helplessly, childlike even, struggling with his impotence.

With Murph's house almost in sight, he became uncomfortably aware of the frenetic movements of the creatures all around him. Bees vibrated in the colorful clusters of wildflowers; frogs croaked and splashed off in the distance; hummingbirds and swallowtails worked the sweet air in search of vacant flower heads; crickets crooned to a soon-to-be-yellow moon. The accumulation of energy filled his heart with dread.

"It's not enough to just pitch for us anymore, Rogers, ya hear?" McNally had told him. "Quinton wants more. We can't take any chances here. We have to insure our path to victory. Now go over there and rattle that boy's cage."

Lefty nodded imperceptibly, almost desperately. "How am I supposed to do that? I mean, I just got out of trouble."

"Don't be such an amateur, Rogers. Christ. I don't know. Think of something. Steal his glove. Throw a rock through his window. You're no choirboy. You'll think of something. But make it good. I want him so rattled that he can't even hold a baseball."

Lefty pressed his fingers against his face like prison bars, as if to force out between them his growing uncertainty. "Okay," he finally said, pulling his hands away from his face. "I guess I'll think of something."

Lefty recalled bitterly the last deal he had made with Quinton. How that rat bastard had hung him out to dry. It still burned his insides. He knew Quinton could not be trusted. Of that he was certain. The enormity of this realization rose up with fury, but did not alter his circumstances. *Remember where your bread is buttered,* he told himself. If it weren't for the opportunity he was being given—to pitch in the postseason for the favorite and possibly resurrect his career—he would have just bolted, turned right around, and told both of them to shove it up their asses.

The tip of Murph's roof emerged out from behind a cloud of blackpoll warblers that erupted out of a sycamore that had all but completely turned color. He reached down and picked up a rock, walked a few more steps, thought some more, then dropped it. He considered slipping in the house and messing with Mickey's things, but decided against that as well. In truth, he did not know what to do. All he really wanted was to pitch.

This indecision had all but paralyzed him when his eye caught sight of two figures, linked at the elbow, walking away from the house in the opposite direction. They were talking and laughing. It was Murph, and on his arm a woman. Opportunity flashed before him. Mickey would be by himself. Alone. Vulnerable. It was perfect.

Lefty was certain that he could talk circles around the dim-witted country boy, enough so that he would be too scared to step foot anywhere near the ballpark.

Before Lefty even saw his victim, he heard him, squeaking the boards on the front porch with the white rocker while feeding Oscar some partially spoiled husks of corn. Lefty smiled. He was thinking and wondering what McNally and Quinton would say when they heard. How they would congratulate him on his initiative. Maybe even leave him alone at last. In a flash he saw himself in the triumphant scene—sipping cognac and puffing away on a Cuban cigar in Quinton's office.

"Well done, Mr. Rogers. Well done."

The sky was darkening. Lefty looked right, then left, before stealing up the worn dirt drive and onto the gravel path that lay just below the porch. The sound of the rocker grew louder under the pale light of the emerging moon.

"Hi ya, Mick," he said cheerfully, startling him. "Remember me?"

Mickey flushed. He looked away, his attention tied up with scratching his porker behind the ears.

"Sure is a nice night, ain't it?" Lefty grinned, mounting each of the three steps one at a time, leaning up against the spindled rail, arms outstretched, once he reached the platform. Then he lit a cigar and puffed on it a few times, the smoke flowing from his mouth in a long, curling ribbon over one of his shoulders.

"Whatcha got there, Mickey?" he asked, feigning interest.

Mickey's soul was naked in his big, dark eyes. "My pig. From home."

"He got a name?"

"Name's Oscar. Oscar."

Lefty rolled the cigar across his bottom lip and over to the other side of his mouth. "Well, that there's a fine-looking porker. Yes, siree. Big one. Pig like that's a beautiful thing. Sure would make a whole lotta bacon." He let go a guttural laugh, his voice grating on Mickey's nerves.

Mickey glared at Lefty, his feelings sharp and bent in the intruder's direction. He sat still now, Oscar by his side, left alone to face the wickedness of a world of which he understood so little.

"You know, Mickey, we got a pretty big game coming up. Yes, sir. Sure gonna be a lot of hoopla that day. Lots on the line. I would sure hate to see you get hurt again." Something smug and self-satisfied was in Lefty's eyes.

"Mickey's not getting hurt, Lefty Rogers. Mickey's just playing ball."

"Well, I'm your friend, Mickey. I feel terrible about what happened to you that night. Really. I could never live with myself if it happened again. I'm here today to warn you—to protect you from that same thing happening, all over again."

Mickey's back was stiff as he picked at a splinter in his hand. He was remembering, with great difficulty, the weeks he'd lost at the hands of his assailants. The recollection drew him deeper inside himself.

"Are you not hearing me?" Lefty said. "I'm saying that unless you sit out the next game, someone is fixing to get you."

"Oscar is nine years old. He's one of the oldest pigs on my farm, back home. One of the biggest too."

"I don't give a good goddamn about your lousy pig, you idiot. I am talking to you." Lefty moved closer, continuing to bulldoze the uncertain boy until the blood at his temples drummed feverishly. "Look at me, ya goddamned water head. Are you listening to me? Answer me!"

Mickey's cheeks, soft and fleshy, crumpled. His pupils were large and strained, his thoughts stinging him at every turn.

"Oscar's smart too," Mickey mumbled. "He can count and play fetch."

"Hobble your lip, you retard!" Lefty hollered. "I am talking to you. But all you care about is that stupid, mangy bag of fat."

Lefty paused, and then like a tiny ledge of ice that suddenly breaks free from its glacial host, his senses left him. His eyes, now fixed firmly on Oscar, burned a fiery red. With his gaze narrowed and his lips wet with bubbling saliva, he swung his foot back and launched his boot into Oscar's ribs, sending the stunned beast, wailing plaintively, hurtling across the floorboards and into the rail with a thunderous crash.

"There you go, moron!" Lefty ranted. "Now ya have something to worry about."

A momentary stillness filled the air. Then Mickey shot out of the chair. All the chords of past oppression sounded simultaneously. He heard the booming shouts of his father, and the soft whimpers of his mother. He felt the weight of bootheels in his gut and dirty hands around his neck. He saw the face of the monster who had orchestrated his abduction—and who had just maimed his dearest friend. Mickey was pure instinct now, a machine devoid of reason and feeling. His body lunged forward and crashed against Lefty's, his hands like an iron vise around Lefty's neck.

With his blood surging to every muscle, he lifted Lefty off the ground and shook him. Lefty's legs flailed. So did his arms—weak, flaccid hammers striking wildly, ineffectually, at a brick wall. Mickey was undaunted. He squeezed tighter and tighter, like a screw being turned slowly, steadily. The protest began to wane. The breath was fainter and the muscles listless. Mickey saw none of it. He was still gone, his eyes glazed with fear and terror and loathing. He had all but completely surrendered to the demon that had seized him when his outburst was arrested by a voice, distant, but soft and soothing.

"'Slowly, silently, now the moon, walks the night in her silver shoon.' "It's 'Silver,' Mickey," Molly called to him. "Walter de la Mare. You remember. I know you do."

The tiny group that had gathered outside the house stood and watched in helpless horror as Mickey released Lefty to the ground in a crumpled heap. They watched as Mickey's eyes slowly returned to him, his lips moving in unison with Molly's.

Sheriff Rosco, who had come shortly after the disturbance was called in, raced to the porch, silver cuffs clanking in his eager hands, only to be thwarted by Murph's body, rigid and strong.

"Let her handle it, Sheriff," he said to him. "She's got him."

Molly climbed the steps of the porch, continuing to recite the magical words. She could see the tears straining in Mickey's eyes.

"'Couched in his kennel, like a log, with paws of silver sleeps the dog.'"

Mickey's lips continued to form the same words. He looked quizzically at the body lying before him. It no longer seemed this menacing, wicked force but rather just a lifeless, inert mass for which he felt nothing more than indifference.

Molly reached the boy just as the two of them completed their recitation. Rosco was right behind her.

"Mickey, sweetheart, it's all right now," she said, running her hand over the damp skin at the back of his neck. Mama's here. It's all right."

Mickey's mouth fell open, and tears slid swiftly down his cheeks. His face flushed with a sudden calm, and he embraced Molly with a quiet, desperate longing.

"It's all right, sweetheart. It's over now. I'm here," she whispered in his ear. Mickey's massive body melted in her arms. She rubbed his back lovingly for some minutes, then pulled away ever so slightly, so that he could see her face.

"Now you'll do something for Mama, right?"

Mickey wiped his eyes crudely with the back of his wrist and nodded.

"Be a good boy for Mama and just tell the sheriff here what happened."

Sheriff Rosco no longer had any use for Molly. He thanked her but pushed her aside and sent her back down the porch steps, instructing her to wait with the others while he conducted his investigation.

"What happened here, son?" Rosco asked. "Did you hurt this man?"

Mickey could not answer. His eyes raced back and forth between the lifeless carcass of his fallen friend and Lefty.

"Boy, I'll ask you again, one more time, and one more time only, because I'm losing my patience. Did you hurt this man? Yes or no?"

Mickey's mouth moved spastically, but nothing came out. Rosco stood, shoulders square and stiff, his face frozen with frustrated rage. Mickey's heart beat frenetically. His eyes were fixed beyond the sheriff, on Molly, as she continued to mouth the words *It's all right.*

"He killed Oscar," Mickey finally cried. "Killed him. Right there. Killed him. That wasn't nice."

"So *you* wanted to kill *him*? Is that right?" Rosco persisted.

"Oscar was my friend."

"Did you want to kill him? Just answer the question."

"He were my favorite porker. Biggest one too."

"What's the matter with you, boy? You stupid or something? I'm talking to you here. And you could be in a heap of trouble. Answer the question. Now."

All at once there was a drumming in Mickey's head. There were too many thoughts, and no place to put them. He placed his hands over his ears and shut his eyes tightly.

"Answer me, boy. Answer me now," Rosco demanded.

A low mutter of thunder moved along the sultry sky, and a moment later some cold drops began to fall to the earth. Then in a voice high and abject, almost inhuman, Mickey began the haunting recitation.

" 'Slowly, silently, now the moon . . . .' "

Rosco was out of patience. He removed the billy club from his waist and pressed the end up against Mickey's throat. Molly gasped and buried her face in Arthur's shoulder. The boy's eyes exploded open, followed by words, desperate and emotive.

"Mickey did not mean to hurt Lefty," he cried loudly. "Oscar's my friend. My friend. I did not know. Mickey does not lie. I just wanted him to stop. To stop hurting us. I did not know. Lefty will get up. Then I can take Oscar. Mickey did not know."

Rosco shook his head. He had a nasty impulse to just cuff the boy and throw him into the back of his car, but the ambulance had arrived and Lefty was coming to.

"Don't let him go nowheres," the sheriff said to Murph before turning his attention to the victim. "He's far from free. I'm gonna have plenty more questions for him."

Molly sobbed out loud before collapsing into Murph's arms. He squeezed her tightly. His wet face, lit now by the flickering glow of the sheriff's car lights, melted into clay, his dream of play-off glory all but gone, once and for all, carted away in the ambulance with the battered body of Lefty Rogers.

The clouds the next morning were thick and restless, a suffocating shroud of steel gray that threatened to burst open at any moment. Murph and the entire team sat in the locker room expressionless, numb from the previous day's debacle. Nobody wanted to talk about it—even think about it—but Murph had Mickey with him, per the request of Sheriff Rosco, who would be by later that day to bring the boy in for more questioning.

"Look, fellas," Murph began. "This ain't easy. For any of us. But we are a family here. Have been all season. And something bad has happened to one of us. We need to stand together here and help Mickey as best we can."

Mickey looked uneasily up at the ceiling and lost himself in the symmetrical pattern of the tiles.

" 'Something bad has happened to *one* of us?' " Danvers repeated scornfully. *One* of us? Like hell! Something bad has happened to the *rest* of us, because of *one* of us."

"Now listen, Woody, there ain't no use in—"

"What the hell was you thinking, Mickey, for Christ sake? One day before the big game. Jesus, how stupid. And over a mangy pig no less. That's what we get for putting all our faith in a retard."

"Stand down, Woody," Boxcar warned. "That ain't gonna do us any good now. The kid is sorry."

"Sorry? He's sorry?" Danvers barked. "Oh, well, isn't that just great. He's sorry. That makes it all better now."

Murph put his hand on Mickey's shoulder. The boy moved around uncomfortably in his clothes and seemed to be buckling beneath the oppressive weight in the room. He looked as though he would just lie down, right there, and shrivel up before them. None of them could watch. They simply hung their heads in quiet desperation, a sort of catatonic state that lasted until an unexpected voice shattered the silence.

"Mickey is sorry," the boy burst out suddenly. "I didn't mean to hurt no one. Honest. I don't know why Mickey did it."

"It's okay, Mick," Murph assured him. "Nobody blames you."

"It felt like a train," the boy continued. "Roaring by Mickey's face. It was loud, and rumbly. My head was shaking. I couldn't hear nothin' in my ears, except that sound. Honest. It would not stop."

Murph felt sick, deep in the pit of his stomach, as the boy unburdened his mind; not because Murph believed he could really have done anything to prevent what had happened, but because it was all just so damn ugly. They all seemed to share the same feeling. The room fell absolutely silent, except for the squeaking of Mickey's sneakers, scraping nervously on the floor. Nobody knew what to say, or do, and they all would probably have remained that way indefinitely had Rosco not come in, blustering about "unanswered questions" and "good old country justice."

"I need him, Arthur," he instructed curtly. "Right now."

Mickey stood, defeated and exposed. His chest began to heave as if there were not enough air in the room for all of them to share.

"Let's go, big boy," Rosco said flatly. Then he pinioned Mickey's arms behind his back, and just like that Mickey was gone.

Later that afternoon, Murph and the Brewers had a casting off of their own, bidding farewell to their dream season. The Rangers made fast work of their archrivals, defeating them in just under two hours by the score of 5–1. With the image of Mickey being dragged away in cuffs still fresh in his mind, Murph found the sight of Chip McNally and his club celebrating on the pitcher's mound intolerable.

"Look at McNally," Matheson said, draping his arm over Murph's sagging shoulder. "Christ, if dumb were dirt, that jackass would be about an acre."

Murph forced a grin. Then he frowned and his lids narrowed

with disappointment. "That may be the case, Farley," he said with resignation, "but that jackass is going to the play-offs."

The loss was so much more than just a loss. For Murph, baseball was the center of his universe. He had come to the game years ago, young and naïve, with the feeling that he was to be, always, at the very heart of it. It was in his blood. He knew no other way. It's why saying good-bye for the winter at each season's end was so painful.

"I'm sorry, Murph," Boxcar said on his way out later that day. He, like all the others, had the contents of his locker in a tan bag flung over his shoulder. "It should have been different."

Murph shrugged his shoulders, as if to suggest that it didn't really matter. But in the darkest, most remote corner of his soul, hanging restlessly from a single strand of sticky filament like an anxious spider, was the unmitigated, undeniable truth.

In the deepening night, ensconced in grotesque shadows, Mickey still struggled with *his* good-bye. His prison cell was putrid. Cockroaches. Pungency of urine. Animal feces. And lurid scrawlings on the walls all around: skull and crossbones; demoniac sketches; the haunting message G.L.R. *was here.* From the moment the cold metal doors slammed behind him, he sat in his cell like some overwound automaton, talking to himself and rocking uncontrollably for hours before finally getting up from his cot and looking out the small window on the far wall, his eyes roving across the burned bed of grass outside to the faint line of trees and rooftops that dozed just beyond Borchert Field. He wiped his eyes with the corner of a dirty rag he found stuffed between the slipshod mattress and wire bedframe and tried to catch a glimpse of something familiar.

"Hey, chucklehead," Rosco's deputy shouted through the rows of black metal bars. "I stand to lose a heap of money 'cause of you. You know that? All because of you. 'The Brewers are a sure thing,' they all said. A sure thing. Right. That was the plan. But then you go and screw it all up with your goddamned retard rage. It's just like you reached your fat paw in my pocket and robbed me. How do you reckon we square that?"

Mickey remained facing the window, his entire body enveloped in spasmodic convulsions.

"'Slowly, silently, now the moon, walks the night in her silver shoon.'"

"What'd you say, boy? Turn around when I'm talking to you."

Mickey just continued to recite, his eyeballs swerving from side to side, lost in the crossing shadows of past and present.

"'This way, and that, she peers and sees, silver fruit upon sliver trees.'"

The baleful deputy burned with agitation, his heart beating furiously beneath his potbelly. In between the cascading folds of fat running from his neck beads of sweat began to form. He swiped at them nervously with a napkin already stained with cooking grease.

"Don't you be mocking me now, boy," he demanded, banging his billy club against the iron bars. "Ya hear now? You is gonna be here awhile, till they sort this whole mess out. So we best come to a goddamned understanding! You got that!"

The clanging of the bars and the vituperative voice of the deputy only made Mickey rock more ferociously and speak louder, with even greater urgency.

"'One by one, the casements catch, her beams beneath the silvery thatch. Couched in his kennel, like a log, with paws of silver sleeps the dog.'"

Mickey's words seemed to the deputy to be nothing more than mockery. His pupils narrowed and his lips trembled. Outside, it was completely dark now, save for the blurred glow of two naked exterior lights just outside the tiny jailhouse. The irate officer checked the clock on the wall and unfurled a devilish smile. Rosco would not be back for another hour, and the cell next to Mickey's was empty.

"Batter up, freak show," the Deputy called out loudly.

Mickey turned and let his eyes fall dead on the deputy's slack-jawed face. For a moment he thought he heard Oscar—a soft, playful grunting coming from just inside the other room. His heart leaped. But the notion faded quickly, leaving only the sound of jingling keys. Then, in the lurid shadows of early nightfall, Mickey watched blankly as the deputy turned the rusty lock and swung open the door, pounding his palm with the billy club in violent rehearsal, certain that no one would be the wiser.

It would have been ugly. No doubt. But just outside the prison door emerged the outline of a figure, maybe two, hidden against the blackening night sky. It moved slowly, stealthily, inside and stood silently by the front desk. Then, becoming conscious of what was transpiring, the figure finally moved, clicking the switch on a dusty lamp. The deputy spun around as if he had been rocked by a violent wind and, with eyes that struggled to adjust to the sudden light, saw a yellow glow falling across a silver-haired man dressed in a neatly pressed suit. He was standing there with a little boy.

"Evening, Deputy," the man said. "Hope I'm not interrupting anything. I'm here to see the young man you have locked up there — and to relieve you of your responsibility for him."

The deputy brushed off the man with a blanching smile. "Well, I'm afraid visiting hours are over, Grandpa. And you're confused. I think you best turn right around and be on your way."

The man released the boy's hand, placed his newspaper on the desk, and reached into his breast pocket, removing a piece of folded parchment. He stood staring at the abrasive officer, his eyes unchanging.

"I'm not going anywhere, sonny, without Mr. Tussler."

The angry deputy sighed and puffed out his cheeks. "And what makes you think that's going to happen?" He laughed scornfully as his hand strayed involuntarily to the revolver affixed to his hip.

Mickey heard the contentious exchange and moved forward, pressing his face up against the bars while straining for a better look.

"Do you know who I am, Deputy?"

The officer shrugged his shoulders and started toward the man.

"The name's Walter Harrigan. *Governor* Walter Harrigan."

The deputy halted dubiously, his heart rocking tumultuously like a boat in a stormy sea.

"And this paper I have, Mr. Deputy, is an official pardon — from my office—that allows me to walk out of here with Mickey—Mr. Tussler." The governor unfolded the white sheet and pointed to its contents as if the deputy could read it from a distance. "Now be a good little soldier and start taking care of that for me."

The disgruntled officer stood momentarily in silent deflation, then went about the jail grumbling to himself and uttering curt laughs. He struggled mightily with his unforeseen loss of authority while the governor and the boy just watched and waited.

Then, neither convivial nor exanimate, Mickey emerged from the darkest recesses of the foul dwelling. He sighed loudly and looked at the governor like a purblind tourist negotiating a once traveled street, trying to place the face. His head swam in confusion, then cleared when he caught sight of the boy.

"Mickey, good to see you again," the governor said. "Remember us?"

Mickey smiled. He came forward and patted Billy on the head. "Yes. Yes. Mickey remembers." Then he sighed again. So many thoughts that had been harbored in the darkest corners of his mind suddenly leaped forward in this moment.

"I told you I would never forget," the governor continued. He smiled with growing satisfaction. "I'm here to take you away from here. Your time here is over."

Mickey blinked nervously and rubbed his head. He thought about the gruesome reality that had touched him so mercilessly. Then he cried.

"Thank you, Mr. Harrigan," he said, wiping his eyes with his shirtsleeve. "Mickey thanks you."

"Not at all, son. It's my pleasure. Truly. I'd do just about anything to see you on that mound again, mowing 'em down."

A shadow fell across Mickey's face. His eyes traveled around the room, looking everywhere except at the governor. "No more baseball," Mickey said, choking on the words. "I reckon Mickey will just have to go back home. To my farm. It ain't so bad. Maybe not. I got me some swell pigs there."

"Go home?" the governor questioned. "You can't do that. You've got the whole world at your feet here. Are you crazy? The sky's the limit. People would die to be in your shoes."

Mickey stood gaunt, hollow-eyed, tugging at his shirt collar. "Mickey doesn't know if he wants to play baseball anymore." He just stood there, in the thickening darkness pouring through the windows—a mere child, lost in the vast and oppressive gloom of the dissolute wilderness that lay just outside the door—just a child, caught up in the rattle of everything, big and small, that had led him to this one moment. The unpleasant vision paralyzed him.

"Well, you have time to decide all that," the governor said. "Things change. Relax. A lot has happened. You're tired. It makes sense. Anyone would feel the way you do. But give yourself some time to think about it. To put all this behind you. Don't rush into any hasty decisions."

The governor laid his hand on Mickey's back and, together with little Billy, guided the young man toward the door. Silently, Mickey continued to sink into the depths of his memory until he appeared to lie lifeless, like a stone at the bottom of a swift river. "Mickey will have to go back to the farm," he whispered again. "I got me some pigs there. The farm. Yeah, farm."

The governor's spirit sagged. He sighed and moved slowly, methodically, toward the door. Mickey took small steps, relying on the governor to steady his erratic gait, as the door to this most troubling chapter closed behind him.